The Love We Brew

Hope and Healing Blend

Ethan Jakob

Runebeast Publishing

Dedication

FOR THE BROKEN KNIGHTS IN SHINING ARMOR AND THE DAMSELS IN DISTRESS THAT LEARNED TO SURVIVE

This book contains highly adult themes

From the author of Lavender and Ginger: A Callus Kordec Tale, a high fantasy novel.

instagram.com/ethan_jakob_author
Instagram: ethan_jakob_author
www.linktr.ee/ethanjakobauthor

Contents

Chapter 1: A Ghost in the Street

Connor

THE MIGRAINE HAD BEEN creeping down my spine for the last few hours. Acetaminophen, ibuprofen, even the mild narcotics I had been given by Manu, my lead programmer, had done nothing to dull the ache. Damn sure dulled my wits. That's the only reason I can think of that I would have allowed this meeting to have lasted this long. I love game development. Ever since I got my hands on the original Donkey Kong. Ask most people on the street when the beloved Italian plumber, Mario, first appeared in video games and chances are they will say 'Mario Bros.' However, he was first the protagonist of Donkey Kong.

But I digress. That game was the start of my love for gaming. A love that evolved over the ages through consoles and custom-built gaming PCs all the way to where I sit now. At head of a conference room table zoning out while listening to two artists go back and forth on whether or not it makes more sense for the starting loin cloth of the main character of Rune Beast to be white, green or black.

Manu taps my foot from under the table and I pull my fingers that were pinching the bridge of my nose away and find him staring at me. Looking at me as though I am supposed to say something. I have heard everything the two artists argued about but much in the same way that a person will sudden realize they've heard the chime of a clock and know it has gone off four times already even though they weren't paying it much attention.

I clear my throat and look first at my empty coffee cup and second at my two artists whose faces are nearly beat red from a needless argument.

"Make it purple." I say flatly.

"But Mr. Ebin?" Artist number one starts.

I probably should have bothered to learn their names by now. These two were directly under our lead artist that sadly passed away two weeks ago. The doctors suspected heart failure from an 'insane use' of energy drinks. That is a direct quote from a doctor, no bullshit. My assistant, Ashlyn, had told me that these two were reportedly getting more heated in their disagreements since the position of Lead Artist was now open. The whole purpose of this meeting was to discuss the new warlock class being added to the game and its animations. It's devolution into a color question that I could not give half a shit about made me no longer feel the slightest bit of guilt about not learning their names.

I stand and hold my hand up to stop anymore arguing or pleading. "Look at the bright side, now you are both wrong. If you cannot agree over something this minor on your own, then perhaps you are not the right people for this job."

Artist number two, a young woman in her mid-twenties that almost takes the lax dress code a little too far, apologizes smoothly and with a relaxed breath. "Yes, Mr. Ebin. It won't happen again."

Artist number one, on the other hand, seems to feel a bolder approach will get his point across. "This is ridiculous. That color wasn't even an option we had discussed!"

His raised voice causes any who were not paying much attention to look up. I place my hands down on the conference table and look at him. The man's pinched and puckered face makes me think of a cat's winking asshole. Perhaps that is why I am about to fire him, or it could just be that I don't like his tone.

"Pack your things. Be out of the offices by five." I say as I button my suit jacket. I may have a lax dress code for the office but other than running a game development company I also always wanted to have the kind of job where you could where a good suit. My father was a lawyer. He always wore suits, and everyone always looked at him differently than the other men around him. *'Suits command respect'* he had always told me. I was old enough now to know that was not always the case, but I had plenty of money after five solid triple A game releases to pretend that I didn't.

I look to Artist number 2. "Congratulations, you are our new Lead Artist. As long as questions like this never get brought to me or a conference room ever again."

Her eyes light up and she clutches her laptop to her chest before stifling an excited hop. "Yes, Mr. Ebin."

Ashlyn and Manu rise behind me and follow me out of the room and down the hallway to my office. "What is that young woman's name?" I ask either of them.

Manu shrugs. "Fuck if I know. I'm going to wrap up for the day, Connor. Have a good day, dipshit."

"Bitch." I shake Manu's hand before he sets off. He's a long time friend and one of the only people in this company I feel a real solid kinship with that isn't solely based on video games. It doesn't hurt that we are also the only men in our forties in the entire office.

Ashlyn shakes her head at both of us and says, "Rosalia Morris. Her name is Rosalia Morris."

I nod. "Give HR the details they need for the promotion, please."

"Of course, Mr. Ebin." She looks at me somewhat apologetically, but I know she did that on purpose. She likes to call me Mr. Ebin when she feels that I have acted like a child on a power trip. I give her a look of mild annoyance.

Ashlyn has been my assistant since the start of the second game I led the development for, Critical Chaos in Chains. It was a roguelike dungeon crawler with high stakes high reward mechanics. We didn't think it would amount to much at first, but it burst onto the scene right as people were starting to become professional game streamers and it took off like mad. It won 'Best Game from a New Developer 2012.' Ashlyn had also been my wife's best friend since college but that never stopped the whole office quietly calling her my work-wife. Something she used to tease Olivia with by saying, 'All of the drama and none of the perks.'

Olivia. My soulmate. My… everything. We were together for eleven of the most wonderful years of my life. Our love gave us Desiree, our daughter. No one can ever understand how much of your soul is ripped from your very existence when you lose the people that helped make you who you are. No one except those that have been through it themselves.

I had stayed late for a meeting that night, much like the one I just left. A pointless meeting that could have waited until the following Monday, but I just had to get it over with. Had I not stayed, had I just gone home, then I would have been the one driving. Olivia hated driving. She wasn't bad at it mind you. She just preferred someone else to do it. I would have been the one to pick Desiree up from her Little Rollers jiu jitsu class. Maybe I would have seen the truck coming and avoided him. Maybe I would have decided to take Desiree to her favorite bubble tea shop before going home and we would have avoided that entire intersection all together.

I make my way down to the parking garage, each step echoing off concrete walls that feel like they're closing in with every step. My Lexus LS sits there waiting - another expensive toy that doesn't fill the void. The leather seat creaks as I sink into it, that new car smell still lingering even after six months. I should feel grateful. Successful. Content.

Instead, I grip the steering wheel until my knuckles turn white.

"Not here," I whisper to myself. "Just get home first."

But my throat's already tightening. The parking garage blurs as tears well up, and I slam my palm against the dashboard. The sharp sting doesn't help. Nothing helps.

I fumble for my phone, pulling up my photo gallery like I do every damn day at this time. There they are - Olivia and Desiree at the beach several summers ago. Des has ice cream all over her face, and Liv is laughing, her hair catching the sunset. I remember taking the picture and feeling like the luckiest man alive.

A sob rips through me, and I let my head fall forward onto the steering wheel. The tears come hot and fast now, like they always do. Five years, and it still feels like yesterday. Still feels like I might walk through the front door and smell Liv's delicious baking or hear Des practicing her BJJ moves on the dummy I bought her in the living room.

"I'm sorry," I choke out to the empty car. "I'm so fucking sorry I wasn't there."

My fingers trace the double fox tattoo through my shirt sleeve - black and white foxes, forever frozen in a playful chase. Just like my girls, forever out of reach.

I don't know how long I sit there, shoulders shaking, but eventually the tears slow to a steady drip. They always do, my energy has to run out at some point. I'll pull myself together, drive home to my empty house, and do it all again tomorrow. Because what else can I do?

I wipe my face with my sleeve, probably ruining another expensive suit jacket. Liv would've told me not to worry, it was just a jacket. The thought brings a wet laugh that sounds more like a hiccup.

CONNOR

I pull out of the parking garage into Seattle's endless rush hour traffic. The setting sun glints off glass buildings, turning everything into a maze of orange reflections. I crack the window, letting the spring air wash over me and to help dry my face. Maybe it'll clear my head too.

The radio comes to life with Foreigner's "I Want to Know What Love Is." Really? The universe has a sick sense of humor sometimes. I switch stations until I find Def Leppard's "Pour Some Sugar On Me." Much better.

Traffic inches forward on 5th Avenue. A homeless guy with a cardboard sign shuffles between cars. I've seen him before - he's got a system, working this same intersection every evening, but he seems likeable and I give him what change I have. The light turns green, and we crawl forward another block.

That's when I see her.

A young woman steps off the curb, head down, oversized flannel shirt hanging loose on her thin frame. Something about her catches my eye - maybe it's the way she moves, or the auburn waves of her hair. She reminds me of...

"WATCH OUT!" I slam my hand on the horn as a BMW, driver clearly texting, drifts toward her. The sound makes her freeze mid-step, and the BMW swerves back into its lane with inches to spare.

She turns toward my car, and my heart stops.

Those eyes. That face. It's like seeing a ghost - no, two ghosts merged into one. She has Olivia's delicate features, softened by Desiree's gentle expression. My hands start shaking on the wheel.

It's impossible. I know it's impossible. But for a moment, I can't breathe. Can't think. Can't do anything but stare at this stranger who somehow carries echoes of both my girls.

She meets my gaze for a split second, then hurries across the street, disappearing into the crowd on the other side. I lean forward, trying to keep sight of her, but she's gone.

My chest feels too tight. I reach up to loosen my tie, realizing I'm covered in cold sweat. The radio's still playing, but I can't hear it anymore over the pounding in my ears.

Chapter 2: Give Me Shelter

Shelly

MY HEART POUNDS AGAINST my ribs as the sleek black car disappears around the corner. The man's warning probably saved my life - I was so lost in thought about finding a bed tonight that I didn't see the damn car racing through the intersection.

I raise my hand in an awkward and cringeworthy belated wave, but he's long gone. Something about his face strikes me as familiar, though I can't place where I might have seen him before. His expensive suit and car mark him as someone way above my social circle. Fuck, everyone is above my social circle. I don't even have a circle.

A gust of wind whips down the street, cutting through my thin flannel shirt. I pull it tighter and pick up my pace toward Soaring Angels. The shelter fills up fast, especially on cold nights like this. Last week I had to sleep in the doorway of a closed taco shop because I arrived too late.

The sun dips behind Seattle's skyline as I round the corner onto Pike Street. Other women hurry toward the shelter's entrance, some with children in tow, their faces drawn with the same desperate hope I feel. A mother clutches her toddler's hand while balancing a worn backpack, and two elderly women huddle together against the growing chill. My stomach sinks. This many people already in line means my chances aren't good. I count at least fifteen ahead of me, and Soaring Angels only has thirty beds available on a normal night. Some of the regulars told me they've been turning people away even earlier lately, now that winter's coming.

I take my place at the end and do a more accurate headcount. Sixteen women ahead of me. That isn't counting their children. The woman in front of me rocks back and forth, muttering to herself. Her unwashed hair hangs in greasy strands around her face.

Unbidden, the image of the man in the car flashes through my mind again. His eyes had looked so...concerned? Surprised? It's been a long time since anyone looked at me that way. Most people's gazes slide right past like I'm invisible. Part of the street furniture.

The line inches forward as shelter staff begin processing everyone. I bounce on my toes, trying to stay warm. Six more people join the line behind me. At least I'm not last. Maybe tonight I'll get lucky and score a bed. Maybe I'll even get one of the ones by the heating vent.

One of the Soaring Angels staff peeks her head outside the door, clipboard in hand. I already know what she is going to say, "Sorry ladies, we're full up. No more beds." Her voice cracks with regret.

My shoulders slump. Another night trying to find a safe doorway or spot behind a dumpster. I make a mental note to find more cloths and old clothes to stuff my aging backpack. It is the closest thing to a pillow I can get out here and right now it only contains my state issued ID, social security card and another set of clothes; if I can call them that. The panties might as well be a paper napkin at this point.

I check my pockets and find just enough to cover the only thing that will take my mind off the disappointing night, even if just for a few moments. It isn't a long walk. The neon "Open" sign of Books and Beans glows like a beacon through the deepening twilight. My last three dollars and forty-seven cents sit clutched in my hand inside my pocket - just enough for their cheapest drip coffee. The bell chimes as I push through the heavy wooden door, and warmth wraps around me like a blanket.

The aroma of fresh coffee and old books fills my lungs. I breathe it in deep, letting it chase away thoughts of another night on concrete. The Books and Beans is the type of place college kids and book fanatics dream of working at. Polished wooden walls with numerous old books shelves line the outer edges of the interior. Books for purchase and books you can check out while you sit and drink. There are several nooks and crannies with soft plush chairs that you can tuck yourself away in. That is the main reason I love this place. I can be reasonably unseen. A few customers occupy the scattered armchairs, most with laptops open or books propped on their knees.

"Small drip, please." I slide my crumpled bills across the

counter.

Jenny, the barista nods, her nose ring catching the light. "Room for cream?"

"No thanks." Can't waste precious caffeine space on cream.

She hands me the steaming cup, and I claim the armchair in the far corner. It's partially hidden behind a towering bookshelf of mystery novels. Perfect spot to stretch out one cup for hours without drawing attention.

I wrap my cold fingers around the warm ceramic, letting the heat seep into my bones. The coffee's bitter but I don't mind. It'll keep me alert tonight when I need to stay awake. Can't risk falling asleep in the wrong place again - learned that lesson the hard way last month when someone stole my ratty old jacket that doubled as a blanket while I dozed.

I take tiny sips, watching the clock crawl toward closing time. The shop stays open until ten - that's four more hours of warmth before I have to face the streets. Five hours to plan where I'll spend the night. The library's alcove might work, or maybe that loading dock behind the grocery store. Somewhere out of the wind at least.

The coffee's gone lukewarm but I keep holding it, pretending to drink. Can't give them any excuse to ask me to leave. Not yet.

Connor

I push through my front door, letting it close behind me with a soft click that seems to echo through the emptiness. The sound reminds me of a coffin lid shutting – Gods, where did that thought come from? My keys clatter into the ceramic bowl Desiree made in art class, the one with the uneven edges and too much glitter that somehow survived when my world fell apart. It is odd to me that it hurts to look at it but brings me a sliver of joy at the same time.

The silence is oppressive, pressing against my eardrums like I'm deep underwater. I'm reminded of panic attacks I used to have before I met Olivia. Four bedrooms, three-thousand square feet of premium Seattle real estate, and it feels like a tomb. Note to self: stop with the death metaphors, you're not helping yourself here.

My gaze drifts to the spot where Olivia's easel used to stand by the window. Now there's just a potted plant that's probably plotting its suicide, given my track record with keeping things alive. The wall still has that slightly lighter rectangle where Desiree's finger-painting masterpiece used to hang. I'm filled with a sudden pang of guilt at its absence. Shortly after…I lost control and nearly destroyed the apartment. Her painting was one of the worst causalities of that event.

Fuck this silence.

I practically lunge for the stereo controller, my fingers trembling slightly as I pull up my "Emergency Happy" playlist. The opening notes of Hall & Oates blast through the apartment, and I crank it until the bass makes the windows vibrate. "What I want, you've got..." Daryl Hall's voice drowns out the thoughts trying to creep in from the corners of my mind.

I used to dance to this with Olivia in the kitchen while making Sunday breakfast. She'd do this ridiculous shimmy with her hips while flipping pancakes, and Desiree would giggle at us from her perch at the counter, syrup already sticky on her chin.

The music's not loud enough. I turn it up another notch, until it's probably pissing off my neighbors. Let them complain. It's better than letting the silence win, better than remembering how it felt when the police showed up at my door that night after I'd come home to an empty apartment and Liv wouldn't answer her phone, better than–

"You make my dreams come true..." The song insists, and I want to laugh at the irony, but I'm afraid of what might come out if I start.

My fingers twitch at my tie, wanting to yank it off and leave a trail of expensive designer clothes across the floor like breadcrumbs. But even in my worst moments, some habits die hard. "You don't need the suits babe. You are the CEO of Eldritch Magic. Wear what you want to. But if you're going to insist on these damn suits then stop putting wrinkles in them," Olivia's voice echoes in my head. She used to lay out my clothes every morning, each piece perfectly pressed. I always told her I would take care of it but she never let me.

I methodically remove each item, folding them with mechanical precision. The Armani suit goes into the dry cleaning bag – there's probably a small fortune's worth of clothing in there already, but who's counting? At least it gives Alicia, my housekeeper, something to do when she comes by twice a week since I don't do much in here anymore but lounge, cry, mope and sit at my computer .

In the bathroom, I crank up the shower until steam billows around me. The smart stereo follows me in here too – thank the Gods for whole-house audio systems. Queen's "Under Pressure" feels appropriate as I step under the scalding spray. The water pressure pounds against my shoulders, and I brace my hands against the marble tile, letting my head hang down.

"Pressure pushing down on me, pressing down on you..." Freddie Mercury gets it. The hot water runs down my face, and I tell myself it's just shower spray in my eyes. Nothing else. Definitely not tears.

The girl from the crosswalk flashes through my mind – that splash of red hair, those freckles. It's like seeing a ghost that is already targeting me for haunting. The rational part of my brain knows it's impossible, knows that grief can play tricks on your mind. But that doesn't stop my heart from doing that painful little stutter it does whenever I think I catch a glimpse of them in a crowd.

I turn my face directly into the spray, letting the water drown out everything else. The temperature's hot enough to turn my skin pink, but I barely feel it. David Bowie's part of the song kicks in, and I focus on the baseline, trying to let it ground me in the present instead of sliding back into memories of bath time splashing wars and Desiree's giggles echoing off these same tiles.

I step out of the shower, wrapping a towel around my waist as Queen fades into something by Journey. The bathroom mirror is completely fogged over – probably for the best, I'm not sure I want to see my own reflection right now.

Padding into the master bedroom, I make the mistake of looking up. There it is, the photo I will never take down and yet every time I see it it feels like a surprise. Olivia holding Desiree at the top of a mountain we hiked in Tennessee, both of them squinting with identical grins as the sun peaks through the canopy of trees. Desiree holding a deer bone she found and refused to put down and Liv staring at me with a look of desire in her eyes. Hikes had always been a, I'll just say an energy booster for her.

My chest constricts. The room suddenly feels too small, the air too thick. My hands start to shake as I fumble through my dresser, yanking out the first t-shirt I touch – some old Pantera concert thing that's seen better days. Jeans next, nearly tripping as I pull them on with trembling fingers.

"Not now, not now, not now," I mutter, but the panic is already clawing its way up my throat. The photo seems to be watching me, those twin smiles now feeling more like accusations. Why aren't you with us? Why are you still here when we're not?

I grab my boots from the closet, not even bothering to properly lace them. My wallet and phone go into my pockets with mechanical efficiency – muscle memory taking over while my brain spirals. Need to get out. Need air. Need... coffee. Books and Beans. Yes. The familiar smell of coffee and old books might ground me, might keep me from completely losing my shit.

I'm out the door before I realize I've forgotten my jacket, but the bite of the evening air against my arms is almost welcome. It gives me something else to focus on besides the way my heart is trying to hammer its way out of my chest. The walk to Books and Beans isn't terribly long, and movement helps. One foot in front of the other. Just keep moving.

Chapter 3: Books & Beans

Shelly

I WRAP MY HANDS around the coffee cup, pretending its still warm so no one catches on to how long it has actually been nearly ice cold. Two hours and counting on the same cup - probably some kind of record. A barista I'm not familiar with keeps giving me these looks, like she's trying to decide if I'm trouble or just pathetic. Joke's on her - I'm both.

My flannel sleeve slips down again as I reach for another sugar packet, more to have something to do with my hands than any desire to actually sweeten what's left of my drink. The frayed cuff is starting to come apart at the seams. I should probably try to find a needle and thread somewhere, but that feels like admitting this is my life now. Aging out of foster care with a shit for brains case worker, no high school education and no work history pretty much sets you up to be where I am at right now.

A group of college students bursts through the door, all designer bags and perfectly styled hair. One of them wrinkles her nose as she passes my chair in the corner, and I resist the urge to shrink into myself. Instead, I straighten my spine and stare right back at her. Yeah, I'm wearing the same Gojira shirt I've had on for three days. So what? At least I actually know their music, unlike that poser you're with in the vintage Metallica tee who probably thinks "Enter Sandman" is their only song.

My defiance deflates a bit when I catch my reflection in the window. The fluorescent lights do me no favors, highlighting the dark circles under my eyes and making my already pale skin look almost ghostly. For a moment, I let myself imagine what it would be like to be one of those girls - to have somewhere to go home to, to not count every penny, to not be planning which alley might be safest to sleep in tonight.

The coffee's gone completely stone cold now. I consider asking for a water refill just to buy more time, but my pride won't let me. The barista has moved from suspicion to concern. I think she has realized why I'm still here. I see Jenny tap her on the shoulder as if to say, '*Stop staring*.' But it's too late. The look of pity reddens my face with frustration and I force myself to look out the window as I fight off tears of anger and shame.

The clock on the wall ticks closer to 8PM, each movement of the minute hand making my stomach clench tighter. I've been mapping out possible sleeping spots in my head for the last hour - the alcove behind the dumpster at Pete's Pizza is usually empty, but the rats are bold there. Maybe the covered bus stop on 4th, though last time a drunk guy tried to...

"Excuse me?"

I look up to find one of the baristas hovering near my table, the one with the looks of pity. Her name tag reads 'Bethany' and I find myself wishing it was Jenny. Bethany's fidgeting with her apron strings, clearly uncomfortable. "Are you finished with your coffee?"

Before I can answer, a sharp voice cuts through the quiet atmosphere. "Obviously she's done. She's been nursing that same cup for hours."

A couple stands behind Jenny - both wearing expressions like they've smelled something rotting. The guy has his arm wrapped possessively around his girlfriend's waist, designer watch glinting under the lights.

"We'd like that chair," the girlfriend announces, as if declaring ownership of a small country. "And honestly, you really should do something about people who abuse the space like this. We come here all the time, and it's not fair that paying customers can't sit because homeless people use it as a haven."

My face burns hot enough to probably light up the whole shop. Bethany looks mortified, her eyes darting between me and the couple.

"I'm sorry," she says softly to me, "but you have been here for awhile, I do need to ask you to leave."

I stand up quickly, my chair scraping against the floor. The couple steps back like they're afraid poverty might be contagious. With trembling fingers, I grab my backpack and sling it over my shoulder, keeping my eyes fixed on the ground.

"Thank you for the coffee," I mumble to Bethany, my throat tight with humiliation.

I'm halfway out of the alcove, shame burning through my

chest, when a soft but commanding voice cuts through the tension.

"There you are! Sorry I'm late - traffic was awful."

I freeze, looking up to see the same man who warned me about the car earlier. He's holding two steaming cups of coffee and wearing the kind of casual confidence that makes the entitled couple take an instinctive step back. His salt-and-pepper beard catches the coffee shop lights as he smiles, but there's steel beneath the warmth in his eyes. Behind him I see Jenny. She gives me a reassuring nod with a hint of a smirk.

"I got your usual," he continues smoothly, setting one cup in front of my abandoned chair. "Though I see you started without me."

The couple exchanges uncertain glances. The girlfriend's perfectly manicured hand tightens on her purse strap. "We were just-"

"Just leaving, I hope?" His tone remains pleasant, but there's an edge there that makes me think of corporate boardrooms and power plays I've only seen in movies. "As you can see, this corner is occupied. I'm sure there are other seats available that would better suit your needs."

The boyfriend tugs at his collar, suddenly looking less certain about his position in the social hierarchy. "We didn't realize-"

"What? Didn't realize that someone was already sitting here waiting for someone? Maybe if you had simply asked." The man gestures toward the other side of the café. "I believe I saw some empty tables over there."

They retreat like scolded children, and I'm left standing awkwardly, my backpack still half-slung over my shoulder. He motions to the cushioned armchair again, his expression gentling as he meets my eyes.

"Please," he says quietly. "Sit. Your coffee's getting cold."

I hesitate, years of foster care instincts screaming at me not to trust this sudden kindness. But something in his face - maybe the hint of sadness around his eyes, or the way he's careful to keep his movements slow and non-threatening - makes me slowly sink back into the chair.

"I'm Connor, by the way. Connor Ebin." He settles into the chair across from me, his movements casual but somehow precise. "I got you a white chocolate mocha. I hope that's okay - it seemed like a safe bet."

I wrap my hands around the warm cup, trying not to look too eager even though the heat seeping into my cold fingers feels like heaven. "Thank you. For the coffee, and just now with..." I trail off, not wanting to relive the humiliation of moments ago.

He waves off my thanks with a slight frown. "People like that - they think their bank accounts give them the right to treat others like they're less than human. I can't stand it. They are the same type of people that will crumble to the least bit of hardship." His eyes meet mine, and there's a flash of recognition. "That was you earlier, wasn't it? At the crosswalk?"

I nod, taking a small sip of the mocha. It's perfect - sweet and rich and exactly what I needed. "Yeah. I'm Shelly."

"Shelly. Well, Shelly," he says, running a hand through his

salt-and-pepper hair, "I want you to know that I can move to another spot once those two leave if you'd prefer to be alone. I don't want to intrude or make you feel like you have to accept my presence. I just..." He pauses, something flickering across his face that I can't quite read. "I couldn't walk past and pretend I didn't see what was happening. Nobody deserves to be treated that way."

The sincerity in his voice catches me off guard. I've learned the hard way that kindness usually comes with strings attached, but something about Connor feels different. I read a book about auras once. How some people naturally make you feel happiness or dread. Maybe that's what it is, he has a calming aura? Or maybe it's the gentle authority in his manner, or the way he's carefully keeping his distance and making sure he moves slowly. Like right now as he shifts in his own armchair across form mine. Or maybe I'm just tired of talking to myself all the time and his blatant kindness is catching me way off my game.

I watch Connor shift around in his chair like he's thinking about getting up to leave. I realize it's been several minutes and I haven't said anything. He probably feels like he's making me uncomfortable. Something tightens in my chest - maybe it's my nerves acting up again, or just the familiar weariness that comes from spending so much time alone. No, it's because if he leaves now then those assholes will try and get me to vacate my chair again.

"You can stay," I blurt out, surprising myself. "If you want to, I mean."

Relief softens his features as he settles back into the chair.

He's trying not to stare at me, I can tell. His eyes keep darting away whenever they meet mine, like he's seen something that bothers him. Great. Even the nice ones probably think I'm weird.

"So," he says, clearing his throat, "what brings you here for coffee this late? Are you studying at one of the universities nearby?"

I nearly choke on my mocha. Me, a university student? Has he even looked at my clothes? The Gojira shirt that's got more holes in it than my jeans, the flannel that's practically falling apart at the seams? But then I see it - the hopeful look in his eyes, like he believes asking me about what I could be studying will get me excited. Like I'm just some normal college kid taking a study break.

"Yeah," I lie, hating how easily it comes. "Just needed a break from the books, you know?" I curl my fingers tighter around the warm cup, willing myself to look casual, like someone who actually belongs in this nice coffee shop, someone who has a dorm room to go back to later. Still, as the words come out they carry the obvious tone of a lying anime character. I nearly cringe.

The lie tastes bitter in my mouth, worse than the cold coffee from earlier. But it's better than the truth. Better than watching that kindness in his eyes turn to pity when he real-izes what I really am.

"I can only try to sympathize with needing study breaks," Connor says, a self-deprecating smile playing at his lips. "Never went to college myself, actually."

I nearly spill my mocha. He speaks with so much confidence and then there is the expensive watch and perfect haircut that stand out among his casual clothing. He didn't go to college? He must be joking. Before I can process this revelation, he leans forward slightly.

"What's your major?"

My stomach drops. Stupid, stupid, stupid. Of course he'd ask that. I frantically scan the coffee shop for inspiration, anything to keep this lie from falling apart. My eyes land on the TV mounted in the corner, currently playing commercials. A massive Viking warrior fills the screen, his tattooed skin glowing with mystical runes as he transforms into some kind of beast.

"Video game design!" I blurt out, immediately wanting to sink through the floor. Of all the majors I could have picked...

Connor's face lights up. "Really? That's fantastic! I actually work in that field myself."

Oh no. No, no, no. I watch in horror as the commercial continues, showing behind-the-scenes footage of the game's development. And there he is - Connor, standing in what looks like a motion capture studio, gesturing enthusiastically as he talks about something called "Rune Beast."

The caption underneath reads: "Connor Ebin - CEO, Eldritch Magic Gaming."

My mouth goes dry as I realize I just told the CEO of one of the biggest gaming companies in the world that I'm studying video game design. The mocha suddenly tastes like ash in my mouth as I try to figure out how to backpedal from this massive mistake.

I'm trying to figure out how to escape this lie I've created when Connor's attention shifts to the TV behind me. He curses under his breath and groans. His groan makes me turn to look too, and - oh. Oh wow. While I don't know if what I see is the reason for his groaning, the camera angle and the lighting in the studio make something terribly obvious.

The motion capture suit leaves absolutely nothing to the imagination. Like, nothing. I feel my cheeks heat up as I quickly avert my eyes, but not before getting an extremely detailed view of what Connor's packing beneath those slightly worn jeans. The skin-tight material of the mo-cap suit might as well be painted on, and the way he's gesturing animatedly in the commercial just makes everything... bounce.

"They promised they'd edit that part out," Connor mutters, running a hand through his hair in obvious discomfort. "Apparently marketing thought it would 'humanize' me to the gaming community. Because nothing says 'relatable CEO' like…" He cuts himself off after realizing he was talking louder than he intended.

His reaction is more humanizing than his…predicament. I bite my lip to keep from laughing at his obvious mortification. He's staring intently into his coffee cup now, a slight flush visible beneath his salt-and-pepper beard. It's kind of adorable how this clearly powerful man is reduced to embarrassed fidgeting by a poorly edited, or perhaps purposefully unedited, commercial.

"At least they didn't zoom in?" I offer, immediately wanting to smack myself. Real smooth, Shelly.

He lets out a surprised bark of laughter, some of the

tension leaving his shoulders. "Small mercies, I suppose. Though my marketing team suggested that might boost our female demographic. My social media messages suggest the opposite. Whole lot of unsolicited wiener sent my way."

Now we're both laughing, and for a moment I forget about being homeless, about lying about being a student, about everything except how nice it feels to share this awkward moment with someone who seems genuinely kind.

The laughter fades into a comfortable silence. I sip my mocha slowly, savoring each sweet mouthful because who knows when I'll get another one. Connor seems content just sitting there, occasionally running his hand through his hair like he's lost in thought.

"So..." I venture, surprising myself by breaking the quiet first. "What brings you here this late for coffee?"

He blinks, like I've pulled him out of deep thoughts. For a split second, something raw and painful flashes across his face - the kind of look I've seen in the mirror too many times to count. But it's gone so fast I almost think I imagined it.

"Ah, just trouble sleeping," he says, forcing a casual shrug that doesn't quite match his eyes. "Figure if I'm going to be awake anyway, might as well go for a walk and enjoy some decent coffee. Better than staring at the ceiling, right?"

He takes a deliberately long sip from his cup, and I recognize the move for what it is - a way to hide whatever's really going on behind those eyes. I know that trick. I've used it myself plenty of times when shelter workers ask how I'm "really doing."

The silence settles back in, but it's different now. There's a weight to it, like we're both pretending not to notice the other person's carefully constructed walls. I wrap my hands tighter around my cup, soaking in the last bits of warmth as the coffee slowly cools.

The silence stretches between us like a rubber band ready to snap. I can see Connor fidgeting with his coffee cup, probably trying to figure out a polite way to excuse himself. I should make it easier for him - tell him thanks for the coffee and the save from those pricks, then let him get back to his obviously much more important life.

But before I can speak, his eyes light up as he spots something on the lending shelf behind me.

"Hey, they have Settlers of Catan," he says, his voice warming with what sounds like fond memory. "Have you ever played?"

I shake my head, watching as he glances around the now quieter coffee shop. Those awful people from earlier are gone, leaving just a few other customers scattered around reading or working on laptops.

"We've got about an hour before they close," he says, then quickly adds, "Unless you need to go? I don't want to keep you if you have other plans. And if you'd rather have some privacy now that those..." He pauses, clearly choosing his words carefully, "...those individuals have left, I completely understand."

There's something in his expression - a mix of hope and hesitation - that makes my chest ache. Like he genuinely wants to spend more time with me but is afraid of pushing too hard. I should say no. Should protect myself from whatever this is. But...

"I've never played," I admit softly. "But I'd like to learn. If you're willing to teach me?"

The smile that breaks across his face makes him look younger somehow, less burdened. "I'd love to. It was..." He swallows hard, something flickering behind his eyes. "It was a family favorite."

Connor

Beyond thrilled that she agreed to play, I'm already pulling my phone out, fingers flying to the YouTube app. "It's fun board game. I'll explain the rules. They aren't too complicated." I pull up a YouTube video that explains the rules much faster than the rule book, which is a good thing since it appears to be missing from the box anyway.

I wave down Jenny, probably too enthusiastically. "Two more coffees, please! And... oh, that cream cheese danish looks amazing. We'll split that."

Mid-tap on my phone screen, I freeze. Shit. I didn't even ask if she wanted more coffee. Or if she likes danish. Or if she's a fan of cream cheese. Or if she even really wants to stay and learn a strategy game from some random guy who's acting like an overeager puppy at a dog park. I hope she's not just going along with this because she feels like she's obligated.

Get it together, Connor. You're not eight years old showing off your new Pog collections. Hell, do Pogs even exist anymore? I should look that up later.

"I'm sorry," I say, trying to rein in my excitement. "I just completely steamrolled over you there, didn't I? You don't have to have any of that if you don't want to. Or stay, for that matter. I got carried away."

Shelly's watching me with this careful, measuring look that makes me feel simultaneously exposed and intrigued. There's something in her eyes – a wariness, yes, but also a spark of curiosity. It reminds me of how Desiree used to watch street performers, like she was trying to figure out their tricks while still wanting to believe in the magic.

"I just..." I run a hand through my hair, somehow still feeling the dampness from my rushed shower. "I haven't played this with anyone in a long time. But please, don't feel obligated. The coffee and danish are yours either way."

Jenny approaches with our order, and I notice Shelly's shoulders tense slightly. But she doesn't leave. Instead, she leans forward just a fraction, eyes flickering between me and my phone screen where the game's tutorial is loading and says, "I'm good."

As the video plays, I feel something stirring in my chest – a lightness I haven't experienced since... well, since before. It's unsettling how familiar it feels, like putting on an old favorite sweater you forgot you owned.

Don't go there, Connor. Don't make this weird.

But damn if she doesn't look just like Olivia when she's concentrating, the way her brow furrows slightly as she watches the tutorial. Same thoughtful head tilt, same subtle lip bite. I force myself to look away, focusing instead on setting up the game board with probably more attention than hexagonal cardboard tiles deserve.

The tutorial ends, and I clear my throat. "Any questions? It can be a bit overwhelming at first."

She shakes her head. "No, it seems pretty straightforward."

For the next hour, we speak only in terms of resources, development cards, and trading. And holy shit, does she play like a seasoned pro. Every move is calculated, every trade purposeful. Before I know it, she's sitting there with ten victory points while I'm still struggling to maintain my longest road.

"Okay, wait a minute," I say, throwing my hands up in mock surrender. "Are you sure you've never played this before? Because I'm pretty certain I just got absolutely demolished by a Catan savant."

The corners of her mouth twitch upward – the closest thing to a smile I've seen from her all evening – and something in my chest does that weird flutter thing again. Then I begin to feel guilt creeping in. The flutter isn't what you're thinking. She just looks so much like my girls and it briefly makes me feel as if I am getting a glimpse into the future of an alternate universe where they are still alive. I'm playing the game with Desiree while she is on break between classes at she'll never take at UW, waiting for Liv to walk through a door she's never coming through again. I almost start to argue with myself. I seem incapable of allowing myself to enjoy anything. I wonder, not for the first or even thousandth time, if I can't let myself feel joy because I don't know if they can, wherever they are now.

Focus on the game, Connor. Just the game. The game that was apparently over before it started.

"And that's game," I announce, watching her place her final settlement. "You absolutely destroyed me. You, young lady, are a hustler. Glad I wasn't gambling."

She shakes her head, but there's that ghost of a smile again. As I start packing away the pieces, I notice her glancing out the window at the darkened sky, her shoulders tensing slightly. There's something in her expression – worry, maybe? – but it's gone before I can be sure.

Standing up, she tugs at the sleeve of her oversized flannel. "Thank you for the game. And the coffee. And... earlier."

"Thank you for humoring an older guy who needed his ego checked," I say, trying to keep things light. "If I see you in here again I'll want a rematch. Keep your head up out there. Seattle drivers are assholes."

She nods quickly and hurries out the door before I can say anything else. I watch her disappear into the cooling evening before heading to the counter.

"Hey Jenny, quick question – that young woman, does she come in often?"

Jenny glances toward the door, her usual cheerful expression faltering. "A few times a week, maybe? Always orders the cheapest drip coffee we have. Pretty sure she's..." She hesitates, lowering her voice. "I think she might be homeless."

My chest tightens. I'd suspected as much, but hearing it confirmed makes it real. "Yeah, I was afraid of that. Listen, next time she comes in? Whatever she wants, put it on my tab. I'll take care of it."

Jenny nods with her usual smile. "I will do just that, Mr. Ebin."

Walking back to my car, I spot Shelly's silhouette in the distance, getting smaller with each step. The warmth from our game session evaporates as I think about heading back to my empty apartment. The silence waiting for me like a predator toying with its food.

Chapter 4: Bitter Dessert

Shelly

I'M SEVERAL BLOCKS FROM the Books and Beans when my feet automatically shift into what I think of as my "don't fuck with me" walk - head high, shoulders back, purposeful stride. It's amazing how much safer you are when you look like you know exactly where you're going, even when you don't.

Connor's face keeps floating through my mind as I navigate the dimming streets. The way his eyes crinkled when he laughed at my brutal takedown in the game. How he didn't treat me like I was something gross stuck to his shoe, the way most people do when they see me in my raggedy clothes. The knowledge that just not being treated like shit by someone makes me feel good is concerning. Still, for a moment there, I felt... normal. Like I was just a regular person having coffee with a friend.

Friend. The word sits weird in my chest, both warm and scary at the same time. It's like finding a twenty dollar bill on the ground - you want to believe it's real, that it's meant for you, but you're terrified someone's going to show up and snatch it away. I haven't had a real friend since... well, maybe never. Foster kids learn quick that "friend" usually means someone who's either leaving soon or wants something from you.

A gust of wind whips through my flannel shirt, and reality crashes back in. Time to figure out where I'm sleeping tonight. The university library's open until midnight, but the security guard there knows my face now. There's that semi-sheltered spot behind the dumpster at Pete's Pizza, but last time some drunk asshole tried to piss there at 3 AM and of course there were the damned rats. If I didn't know better I would say they were bred to be fighting rats. There's a secluded park bench near the marina that is usually quiet, but it's supposed to drop into the low 40s tonight.

I imagine the coffee cup still warming my hands - the fancy mocha Connor refilled me with before I crushed him at the game. It's been out of my grip for going on an hour now, but I can't bring myself to forget about it yet. Something about pretending to hold onto the small piece of kindness for just a little longer.

My practiced stride carries me past the neon signs and evening crowds, my mind still caught between the warmth of those moments in the coffee shop and the cold reality of finding a safe spot to curl up for the night. It's weird how a few hours of normalcy can make everything else feel that much harder. In my defense, when I landed on the streets it was a few weeks from spring. This is my winter out in this shit.

The shopping center on 43rd floats into my mind - one of

those older strip malls with the deep overhangs that actually keep the rain off, unlike those useless modern designs. It's been what, two months since I tried staying there? Long enough that the security guard who hassled me last time might have moved on to an easier gig.

I adjust my route, cutting through the alley behind Mike's Auto Parts. The back corner of the shopping center, where it meets the chain-link fence, creates this perfect little nook. If you arrange yourself just right, you're invisible from both the street and the parking lot. Plus, the brick walls block most of the wind, which is starting to bite harder as night creeps in.

My stomach growls, reminding me that fancy coffee isn't exactly dinner. Sweet Dreams Bakery is right there on the end - they often toss their day-olds in the dumpster out back around closing time. The owner caught me once, but she just looked away and pretended not to see me. Some people have that kind of kindness in them, the quiet kind that doesn't need attention.

I slip my hands into my flannel pockets, feeling the worn fabric. These pockets are deep enough to hold quite a bit - a survival hack I learned early on. Even stale donuts and rock-hard bagels are better than nothing, and sometimes you get lucky and find something that's still pretty good. You just have to check carefully for mold in the dark, which is always fun. Like a really sad version of those food challenge shows on TV.

The thought makes me snort-laugh, and for a second I remember Connor's face when he got embarrassed by the commercial for his game. I shake my head as if it will reset my mind to focus on the present. Just like that the warm feeling fades quickly though, replaced by the practical reality of my situation. Time to scope out my corner and see if anyone else has claimed it since I was here last.

The gap in the fence is exactly where I remember it - a loose section you can shimmy through if you're skinny enough. And hey, being homeless has definitely helped in that department. The back lot of Sweet Dreams feels different tonight though. The usual trio of security lights is down to just one sad bulb, flickering like it's having an existential crisis. Shadows stretch across the pavement like grasping fingers, and I have to remind myself I've done this several times before.

My heart leaps when I spot a donut box perched right on top of the dumpster - usually I have to dig for these treasures. But when I pop it open, my excitement deflates faster than a dollar store balloon. Half a strawberry-frosted donut sits there like a sad little pink moon. I've never liked strawberry. It has always baffled me how so many women love the taste. I think some of them are faking it just because they're told girls are supposed to like it. Still, food is food. I scarf it down, trying not to think about how many days it's been since my last real meal. The cream cheese danish earlier was wonderful but really only served to remind my stomach that it had been a barren pool of acid for far too long.

The space between the dumpster and wall is tight but familiar. I gather some flattened boxes, laying them out like the world's saddest mattress. One piece gets propped up as a makeshift windbreak - my own personal interior decorating touch. Very chic, very homeless-couture.

Lying down, I can feel every point where my hip bones dig into the ground, even through the cardboard. It's weird to remember how I used to actually have real curves, back when the foster system at least made sure I got three meals a day. Now I'm all angles and sharp edges, like someone took an eraser to parts of me.

I shift, trying to find a position where something isn't jabbing into me. The cardboard crinkles with every move, a constant reminder that this is what passes for a bed these days. Foster care might have sucked, but at least I had a real mattress.

The sound of off-key whistling cuts through the night air, and my entire body goes rigid. I know that whistle - it's been haunting my nightmares for weeks. The tune's some old pop song, but he always mangles it into something sinister.

I peek around the edge of the dumpster, moving slow like I'm underwater. Bertrand's massive frame sways down the alley, and my throat closes up so tight I can barely breathe. The security light catches his face in grotesque shadows, highlighting the scabs where he's been scratching. My fingers dig into the cardboard beneath me, and I'm pretty sure I'm shredding it, but I can't make myself stop.

The last time I saw him... God, I can still feel his rough hands pawing at my clothes, the stink of his breath. If I hadn't woken up when I did and screamed-

He staggers closer, and that's when I notice it - the dirty rubber tubing still wrapped around his upper arm. His eyes are glazed, pupils pinned to dots. Not drunk then. Heroin.

Sometimes that makes him slower, sloppier. Other times it makes him mean as a kicked hornets' nest. He causes trouble for everyone of us on the streets.

I press myself further into the shadows, trying to make myself smaller. The cardboard beneath me feels like it's amplifying every breath, every heartbeat. He's close enough now that I can hear him mumbling between whistles, something about "pretty little thing" and "gonna find you."

My whole body's screaming at me to run, but movement would give me away. So I stay frozen, watching him weave through the dim light, praying to whatever might be listening that he doesn't decide to check behind this particular dumpster.

"Come out, come out, wherever you are..." Bertrand's voice slides through the darkness like oil on water. "I saw that sweet little ass walking this way. Bet you thought you were being sneaky, didn't you?"

I press my face against the rough brick, willing myself to melt into it. The cardboard beneath me feels like quicksand holding me in place.

"Remember last time?" He lets out a wet chuckle that makes my skin crawl. "I was just getting to the good part." His footsteps scrape against the pavement, getting closer. "I bet those little perky tits taste sweet. Been thinking about them, you know?"

My throat closes up so tight I can barely breathe. Again the security light exaggerates the monster and casts his elongated shadow across the ground. I watch it stretch toward my hiding spot like a grasping hand.

"Want to pick up where we left off, baby girl." The words slur together, riding on heroin-heavy breath. "No interruptions this time. Be a good little whore."

There's nowhere to run. The fence behind me is too high, the gap I squeezed through earlier suddenly feels like a trap. The only way out is past him, through the narrow alley space between the dumpster and wall. My heart pounds so hard I'm sure he must hear it.

His shadow looms larger. Closer. The scrape of his boots against concrete sounds like sandpaper on my nerves. I curl into myself, trying to become invisible, but the space suddenly feels impossibly exposed. He's going to find me. There's no way he won't.

"Come on out, pretty thing," he croons. "I know you're back here somewhere..."

The sound of a zipper being pulled down makes my blood run cold. Bertrand's heavy breathing gets closer as he yanks away my cardboard wall. His silhouette blocks what little light remains, and the smell of unwashed body and chemical sweat hits me like a physical blow.

"There you are, little whore." His gnarled dick is already in his hand, and bile rises in my throat. "Gonna make you take it all. Only question is where."

I press my palms against the rough concrete, muscles coiled to run. Even strung out, he's huge - but he's also high as fuck. I can outrun him. I have to, but in case I cant, I reach for a shard of broken glass that shines under the dumpster like a beacon.

"Such a pretty little mouth," he slurs, taking another step

closer. "Gonna stuff it full-"

A flash of blue and red light suddenly paints the alley walls. Bertrand whips around, nearly losing his balance, and I don't hesitate. I flatten myself and slide under the dumpster, ignoring the way the concrete scrapes my arms raw. For once, I'm grateful for how much weight I've lost - six months ago, I wouldn't have fit. I think to call out for help, but at the same time I'll expose myself and be told I am trespassing and I need to vacate the premises.

"Hey!" A firm voice cuts through the night. Car door slams. Heavy boots approach. "Sir, what do you think you're doing back here?"

From my hidden vantage point, I can see Bertrand hastily stuffing himself back in his pants. "Just taking a leak, officer."

"This is private property," the cop says. "And public urination is illegal. Move along before I run you in."

"Fuck you, pig," Bertrand spits, but he's already backing away. "I ain't done nothing wrong."

"Now," the officer commands, and even Bertrand isn't stupid enough to argue further.

I stay perfectly still under the dumpster, barely breathing, as Bertrand's uneven footsteps fade into the distance.

I wait under the dumpster until my arms go numb from the cold concrete, counting my breaths like I used to do during panic attacks in foster care. One-two-three-four. The cop car's long gone, but I can't make myself move yet. When I finally do crawl out, my whole body's shaking so bad I can barely stand.

The tears come without warning, hot and silent down my

cheeks. I slide down the brick wall, hugging my knees to my chest, and let them fall. Fuck. Just... fuck everything.

"You'll be fine on your own," Mrs. Patterson had said when I aged out, not even bothering to look up from her phone. "You're so good with the little ones, I'm sure you'll find work as a nanny or something."

Right. Because who wouldn't want to hire a homeless teenager with no real diploma and zero job history? The bitch had made sure of that, keeping me trapped in that house 24/7 to watch her revolving door of foster kids while she and her husband collected checks for all of us.

"We're homeschooling Michelle," she'd tell the social workers with that fake-ass smile. What she meant was I spent my days changing diapers and making meals while she went shopping or got her nails done. No GED prep, no actual education - just endless hours of being their unpaid servant.

I dig my fingers into my arms, remembering all the times I'd asked to get a part-time job. "But who would watch the children?" Mr. Patterson would say, like I was being selfish for wanting something - anything - for myself. They'd had it all figured out - free childcare courtesy of the foster system, with bonus government checks for their trouble.

A sob catches in my throat, raw and ugly. One whole fucking year on the streets because they made damn sure I couldn't stand on my own two feet. No skills, no education, no references - nothing but the clothes on my back and a system that stopped giving a shit the minute I turned eighteen.

My hands won't stop shaking as I gather what's left of my cardboard. No way in hell I'm staying here - Bertrand knows this spot now. The thought of him coming back, maybe with friends this time...

Something glints in the security light near the bakery's back door. A bread knife, probably tossed out after breaking. The serrated edge is still intact, though the handle's split. It's not much, but it's better than the shard of glass I was reaching for earlier. I slide it carefully into my flannel's deep pocket, trying not to think about whether I'd actually be able to use it if I had to.

Pete's Pizza is a twenty-minute walk, and every shadow makes me jump. I would rather put up with the aggressive super rats, and the smell of stale piss even though it is enough to make your eyes water, but at least there are usually other people around. Safety in numbers, even if those numbers are mostly passed-out drunks and fellow street residents.

The alley behind Pete's comes into view, and I spot three familiar shapes huddled around a steam vent. They aren't friends by any stretch but we still share nods of acknowledgment. More people means less chance of getting jumped. Sure, someone might try to steal my shoes while I sleep, but that's better than... I push away the memory of Bertrand's hands, his voice, that sickening zipper sound.

I find a spot against the wall, far enough from the steam vent to avoid attention but close enough to see if anyone approaches. The knife in my pocket presses against my hip - not comfortable, but comforting in a way I don't want to examine too closely.

It takes me longer than I would like to fall asleep. Truth be told after the altercation earlier I fight sleep off for a bit, but I eventually close my eyes and let sleep find me.

Chapter 5: Admissions & Secrets

Connor

THE SEATTLE SKYLINE STRETCHES out before me, all steel and glass catching the morning light, but I'm not really seeing it. My mind keeps drifting back to the board game at Books and Beans, to the way Shelly's eyes lit up when I admitted my crushing defeat. I've stayed away from my favorite coffee shop for three days. I deliberately tried to keep it from my mind, though every fiber of my being wanted to go back. The last thing that girl needs is some creepy older guy making her uncomfortable at one of the few places she can find refuge. I did end up going back on day four, but she hadn't been there and neither was Jenny, so I couldn't ask her. It had been another three days since then.

Christ, she looks so much like my Liv.

I drum my fingers on my desk, wondering if Jenny's been keeping track of my secret tab, if Shelly's been getting enough to eat. The thought of her sleeping rough makes my stomach churn. But what am I supposed to do? Roll up in my Lexus and play white knight? That would probably send her running for the hills. Hell, she would probably assume I was trying to pull a Pretty Woman on her. I chuckle to myself knowing she probably has no idea that movie even exists.

"If you stare any harder at that window, you might actually succeed in burning a hole through it."

Manu's dry voice snaps me back to reality. He's leaning against my office doorframe, arms crossed, wearing that knowing smirk that makes me want to throw a stapler at him.

"I was thinking about the Rune Beast character models," I lie, straightening in my chair.

"Sure you were." Manu walks in and drops a folder on my desk. "And I'm secretly a K-pop star. Want to tell me what's really eating at you, or should I pretend to believe you're actually this invested in polygon counts?"

I run a hand through my hair, catching a whiff of the lavender and ginger beard oil that Liv bought me long ago and that I refuse to stop getting. The act of stopping the reoccurring order feels like betrayal to me for some reason. "It's nothing. Just... lost in thought."

"Uh-huh." Manu raises an eyebrow. "Well, when you're done being 'lost in thought,' we have actual work to do. The dev team's waiting for your input on the combat mechanics."

"We can deal with that in a minute. I want to hear more about your secret K-pop life."

Manu rolls his eyes. "You know, sex, drugs and exotic foods. The good life."

"The dev team wants to go over the differences between console and PC mechanics?" I ask, already knowing the answer. The ache in my shoulders tells me I'll be spending hours hunched over multiple team members shoulders as they show me what does and doesn't work well in the conversion.

"Yeah. Keyboard and mouse versus controller is giving them fits with this one for some reason," Manu confirms, settling into one of my office chairs. "But while we're on the subject of development..." He leans forward, that gleam in his eye that usually means I'm about to end up with more work. "I had an idea about the Rune Beast and the Seidr Witch's relationship."

I raise an eyebrow. "I'm listening."

"We already have a romance established between them, but what if they could 'commune' together? Like, intimately." Manu's face remains perfectly neutral. "It could unlock special power upgrades for the Rune Beast at different intervals through out the game."

"You mean full on adult animation scenes like last years Game of the Year?" I lean back, stroking my beard thoughtfully. "Their romance scenes practically broke the internet."

"Exactly. But we'd need to do it right. No half-assing it."

I nod slowly. "It could work. The marketing practically writes itself. 'Forge a deeper connection with—'" The realization hits me. "Oh fuck no."

Manu's smirk grows wider. "You're our motion capture guy for the Rune Beast. Back in the suit you go."

I groan and slump forward, forehead hitting my desk with a dull thud. "I hate you so much right now. The last time I wore that suit, I had sensor dots stuck in my beard for three days and then our wonderful marketing assholes left my perfectly outlined hog in the damn developmental update video for everyone to see! You know what that is like?" The memory alone makes me itch.

"To have people whispering about my dick? Not in the way they were whispers about yours." Manu says with a flat smile. "Think of it this way – at least you can get up close and personal with Maddison again when she does the Seidr Witch's mo-cap."

I groan. Maddison is a lovely woman but haven't been able to get myself in the frame of mind for anything like that in the last five years. Manu turns and closes my office door before sitting down across from me at my desk. "I'm not leaving until you tell me what you were really spacing out about."

I sigh, knowing Manu won't let this go. He's like a terrier with a bone when he senses something's up. Plus, if anyone would understand this situation without jumping to conclusions, it's him. He knew me before Liv, was at our wedding, helped me pick out Desiree's first bike.

"Remember when I left early last week?" I lean back in my chair, studying the ceiling. "I ran into this homeless girl who almost got hit by a car. She..." My voice catches. "She looks like them, Manu. Like if you mixed Liv and Des together."

Manu's expression shifts from curiosity to concern at the tone of my voice. "Shit."

"Yeah." I rub my beard again, the familiar scent of Liv's oil grounding me or haunting me. I honestly can't tell. "Ended up running into her again at Books and Beans. We played that Settlers of Catan game Liv and Des loved to play. She kicked my ass, actually." I can't help but smile at the memory.

"And now you're worried about her," Manu states. It's not a question.

"She's sleeping on the streets, man. In fucking Seattle. Winter's coming."

Manu studies me for a moment. "Connor, is she hot?"

"For fucks sake!" I snap, then force myself to calm down. "…yes, she's attractive, but that's not… it's not like that. She's just a girl that needs help."

"Mmm." Manu nods slowly. "Probably best not to mention this to Ashlyn. You know how she's been about getting you 'back out there' and you have repeatedly told her you are not ready. Finding out you're spending time with a much younger woman – even innocently – might set her off or give her the wrong idea."

"Yeah, good call." I grimace, remembering Ashlyn's last attempt to set me up with her yoga instructor. "The last thing I need is her getting the wrong idea about this and then to start meddling."

Manu shrugs. "You might not even see this girl again for all you know. She could have been just passing through and heading to somewhere else in the city."

"Jenny said she usually comes in a few times a week with just enough to buy their cheapest coffee so I'm pretty sure she stays around here. Hopefully at the shelters."

Manu sighs with a look of mild concern. "You remember when we did that charity drive two winters ago to help fund the shelters around Seattle? I talked with our public relations officer then and he said that many of the shelters are first come first serve everyday. Those that aren't, he said, don't tend to be the types of shelters women should stay at alone. It's mostly men with addiction or mental health issues. Not to bring your day down even further. You already know you have to model your dick for a room full of people again I'm just making things worse."

His attempt to lighten the mood at the end of his rant did work, but only enough to get me to smirk.

I sit forward and hit the button on my office phone that calls Ashlyn directly. She answers with her usual sweet tone that I have heard turn to ice when people give her attitude about my schedule. "Yes, Connor?"

"Get with public relations and get the fundraiser and donation for the shelters going again, please."

"Sure thing, Connor. Anything else?" I can hear the prodding tone in her voice.

"Actually, contact Maddison Ball and let her know we have some scenes to shoot. Please inform her they are…intimate." I bite my lip right after saying the words, knowing Ashlyn will read too much into them.

"Really? Does this me-"

"That is all." I quickly hang up the call and ignore Manu's wicked smirk.

"She is really pushing for it. She'll wear you down and get you to start dating again eventually. Even if it's only to get her to shut up about it. If she hadn't been Olivia's best friend I don't think she would be pushing so hard. I think she feels like it's what Olivia would want for you." This is one of the most serious things the man has said to me in all our years as friends.

"Change of subject please." I rub the palms of my hands into my eyes.

"Speaking of changes," Manu shifts in his chair, his expression darkening slightly. "I had to let Trevor go this morning."

"The junior dev? What happened?"

"Caught him trying to push the inclusion of micro-transactions to other devs again. Third time this month." Manu's jaw tightens. "Kept insisting we were 'leaving money on the table' by not monetizing character skins and rune upgrades."

I feel my blood pressure spike. "Jackass. After what happened with that Septic Tank Studios disaster last year?"

"Exactly. I told him our stance on that bullshit when we hired him. No predatory mechanics, period." Manu shakes his head. "Anyway, you're still coming over Saturday for the triple threat match, right? Champion's defending against both challengers. Triple threat match my man. There will be tables, ladders and chairs." He dangles the last sentence at me like a carrot to a horse.

The thought of wrestling night at Manu's place brings a genuine smile to my face. It's one of the few normal things left in my life. "Wouldn't miss it. I've got money on the Blackfang taking it."

The rest of the day passes in a blur of meetings and development reviews. When I finally make it to my car, I grip the steering wheel and feel that familiar tightness in my chest starting to build. The parking garage is too quiet, too empty. But I refuse to let it happen again. Not today.

Instead of sitting there drowning in memories, I force my-self to start the car and head straight to the gym. Brazilian jiu jitsu practice will help keep the demons at bay, even if every time I walk into the dojo I expect to see Des's little gi-clad form bouncing around the mats, begging me to watch her new moves.

Chapter 6: 'Sisterly' Sanctuary

Shelly

THE RATS ARE GETTING bolder. I swear one of them sized me up last night like it was considering whether I'd make a good meal. Pete's Pizza isn't exactly five-star accommodations, but at least the brick wall blocks some of the wind and there are a few heating vents that intermittently give out a blast of warmth. My threadbare flannel doesn't do much against the autumn chill anymore.

Sleep over the last several nights has come in fragments between the scuttling of tiny feet and drunken shouting from the late-night customers. Every time I would start to drift off, someone stumbled out the back door, usually to puke or worse. The smell of garlic and pepperoni that used to make my mouth water now just turns my stomach.

I look over at the digital marque outside the gas station down the block and see that its 5:37am. If I hurry, maybe I can beat the morning rush at Soaring Angels. Last night was particularly rough enough that I'd kill for an actual bed, even if it means dealing with the shelter drama.

The streets are quiet this early, just delivery trucks and the occasional early commuter. My boots scrape against the sidewalk as I quicken my pace, trying to generate some warmth. I hope that perverted asshole Bertrand got himself arrested or something. The memory of his leering face makes my skin crawl.

I step onto the same block as Soaring Angels when I hear someone call out my name. "Michelle? Oh my God, Michelle!"

I freeze. That voice - I haven't heard it in what, seven years? Across the street, Heidi Mason is practically bouncing up and down, her perfect blonde hair catching the pre-dawn light. Her facial features look almost exactly like she did when we shared a room at the Hendersons', except grown up and somehow even prettier. The rest of her on the other hand is much different. She's dressed in rainbow colored fishnets, a huge shiny and plush red jacket and heels that I can't begin to understand how she is standing in, let alone walking.

"Shell, wait right there!" she calls out, already dodging through early morning traffic to reach me. Her excitement feels like a spotlight, making me painfully aware of my un-washed hair and ragged clothes.

I consider running. Seven years is a long time, and I'm not exactly in a position to catch up over coffee and croissants. But before I can decide, she's already here, wrapping me in a hug that smells like expensive perfume, vape scent and a sex? Still probably a more normal life than I have achieved.

"Oh my God, Shell, I can't believe it's really you!" Heidi's enthusiasm hits like a sugar rush, making me dizzy. "You look... well, you're still so pretty! Those eyes of yours, I swear they got even greener!"

I shuffle my feet, trying to find words that won't make this more awkward than it already is. "You look good too, Heidi." My voice comes out smaller than I intend.

"What have you been up to? Are you working around here?" Her smile is genuine, which somehow makes this worse.

I gesture weakly toward the Soaring Angels sign down the block. Understanding floods her features, followed by determination. "Oh hell no, that place is a shithole. You're coming with me."

"I don't need-"

"Just got off work at Madame's Lust," she continues, talking over my protest. "Got a sweet little one-bedroom nearby. You can crash on my couch, get cleaned up, wash your clothes..." She eyes my flannel shirt. "Or maybe we can find you some new ones."

The mention of a shower makes my resolve waver. When was the last time I had hot water that wasn't from a gas station bathroom sink? "I appreciate it, but I can't-"

"Can't what? Accept help from family?" Her perfectly manicured fingers wrap around my wrist. "We were sisters once, remember? For like six whole months?"

"Foster sisters," I mutter, but she's already pulling me along.

"Same difference. Come on, I'm not taking no for an answer. Consider it payback for that time you took the blame when I broke Mrs. Henderson's ceramic cat collection."

I remember that day. I also remember how she snuck me extra desserts for a week after. Maybe... maybe just one shower wouldn't hurt. Wait, did she say Madame's Lust? Isn't that the strip club? That explains the fishnets and high heels that probably require acrobatic skills.

Heidi's apartment is... something else. Every surface seems covered in feather boas, glittery outfits, and what I'm pretty sure are various types of bondage gear. A hot pink riding crop hangs from a decorative hook next to what appears to be a very expensive leather corset.

"Sorry about the mess," Heidi says, tossing her keys into a bowl shaped like, um, male anatomy. "Occupational hazard. When you're in the business of making fantasies come true, the props tend to follow you home."

I shift awkwardly, trying not to stare at what looks like a collection of whips arranged in a fan pattern on one wall. "It's... unique."

"That's one word for it." She grins, gesturing broadly. "Welcome to my den of iniquity. Where the furniture's like me - looks expensive but has seen some shit."

The unexpected joke startles a laugh out of me. "I guess you could say it's all been... thoroughly used?"

"Oh my God, Shell!" Heidi cackles, shrugging off her puffy red jacket. "You actually made a dirty joke! I'm so proud."

My amusement fades as I take in her outfit - or what there is of it. A sparkly halter top that dips very low and matching bottoms that are so tight they leave very little to the imagination. I mean, hell, her labia are nearly spilling out of what has to be the thinnest thing that can pass for fabric. Her figure is absolutely incredible, all curves and smooth skin. I glance down at my own boy-ish, no that's not the word, that makes is sound like I have no curves at all…tomboy-ish frame, feeling suddenly very small and underdeveloped.

"Hey, none of that," Heidi says, catching my expression. She cups her generous chest with both hands. "These babies? Cost five grand, courtesy of Derek the dickhead ex-boyfriend. At least he left me with something useful when he lost his job in an embezzlement scandal."

"Bathroom's through there," Heidi points to a door adorned with what appears to be a poster from some kind of adult film. "Just toss your clothes outside the door, and I'll get them in the wash. Don't worry about borrowing mine - I've got some normal clothes too, believe it or not."

I nod gratefully, clutching my flannel shirt closer. "Thanks, really. This is… nice of you."

"That's what sisters are for, right?" She winks and heads toward what I assume is her bedroom.

The bathroom is… well, it's…I'll just say it, it looks like a sex dungeon in a bathroom. Every surface seems to have some kind of exotic item that makes my cheeks burn. I try to focus on the actually relevant things - like the fluffy purple towels and fancy-looking shampoo bottles. I'm no prude but the items in here are not the standard sexual enhancement toys that most women have in their nightstands.

Something catches my eye on the wall and - oh. Oh my. That's… definitely not a normal shower accessory. It's purple and has ridges and what appear to be small horns and… I flick it with my finger before I can stop myself, watching it wobble obscenely.

"Everything okay in there?" Heidi calls out. "Feel free to use anything you find - it's all sanitized after use!"

"O-okay!" My voice comes out as an embarrassing squeak. I remove the broken bread knife from my flannel and nearly panic. Heidi's is going to think she let a psycho killer in her place if she sees this. I quickly stash it behind cleaning supplies under the bathroom sink. I slowly strip off my clothes, bundle them up, and crack the door just enough to set them outside.

I turn and catch my reflection in the full-length mirror mounted on the back of the bathroom door. Jesus. When did I get so... small? I mean, I was never curvy like Heidi, but there used to be more of me. Now my hip bones jut out like they're trying to escape, and the space between my thighs could probably house one of those rats from Pete's Pizza.

Cupping my breasts, I give them a gentle squeeze. They're still perky at least, but definitely less full than they were even six months ago. My large puffy areolas look almost too big for them now. A flash of dark hair under my arms catches my attention, and I grimace. My eyes trail down my flat (too flat) stomach to the wild forest I've got going on below.

"Fuck's sake," I mutter, running fingers through the unruly mass of auburn curls. "I look like a seventies porn star down here."

It reminds me of all those post-apocalyptic shows I used to watch at the library. You know, the ones where civilization has completely collapsed, but somehow every female character still has perfectly smooth legs, pristine armpits, and a probably completely bare pussy (can't be sure since they never showed that). Not to mention the perfectly applied makeup and styled hair. Like, really? You're fighting off zombie hordes but still finding time to maintain a Brazilian wax?

Steam starts to fill the bathroom as turn the shower on full blast. On a small glass pedestal in the shower stall, I spot some precision scissors and a razor among various shower products. The razor... no, that feels too intimate to share. But maybe the scissors...

First though, I'm going to stand under this hot water until my skin turns lobster red. It's been way too long since I've felt actual warm water that didn't come from a public sink.

The water running off my body looks like something out of a horror movie - weeks of grime and city filth turning it a murky brown. I should probably feel disgusted, but the heat feels too damn amazing to care. My muscles practically sing as the water pounds against them, releasing tension I didn't even know I was carrying.

I grab a bottle of shower gel that smells like a candy store threw up in it. Normally I'd gag at something this sweet, but right now it's exactly what I need to feel human again. The lather builds up thick and pink, washing away the streets, the cold nights, the lingering fear.

My eyes keep drifting to those scissors sitting on their little glass throne. Fuck it. I grab them and start working on the jungle between my legs. It takes some careful maneuvering, but eventually I can actually see my labia again instead of just a mass of tangled curls. Moving to my armpits, I hesitate. The scissors would work, but...

"In for a penny," I mutter, reaching for Heidi's razor. My armpits go first, smooth skin emerging from beneath dark stubble. Then I look down at my legs. The hair there actually provides a bit of warmth on cold nights, but...

"Fuck it." The razor glides up my calf, leaving a clean stripe through the forest. It feels ridiculously luxurious, this simple act of grooming.

"Hey Shell?" Heidi's voice carries through the door. "I can hear the shower running. Girl, stop that nonsense and take a bath. You deserve a proper soak - doctor's orders! Treat yourself babe!"

My throat tightens unexpectedly. When was the last time someone cared about what I "deserved"? Connor. Connor did too, or at least he seemed to. Why does that man keep invading my mind? I blink back tears as I reach for the drain plug.

"Thanks, Heidi," I manage to croak out, switching the water to fill the tub. The simple kindness of being treated like a real person again hits harder than I expected.

The warmth of the bath seeps into my muscles, making my eyelids heavy. I can't remember the last time I felt this... safe. The lock on the door is solid, I'm surrounded by four walls and Heidi's taste in music, while not exactly my style, creates a cocoon of sound around me. Still I would prefer some heavy or goth metal like The Nightfallen.

Some bass-heavy pop song with synthesizers thumps through the walls. That ridiculous purple monster on the wall actually vibrates with each beat, making me snort with unexpected laughter. The sound of my own genuine amusement startles me.

Surrounded by all of this sex wakes me up. I'm alone. Actually, properly alone. Not the fake alone of a library bathroom stall or the tense alone of a hidden corner in an alley. But real, door-locked, music-blasting, no-one-can-get-to-me alone.

My eyes drift over the collection of toys scattered around the bathroom. That demon dick is definitely out of the question - looks more like a weapon than a pleasure device. Some of the others though... No. That's crossing a line. These are Heidi's personal items, and I've already borrowed her razor.

Still... it has been so long. The few times I've managed to touch myself this past year have been rushed, paranoid affairs. Always one ear listening for footsteps, always nervous and ready to be interrupted. Yet another thing most people do every day and take for granted.

I glance at the door again. The lock gleams reassuringly in the soft bathroom light. The music throbs louder, as if encouraging me. My hand slides down my newly nearly smooth skin, finding that familiar spot. For once, I don't have to rush. For once, I can just... feel.

I let my head fall back against the tiled wall, warm water lapping at my shoulders. My fingers trace lazy circles around my clit, building that familiar tension. I dip lower, teasing my entrance, gathering wetness that has nothing to do with the bath.

My free hand finds my breast, rolling my nipple between thumb and forefinger. The sensation sends little sparks of pleasure down my spine, but something's missing. I've never been good at just focusing on the physical - my mind needs somewhere to go, some fantasy to latch onto.

My thoughts drift to Tommy, my foster 'brother' from the Williams' place. Nope. That memory kills any arousal instantly. Those self-righteous assholes shipped me off like I was damaged goods after they found out what we were doing. Moving on.

What about Chris from next door at the Pattersons'? Now there's a better memory. We'd been fooling around in his room while his parents were at work. My hand down his pants, his mouth hot on my breast. I remember how hard he was when I finally freed him from his jeans, how eager we both were. Then he bucked his hips and knocked over a scalding cup of coffee from his folding table. I yanked my hand away just in time, but his dick took a direct hit.

A snort of laughter escapes me at the memory. Poor Chris, hopping around his room clutching his crotch, face red from both embarrassment and pain. Not exactly spank bank material either.

The memory of spilled coffee leads my thoughts naturally to that night at Books and Beans. Connor, sitting across from me, his salt-and-pepper beard catching the warm café lighting. Those dark eyes focused entirely on me, like I was actually worth seeing.

My fingers still between my legs as a pulse of unexpected arousal catches me off guard. Well, that's... interesting. I mean, yeah, he's attractive - that whole silver fox vibe definitely works for him. But he has to be what, early forties?

That's twice my age.

Then again... My fingers resume their slow circles as I picture his strong hands shuffling those game cards. The way his shirt stretched across his chest when he leaned forward. How his eyes crinkled at the corners when he smiled. That warm, rich laugh when I destroyed him at the game.

The tension builds faster now, my breath catching. There's something incredibly hot about the way he just... took care of things. Handled that couple giving me trouble. Bought me coffee without making me feel like a charity case.

I mean, really, what's the harm in a fantasy? Women everywhere get off thinking about thousand-year-old vampires and immortal elves ravishing them. At least Connor's real. Real, and successful, and genuinely kind...

My hips rock against my hand as I imagine those strong arms wrapping around me, keeping me safe. His large hands touching me with the same focused attention he gave everything else. That deep voice murmuring that he'll take care of me...

The mental image sends another throb through my core. Fuck it. If I'm going to indulge in impossible fantasies, I might as well enjoy this one.

I lose myself in the fantasy. The image of those dark eyes focused on me now as he lowers his head, kissing a trail down my neck, sends another jolt of want through me. In my fantasy, I let him. I imagine the coffee shop disappearing, just the two of us left in the dim light.

Strong arms wrap around me, lifting me easily onto the counter. My breath hitches as he settles me there, his hands firm but gentle. His lips find the sensitive spot just below my ear, sending shivers down my spine. One hand slides up my body, under my shirt, and cups my breast with a possessive confidence that makes my breath catch.

"I'll handle everything," he murmurs, his voice a deep rumble that makes my core clench. "Don't worry, Shelly."

The sound of my name on his lips nearly undoes me. I arch my back as his fingers tease my nipple through the fabric of my bra, my imagination taking care of the details, providing the sensations I crave. That beard of his against my thighs as he kneels, his mouth finding the core my own wetness.

I moan, picturing him there, face buried in my lips as he feasts on me like a man starved. I run my fingers through his hair, the soft texture soothing to the touch. He pulls back, eyes dark with hunger with a look that says he's just getting started.

I'm gasping now, back arching harder as my imagination fills in the exquisite torture of his tongue swirling around my clit, his breath hot against my pussy. I grasp his hair as I picture myself hovering on the edge of the counter, his firm hands gripping my thighs to hold me in place while he devours me.

I have a brief moment where I realize how shocked I am that I am letting this fantasy take such a large hold of me. I'm imagining things I've only ever seen in movies or read in books. Look, I know I just made fun of those women a little bit, but when you spend enough time in the library to take refuge from whatever weather Seattle is throwing out at the time you get curious enough to see what all these women are raving about.

The tub is forgotten as my fantasy shifts us to the chair he sat in at Books and Beans. My legs wrap around his waist as he sits, cradling me close. I can feel the hardness of his length through his pants as he settles me in his lap.

The sensation of his mouth on mine is so real, I swear I can taste him. One hand tangles in my hair, tilting my head back to deepen the kiss, while the other slides down my body, pulling my panties aside again. His fingers find my clit, rubbing slow circles that match the rhythm of his tongue in my mouth.

My hips buck involuntarily as my fantasy fully takes over, my imagination filling in the sweet torture of his touch. I'm so close, riding that knife-edge of pleasure. Next thing I know my vision shifts and he's inside me, my imagination so vivid right now that I can almost feel his girth filling me up. I ride him while he holds me tight. His eyes locked with mine, those dark sweet eyes, they tell me he doesn't just want my body, he wants all of me.

That's it. Right there. It's not the hardcore sex, although that is definitely helping, it's that look that tells me 'You have nothing to worry about, Shelly. I'll take care of you.' That's what sends me over the edge. My entire body shudders in the most explosive and pent up orgasm I have ever felt in my entire life.

Then reality intrudes in the form of a throbbing ache in my shoulder and wrist. The fantasy fades as I realize my hand is clenched around the shower curtain, my neck stiff from being arched for so long. With a soft groan, my hand releases, sitting back in the tub as I realize I've been in the tub long enough for the water to start to cool.

The remnants of my fantasy still cling to me as I sink down further, the water now covering my breasts. Connor's face floats in my mind's eye, dark eyes fixed on me, lips parted as if waiting for mine.

I shake my head, sending droplets of water flying. Get a grip, Shelly. The man is like twenty years older than you. It was just a game, a damn cup of coffee. He probably doesn't even think about you at all.

I reach blindly for a washcloth, needing to just... scrub away this weird feeling coiling inside me. This longing for someone who's probably forgotten all about me and that I have probably romanticized beyond all reason.

But even as I scrub, I find my mind drifting to impossible dreams. That is until Heidi knocks at the door again to ask if I'm OK. "I'm getting out now, I think I drifted off for a second."

Somehow even through the door I sense that she knows I'm lying.

Chapter 7: Friend Request

Connor

THE MAT SQUEAKS UNDER my feet as I bow to Professor Armando. My gi is soaked through with sweat, and my muscles have that pleasant ache that comes from a good training session. Tonight's rolling helped quiet my mind, but not enough. Not nearly enough.

The locker room's familiar mix of bleach and foot funk hits me as I strip off my gi. The shower's hot water pounds against my shoulders, and I try not to think about how Desiree used to practice her breakfalls on these same mats, her little face scrunched up in determination.

Fuck.

I bang my forehead against the tile, letting the water run down my back. This is exactly what I'm trying not to do – spiral into memories that'll leave me a mess. I want so badly to be like others and just look back on these kinds memories with fondness, but for some reason I can't stop feeling over-whelming sadness and at times guilt. The shower's getting cold, so I step out and start drying off.

My suit from work feels oddly formal after the gi, like I'm playing dress-up. Olivia's lavender beard oil I keep in my gym bag helps tame the post-shower mess of my beard, but there's no saving my hair – it's going to do whatever the hell it wants tonight. Running my hands through it only makes it worse, so I give up.

The thought of going home to that empty apartment makes my chest tight. The silence there has teeth lately, and I'm not ready to face it. Books and Beans is open late on Fridays – maybe I can lose myself in a book for a few hours, let the ambient coffee shop noise drown out the thoughts I'm trying to avoid. Maybe she'll be there.

I grab my gym bag, nod goodbye to Professor Armando, and head out into the Seattle night. The suit feels like overkill for a coffee shop, but it's better than the alternative of sitting alone in my living room, trying to decide what show to watch or what game to play until I get overwhelmed and do nothing again.

The bell above the door chimes as I enter Books and Beans. Jenny's already reaching for my usual Bean Club Mug before I hit the counter. Olivia and I both joined their Bean Club years ago when they first opened their doors. It was one hundred dollar to join, but you got a mug with your name on it and half priced coffee for the first year. She had made a joke that while their beans were half off, hers was free and I could put my lips on it whenever I wanted. She had a habit of saying the most out of pocket things when she was sure people around us could hear. Olivia's mug has sat next to mine on their Club Shelf for a lonely five years now.

"Still haven't seen her, Mr. Ebin," Jenny says, anticipating my question. Her ponytail swishes as she shakes her head. "I've been keeping an eye out, like you asked."

"Thanks, Jenny." I try to keep my voice neutral, professional. "I hope that means she found somewhere safe to stay." The alternative – morgue drawers, hospital beds, police reports – tries to crowd into my mind, but I shove it back.

She hands me my coffee, and I drift to the spot where Shelly demolished me at Catan. The chair feels different, but the view of the street's the same. Steam rises from my cup as I watch people hurry past in the growing dark, none of them the person I'm hoping to see.

The borrowing shelf catches my eye, and I grab a book at random. My breath catches when I see the cover – "Lavender and Ginger: A Callus Kordec Tale." The spine's cracked and well used.

I used to read this to Des before bed. She loved the adventure parts, the magic, the intrigue. When it got to the steamy scenes, I'd just say "and then they kissed a lot" and skip ahead while she made exaggerated gagging noises. Liv would stand in the doorway sometimes, trying not to laugh at my creative editing.

The beard oil I'm wearing right now – that was Liv's idea after reading this together the first time. "If Callus loved the smell of lavender and ginger," she'd teased, "then so can my sexy husband." She bought me my first bottle the next day. Now I can't bring myself to use anything else.

I set the book down without opening it. Some memories are still too sharp, even after all this time.

My eyes dart to the door for what feels like the hundredth time tonight. A flash of auburn hair makes my heart jump, but it's just some teenager with their nose buried in their phone. This keeps happening – my brain desperately trying to transform random strangers into her. The girl with the backpack crossing the street. The woman huddled at the bus stop. Each time, my pulse quickens, and each time, reality crashes back in.

I try to focus on my coffee, now lukewarm and forgotten. The bell chimes again, and I force myself not to look. But then-

"Connor? I thought that was you!"

Ashlyn's voice, not Shelly's. She's wearing one of those floral dresses she favors, looking fresh despite the late hour. I watch as she orders something that sounds more like dessert than coffee – caramel this, whipped cream that, enough sugar to give an elephant diabetes.

"Mind if I join you?" She's already pulling out the chair across from me, not really waiting for an answer. "How long have you been camping out here?"

"Just got here," I lie, straightening up like I haven't been slouching here for the past hour watching the door. "Needed some coffee after jiu jitsu class."

The lie feels hollow in my mouth, but Ashlyn just nods, stirring her liquid candy with practiced precision. I notice she's wearing the earrings Olivia got her for her birthday years ago. She wears them a lot, actually. I wonder if it's her way of keeping Liv close, like the beard oil is mine.

"So," Ashlyn stirs her drink, the spoon clinking against the ceramic in that way that always makes my teeth itch, "any plans this weekend?"

"Yeah, heading to Manu's tomorrow. Wrestling pay-per-view." I take a sip of my now-cold coffee. "Want to watch Blackfang take the title."

She sets her spoon down, and something in her expression shifts like a trap has sprung. "Why don't we ever hang out anymore, Connor? Just us?" Her fingers trace the rim of her cup. "I was your friend too, not just Liv's."

The question hits me like a sucker punch. My throat tightens as memories flood back – the three of us sharing plates of nachos at dive bars, Ashlyn and me supporting each other through those first raw months after the accident. Movie nights where we'd both pretend not to notice the other crying during romantic scenes.

"I miss that," she continues, softer now. "Miss being able to talk to you."

I run my hands through my hair, a nervous habit I can't shake. She's right – we did drift apart. About a year ago, Ashlyn had started pushing – trying to set me up on blind dates. Sending links to dating apps. Showing me pictures of her "really sweet" single friends.

Each suggestion felt like a tiny betrayal, like she thought Liv was replaceable. I know that wasn't her intent – she was just trying to help in her own way. But it made every conversation feel like walking through a minefield, waiting for the next well-meaning push toward "moving on."

"I wasn't ready," I say finally, studying the coffee grounds at the bottom of my cup. I see her confused expression as I briefly look up. "You were really pushing me to start dating again and I wasn't ready. Still not sure I am. And it felt like... like I couldn't just talk with you anymore. I worried when you were going to squeeze in the next single friend of yours into our conversation. I'm not saying I'll never date again, but I'm not actively looking for anything either. I don't know that I ever will."

Ashlyn's face crumples, and I can see her trying to hold herself together. She always been a sweet person and has never been able to stand upsetting someone she loves. I hate seeing that look – the same one she wore at the funeral when she couldn't find the right words when it was her turn to speak.

"God, Connor, I'm so sorry." Her voice catches. "I just... I couldn't stand watching you disappear into yourself. Some days it felt like I was losing you too, and I panicked. I thought if I could just get you to connect with someone – anyone – it would pull you back from wherever you were going."

She slides her chair closer, and the sound of wood scraping against floor makes me wince. "But you have to know," she continues, her eyes getting glassy, "Liv would be devastated seeing you punish yourself like this. She loved you so completely, and the thought of you spending years just... existing? It would break her heart."

I start to protest, but she cuts me off. "I'm not saying you need to date or even look at another woman ever again. But Liv would want you to find some kind of peace, some way to be okay again. Maybe not whole – I know that's impossible – but at least not in constant pain."

She reaches across the table, her hand hovering uncertainly over mine. After a moment's hesitation, I take it. Her fingers are warm from holding her coffee cup, and the simple human contact makes my throat tight.

"I miss them so much," I whisper, the words feeling raw in my mouth. "Every single day."

"I know," she squeezes my hand. "I miss them too."

Chapter 8: Shattered Illusions

Shelly

I WAKE TO THE soft thrum of pop music, my body luxuriating in the plush comfort of Heidi's couch. It's been so long since I've slept somewhere this soft that my muscles feel like they're melting into the cushions. The oversized 'Party Princess' shirt I'm wearing has twisted around my torso during my sleep, and I vaguely remember Heidi lending it to me along with some too-big panties and shorts I had to MacGyver into staying on my waist.

"Morning, sleepyhead!" Heidi's voice carries from the kitchen. "Want some coffee?"

The word 'coffee' hits me like a splash of cold water, and suddenly I'm thinking about Connor at Books and Beans again. He's haunting me. Those kind eyes, the way he stepped in to help me, how his fingers drummed against the game board when he was thinking about his next move. My mind drifts back to this morning's shower fantasy - his hands instead of mine, his beard against my neck...

I feel my cheeks flush hot and I squirm a little on the couch. "Um, yeah," I manage to squeak out, trying to shake off the lingering effects of that particular daydream. "Coffee would be great."

The borrowed shorts slide down my hip a bit as I stand up, and I have to retie the makeshift knot. My mind keeps wanting to wander back to Connor, but I force myself to focus on the present. One night of decent sleep doesn't change the fact that I'm still basically homeless, just with a temporary reprieve.

I pad over to the kitchen counter, the borrowed panties threatening to slip down within my shorts with each step. The marble countertop is cool against my forearms as I settle onto one of the barstools. "Thanks again for everything, Heidi. I can head out after coffee if that works for you."

Heidi whirls around from the coffee maker, her blonde hair fanning out dramatically. "Absolutely not. You're staying here for at least a week or two. Maybe longer." She points a spoon at me like it's a magic wand. "You need a stable address and a phone number for job applications."

My stomach twists. "About that..." I trace invisible patterns on the counter with my finger. "My last foster parents, they never let me get a job. Said I had to focus on school." I let out a bitter laugh. "Except they were supposedly homeschooling me and never actually did. I don't even have a GED."

The coffee maker gurgles and spits, filling the silence between us. I watch the dark liquid drip into the pot, avoiding Heidi's gaze. "I don't know what kind of job I can even get without that."

Memories of those last foster parents surface - servitude, the "homeschooling" that consisted of me babysitting the other kids while they collected their checks. The way they'd tell social workers I was "difficult" whenever questions came up about my education.

Heidi gestures toward a sleek laptop on a short table by the window. "You can use my laptop to look for jobs. I've got decent wifi, and..." She glances at her phone, cursing under her breath. "Shit, I need to start getting ready. Friday nights are themed at the club and the men go ape shit. Tonight is super heroes."

She bustles around the kitchen, mixing our coffees with practiced efficiency before sliding a mug my way. The warmth seeps into my palms as I lift it to my lips. The moment the liquid hits my tongue, I nearly spit it back out. Heidi does the same, her face scrunching up in disgust.

"Fucking coffee maker!" She slams her mug down. "I've cleaned this piece of shit three times this week, but every third brew tastes like someone mixed vinegar with dirt." She yanks open a drawer and pulls out some cash. "Here, go get yourself some real coffee somewhere. I can't have a guest in my house living without caffeine. And help yourself to anything in the fridge."

I stare at the money in my hand, that familiar suspicion creeping in. "Why are you doing all this? Trusting me with your place, your stuff..." I swallow hard. "You don't even really know me anymore."

Heidi's expression softens as she leans against the counter. "Because three years ago, I was you. Aged out, nowhere to go, scared shitless." She sets her hand on her hip. "This woman, Sandra, found me sleeping in her apartment building's laundry room. Instead of calling the cops, she gave me her spare room for two months. Got me on my feet." A small smile plays at her lips. "Just paying it forward or whatever. Besides, I remember you being the only foster sister who didn't steal my shit."

I let out a small laugh, fidgeting with my coffee mug. "Okay, fine. I might have borrowed your cherry lipstick a few times back then. But only because you always looked so damn good wearing it!"

"Oh. My. God." Heidi clutches her chest in mock horror. "That's it, you thieving little monster. Out on the streets with you! Go work the corner like the criminal you are!"

Her eyes scan me up and down, and a mischievous grin spreads across her face. "But for real though, with that tiny little body of yours? Rawr! You'd make bank, girl."

"You're such an ass!" I feel my cheeks burning as I chuck a nearby dish towel at her head. She dodges it with practiced grace, cackling as she disappears into her bedroom. I smile from the corner of my mouth feeling normal.

When she emerges, she's transformed. Skin-tight leggings disappear into cozy Ugg boots, and a massive red fluffy coat envelops her like a glamorous cocoon. Whatever she's wearing underneath remains a mystery, but I can guess it's probably not much.

"Hey," she says, pausing by her bedroom door. "Help yourself to anything in my closet. You can't go running around in borrowed PJs in this weather - you'll freeze your cute little ass off." She grabs her purse from the counter and set down a spare key for me. "Seriously, raid away. Most of that stuff is too small for me now anyway."

After Heidi leaves, I settle onto her couch with the laptop, my borrowed shorts bunching awkwardly as I cross my legs. The screen's glow illuminates my face as I type "entry level jobs Seattle" into the search bar. My fingers hover over the keyboard as I stare at the results. There's something surreal about job hunting from a warm apartment instead of a library computer with a time limit ticking down.

I create accounts on Indeed, ZipRecruiter, and Monster, copying and pasting Heidi's address and landline number into each application. The familiar ding of alerts from my old email - PunkPrincess2018@gmail.com - makes me cringe. God, I was such a dork back then, spending hours in anime chatrooms pretending I had a normal life and friends.

The rejections start rolling in almost immediately. Each automated "thank you for your interest" feels like a tiny punch to the gut. I try not to let it get to me - this is just how it goes, right? Everyone deals with rejection. But after the fifteenth "unfortunately" email, I start to be torn between anger and despair.

Then I see it. Subject line: "Phone Interview Request - Junior Data Entry Position."

My heart skips as I read the email. It's from some company called Flex Data Flight Solutions, asking if I'm available for a phone interview tomorrow at 2 PM. The position requires "attention to detail and basic computer literacy" - no experience necessary, no education requirements listed.

My hands are shaking as I hit reply, trying to sound professional while confirming the interview time. I glance at the phone number Heidi left me, already memorizing it. This could be it. This could be my chance to actually start building something real.

I close the laptop with a sigh, rubbing my temples. Forty applications. Thirty rejections. One maybe. The numbers dance in my head like mocking little gremlins. The Flex Data Flight interview is something, at least, even if the company's website looks like it was designed when dial-up was still cool.

Heidi's cash sits on the counter, tempting me with promises of decent coffee and warmth. My stomach growls, reminding me that hoarded granola bars the shelter handed out two weeks ago aren't exactly a balanced diet.

I pad over to Heidi's closet, which is basically a small boutique's worth of clothes. Most of it screams "look at me!" in a way that makes my skin crawl. But buried in the back, I find a plain black sweater that looks cozy without being flashy. There's a pair of jeans that might work if I roll up the cuffs about four times, and a belt that'll keep them from falling off my hips.

Looking in the mirror, I adjust the sweater. It's still a little big, but in a way that feels like hiding rather than drowning. I run my fingers through my hair, trying to tame it into something presentable. The girl in the reflection looks almost normal. Almost like she belongs somewhere.

Books and Beans isn't that far, and they have advertise 'Great WiFi', maybe I can take the laptop with me and keep searching. I'll actually look like I belong there for once. That's why I'm going. Not because Connor might be there. Definitely not because I've been replaying our conversation in my head for the past week. Not because I wonder if he noticed I haven't been back, or if he even remembers me at all.

I grab Heidi's key and the cash, tucking both safely into my pocket before packing the laptop in its case and slinging it over my shoulder. My heart does a little skip as I head for the door, and I tell myself it's just the prospect of good coffee making me feel this way.

Yeah. Right. Keep telling yourself that, Shelly.

The Seattle sidewalks feel different today. Maybe it's the borrowed clothes, or maybe it's just having somewhere to go back to, but people aren't doing that thing where their eyes slide past me like I'm a ghost. A guy in a business suit actually smiles and says "hello" as he passes. An elderly woman with a tiny dog gives me a friendly nod. Others ignore me but not in the obviously purposeful way they do when you are clearly a vagabond.

My reflection in store windows doesn't look like someone you'd cross the street to avoid or turn your nose up at anymore. The black sweater hugs my shoulders just right, and even though the jeans needed serious rolling up, they work. I actually look… normal.

Books and Beans comes into view, and my heart does a little flutter. The morning sun catches on the gold lettering above the door, making it gleam like something out of a fairy tale. I'm smiling before I even realize it, already tasting that perfect first sip of coffee.

Then I see him.

Connor's sitting at one of the corner alcoves that seats two comfy armchairs, the same one he sat at with me. For a second, my smile grows wider. But as I get closer, I notice he's not alone. I can't see who he's talking to at first, but then I spot a perfectly manicured hand reaching across the table to rest on his. The owner of that hand leans forward - a gorgeous woman with honey-highlighted hair and an hour-glass form that fill out her floral dress perfectly.

Connor smiles at her, that same warm smile he gave me when we played board games. Something in my chest crumples like tissue paper in a fist.

God, I'm such an idiot. Of course he has someone. Of course a successful, handsome man like that wouldn't be single. And his age, Shelly, what would he want with a girl young enough to be his daughter. What was I even thinking would happen?

I start to retreat when Connor glances up and catches my gaze across the glass pane. Recognition dawns on his face, but I'm already turning and walking away. I am back to the other side of the street and half a block down already when I think I hear him shout my name. For some reason it makes me walk even faster, any more speed and I would be jogging. I have to keep moving. The soles of these loaned shoes tap rhythmically on the concrete while I stride quickly away, the sound of him calling after me drifting in the breeze.

I keep walking, even as he calls out again, even as my eyes start to sting. Stupid, stupid, stupid.

My feet carry me aimlessly through Seattle's streets while

my mind churns like a washing machine stuck on spin cycle. Why am I being such a drama queen about this? It was one conversation, one stupid board game. One kind gesture from a sweet, obviously taken man who probably helps stray puppies and lost tourists as a hobby.

But seeing his hand under hers, that smile I thought was special aimed at someone else... it shouldn't hurt like this. I've got bigger problems - like tomorrow's phone interview, or figuring out how to get my GED, or not screwing up Heidi's generosity.

The evening air bites at my cheeks as I realize I've wandered into unfamiliar territory. Well, mostly unfamiliar. The neon sign for Pete's Pizza glows like a beacon through the darkness, and my stomach growls in response. I check the wrinkled bills in my pocket - Heidi's coffee money that never made it to its intended purpose.

When was the last time I had real pizza? Not the stale slices from behind dumpsters or the rubbery cafeteria stuff from the shelter? Must have been that foster home in Tacoma, the one before everything went to shit. Three years ago? Four? That last foster home with the Patterson's, they claimed pizza was poison and refused to have it in the house. Heresy in my opinion.

The aroma of melting cheese and tomato sauce hits me before I even reach the door, and suddenly Connor's smile doesn't seem quite so important. My mouth waters as I push through the entrance, the little bell announcing my arrival. A blast of warm air carries the scent of oregano and fresh bread, and for a moment, I forget everything else.

Fresh pizza. Real food. Maybe this day isn't completely ruined after all.

I order three different slices. The first bite of pizza makes my knees weak. Warm, gooey cheese stretches between my teeth and the slice, and I have to resist the urge to moan out loud. The Alfredo sauce is rich and creamy, perfectly complementing the spicy kick from the sausage. I demolish it in record time, barely pausing to breathe.

The triple pepperoni is next - a greasy, salty masterpiece that makes my taste buds sing. By the time I get to the chicken and basil, I'm already feeling stuffed, but I soldier on. Each bite is a reminder that I'm not dumpster-diving tonight, that I have somewhere warm to sleep.

I pat my distended belly, feeling like I've swallowed a basketball. The root beer helps wash it all down, but now I'm so full I might actually waddle. Worth it. So worth it.

The digital clock on Pete's menu board reads 9:47 PM. Time to head back to Heidi's. My mind drifts briefly to Connor and that woman, but the food coma is keeping the worst of the sting at bay. Besides, I should focus on the positives right now. That's what matters the most right now, like the couch I am going to lay on and fall into a food coma.

The night air hits my face as I step outside, and I spot an alley between two main streets that'll cut ten minutes off my walk. My feet are tired, and the food baby I'm carrying makes me want to get horizontal as soon as possible.

I'm halfway through the alley when a meaty hand clamps over my mouth. Another arm yanks me backward, slamming me against the brick wall. The impact knocks the wind out of me and I nearly wretch.

Bertrand's face looms in front of mine, his breath reeking of cheap booze and rotting teeth. His hand presses harder against my mouth, fingers digging into my cheeks. My heart hammers against my ribs as I stare into his wild, desperate eyes.

Bertrand's grimy fingers dig deeper into my cheeks as he leans in close. "We got interrupted again, didn't we my little pet. I was all ready for my dessert at the the bakery and you let it be spoiled." His rancid breath makes my stomach turn, pizza threatening to come back up.

My eyes dart around the alley, searching for anything I could use as a weapon. God, why didn't I bring that broken bread knife? It's still stuffed behind the cleaning supplies under Heidi's bathroom sink.

He sneers, looking me up and down. "Look at you, playing dress-up in your fancy new clothes." His free hand paws at my borrowed sweater. "Put some lipstick on a street whore, she's still just a whore."

My heart pounds so hard I can barely hear him over the rush of blood in my ears. Every survival instinct screams at me to fight, to run, but his weight has me pinned against the rough brick wall.

"Done being patient with you," he growls, face twisted in a horrible grin. "Gonna have what I want right here in this alley."

His hand clamps down on my breast, squeezing with bruising force. The pain shoots through my chest like lightning, and I scream against his palm, the sound muffled but desperate. I drop Heidi's laptop case and begin to kick, claw and bite wildly.

Chapter 9: I'm Hot Blooded

Connor

THE COLD NIGHT AIR still clings to my suit jacket as I slump back into my chair across from Ashlyn. My throat feels raw from yelling after Shelly, and something heavy settles in my chest. Was it something I did? Did I come on too strong that night? I forced the coffee and game on her didn't I? Fuck, I was too excited. Maybe she thought…I don't know.

"Okay, what the hell was that about?" Ashlyn's perfectly shaped eyebrow arches as she sets down her cappuccino. "And who's Shelly?"

"She's..." How do I even explain this without sounding like a complete creep? "I met her here early last week. Helped her out when some entitled couple that was giving her grief about taking up space."

"And you just happened to spot her through the window and decided to chase her down the street?" Ashlyn's tone carries that gentle skepticism she usually reserves for when I make what she thinks are questionable business decisions.

"She looked right at me before she ran." The words come out more defensive than I intend. "I thought maybe... I don't know what I thought."

Ashlyn leans forward, her expression softening. "Connor, is everything okay? You seem really…I don't know, invested in someone you met once at a coffee shop. I need more context here. So far you're telling me you chased after someone you helped out of a jam…once."

The truth sits like a stone in my stomach. How do I tell my dead wife's best friend that I met a girl who looks eerily like both Liv and Des? That every time I think about her, it feels like the universe is playing some cosmic joke on me? And that I can't stop letting her slip into my brain. I've tried.

"She just seemed like she could use a friend," I say instead, which isn't entirely a lie. The memory of Jenny telling me about Shelly's situation flashes through my mind. "And now I probably scared her off by acting like a fucking lunatic."

"You? A lunatic?" Ashlyn's laugh breaks some of the tension. "Mr. 'I-Schedule-My-Coffee-Breaks-Down-To-The-Minute'?"

"If I don't do that you guys don't let me breathe." I say it with the intent of a joke but in my current state it seems more accusatory.

I run my hands through my hair and fidget. "Look, when I met her... something clicked. Not in a creepy way, before you give me that look. We played that old strategy game on the shelf for hours, and she absolutely killed me." A genuine smile tugs at my lips at the memory. "It was the first time in five years I didn't feel like I was drowning."

Ashlyn's expression shifts from concern to curiosity. "What do you mean?"

"You know how it is at home. Even with music blasting, even with shows or movies in the background... it's just empty. I can lose myself in a video game every once in a while, but sooner or later I need to sleep. At the gym or Knuckledraggers, I can lose myself in training, but eventually class ends and I am right back to remembering everything I lost. But that night?" I pause, trying to find the right words. "It felt natural. No pressure, no grief hanging over me. Just...peace."

"Connor..." Ashlyn starts, then hesitates. "How old is she?"

I wince slightly. "I don't know. Probably early twenties?"

Her eyes widen, but before she can speak, I continue, "I know how it sounds. Trust me, I do. But it's not like that. She needed help, and for a few hours, we both just...existed without all the baggage. No expectations, no history. Just two people playing a board game."

Something in my voice must convince her because Ashlyn's expression softens. She reaches across the table and squeezes my hand. "I haven't seen you this animated about anything in years. Not since..." She trails off, but we both know she means since Liv and Des.

I don't know exactly how to respond to her words and just sigh to myself.

The silence between us stretches, broken only by the gentle clink of coffee cups from other tables and the whir of the espresso machine. Ashlyn still has her hand on mine, and I'm grateful for the contact – it grounds me, keeps me from spiraling into my own thoughts.

"You know what?" she finally says, pulling her hand back to wrap it around her cooling coffee. "I'm just happy you enjoyed talking with someone. Really talking, not just the polite CEO small talk you do at work."

I snort. "I do more than small talk at work."

"Sure, when you're discussing game mechanics or character developments. Then you won't shut up." She gives me a knowing look. "But when was the last time you just...connected with someone?"

The question hits harder than I expect. I flick at my wrist, a nervous habit I've apparently just decided involuntarily to replace running my hands through my hair. "It's complicated."

"Life is complicated," she counters. "Look, Connor, whatever this is – friendship, attraction, or just someone who makes you feel less alone – pursue it. Figure it out. Unless of course you accidently really did scare her off. I honestly don't think that is possible with you though. And the age difference?" She waves her hand dismissively. "You're both adults. And honestly? After everything you've been through, maybe someone with a different perspective is exactly what you need."

"I'm not looking to replace-"

"I know," she cuts me off gently. "Nobody's asking you to. But Liv..." she pauses, and I can see her gathering courage to continue. "Liv would want you to find whatever makes you feel alive again. Whether that's friendship or something more."

Connor

The coffee shop's warmth fades into memory as Ashlyn and I head to my car. Our laughter echoes in the parking lot, still riding the high of sharing stories about that disaster of a house party. Who shows up to what they think is a casual get-together only to find people swapping keys in fish bowls? (Well, besides us, apparently.)

"I still can't believe you grabbed my arm so hard you left bruises when you realized what kind of party it was," I say, unlocking the car doors.

Ashlyn slides into the passenger seat, her cheeks still flushed from laughing. "Hey, someone had to save you from that woman in the leopard print teddy. She was eyeing you like you were the last cookie at a bake sale."

Ashlyn's fading laughter makes me feel like we are back to being 'us' again, two friends that share nearly everything with each other. The moment I turn the key, Foreigner's "Hot Blooded" blasts through the speakers. Without hesitation, I hit the window controls, letting in the crisp night air.

"Connor! It's freezing!" Ashlyn yelps, hugging herself.

I can't help but grin, cranking up the volume. "House rules, Ash. Liv always said this song requires open windows. Rain, sleet, or apocalypse."

"Liv was insane," she protests, but she's smiling too, and I catch her foot tapping to the beat.

"Completely nuts," I agree, the familiar ache in my chest softening into something warmer as I pull out of the parking lot. "Remember when she made us drive around the block three times because it came on just as we were getting home?"

The wind whips through the car, carrying our shared laughter into the night. I try, just this moment, to allow myself to pretend its like old times. Like maybe some pieces of my life aren't as broken as I thought.

The wind whistles through the car, and I'm about to roll up the windows when a scream pierces the night. My hand freezes on the controls. Another scream, this one closer, more desperate.

"Did you hear that?" Ashlyn asks, but I'm already yanking the wheel hard right, tires screeching as I pull to the curb.

The sound of a man cursing echoes off the brick walls of the alley to my right. "You fucking bitch!" The voice is guttural, angry.

I'm out of the car before I fully process what I'm doing, my dress shoes slapping against pavement as I sprint toward the alley. I see a large shape pinning a much small one to the wall. "Hey!" I roar, letting out all of my recent frustration and sounding like a feral animal. "Get the fuck away from her!"

The large shape detaches from the shadows, and I catch a glimpse of matted hair and wild eyes before he bolts down the opposite end of the alley. But what stops me cold is the small figure crumpling to the ground.

Shelly!

"Go!" Ashlyn shouts, already running to Shelly's side. "I've got her!"

I take off after the bastard, my lungs burning as I push harder. He's bigger than me, but slower, probably high. I catch him at the alley's end, launching myself at his legs in a tackle that would make my old high school rugby coach proud.

We hit the ground hard, and he tries to throw a fist at my face. Amateur. I've spent too many hours on the mats at Knuckledraggers to fall for that. I slip to the side, grab his arm, and use his momentum to flip him. The back of his head bounces off the concrete.

"Motherfucker!" I snarl, driving my fist into his nose. There's a satisfying crunch, and he goes limp beneath me.

Behind me, I hear Ashlyn's voice trying and failing to remain calm. "Yes, we need police at..." She rattles off cross streets while I keep the unconscious attacker pinned, my hands shaking with barely contained rage.

I look behind me to see Shelly curled up and sobbing against Ashlyn. I look back down at the bastard below me and hammer two more fists into his face with gratifying wet gurgles.

My knuckles are bleeding, but I barely notice as I push off Bertrand's limp form. The rage that powered my fists subsides into a cold, nauseating fear as I sprint back toward Shelly and Ashlyn.

Shelly's huddled between Ashlyn and the brick wall, her

shoulders shaking with silent sobs. Her sweater's torn at the collar, and there's a scrape on her cheek that makes my stomach clench. I drop to my knees beside her but still keeping some distance. I quickly wipe my bloody knuckles on my dress pants, worried it might frighten her.

My hand reaches out tentatively, "Shelly?" I keep my voice soft, like I used to when Desiree had nightmares. "You're safe now. I promise."

She looks up, those green eyes – so much like Liv's – wide with recognition. "Connor?" Her voice breaks on my name, and suddenly she's launching herself into my arms.

I catch her, wrapping her tight against my chest as she breaks down completely. Her whole body trembles, and I can feel her tears soaking through my shirt. My own eyes burn, and I don't try to stop the tears that fall into her hair as I rock her gently.

"I've got you," I whisper, one hand cradling the back of her head. "I've got you."

Behind us, Ashlyn paces with her phone pressed to her ear, keeping a sharp eye on the piece of shit that assaulted Shelly while getting updates form the police on their location. Her free hand's balled into a white-knuckled fist, and I know she's fighting the urge to go kick the unconscious bastard herself.

Shelly's fingers dig into my back, clutching my shirt like it's the only thing keeping her from drowning. I hold her tighter, fighting down the urge to go back and make absolutely sure the prick never gets up again.

"You're safe," I repeat, as much to convince myself as her.

"I've got you."

Chapter 10: Safe Harbor

Shelly

I LAY BACK ON the stretcher like it is the most uncomfortable recliner in existence. Which is saying something with the places I am used to sleeping. The fluorescent lights make everything feel too harsh, too real. Across the ER, Connor speaks with two police officers, his hands moving as he describes what happened. There's dried blood on his knuckles and pants – Bertrand's blood.

"Are you absolutely sure there's no one I can call for you?" Ashlyn asks for the third time, her voice gentle. She's been sitting next to me since we arrived, a steady presence, she is calming and I find myself liking her.

"I don't know Heidi's number." My voice comes out smaller than I intend. "And there's... there's no one else."

The words hang there, heavy and true. A lifetime in foster care doesn't exactly build up your emergency contacts list.

I keep watching Connor. Earlier, when he carried me to the ambulance after it arrived, too impatient to wait for them to get to me after finding me in the alley, he made me feel it again - safe. His arms were strong, and he smelled like coffee and something spicy. I didn't want him to let go.

The officer on Connor's left is Sergeant Dinah Wesley, a naturally beautiful and thick Samoan woman, who took my statement and told me Bertrand is under arrest. "Once he's patched up, he's going straight to jail," she'd said, giving me a knowing look. "Your friend did quite a number on him. I'm sure I don't need to tell you it's a good thing they came running when they did, otherwise…" She cuts herself off. Even though he didn't get past groping me it almost feels like he might as well have gotten away with more. "But that bite mark you left on his face? Good girl. You fought back hard."

I touch my lip where it's split, wincing at the sting. The nurse said nothing's broken, just bruised. I got lucky. If Connor and Ashlyn hadn't shown up…

My hands start shaking again, and I tuck them under my thighs. The scratchy sheets on the stretcher crinkle beneath me.

I can't stop watching Connor. The steady rhythm of his gestures as he talks to the police officers gives me something to focus on besides… besides what happened. His presence, even outside the room, feels like an anchor and it's keeping the panic at bay. Every few minutes, he glances over at me, his eyes concerned. Yet they don't make me feel like he is pitying me and I am extremely thankful for that.

Movement catches my attention as Ashlyn stands up. Someone – another woman in business clothes – appears at the entrance to our section of the ER, holding what looks like a shopping bag. They have a brief conversation I can't quite hear.

Ashlyn returns, holding a bundle of folded clothes. "Here," she says softly, setting them on the edge of my stretcher. "I had Sarah from the office bring some of mine. They might be a little big, but..." She trails off, offering a gentle smile.

"Thank you," I whisper, running my fingers over the soft fabric of what appears to be yoga pants and a sweater. The hospital gown makes me feel exposed, vulnerable. Like everything that happened is written all over my skin for everyone to see.

"The nurse said you can change now if you'd like," Ashlyn tells me, her voice still carrying that same gentle tone. "They just want to keep an eye on you a bit longer to rule out a concussion. But you don't have to stay in that gown."

I clutch the clothes closer, grateful beyond words. As grateful as I am, I feel like I am not adequately showing it. I feel numb about everything except when I look at him. At Connor.

Ashlyn and the nurse close the curtain around my bed. The yoga pants are soft against my skin, and the sweater smells faintly of mint and rose. Everything's a bit loose, but still a better fit than the clothes Heidi let me borrow. I wince and close my eyes tight, wondering how she will take the news of her ruin clothes and damaged laptop.

When the curtain pulls back, Connor's there. My heart does this weird little skip that I immediately try to ignore. He's changed his shirt into something provided by SPD – probably because the other one had blood on it. It looks a little funny, dress pants and shoes with a "Seattle's Finest: Back the

Blue" t-shirt and his suit jacket draped over his arm. His eyes find mine immediately, and that anchored feeling returns.

My stomach chooses that exact moment to let out an embarrassingly loud growl. I feel my cheeks heat up, but Connor's already moving.

"I'm getting you food," he says, his tone brooking no argument. "The cafeteria's open. What sounds good? Soup? Sandwich? Chips? Cookies?"

Before I can protest or even answer, he's already striding out the door and still talking. I watch him go, feeling something warm spread through my chest despite everything that's happened tonight.

"You have a really great boyfriend," I tell Ashlyn softly, picking at a loose thread on the sweater she lent me. "The way he just... takes care of things."

Ashlyn lets out a surprised laugh, warm and genuine with the hint of a snort. "Oh honey, Connor's not my boyfriend." She shakes her head, still smiling. "We're just good friends. I used to be close with..." She pauses, something flickering across her face as she looks at me more closely as though she recognizes me. "We've known each other a long time."

I try to ignore how relieved I feel at this news, but my cheeks are probably giving me away.

Ashlyn studies my face, and I know she's caught my blush. I try to look anywhere else, but there's not much to focus on in the ER bay except empty stretchers and medical equipment.

"Listen," she says, her voice dropping lower. "I...Connor is an amazing man, but he's a little fragile. Far more than he seems." She glances toward the doorway where he disappeared, then leans in closer. "He had a wife and daughter. They..." She pauses, and I can see her choosing her words carefully. "They died in a car accident a little over five years ago."

My chest tightens. Suddenly, certain things make more sense – the sadness I caught in his eyes that night, the way he seems to look at me like he's seeing someone else.

"I shouldn't be saying anything. It's really his story to tell, if he wants to," Ashlyn continues, wringing her hands slightly. "It's just, it's still really hard for him to connect with new people and he seems to have made a connection with you. Just, be careful with him, OK?"

"Of course," I whisper, my throat feeling tight. "I won't say anything." I feel like that wasn't the right thing to say but I am at a loss of what else I should say. What was she insinuating? Does she think I'm a gold digger? Wait, for her to think I made some sort of connection with him, that would mean he would have had to talk to her about me right?

The weight of this knowledge settles over me like a heavy blanket. I think about how he's been so kind to me, how he saved me tonight, and I wonder if maybe I remind him of them. The thought brings a complicated mix of emotions I'm not ready to sort through. Ashlyn and I sit in silence for a bit, both seemingly holding something back.

In the distance, I can hear Connor's voice getting closer, I can't quite make out what he's saying but I think he is complaining that the signs directing people to the cafeteria are wrong and he needs to get someone food badly.

"How long were you living on the street before Heidi took

you in?" Ashlyn asks, her voice still carrying that gentle concern that makes my walls want to crumble.

I fidget with the hem of her borrowed sweater. "Almost a year, give or take. Since I aged out of the system."

Something in her expression makes me want to tell her more, despite every instinct screaming at me to keep quiet. Maybe it's the leftover adrenaline from tonight, or maybe it's just that she reminds me of one of the few good social workers I had or that she shared Connor's tragedy with me.

"Foster care wasn't... great," I find myself saying. "Fourteen homes in eighteen years. Some were okay, most weren't. The last one..." I swallow hard. "... I was counting down the days until the summer after I turned eighteen."

Ashlyn's hand finds mine, and I'm surprised to find I don't want to pull away.

"I have a phone interview tomorrow," I tell her, trying to sound hopeful. "Or, had. I don't know if Heidi will still let me stay once she finds out about her laptop."

"Here." Ashlyn pulls out a business card, writing something on the back. "That's my personal number. Call me anytime for anything, okay? I mean it. This isn't one of those hollow attempts to make someone feel good for a moment, I promise you. And if this interview doesn't work out, I might be able to help with at least a temp position somewhere at Eldritch Magic."

"I appreciate that, but..." I bite my lip, wincing as I forget about the split. "I don't want handouts. I need to earn my way."

"I understand completely," she says, and somehow I believe her. "The offer stands though. No strings attached."

I hear Connor's footsteps approaching before I see him, his voice carrying around the corner as he complains about hospital signage again. Ashlyn stands, gathering her purse and jacket.

"Take care of yourself, honey," she says, squeezing my hand one last time. "Remember what I said – call anytime."

Connor appears in the doorway, arms laden with what looks like half the cafeteria's inventory. A woman I assume is Sarah, stands behind him, trying not to laugh at his determined expression.

Ashlyn meets him with a warm hug, and they exchange quick kisses on the cheek. It's clearly a comfortable, familiar gesture between old friends. "Text me when you get home," he tells her.

"Always do," she replies, then leaves with Sarah, their heels clicking in sync down the hallway.

I watch in amazement as Connor starts unloading his haul onto the bedside table. Three different wrapped sandwiches, multiple bags of chips, cookies, fruit cups, and – is that pudding? He saves the best for last, carefully setting down a steaming bowl of potato soup and a handful of cracker packets.

"I, uh, wasn't sure what you'd like," he admits, rubbing the back of his neck. "So I might have gotten... everything?"

A laugh bubbles up from somewhere deep inside me, surprising us both. It feels foreign after everything that's happened tonight, but genuine. His face breaks into this adorably sheepish grin that makes him look years younger.

"Might have?" I gesture at the mountain of food. "The cafeteria staff probably thinks you're feeding an entire ER."

"Well," he says, arranging things more neatly, "at least you'll have options."

The warmth in my chest expands, and I find myself smiling despite my split lip. There's something so endearing about this man standing here in his mismatched outfit, practically glowing with pride at his ability to provide snacks.

Chapter 11: A Shoulder To Sleep On

Connor

THE DASHBOARD CLOCK READS 2:17 AM as I navigate the empty streets. Shelly's quiet beside me, rustling through her discharge papers. I catch her sharp intake of breath less from the sound and more from her body language in my peripheral vision.

"You paid for this?" Her voice carries an edge I haven't heard before. "This is... this is thousands of dollars."

I keep my eyes on the road, trying to maintain a casual tone. "It's not a big deal."

"Not a big-" She cuts herself off, papers crinkling in her grip. "Mr. Ebin, this is way too much. I can't... I won't accept this."

My hands tighten slightly on the steering wheel. Hearing her be formal with me feels like a dagger in my chest. "Connor," I correct gently. "And yes, you will. It's already done. I suppose I could take you back and you could try and get a for profit hospital to turn down guaranteed payment. Look

Shelly, the last thing you need right now is medical debt hanging over your head when you're trying to get back on your feet. Besides, all I have to worry about is myself. Might as well use my money to help someone who deserves it."

She gets quiet for a second, in that way you do as you quickly mull over whether or not saying a particular something might be a mistake. I can tell by her mannerisms that she decided not to say what she was thinking. "I'm going to pay you back," she says firmly, and there's something in her tone that reminds me so much of Liv when she'd made up her mind about something that it makes my chest ache. "Every penny."

I flick my wrist a few times and nod. "If that makes you feel better, we can work something out. But, focus on getting stable first." The words are hollow on my end. There is no working something out. She could win the lottery and I still wouldn't take her money.

She's quiet for a moment, then lets out a small sigh. "Thank you," she whispers, so softly I almost miss it.

The words hang between us as I turn onto the street where Heidi's apartment building stands, dark and quiet in the late night hours.

I pull into the dimly lit parking garage, finding a spot near the entrance. The whole drive, I've been noticing how Shelly keeps glancing around herself, her body tense like a coiled spring.

"I know this is probably weird," she says as we reach Heidi's door, "but would you mind coming in? Just until I make sure everything's okay inside?"

"Of course." The moment she opens the door, I'm assaulted by what can only be described as a bordello throwing up in an apartment. The walls are adorned with artful (if I'm being generous) nude photographs, and there's at least one stripper pole that I can see. I bite back a laugh. "So... your friend runs a home-based brothel, or...?"

Shelly shoots me an amused look, her lips quirking up slightly.

I do a quick sweep of the apartment - bedroom, closets, behind the shower curtain - while trying not to look too closely at some of the more... interesting decor choices. When I'm satisfied everything's secure, I grab a notepad from the kitchen counter and scribble down my number.

"Call me if you need anything. I mean it - any time, day or night. Please."

She takes the paper, then hesitates. "Connor, would it be really weird if... could you maybe stay until I get out of the shower? I just... I don't want to be alone in there and not know what's happening out here. I know it's dumb but I just…"

"Not weird at all." My eyes drift to the bathroom and lock onto what appears to be a purple demon-themed dildo mounted on the wall like some kind of trophy. I can't help the concerned glance I shoot her way.

She catches my look and smacks my arm. "I can't control what Heidi's into."

I raise my hands in surrender and settle onto the couch. "No judgment here. I'll keep watch." What I absolutely do not say is that Olivia had one similar, only not as big as that monstrosity. I have no idea how Heidi's could fit into anything smaller than a horse.

I try to focus on my phone, scrolling through emails I've already read, but my eyes keep drifting around Heidi's apartment. The sound of the shower running provides a steady backdrop as I fight the urge to catalog every potential red flag. It's not my place. I'm not her father, not her guardian, not even really her friend yet. Am I?

Still.

The stack of mail on the counter catches my eye - some of it looks like past-due notices. There's a business card for "Madame's Lust" tucked into the corner of a mirror. I know that place, it's one of those full-nude clubs on the edge of town. Pretty sure I recall an article about a drug bust there a few years ago. Olivia and I almost went there once. We were drunk and each dared the other, just waiting for one of us to chicken out. We almost got into the door and then Liv lost her alcohol on the doorman's shoes.

I drum my hands on my thighs, trying to calm the protective instinct surging through me. Why am I sitting here playing detective? I just met this girl. But even as I think it, I know exactly why - those eyes, that auburn hair, the way she carries herself. She's not them, I know she's not them, but...

The memory hits me like a punch to the gut: Desiree's tiny hand in mine as we crossed streets, me teaching her to always look both ways. "I'll always keep you safe, tiny fox." The words I'd promised her a thousand times.

I couldn't keep that promise. I couldn't protect either of them.

But maybe... maybe I can protect Shelly. Not because she's some replacement for what I've lost - that wouldn't be fair to any of them. But because she needs someone in her corner, and for whatever cosmic reason, our paths have crossed.

I hear the shower stop and a few moments later, Shelly darts across the living room wrapped in a towel, her wet hair leaving droplets on the floor. She disappears into what I assume is Heidi's room, emerging minutes later in an oversized t-shirt and sweatpants.

"Thank you again," she says, hovering awkwardly by the couch. "For everything."

"You good if I head out?" The words feel heavy in my mouth, but it's late and I shouldn't overstay my welcome.

She hesitates, something flickering across her face - fear maybe, or uncertainty. But then she nods, wrapping her arms around herself. "Yeah, I'm good."

We both take a half-step toward each other, then stop. The air feels thick with unspoken words and aborted movements. I want to hug her, to tell her everything will be okay, but I'm not sure if that would help or make things worse. Instead, I give her a small wave and head for the door.

I hear it close behind me and I turn, walking away and hating every step. I'm almost to the end of the hallway when I hear her voice, tight with panic.

"Connor!"

I spin around and sprint back, my heart hammering. She pulls me inside the apartment, her hands shaking as she closes the door. She paces back and forth, tears starting to stream down her face.

"I can't- I can't breathe right," she gasps, her hands trembling violently. "My hands won't stop- I don't know what's happening-"

Without thinking, I pull her into my arms. She stiffens for a split second before collapsing against me, her tears soaking into my shirt. Her arms wrap around my waist, holding on like I'm the only thing keeping her from drowning. The shaking subsides, replaced by deep, wracking sobs.

I hold her tighter, remembering how Liv used to ground me during panic attacks after particularly rough days at work. Sometimes just having someone there makes all the difference.

I hold Shelly firm and secure, fighting the overwhelming urge to press my lips to her hair like I used to do with Des when she'd cry. My hand moves in slow circles on her back, feeling each trembling breath she takes.

"It's not fair," she chokes out against my chest. "Everyone else just... just gets to be normal. They walk around and go to coffee shops and nobody looks at them like they're garbage. Nobody crosses the street to avoid them because they look homeless or dirty."

Her fingers clutch at my shirt. "I had one night - just one fucking night where I felt like a real person. I had clean clothes and Heidi's laptop and I was going to sit there like everyone else does. Nobody was giving me those looks. The ones where they either think you're disgusting or they pity you so much it makes you want to puke."

My chest tightens at her words. I think about so many of us train ourselves to not see the homeless. Not to literally ignore them, but to pretend to not have pity or mistrust and just look right past them like we do with everyone we pass by on the street. Pretending we aren't all secretly praying we never end up in the same boat they are in.

"And then... then that bastard-" her voice cracks. "He just... he took it all away. The laptop's destroyed and Heidi's probably going to kick me out and I'll be back on the streets and-" She breaks off into fresh sobs.

I tighten my hold on her, wishing I could somehow shield her from all of it. From the unfairness, from the cruelty, from the sideways glances and crossed streets. But I can't. All I can do is stand here and let her cry, my hand continuing its steady circles on her back while she lets out years of pain and frustration against my tear-soaked shirt.

I don't mean to do it. It's pure instinct, muscle memory from years of comforting Des after nightmares or Liv after she got too invested in a sad novel. Before I can stop myself, I press my lips to the crown of Shelly's head in a gentle kiss.

She tenses in my arms, and I immediately curse myself. Stupid. Fucking stupid. I've crossed a line, made her uncomfortable when she's already vulnerable, and after that asshole forced himself on her. I literally about to recoil away from her and apologize like my life depends on it. But then she squeezes me tighter, her sobs quieting to soft hiccups against my chest.

"Why are you being so kind to me?" Her voice is muffled against my shirt, but I can hear the confusion, the wariness beneath the question. "Nobody's just... nice. Not without wanting something."

The words hit me like that first drop on a roller coaster, only without the excitement. I wrack my brain for the right words. How do I explain that seeing her in pain physically hurts me? That every protective instinct I have is screaming to keep her safe? That yes, she reminds me of my wife and daughter, but that's not why I want to help? Why I wanted to get to know her, maybe. But not why I want to help.

"I don't want anything from you, Shelly," I say softly, keeping my arms loose around her so she doesn't feel trapped. "I know you have no reason to believe that. But it's true."

She pulls back slightly, looking up at me with those piercing green eyes that are so familiar and yet entirely her own. I can see the war behind them - hope fighting against experience, trust battling with learned suspicion. It breaks my heart that someone so young has already learned to question every kindness.

Shelly swallows hard, her fingers still gripping my shirt. "Is it... is it because I remind you of them? Your wife and daughter?"

The question hits me like ice water. I step back slightly, my hands dropping to my sides. "How? Ashlyn told you, didn't she?"

"Don't be mad at her," Shelly says quickly, wrapping her arms around herself. "I kind of... dragged it out of her. While you were getting snacks at the hospital. I just..." She looks down at her feet. "I wanted to understand why you looked so happy but sad at the same time. Or if it was just when you were around me, if I made you sad somehow."

I run a hand over my face, feeling suddenly exhausted. Part

of me wants to be angry at Ashlyn, but I can't blame her. Not really.

"It's complicated," I admit, leaning back against the door. "When I first saw you on the street, yes, you reminded me of them. But that's not why I'm here now. That's not why I want to help."

I pause, trying to find the right words. "Meeting you... it woke something up in me. Something I thought died with them. But you're not them. You're you. And that's more than enough reason to care about what happens to you. If I am fully honest, I don't truly know."

Shelly steps back, wiping her eyes. "I'm sorry. I shouldn't have asked about them. I probably just ruined whatever... this is." She gestures vaguely between us.

"You didn't ruin anything," I say softly. "And you don't need to apologize."

She moves forward and wraps her arms around me again, this time initiating the hug herself. "I'm so sorry you lost them."

My chest feels warm, like embers being gently blown back to life. I hold her close, letting the feeling spread through me. It's been so long since I've felt anything but cold emptiness.

After a few moments, I pull back slightly. "You okay if I head out now?"

She shakes her head, her hands trembling slightly. "Can you stay a little longer. Unless you really need to go. My skin still feels like it's buzzing. Like everything's too loud and too quiet at the same time. Does that make sense? I shouldn't be asking you to do this. It's really late." She's babbling.

"No, it makes perfect sense. Believe it or not I know exactly what you are describing." I guide her to the couch. We sit in comfortable silence for a minute before I turn to her. "What's your favorite movie? We could watch it until you feel more settled."

"I can't..." She rubs her temples. "I can't think straight right now."

I grab the remote and pull up a streaming service. "Oh hey, '10 Things I Hate About You.' Have you seen this?"

"No, but I like Heath Ledger."

"What?" I feign outrage. "Not seeing this movie is literally a crime. You have to watch it now or face serious prison time. I don't make the rules but I will enforce them. Next thing you'll say you haven't seen the Lord of the Rings Trilogy."

She laughs softly and smirks with a questioning eyebrow raised.

"No. You have got to be kidding."

"No, no," she cuts me off with a grin. "I've watched all the extended versions."

"Good girl," I say without thinking, and I swear I see a blush creep across her cheeks in the dim light of the TV.

Chapter 12: Danish Data

Shelly

THE SOUND OF A door slamming jolts me awake. My head is nestled against something warm and solid - Connor's chest, I realize with a start. His arm is draped around me, protective even in sleep. The morning light filtering through Heidi's gaudy pink curtains makes everything feel surreal.

Connor stirs beside me, and our eyes meet. There's this moment of mutual "oh shit" that passes between us, and I quickly sit up straight, trying to smooth down my probably-disaster hair. My cheeks feel hot enough to fry an egg on.

"Well, well." Heidi's voice carries from the kitchen doorway. "I was just teasing about you working the street last night. I had not idea you would take it serious and bring home a sugar daddy."

I shoot her my best 'what the actual fuck' look. Really, Heidi? Now?

Connor clears his throat and stands, straightening his rumpled shirt. "I should probably introduce myself properly. Connor Ebin." He extends his hand to Heidi, ever the professional, even with couch creases still marking his cheek. "You have a lovely apartment."

I catch his subtle glance at the assortment of toys sitting on the bookshelf like several naughty gargoyles, and have to bite my lip to keep from laughing.

Heidi shakes his hand and looks him up and down before embarrassing me even more. "If you're looking to reenact 'Pretty Woman' I might be available."

I don't catch the reference but judging by the look that swiftly passes over Connor's face before he laughs I should be mortified, and so I am.

"I should get going," he says, running a hand through his disheveled hair. "Early meeting."

We both stand there for a moment, doing that awkward dance of not knowing how to say goodbye after accidentally sleeping on someone's couch together. Finally, I step forward and give him a quick hug. He somehow still smells like coffee and something woodsy, and for a split second, I don't want to let go.

But I do, and he leaves, the door clicking shut behind him much more gently than Heidi's entrance.

Heidi's smile turns predatory as she sinks into the armchair across from me. "So... want to tell me what that was all about?" She wiggles her eyebrows suggestively.

I open my mouth to explain, but she suddenly freezes, her playful expression vanishing. "Holy shit, what happened to your lip?" She practically leaps across the space between us, tilting my chin up to examine the split.

"Did he-" Her eyes narrow dangerously.

"God, no!" I jerk back, horrified at the suggestion. "Connor's the one who saved me. This guy... this creep who's been harassing me..." I take a shaky breath and tell her about Bertrand, the attack, and how Connor and his friend Ashlyn came to my rescue. When I get to the part about her laptop being smashed, my voice cracks.

"I'm so, so sorry about your laptop. I have a job interview at two today - I'll buy you a new one as soon as I start getting paychecks, I promise."

Heidi's face softens, and she grabs my hands in hers. Before I can react, she pulls me into a tight hug. The familiar scent of her vanilla perfume brings back memories of the foster home where we met, how she'd always share her body spray with me.

"Screw the laptop," she says fiercely into my hair. "That old thing was basically a paperweight anyway. Everything I used that one for I do on my phone now." She pulls back, holding me at arm's length. "I'm just glad you're okay. That's all that matters."

The sincerity in her voice makes my throat tight. It's been so long since anyone has cared about my wellbeing like this and now I have at least three people that do.

Heidi flops onto the couch next to me, tucking her feet under herself. "Okay, spill. What's the deal with Mr. Tall-Dark-and-Loaded?"

I pick at a loose thread on my sleeve, trying to figure out how to explain Connor. "We met at Books and Beans. He... he saved me from being kicked out when this couple were being jerks about me taking up space." The memory makes me smile despite myself. The smile pulls at the cut on my lip but I barely notice it. "Then we played this board game. I won, by like a lot."

"And?" Heidi prompts, poking my leg with her toe.

"And nothing. He's just... nice." I shrug, but my chest feels warm thinking about how he stood up for me, how he put his credit card down at the hospital without hesitation. "He reminds me of those stories we used to read in foster care. You know, the ones about knights and protectors?"

"And you want to be the milkmaid he takes a shine to and saves from her life of anguish?" She says playfully.

But when I don't respond and look down at my hands Heidi's teasing expression softens. "Shell, do you like him?"

"I..." My voice trails off as I consider it. Do I like Connor? The way my heart skips when he smiles at me probably answers that question. "Maybe? But it doesn't matter. He's successful, older... and his wife and daughter…they died in an accident. I don't think he's looking for anything. Probably definitely not with someone as young as I am."

"Oh." Heidi's eyebrows shoot up. "That's heavy."

"Yeah." I pull my knees up to my chest. "Besides, he probably just feels sorry for me. The homeless kid that somehow reminds him of what he lost" The words taste bitter coming out and I immediately know they aren't true.

"Hold up - did he say that? That you remind him of his wife and kid?"

I nod, remembering how he'd stared at me that first day on the street, like he saw a ghost. "Not in so many words, but yeah. That's probably why he's being so nice."

"Shell..." Heidi reaches over and squeezes my hand. "From what I saw this morning, that man wasn't looking at you like you're some ghost from his past. He was looking at you like... well, like you're you."

"I hope you're right," I whisper, not trusting my voice to be any louder. The flutter of possibility in my chest feels dangerous, like hoping for too much will make everything crumble. But Heidi's words echo in my head: *looking at you like you're you*.

Heidi stretches and yawns dramatically. "I need a shower and some beauty sleep before work tonight. You good out here by yourself?"

I nod, even as my heart rate picks up slightly. "Yeah, I'll be fine. Thanks for... just thank you."

After Heidi disappears into her room, I get up and check the front door lock. Then check it again. And once more, just to be absolutely sure. The deadbolt is solid under my fingers. I test the windows next, though we're three floors up. Can't be too careful.

Finally satisfied that everything's secure, I curl up on the couch where Connor and I fell asleep. His scent still lingers on the cushions - that mix of coffee and is that lavender? I press my face into the spot where his shoulder was and breathe deeply, feeling ridiculous even as I do it. But it's... comforting. Like the memory of being held, of feeling safe.

The TV screen still has the description of '10 Things I Hate About You' on it and I think of how we laughed at the same spots and how I teared up at the end when Julia Styles' character professed that she didn't hate Heath Ledger's. He cried too. I could tell from the sniffles he was trying to hold back and that he kept moving his hand to his cheeks. I see his number written on the notepad that now rests on the coffee table. Just knowing that it's there makes me feel less alone.

I pull the throw blanket over myself, listening to the sound of Heidi's shower running and the distant hum of traffic outside. The couch still holds a trace of warmth where we sat together, and I find myself drifting off to sleep with the ghost of his arm around my shoulders.

A gentle knock startles me from my doze on the couch. My heart immediately starts racing, and I press myself deeper into the cushions, holding my breath. I don't know how long I was asleep. The knock comes again, followed by retreating footsteps.

I creep to the door, my sock-covered feet silent on the carpet. Through the peephole, I watch a woman in a bright green delivery vest disappear down the hallway. I count to thirty, twice, before working up the courage to crack open the door.

A large brown paper bag sits innocently on the welcome mat, the familiar Books and Beans logo making my stomach do a little flip. I snatch it inside quickly, securing both locks before allowing myself to investigate.

The rich smell of coffee and pastries hits me as I open the bag. Two large white chocolate mochas - still hot - and an assortment of Danishes that makes my mouth water instantly. There's apple, cherry, cream cheese... all of them from the browsing display case that I could barely ever afford.

The receipt catches my eye, and I pull it out with trembling fingers. Circled in highlighter at the bottom, typed in neat computer font:

'Good luck with your interview today. I know you'll nail it. -Connor-'

I press the paper to my chest, a giddiness spreading through me that has nothing to do with the coffee. My lip stings a bit as I bite it, trying to contain my smile, but I don't care.

Is he real? People like this don't actually exist, do they? Knights in shining armor who chase away bad guys and send coffee and breakfast just because... but here I am, holding proof in my hands that they do. That he does.

I take a sip of the mocha - perfect temperature, exactly how I like it - and let myself believe, just for a moment, in fairy tales.

I realize that he even thought of my friend as I set what must be Heidi's mocha and half the pastries by the fridge, staring at the coffee with genuine remorse. It feels almost sacrilegious to refrigerate something so perfect, but Heidi needs her beauty sleep before another night at the club. After a moment's hesitation, I slide it onto the shelf next to her almond milk.

Settling at the small kitchen table with my own breakfast, I take a bite of the apple Danish. The pastry practically melts in my mouth, and I have to stop myself from making em-barrassing noises. When was the last time I had something this fresh and delicious? The pizza, but that was more savory than delicious. Is there a difference? Does it matter? No.

My eyes drift to Heidi's... unique decor choices while I eat.

The collection of sex toys arranged like some kind of modern art installation on the bookshelf makes me wonder about her thought process. Is it a statement? Maybe she's just run out of drawer and dresser space - judging by the sheer variety, that's entirely possible.

Most of them have the Naughty Wyvern logo stamped on the base. Some look intriguing enough that I catch myself blushing, while others... well, they look more like medieval torture devices than anything meant for pleasure. There's one that seems to have actual scales, and I'm not sure if I'm impressed or terrified by the engineering involved.

I take another bite of Danish and try not to make eye contact with the anatomically ambitious dragon dildo that seems to be watching me from its perch between "Fifty Shades of Grey" and "The Joy of Cooking." At least now I know why Connor kept glancing at the bookshelf last night with that mix of fascination and horror.

I savor the second Danish, the cream cheese one, and stash the remaining Danish in the fridge, letting my fingers trail over the smooth paper bag one more time. The Books and Beans logo makes me smile, thinking of Connor's thoughtfulness.

Back at the kitchen table, I eye the clock on the microwave. One hour until the phone interview. My stomach does a nervous flip that has nothing to do with the pastries I just inhaled.

I fish through Heidi's kitchen drawer until I find a notepad decorated with cartoon penises (seriously, Heidi?) and a pen that actually works. The glass of ice water I pour myself sweats onto the table as I sit down, and I absently wipe at the puddle with my sleeve.

A real job. My first real job. The thought makes me light-headed with possibility until reality crashes in like a bucket of ice water.

The laptop. Shit.

My pulse quickens as panic starts to set in. The data entry position requires a computer - it's right there in the job description. The one Heidi had is in pieces thanks to that son of a bitch, and I don't have...well, anything.

I take a long drink of water, trying to calm myself. Think, think. Maybe I could tell them I need a week before starting? But who am I kidding? Even if they agree, where am I going to get a laptop in a week? They're not exactly giving those away at shelters. Maybe I could use one of the computers at the library? Will they let me use it for that long at a time? Shit, the information probably needs to be from a dedicated and secure wifi source and not a public one.

My hands shake as I write "NEED LAPTOP" at the top of the penis-decorated paper, then immediately scratch it out. As if writing it down will somehow make a solution appear.

The clock keeps ticking, each minute bringing me closer to an interview for a job I'm already setting myself up to fail. I press my forehead against the cool table surface and try to breathe through the rising panic.

Chapter 13: Tarot Cards & Turnbuckles

Connor

THE MOONLIGHT STREAMS THROUGH our bedroom window, casting soft shadows across Olivia's bare skin. Her auburn hair cascades down her shoulders as she takes me in her mouth, her tongue working magic that makes my toes curl. I run my fingers through her silky strands, letting out a contented sigh as she releases me with a playful pop.

"You're mine," she whispers, climbing up my body. Her breasts brush against my chest as she positions herself above me. When she sinks down, taking me inside her, the feeling is exquisite - familiar yet electric. Her hips roll in that perfect rhythm we perfected over years together.

I grip her waist, drinking in every detail - the constellation of freckles across her collarbone, the way her lips part slightly when she moans. With one fluid motion, I flip us over, pinning her beneath me. Her legs wrap around my waist as I thrust deeper, our bodies moving in perfect sync.

Her fingers dig into my shoulders as I kiss her deeply,

tasting traces of myself on her tongue. We're both close, our breathing ragged. I pull back to look into those piercing green eyes I've loved for so long, but something's different. The face beneath me has shifts - it's Shelly now, her younger features soft with trust and adoration. Her eyes hold that same vulnerable longing I remember from the coffee shop, but there's something more there now. Something that makes my chest thrum.

I jolt awake, sheets twisted around my waist. For a moment, I hold onto the lingering warmth of the dream, a smile playing at my lips. Then my eyes land on the framed photo on my nightstand - Olivia beaming at the camera in front of the Sensō-ji Temple, cherry blossoms caught mid-fall around her.

The smile dies on my face. Shame crashes over me like a cold wave, and I roll onto my back, pressing the heels of my hands against my eyes until I see stars. What the fuck is wrong with me?

I swing my legs over the bed and try not to look at Liv's picture - worried it will come to life and she'll be in tears at my betrayal. I walk to our massive closest, that doubles as a vanity, to the bathroom a cold shower on my mind. Ashlyn's words pop into my head, 'Liv would want you to find whatever makes you feel alive again. Whether that's friendship or something more.' I can't help but feel that if that were the truth then I wouldn't feel this overwhelming guilt.

The cold water cascades over my shoulders as I examine my bruised knuckles. Purple and red bloom across the skin like watercolors. Worth it. Every fucking hit was worth it. I hope that piece of shit gets passed around the prison yard like a party favor.

I turn the water all the way to hot and as steam fills the bathroom I let my head fall forward, watching water spiral down the drain. My mind drifts to Tokyo, to our honeymoon suite with its floor-to-ceiling windows overlooking the neon-painted skyline. Liv wore nothing but my dress shirt, the fabric barely covering her ass as she pulled me onto the balcony at midnight.

"We're going to get arrested for public indecency," I'd whispered against her neck.

"Then make it worth the fine," she'd purred back, already undoing my belt.

The memory is so vivid I can almost feel her skin under my fingers, hear her gasps mixing with the distant city sounds as I took her against the railing. We didn't care who might see us. In that moment, we were the only two people in the world.

My chest constricts painfully as reality crashes back in. The shower tiles blur through my tears, and I have to brace myself against the wall to stay upright.

"Liv..." My voice breaks on her name. "I can't do this much longer. You and Des made me who I am. Every breath is me grasping for the desire to keep going. Help me, please."

The only answer is the steady drumming of water against tile.

I step out of the shower, toweling off with more force than necessary like I can somehow scrub away these conflicting feelings. The gym seems like the perfect escape right now

- nothing clears the head like pushing weights until your muscles scream and it's a deadlift day - my favorite.

Pulling open my dresser drawer, I find it suspiciously empty. Alicia. She must have done her ninja housekeeper routine yesterday while I was at work. The woman's obsessed with getting my gym clothes "properly" cleaned, insisting my high-end washer and dryer combo can't handle the task. I can practically hear her saying "That fancy machine of yours can't get the stink out like industrial cleaning can, Mr. Ebin."

Digging deeper for my backup gear, my hand brushes something wrapped in soft fur. The bundle tumbles to the floor, cards spilling across the hardwood. My throat tightens as I recognize Des's last birthday gift to Liv - her tarot deck. She'd been so proud of picking it out herself, knowing her mom's fascination with all things mystical and occult.

Two cards have separated from the rest: The Lovers and the Ace of Cups. I know enough about tarot from Liv's excited explanations to recognize The Lovers - union, relationships, choices of the heart. My fingers tremble as I pick up the cards, and for a moment I swear I can smell Liv's hair.

"Are you trying to tell me something, baby?" I whisper, carefully gathering the deck and place the bundle on my dresser next to my watch collection, where the morning sun catches the gold leaf edges of the cards. The familiar ache in my chest feels different somehow. Not lighter exactly, but... clearer.

I think she's telling me not to give up.

The apartment's gym fluorescent lights hum overhead as I adjust the weight plates. The familiar smell of rubber flooring and metal fills my nostrils - it's comforting at this point. My reflection catches my eye in the wall-length mirror, and I notice the dark circles under my eyes. That dream really did a number on me.

I chalk my hands, the fine powder creating a small cloud as I clap them together. The warmup sets flow smoothly - 135, 225, 315. Each pull feels better than the last, my form locked in after years of practice. The empty gym means no one's here to witness me talking to myself between sets, a habit Liv used to tease me about mercilessly.

"Come on, old man," I mutter, strapping my lever belt tighter. "Time to earn your protein shake."

More plates go on: 405, 495, 545. The knurling of the bar bites into my palms as I set up for my final attempt. 605 pounds. A new PR. My heart hammers against my ribs as I brace against the belt.

Deep breath in. Hold. The first pull breaks the weight off the floor - it feels like trying to uproot a tree. My quads shake and my hamstrings scream as I push through my heels, keeping the bar close. Everything narrows down to this single moment of strain and determination. The lockout is smooth, and for a split second, I'm on top of the world.

The plates crash back to the platform with a satisfying bang that echoes through the empty gym. I undo my belt, grinning like an idiot, but the victory high fades fast as the room starts to spin. My knees buckle, and I barely make it to the nearby bench before collapsing. At least I am sitting and didn't fall over.

Shit. I should've eaten something before this. The ceiling

tiles swim above me as I lay back, trying to get my breathing under control. Note to self: emotional turmoil and heavy deadlifts don't mix well on an empty stomach.

I blink hard several times, willing my vision to clear. The gym slowly stops spinning, and as I catch my breath, my eyes drift to the far corner. Something's different. The spot where Liv's epic battle with the slam ball ended in defeat - it's gone. The dent that's been there for years, a constant reminder of her laughing "I meant to do that" as she rubbed her bruised ego, has been patched and painted over. The repair looks fresh, probably done last night based on the paint sheen.

Harold, our maintenance supervisor, pushes through the gym door, clipboard in hand. "Morning, Mr. Ebin. Just checking on the repair work. Don't let me bother you. Damn, did you just lift that?" He gestures to barbell in front of me.

I sit up straighter, still a bit light-headed. "Just barely." I then point over to the repair. "Why now?" The words come out rougher than intended. I flick at my wrist, trying to keep my voice steady. "That dent's been there for years."

Harold adjusts his glasses, squinting at the wall. "Funny thing, actually. No one ever reported it until a few days ago. Honestly went completely unnoticed." He shrugs, making a note on his clipboard. "Sometimes things just blend into the background, you know? But even old wounds get patched up eventually I suppose. Unless our checks ever bounce of course." He chuckled as if knowing that with the people in this building, coupled with the rent they pay will make sure that never happens.

I do know what he means about blind spots though. I've

spent years carefully cultivating my own, choosing which memories to preserve and which to paint over. But this one - this tiny imperfection that made Liv laugh so hard she snorted - I wasn't ready to lose it. It feels like everything in the world is moving forward but me.

I force myself to finish my workout routine. Pull-ups, rows, face pulls and some bicep curl variations. I check my cell phone and see that I only have about three hours before I need to be at Manu's place.

As if I added a speed race to my routine today, I race upstairs, shower and change to try and get some gaming time in. If I keep my mind busy…

The gaming rig hums to life, its RGB lighting casting a soft glow across my desk. I pour vodka over ice, add ginger beer and a splash of lime - my go-to Moscow Mule. I swapped out the usual copper mug for a standard cocktail glass years ago during one of my extremely rare bar visits when I noticed everyone with a copper mug had a manbun, greasy pointed beard and pants so tight they belonged on a child sized yoga pants. I shake my head at the thought and take a sip from my glass, letting the spicy-sweet burn chase away the lingering gym fatigue.

My eyes catch on a discarded Books and Beans cup in the trash. Wonder if Shelly nailed that interview? The thought of her sitting on the phone talking to some HR rep using her best "please hire me" voice makes my own lips twitch upward. She's got more grit than most of the trust fund kids we interview these days.

The cocktail hits my empty stomach like a punch, and

the room does a lazy spin - right, food. Probably should've learned my lesson after nearly face-planting in the gym. I shuffle to the kitchen, pulling out an obscene amount of turkey, ham, and roast beef from the deli drawer. Alicia keeps me stocked like she's preparing for a meat shortage.

The sandwich I construct is a monstrosity that would make any food photographer weep. Three types of meat, double cheese, lettuce, tomato, and enough mayo to have my cardiologist not understand how my labs are still normal. While I'm at it, I mix up a protein shake - peanut butter of course, because I'm not a savage who drinks vanilla. Ok, I actually love vanilla but most vanilla protein powders taste like nothing but chemicals.

Back at my desk, I balance the plate precariously next to my keyboard. The mechanical clicks of my custom switches fill the room as I log in, my character's idle animation playing across my ultra-wide monitor. I load up Guardians of Havoc Fire, an incredible turn based role play game with so much character customization it made you feel a little uncomfortable. Why anyone should care about the shape of your character's nipples is beyond me, but it won Game of the Year 2019. It beat our own nominated entry of Tales of Fallen Embers. I hated that I had to admit that I believed there's was better, only to myself and Manu of course.

I take a massive bite of my sandwich, letting out an embarrassingly satisfied groan. Sometimes the best meals are the ones that would make a food critic cry.

I decide on star shaped nipples. Why? I don't know, they made the breasts physics look better. I joke with myself that perhaps we should change the shape of the Seidr Witch's nipples for Rune Beast and I think I might jokingly bring it up to the art department just to see if they think I'm serious.

After my sixth failed attempt at the Demon Lord boss fight, I finally admit defeat. The star-shaped nipples didn't give me the edge I was hoping for. I check my watch - shit, I need to head to Manu's. The Moscow Mule has left a pleasant buzz humming through my system, but I'm nowhere near impaired.

I grab my keys and leather jacket, then head down to the parking garage. The liquor store near Manu's place is my first stop. Their craft beer selection is impressive, and I know exactly what I'm looking for - Three Dark Jarls Imperial Stout. It's this ridiculously delicious beer that Manu absolutely loves, complete with Norse-style artwork on the label. We were actually pretty heavy into rounds of it when we came up with the idea for Rune Beast.

His condo building always reminds me of a giant glass Jenga tower. I park in the visitor spot he always reserves for me and take the elevator up to the 23rd floor. The hallway still smells like fresh paint from their recent remodel.

"Perfect timing," Manu says as he opens the door before I can knock. He eyes the six-pack in my hands and grins. "And you brought the good stuff."

"Like I'd show up with anything else." I step inside, kicking off my shoes. His place is immaculate as always - minimalist furniture, pristine white walls decorated with framed vintage gaming posters. "Please tell me you ordered food. I'm starving."

"Already handled." He takes the beer from me and heads to the kitchen. "Got sushi coming from Sakura. The good stuff, not that conveyor belt nonsense."

I settle onto his absurdly comfortable couch. "You're a saint. Though, I wouldn't turn down conveyor belt sushi either."

"That's because you'll eat anything." He returns with two opened bottles, handing me one. "But tonight we're celebrating. The Seidr Witch power up mechanic is looking incredible. Between that and the epic pay-per-view we're about to watch - it's going to be a good damn night."

The sushi spread before us looks like an artist's palette - vibrant cuts of fish arranged with a precision that would make a surgeon jealous. I pop a piece of fatty tuna into my mouth, letting it melt on my tongue while watching two graying legends execute a perfect double suplex on their younger opponents.

"Look at that form," Manu says, gesturing at the screen with his chopsticks. "These guys are what, our age? Little older? And they're still throwing themselves around like they're twenty-five."

I wash down my sushi with a sip of the Three Dark Jarls. "Yeah, but tomorrow morning they'll be feeling it in places they didn't know could hurt. Speaking of which-" I rotate my shoulder, still feeling this morning's deadlift session. "When did we get old enough to be in the same age bracket as 'wrestling legends'?"

"Speak for yourself," Manu snorts. "I'm aging like a fine Indian whiskey."

"Is that even a thing?"

"It is now."

We're both laughing when the doorbell chimes. Manu raises an eyebrow at me, but I just shrug. The door swings open to reveal Ashlyn, holding up a bottle of sake with a mischievous grin.

"Boys' night? Without me? I'm wounded." She kicks off her heels and makes herself at home on the couch between us. "Someone needs to class up this operation. You can't have good sushi without sake."

"By all means," I gesture grandly at the spread, "elevate our pedestrian gathering with your superior taste."

"Don't mind if I do." She pours three small cups and passes them around. "Now catch me up - who's winning?"

"The legends are dominating," Manu says confidently, right as both veterans crash through tables with perfect synchronization. The crowd erupts, and I can't help but wince at the impact.

Ashlyn smirks, swirling her sake. "You were saying?"

"That was... unfortunate timing," Manu mutters, reaching for more sushi.

I lean forward, recognizing the shift in momentum. The younger guys are playing to the crowd, but they're making a rookie mistake - taking too long to capitalize. Sure enough, when they finally climb back into the ring, the legends are ready.

"Watch this," I tap Ashlyn's leg with my chopsticks. "Classic setup."

The first veteran feints a clothesline, drawing his opponent in. The move is so smooth, so practiced, you'd never know these guys were pushing fifty. The choke slam that follows is textbook perfection - the kind of move that makes the whole crowd gasp in unison.

"Holy shit," Ashlyn breathes as the second legend ascends the turnbuckle with surprising agility. The flying elbow drop that follows is poetry in motion, ending with a thunderous impact that seems to shake Manu's entire living room.

"That's how you do it old school," I say, raising my sake cup in appreciation. The three-count that follows feels like a mere formality.

"That's what experience gets you!" Ashlyn raises her sake cup in celebration, then grabs my hand. "Speaking of 'experience' - how are those knuckles doing? They looked pretty rough last night."

I flex my fingers, wincing slightly at the stiffness. The bruising has turned an impressive shade of purple-green across my knuckles. "They'll heal."

"Hold up," Manu sets down his chopsticks, eyes narrowing. "What happened to your hand? And why am I just hearing about this now?"

Ashlyn jumps in before I can respond. "Oh my god, you haven't told him? Connor went full superhero last night. We found this creep attacking this girl that Connor is crushing on in an alley and Connor just..." She makes a punching motion with her free hand.

"You what?" Manu stares at me. "How the fuck did you not lead with that story?"

I take a long pull from my beer and look at Ashlyn. "Crushing on? Really?" She just smirks at me as if she knows something I don't. The I turn to Manu. "Honestly? I crashed hard when I got home this morning. Stayed at Shelly's place until her roommate got back - she didn't want to be alone after everything."

"You stayed the night?" Ashlyn's eyebrows shoot up, a pleased smile spreading across her face. "Did you two...?"

"Nothing happened," I say quickly, maybe too quickly based on their expressions. "We fell asleep watching movies on the couch. That's it." I flick at my wrist. "There's... I don't know. There's definitely something there, but it's not like that. We're friends."

"Friends." Manu repeats, clearly skeptical. "Wait, is this the girl you were telling me about? Olivia's clone?"

I sigh. "Yes, the 'clone.' And yes, just friends." I grab another piece of sushi, hoping the conversation will move on. "Can we get back to watching aging wrestlers destroy their bodies for our entertainment?"

I can feel Manu and Ashlyn making eye contact and almost speaking into each other's minds about the whole thing. I ignore it and watch as the entrance music of the next wrestler hits.

The match reaches its climax as Blackfang scales the turnbuckle while pulling the champ with him, his signature face paint gleaming under the arena lights. The crowd's roaring reaches a fever pitch, and I'm not ashamed to admit I'm on my feet alongside Manu and Ashlyn.

"He's got it!" Manu shouts, spilling beer as he gestures at the screen. "No way they're letting anyone kick out of the

Death's Door DDT!"

Then that all-too-familiar entrance music hits. The camera pans to reveal Cassius fucking Osborne, looking impossibly jacked after his eight-month "injury." The crowd loses their collective mind as he charges the ring.

"Oh, come on!" I throw my hands up in disgust. "Such bullshit!"

The inevitable happens - Blackfang gets blindsided mid-move, Benjamin Breakout take the opportunity and covers Blackfang to retain the championship title, and wrestling Twitter is about to explode. Even Ashlyn, who claimed earlier not to care about "sweaty men in spandex," looks personally offended.

"I need to piss," I announce, realizing I haven't moved from this couch in hours. My bladder apparently has an incredible tolerance for craft beer. On my way I finally check my phone.

Two missed voicemails from an unknown number. Normally I'd ignore them - probably spam about my car's extended warranty - but in my half drunken state I press play. The first message starts, and I can't help the smile that spreads across my face when I hear Shelly's voice.

Chapter 14: Sugar Rush

Shelly

I SIT CROSS-LEGGED ON Heidi's couch, staring at the blank TV screen. I replay the words over and over in my head, 'Ms Lockhart, I would like to offer the position to you. It starts next week and pay will be $15.24 and hour, there will be the opportunity for advancement. Are you interested?'

Of course I was. My hands are trembling so much I have to place them under my legs that are also shaking up and down. A real job. Not just some under-the-table cash gig or day labor, but an actual position with benefits and everything.

The taste of cream cheese frosting lingers on my tongue as I reach for the last Danish. Connor's surprise breakfast delivery in my hands again. My stomach actually feels full for the first time in...no that's twice in the last twenty four hours that I have been this full.

"One week," I whisper to myself, trying to make it feel real. The words flutter in my chest like trapped birds. I should be thrilled – I am thrilled – but anxiety gnaws at the edges of my excitement. A laptop. I'm going to need a laptop. I didn't even have to ask to start a week later, that's just when they wanted. Should I have requested more time? Maybe two weeks?

My fingers fidget with the hem of my borrowed t-shirt as I force myself to take another bite of Danish. The sweetness floods my mouth, and I try to focus on that instead of the mounting panic. I catch a glimpse of myself in one of Heidi's many decorative mirrors, this one across the room. My cheeks look a little less hollow than they did a few days ago.

"Keep eating like this," I murmur, brushing crumbs from my lap, "and maybe I'll stop looking like a walking coat hanger." The thought makes me smile despite everything else. It's been so long since I've had regular meals that I'd almost forgotten what it feels like to not be constantly hungry.

I practically bounce on my heels as I hear Heidi's bedroom door creak open. She emerges in boy shorts and a tank top, rubbing sleep from her eyes, blonde hair a magnificent mess.

"Coffee's ready!" I blurt before she can even mumble good morning. "And I got the job! The data entry one!"

Heidi blinks at me, then breaks into a wide smile. "Holy shit, Shell! That's amazing!" She wraps me in a tight hug that smells like sleep and expensive perfume.

She then asks, "Coffee? You fixed the machine?"

"Connor sent some over this morning, from Books and Beans."

"I told you he was a sugar daddy." She says with a sly smile.

I want to glare but I know better. This is her apartment, not mine and she is just being playful, I think. "I need a laptop though and after last night I have no idea how I'm going to—"

"Use my PC," Heidi cuts in, though she winces slightly as

she says it. "I mean, not for work, but..." She runs a hand through her tangled hair. "Look, you can use it to search for something cheap tonight while I'm at the Madame's. Just... don't open anything on the desktop unless you want to see way more of me than you ever needed to."

I tilt my head, confused for a moment before it clicks. "Oh! Your... work stuff?"

"Yeah," she laughs. "Let's just say there are some very creative uses of household 'decor' as you've called it that my subscribers really enjoy. But seriously, use the browser, check Craigslist or whatever. Just stay out of my folders unless you want to see exactly how flexible I am."

I can feel my face burning but I'm laughing too. "Noted. Thanks, Heidi. Really. I'm going to pay you back for all of this somehow. I promise."

"Come on, we're celebrating properly!" Heidi grabs my wrist and practically drags me to her bedroom. I stumble along behind her, trying not to trip over my own feet. Her enthusiasm is infectious, even if I'm still processing everything that's happened in the last twenty-four hours.

Her room is a stark contrast to the living room's carefully curated, albeit exotic, aesthetic. Here, clothes are strewn across a plush purple comforter, and the walls are plastered with vintage band posters. She drops to her knees beside a small wine fridge tucked between her dresser and nightstand, pulling out a bottle of something that looks expensive and deep red.

"Is that..." I squint at the label.

"Merlot," she says, reaching up to grab two wine glasses

from a clever little shelf mounted above the fridge. "And before you say anything about it being too early - this is a special occasion and it is past 5pm now so it's close enough to drinking time."

I perch on the edge of her bed, watching as she pours generous amounts into both glasses. "You know I've never really had wine before?"

"Then you're in for a treat." She hands me a glass and plops down beside me, making the mattress bounce. "Speaking of treats, oh my god, you will not believe what happened at work last night."

I take a tentative sip - it's richer than I expected, and warmer somehow. "What happened?"

"This guy, regular client, comes in absolutely convinced he's in love with me." She rolls her eyes dramatically. "Starts going on and on about how he'll leave his wife, all the things he wants to do with me and for me, how we're meant to be together and how we can just leave the country and never return."

"No way," I giggle, the wine already making me feel lighter.

"Some men, I swear." Heidi takes a long drink. "Like, honey, I'm literally at work. This is my job. The only thing I'm in love with is your credit card limit."

"What did you tell him?" I ask, taking another sip of wine. The warmth spreads through my chest, making everything feel softer around the edges.

Heidi stretches out on the bed, propping herself up on one elbow. "Just enough to keep him coming back. You know, batting my eyes, telling him how special he is." She shrugs.

"Eventually he'll either figure it out or I'll have to be direct. Then comes the inevitable tantrum and security escort."

"That happens a lot?"

"More than you'd think. It's part of the job though - making them feel like they're the only person in the world." She swirls her wine thoughtfully. "At least for as long as they're paying. Another year of building my online following and I can quit dancing altogether. Then I can avoid most of the messiness of the adult entertainment business."

The wine must be hitting me because I don't immediately tense up when she adds, "You know, you could make some serious cash doing cam work yourself. I could show you the ropes..."

"Oh god, no." I laugh nervously, nearly choking on my drink. "Nobody wants to see all this." I gesture vaguely at myself.

"Please," Heidi smirks. "I bet your sugar daddy, Connor, would love a private show."

Heat floods my face and I grab one of her pillows, hugging it to my chest. "He's not my sugar daddy! He's just... being nice and even if he was interested he's not the sugar daddy type. He has the money, yeah, but not that kind of attitude."

"Uh-huh." Heidi's grin widens. "That's why he's sending you breakfast and paying your medical bills. Because he's just such a nice guy."

The pillow makes excellent cover as I try to hide my deepening blush. "It's not like that," I mumble into the fabric.

Heidi takes another sip of wine, her eyes sparkling with mischief. "Well, if he's not your sugar daddy, then he must be falling in love with you."

"Stop!" I smack her arm playfully, but the words send a flutter through my chest that has nothing to do with the wine.

"Has to be one or the other, sweetie." She winks at me over her glass.

I sink deeper into the pillow, but my mind is already wandering. The way Connor looked at me last night, concern etched into his features with no sign of pity. How his arms felt when he held me. The gentle way he made sure I was safe before leaving.

The warmth spreading through me isn't just from the Merlot anymore. Every time I think of Connor, it's like something inside me unclenches – some part of me that's been wound tight for so long I forgot it was there. And I realize, sitting here on Heidi's purple comforter with wine in my system and Danish crumbs still on my shirt, that I'm okay with whatever this feeling is.

Because Connor... Connor is safe. Not just in the physical sense, though god knows he proved that last night. There's something deeper, more fundamental about him that speaks to the scared little girl inside me who stopped believing in fairy tales a long time ago. When he looks at me, I feel seen. Not pitied, not sized up, just... seen.

The thought of him feeds something in me that's been starving far longer than my body has. Something that coffee and Danish can't satisfy, but his smile somehow does.

"Earth to Shelly," Heidi waves her hand in front of my face. "You're getting that dreamy look I see in men at the club."

I lower the wine glass, letting my finger trace its rim. "I do like him," I whisper, the admission making my heart race. "Not because of the money or the food or any of that. When I'm with him, I feel... real. Like I'm not just some ghost drifting through other people's lives anymore."

Heidi sits up straighter, her teasing smile softening into something more genuine. "Tell me more."

"It's stupid," I say, but the words keep coming anyway. "But I have these moments when I'm alone, and everything feels too big and empty? When I'm with Connor, it's like... like the world shrinks down to just the right size. Like I finally fit somewhere."

I take another sip of wine, liquid courage warming my throat. "Last night, when we fell asleep watching that movie? I wasn't scared anymore. Not of Bertrand, not of being homeless, not of anything. For the first time since I aged out of the system, no even before that, I felt whole."

"That's not stupid at all," Heidi says softly, reaching over to squeeze my hand.

"I know he's older, and successful, and probably sees me as some kid he needs to help," I continue, the words tumbling out now. "But when he looks at me, it's like he actually something inside me. Not just another homeless girl, or some charity case. Just... me."

The admission hangs in the air between us, and I feel lighter somehow, like naming this feeling has given it permission to exist.

Heidi pours me more wine and sits back down closer to me. "Tell him, Shelly. You owe it to yourself to see where this leads."

I shake my head but with a smile on my face. "Not yet…I need to get a better idea of how he feels about me. Because if he doesn't feel that way about me I don't want to mess anything up by telling him I like him. I would rather have a friend that looks out for me than nothing. What if he thinks I'm taking advantage of his kindness or that I'm just being a silly fickle girl and I'm going to grow out of this fantasy of mine?"

"If you don't tell him then you'll never know, Shell." Heidi downs the rest of her glass. "Now, unless you want to see the few tattoos I have, vacate the room. I need to shower and change for work."

After an hour of Heidi showering, dressing, painting her face up and bathing in body spray, she is out the door and I find myself sitting at her computer.

I stare at Heidi's desktop, the wine making my head pleasantly fuzzy as I try to process what I'm seeing. The folder names are… descriptive, to say the least. 'Railed Into Oblivion' makes me snort-laugh into my wine glass, though I'm not entirely sure if it's the alcohol or genuine amusement.

"Jesus, Heidi," I mutter, quickly averting my eyes from a folder labeled 'Double Penetration' and opening Chrome instead. My cheeks feel warm, and not just from the Merlot.

Craigslist seems like the logical place to start, though every other listing screams 'SCAM' in neon letters. Fifty dollars for a gaming laptop? Yeah, right. And I'm secretly a Nigerian princess. The legitimate-looking ones are still way out of my reach – even at three-hundred dollars, it would take forever to pay Heidi back.

I'm about to give up when a new listing catches my eye: "Computer Store Liquidation - Everything Must Go!" The description mentions laptops as low as one-hundred dollars, with some being given away free if you're willing to take a chance on whether they work or not.

My heart starts racing as I read through the details. The store is closing this Tuesday, and they're practically giving things away just to clear the space. Even the working laptops are marked down to almost nothing.

"This could actually work," I whisper to myself, bookmarking the page. The wine makes me feel bold enough to hope, to imagine waking up to do my new job with an actual computer of my own. Even if I have to get one of the free mystery machines, it's worth checking out.

I take another sip of wine, trying to steady my excitement. After all the times life has kicked me down, it feels strange to have things potentially working out.

I quickly grab a pen and a stickynote from a draw in Heidi's computer desk and write down the address and phone number of the store. I go to put the pen back and my hand freezes on the drawer handle. The little baggie is tucked behind some paperclips, probably meant to stay hidden, but I know what it is. A year on the streets teaches you to recognize certain things, whether you want to or not. My stomach drops as I carefully close the drawer, trying to pretend I never saw it. Cocaine.

"Not my business," I whisper to myself, though disappointment sits heavy in my chest. Heidi's been so good to me, and she seems to have her life together far better than I do. Who am I to judge?

Back in the living room, I realize I've spent way too long at the computer. The wine bottle is mostly empty now, and my head feels pleasantly fuzzy. Connor's number catches my eye from where it sits on the coffee table, scrawled in his neat handwriting.

"This is such a bad idea," I mutter, even as my fingers are already dialing. Each ring makes my heart beat faster, until his voicemail clicks on. His voice, even recorded, sends warmth down to my toes.

"Hi Connor," I start, then giggle nervously. "It's Shelly. I got the job! The data entry one. But um, funny thing… I need a laptop since…anyway there's this sale on Tuesday…" I pause, twirling a strand of hair around my finger. I catch myself and wonder when in the hell I became the girl that plays with her hair. "I was wondering if maybe you could take me? To the store? I just… I feel safe when you're around. So safe…and taken care of…"

I hang up quickly, my face burning. "Oh god, why did I say that?" I groan, flopping back on the couch. The room spins slightly, and I know tomorrow I'm going to regret every word of that voicemail.

I remember seeing in a TV show once that made it look like you can call a number back and delete a voicemail if it hasn't been listened to yet. I frantically call him back and thankfully he doesn't answer. As the voicemail kick over I hit *57, then* 69. None of it is working. "Shit, fuck. Delete. Delete. Delete voice mail." I realize all I am doing is leaving another voice mail of shame and hang up, throwing my head back and groaning in defeat. "Well, I'm fucked." I sink into the couch and let the wine put me to bed.

The phone's ring jolts me awake, and I nearly fall off Heidi's couch. My head is fuzzy from the wine, and it takes me a moment to focus on caller ID. When I do, my stomach drops.

Connor's name blinks up at me accusingly.

"Fuck, fuck, fuck." I stare at the phone like it might bite me. He's definitely heard the embarrassing voicemails. Now he's calling to let me down easy, to explain why he can't be around someone so obviously crushing on him like some little girl.

I should let it go to voicemail. That would be the smart thing to do.

My thumb betrays me, hitting 'accept' before my brain can stop it.

"Hello?" My voice comes out small and squeaky.

"Shelly!" Connor's voice is warm and... slightly slurred? "Got your messages… both of them." He chuckles, and I want to die right there on Heidi's couch. "Course I'll take you Tuesday. But only if we get food first. Deal?"

I blink, processing his words. He doesn't sound upset or uncomfortable. If anything, he sounds... happy?

"I... yeah, that would be nice," I manage.

"Great! It's a..." he pauses, and I hold my breath. "It's gonna be fun."

The words "I like you" bubble up in my throat, wanting to spill out. But I swallow them back down. "I'll see you Tuesday, Connor."

I hang up and press my face into a throw pillow, trying to suppress the ridiculous grin spreading across my face. Maybe the wine hasn't completely worn off, or maybe this feeling in my chest is something else entirely.

Chapter 15: Breakfast Club Revelations

Shelly

I WAKE UP SUNDAY morning with a mild hangover and an empty apartment. No sign of Heidi coming home last night. Strange. I try her cell, but it goes straight to voicemail. A knot forms in my stomach - I've learned the hard way that people disappearing isn't usually a good thing.

"Hey Heidi, just checking on you. Call me back?" I hang up, trying to ignore the worry creeping in.

The kitchen feels too quiet as I scramble some eggs. What I wouldn't give for coffee right now. For someone who practically mainlines caffeine, it's weird Heidi hasn't replaced the coffee maker. Especially considering that she makes pretty good money. Add it to the growing list of things that don't quite add up.

Standing at the sliding glass door to her balcony, watching pigeons strut across the railing, an idea hits me.

Before I can talk myself out of it, I text Ashlyn: "Hey, got a minute to talk?"

The phone rings almost instantly. Taking a deep breath, I answer.

"Hi Shelly, everything okay?" Ashlyn's voice is warm, concerned.

"Yeah, I um... I got that data entry job." I twist a loose thread on my shirt. "But I need a laptop by next week. Connor's taking me to this sale on Tuesday, but..." I trail off.

"But you don't want him paying for it," Ashlyn finishes.

"Exactly. I was wondering... is there anything I could do at Eldritch Magic? Just temporary work to earn enough before Tuesday?"

There's a pause on the other end, and I hold my breath. Maybe this was a stupid idea.

There's a few seconds and the sound of a keyboard on the other end before Ashlyn speaks up. "Actually, have you ever watched any streamers?

"Like video game streamers? Yeah…"

"We had one of out moderators call in for tomorrow. How fast do you read and how quickly can you learn a handful of typed commands?"

"Pretty quickly I think and as fast as I need to."

"Be ready to leave your friend's apartment tomorrow morning at 6am. I'll pick you up."

"Thank you so much, I really appreciate-"

"Hold that thought," Ashlyn cuts in, a hint of amusement in her voice. "Trust me, after eight hours of watching chat scroll by faster than a caffeinated and cracked out hamster on a wheel, you might not be so grateful."

I bite my lip, picturing the chaos of the streaming chats I've lurked in before. "That bad?"

"Let's just say there's a reason we pay our mods well. Speaking of which - you'll walk away with about three hundred for the day."

My heart skips. Three hundred dollars? That's almost enough for a decent refurbished laptop, even without the electronics sale. I press the phone closer to my ear, afraid I've misheard. "Wait, seriously?"

"Seriously. Though you'll earn every penny dealing with the spam bots and hormone-fueled teenagers. See you tomorrow."

I stare at the phone for a moment after Ashlyn hangs up, still processing how quickly my laptop situation might be resolved. Three hundred dollars. It feels surreal, like finding money in an old jacket pocket, except this time I'll actually earn it.

The apartment feels different in daylight - less like a refuge and more like what it really is: someone else's space that I'm borrowing. My eyes drift to Heidi's bedroom door, guilt gnawing at me for snooping last night. The baggie I found keeps nagging at my thoughts. Should I say something? It's not like I have any room to judge, considering I'm basically squatting here.

I think about going shopping for the laptop with Connor and heat rushes to my face as fragments of our drunk mini conversation float back. God, I actually asked him to go electronics shopping with me. At least I didn't mention the folder I shouldn't have opened on Heidi's computer. Did I?

The day stretches ahead, empty and full of possibility. I

could job hunt more, maybe look up some tutorials on data entry to prepare for the new job. Or I could shower again - yeah, that should probably come first. After a year of taking a real honest hot shower probably twice a month I am taking full advantage of this place. The hot water's been surprisingly reliable here, unlike most places I've crashed.

I grab a plush pink towel. First shower, then maybe I'll walk to the library and see what free resources they have for office skills. And hopefully Heidi will be back soon.

Still, it's hard not to feel a tiny spark of optimism. Between the new job, tomorrow's moderating gig, and people like Connor and Ashlyn actually wanting to help... maybe things are finally looking up.

I catch my reflection in the bathroom mirror and quickly look away. I force myself to turn and look again. The young woman staring back at me seems so much older than the one from even a handful of days ago. Don't get me wrong, I still look the same. I guess I just see myself differently now.

The shower spray hits just right and I lean back against the cool tile, letting my mind drift. My hand slides lower, finding that familiar rhythm as steam curls around me. Connor's face flashes through my thoughts - those sweet eyes, the way his arms felt around me that night. Heat floods my cheeks even as my fingers move faster. I shouldn't be thinking about him like this, but...screw that. I can do whatever I want in my own head and no one needs to know about it.

A few minutes later, I'm toweling off on shaky legs, trying to push away the slightly guilty pleasure of those fantasies. Focus on practical things, like clothes. Opening Heidi's closet, I'm hit with a wall of sequins, leather, and things that would make a stripper blush.

I dig through hangers, looking for anything remotely normal. There's got to be something left that won't make me look like I'm advertising. Most of her stuff hangs loose on my frame anyway - she's got curves I definitely don't. After some searching, I find a plain black t-shirt dress that only shows a little cleavage and some thick warm leggings. They'll have to do.

Grabbing my keys, I double-check that everything's locked up tight. The sunshine feels good on my face as I head toward the library, but I keep to the main streets. No shortcuts today, no matter how much my feet hurt in these borrowed flats. I've learned that lesson.

My eyes scan constantly - ahead, behind, across the street. Old and renewed habits. A group of guys hanging outside the corner store makes my pulse quicken, but I keep my pace steady, my face neutral. Just another person going about their day. Nothing to see here.

I stick to the sunny side of the street, avoiding even the shadows of buildings. Funny how something as simple as walking down a public sidewalk becomes a tactical exercise when you've lived on the streets and... but hey, at least I have somewhere safe to go back to now. For a while, anyway.

The library's familiar musty smell wraps around me as I push through the heavy doors. At least this place hasn't changed - same scratched wooden tables, same soft lighting, same elderly librarian who used to let me hide out here after middle school when the weather was bad.

"Well, look who it is," Mrs. Baker whispers, her wrinkled face breaking into a smile. "Haven't seen you in ages, dear."

I manage a small wave, throat tight. She doesn't know I've been sneaking in through the side door for months, using the bathroom to wash up when the shelters were full.

The computer area is mercifully empty this early. I slide into a chair and pull up Google, typing "data entry basics" with slightly trembling fingers. A flood of results appears - Excel tutorials, typing tests, office software guides. I click through several tabs, scribbling notes on a scrap of paper.

After an hour of research, my hand cramps from writing. Time to find some actual books. The business section yields three promising titles: "Data Entry for Beginners," "Microsoft Office Essentials," and "Professional Skills for Office Work."

At the checkout desk, Mrs. Baker beams when I mention having an address now.

"Let's get you set up with a card then," she says, pulling out a form. "It's wonderful to see you getting back on your feet."

I freeze, pen hovering over the paper. "You knew?"

She adjusts her glasses with a gentle smile. "Dear, I've worked here thirty years. You learn to notice things." She slides the completed form closer. "These books will help with your new job?"

"Yeah," I manage. "Data entry position. Starts next week."

"Wonderful." She stamps the due date cards. "And Michelle? The computer lab opens at 9am if you ever need extra practice before you start."

I clutch the books to my chest, fighting back tears. "Thanks, Mrs. Baker. For everything."

I start for the door when I see an old book I used to love reading as an early teen. 'The Maiden and the Lycanthrope,' a modern dystopian retelling of 'Beauty and the Beast.' It's one of those YA novels that should definitely not be YA. Connor shared a movie he loved with me the other night and then recommended I watch 'The Breakfast Club' as well, I still need to watch that one. Maybe when I get back to the apartment. But I wonder if I could convince him to read this book? He shares some media he loves and exchange some that I love. Maybe it could be a thing we start to do with each other.

I turn back around and check out "The Maiden and the Lycanthrope" as well, Mrs. Baker giving me another warm smile as she stamps the card. The walk back to Heidi's feels lighter somehow, like the weight of the books in my arms is centering me to this new reality where I have an actual address to put on library cards.

The apartment is quiet when I unlock the door, Heidi's purse sitting on the kitchen counter. A folded note sits on the coffee table: "Rough night at work. Please keep it down. -H"

I set my stack of books down as quietly as possible, padding to the kitchen in my sock feet. The refrigerator hums as I grab a pop, the can's sharp crack seeming too loud in the stillness. I wince, glancing toward Heidi's closed door, but no sound comes from within.

Netflix loads silently on the TV as I curl up on the couch, with the volume down almost as low as it will go. The Breakfast Club queue's up - might as well see what Connor was talking about before diving into all those office tutorials. The opening notes of "Don't You (Forget About Me)" start playing as I take a sip of my soda. I can study more tonight after the movie. Right now, it feels good to just... exist. To sit on a real couch, in a real apartment, watching a movie someone recommended because they thought I'd like it.

It's such a small, normal thing. But after the past year, normal feels like a luxury I'd forgotten existed.

I am so lost in the movie that before I know it the credits are rolling as I wipe at my eyes, still processing. Damn, Connor was right about this movie. I definitely see myself in Allison - the basket case who keeps to herself, watching everyone else from the sidelines. Though thankfully my dandruff situation has never been quite that dramatic.

I catch myself trying to match Connor to one of the characters and laugh softly. He's got that bad boy look like John Bender, especially with the beard, but his personality is nothing like that. Maybe more like Brian Johnson mixed with Andrew Clark? That same mix of intelligence and protective instinct, but without the pressure to be perfect.

Heidi would totally be Claire, but with an edge that would make even Bender nervous. The thought makes me smile until I glance at the clock - 5:47 PM and still no sign of her beyond that note. My stomach knots up as I remember the baggie in her drawer. What if something happened? What if-

The sudden sound of the shower running makes me jump. Relief floods through me, followed by guilt for snooping and then worry all over again. I should say something about what I found, right? But how do I even start that conversation?

I grab one of the data entry books and flip it open, trying

to focus on keyboard shortcuts and proper posture instead of all the ways tomorrow could go wrong. The shower keeps running as I highlight another passage about Excel formulas, the steady white noise almost drowning out my racing thoughts.

Almost.

The shower cuts off abruptly, and I hear Heidi moving around in her room. Drawers open and slam shut, hangers scraping against the closet rod. I try to focus on my book, but the words blur together as I strain to listen.

Her bedroom door flies open and Heidi bursts out like she's being chased. She's wearing her usual plush red jacket, but something's off. Instead of just her oversized purse, she's also clutching a small handbag close to her body. Large designer sunglasses hide half her face, which wouldn't be weird except it's almost sunset and she's still indoors.

"Sorry Shell, running super late!" she calls out, already halfway to the front door. "We'll catch up tomorrow, okay?"

Before I can respond, she's gone, the door clicking shut behind her. The apartment feels suddenly hollow, like all the air got sucked out with her exit. I stare at my highlighted page about proper spreadsheet formatting, but my mind keeps circling back to that damn baggie in her drawer, the way she wouldn't meet my eyes just now. She didn't even look at me.

In her rush she didn't even lock the door. I nearly panic and launch myself at it to quickly lock the knob and the deadbolt as well as flip the security latch. My curiosity gets the better of me and I go to her room and peak inside. It's a disaster in here. Clothes from the dresser and closet are on the floor, bed and thrown over nearly everything in her room.

My hands shake as I step into Heidi's room, guilt and worry warring in my chest. The drawer slides open with a soft scrape, and my stomach drops - the baggie is gone. Not just moved, but completely vanished along with whatever else had been stashed in there.

The closet catches my eye, clothes strewn everywhere except for one oddly empty space in the back. I inch closer, pulse racing as I spot the fine white powder dusting the shelf. It's like looking at a crime scene in reverse - not what's there, but what's missing that tells the story.

Before I can stop myself, I'm running to the phone and hitting Heidi's number. Each ring feels like an eternity until-

"Yeah?" Her voice comes through breathless, rushed.

"Hey, I just... are you okay? You seemed kind of-"

"I'm fine, Shell, totally fine!" The words tumble out too fast, backed by what sounds like traffic noise. "Just super busy right now. And hey, could you do me a favor and stay out of my room? It's such a disaster in there, I'm honestly embarrassed."

My throat tightens as I stare into her room from the kitchen. "Heidi-"

"Look, I gotta go. We'll talk later, okay?" The call cuts off before I can respond.

I stand frozen at the kitchen counter, phone still pressed to my ear, trying to process what I just found - or rather, what I didn't find. The empty spaces seem to mock me with their implications.

Chapter 16: Epiphanies in Moderation

Connor

THE MASSIVE SCREEN DISPLAY that lines the north wall comes to life, casting a harsh glow across the board room table. I drum my fingers against the polished surface, watching as beta testing metrics scroll across the screen. As usual, the numbers look good. Really good. The same can't be said for alpha testing, that was a disaster.

"So what you're telling me," I lean forward, addressing Tobias from Testing, "is that we've actually managed to optimize this monster gpu hogging game for mid-range systems without sacrificing visual quality?"

"The frame rates are solid," he confirms, swiping to the next slide. "Even on older cards, we're maintaining 60fps with only minor dips during the most intense combat sequences."

Manu's usual stoic expression cracks into a slight smile. "The combat mechanics are testing particularly well. Players are responding positively to the weight of the attacks, especially the berserker transformations."

"Though we should probably address the bath scene glitch," Tanimoto Aimi, our Cinematic Lead that we may or may not have stolen from a competitor chimes in, trying and failing to suppress a laugh. "Having our protagonist suddenly start flailing around like a possessed ragdoll kind of kills the mood we're going for. I don't recall you trying to breakdance in the tub during that motion capture Connor."

I can't help but chuckle at that short video clip. "Yeah, maybe tone down the water physics a bit. What's the timeline on fixing the clipping when moving to a different region on the map?"

"End of week," Tobias assures me, tapping his tablet. "It's just a matter of adjusting the load triggers. Nothing major."

"Overall engagement metrics are through the roof," Ashlyn adds, sliding a report across the table. "The testers are actually putting in more hours than required. That's usually a good sign."

I lean back in my chair, allowing myself to feel genuinely proud of our efforts over the last several months. The game is coming together better than we'd hoped. Maybe all those sleepless nights were worth it after all.

"Speaking of engagement metrics," Manu interjects, his usual deadpan expression taking on a hint of satisfaction, "the power-up mechanics from the Rune Beast and Seidr Witch's intimate scenes are testing exceptionally well. The integration feels so natural, you'd think we planned it from day one."

"That's a relief. I was worried it might come across as gratuitous."

"Actually," Ashlyn cuts in, her tone carrying that particular note that usually precedes complicated news, "about those scenes - I just got off the phone with Maddison Ball's agent earlier this morning. She's more than willing to come back for the mo-cap work, but there's a scheduling issue."

My stomach drops. "Define 'issue.'"

"She has exactly one day available before our deadline, and it's literally the day before." Ashlyn grimaces. "If we can't make it work, we're looking at another delay. We're already two months behind."

"Fuck." The word escapes before I can catch it. "Sorry. But we really can't afford another pushback."

Aimi leans forward, already pulling up the shot list on her tablet. "The scenes aren't that extensive, Connor. Steamy, yes, but brief. If we prep everything properly, we could knock it all out in one day."

"She's right," Manu agrees. "The animations are already blocked out. We just need both you and Maddison's performance to polish them."

I nod slowly, doing mental calculations. "Alright. Aimi, you'll need to run full point on this. Make sure everything's ready to go the moment Maddison walks in. We can't waste a single minute."

"Already on it," she responds, fingers flying across her screen. "I'll have the studio prepped and the capture rigs tested well in advance."

I start gathering my papers, ready to wrap this up, when Ashlyn clears her throat in that particular way she does when

I'm pushing things along too quickly.

"One more thing," she says, practically bouncing in her seat. "I got a call from the People's Video Game Awards committee this morning."

My hand freezes midway through collecting my tablet. The PVGAs are basically our industry's Oscars, and we've won many awards over the years, but we don't have any games that fit within the timeline for this year's awards so I'm a little confused on why they contacted us.. "Don't keep us in suspense, Ash."

"They want you to co-present Game of the Year with Dahlia Nightfall." Her grin spreads wider. "Since she voices the Seidr Witch and The Nightfallen did such an amazing job with Rune Beast's soundtrack, they thought it would be perfect symbolism - gaming and music coming together."

"Holy shit," Manu's surprise is palpable, but I know its not necessarily for me. He has been pining for Dahlia ever since he saw her and her band tour the Eldritch offices for a PR stunt early last year. He starts clapping, followed quickly by Aimi and Tobias.

I can't help but smile. The Nightfallen's haunting melodies and powerful vocals had elevated our game's atmosphere beyond what we'd imagined. Dahlia's voice in particular brought a depth to the Seidr Witch's scenes that still gives me chills.

"So?" Ashlyn prompts, "What do you say?"

"Of course," I nod, feeling a surge of pride for our team and what we've accomplished. "It would be an honor."

"Alright everyone, let's wrap this up. Great work today." I

gather my things as chairs roll against the floor, except for Aimi's yoga ball that nearly flies into my leg as she leaps up. "I thought the yoga ball was going to help with the ADHD Aimi."

She smirks and kicks it at me again for good measure before leaving and pretending to be offended.

I'm halfway to my office when Ashlyn's hand catches my elbow, pulling me aside with that conspiratorial grin she gets when she's sitting on juicy information.

"So," she whispers, glancing around dramatically, "guess who's working in the building today?"

I look at her with sincere confusion. "The bagel guy with the everything bagels I like?"

"Shelly's downstairs moderating on one of our stream channels." Her grin widens. "And before you ask - yes, she specifically asked me for work because she wanted to earn money for a laptop herself. She knew you'd try to buy it outright."

Heat creeps up my neck. "I wouldn't have-"

"Please," she cuts me off with a knowing look. "You absolutely would have. And speaking of tomorrow's shopping date..."

"It's not a shopping date," I protest weakly. "I'm just helping her check out some equipment."

"Uh-huh." Ashlyn's eyebrows climb higher. "That's why you've been checking your watch every five minutes since this morning?"

"Look," I say, probably more defensively than necessary, "what's wrong with wanting to help someone out? I have more money than I know what to do with. If I can make someone's life a little easier-"

"Connor," she interrupts gently, "I didn't say there was anything wrong with it. I think it's sweet."

The sincerity in her voice catches me off guard. I deflate a little, running a hand over my beard. "I just... I want to do this right, you know? I don't want her to feel like a charity case though...but I also want her to understand that it is okay to accept help sometimes."

Ashlyn's expression softens, and she gives me that look - the one that says I'm being dense about something obvious.

"Connor, think about it. From the little bit that Shelly told me at the hospital, she's had to handle everything on her own for most of her life. She probably doesn't know how to react when someone genuinely wants to help. Especially when that person doesn't expect something in return."

The truth of her words hits me harder than I expected. Of course. Growing up in the system, aging out, living on the streets - help always came with strings attached.

We make our way down to the fourth floor, where our streaming setup occupies most of the space. The moderation pods are soundproofed little rooms, each with its own monitoring station. Ashlyn leads me to one of the windows, and we peek inside.

Shelly's completely in the zone, her fingers flying across the keyboard at what looks like light speed. Her brow is furrowed in concentration, and she's leaning forward so close to the monitors that her nose is practically touching them. She looks like she's either having the time of her life or about to burst a blood vessel - maybe both.

I can't help but smile. Despite the intensity of her focus (or maybe because of it), she looks... happy. Really happy. It's a good look on her.

"See?" Ashlyn whispers, nudging my arm. "She's a natural."

I can see the wide smile on Ashlyn's face out of the corner of my eye. She looks like a Cheshire cat as her own eyes go from Shelly and back to me. The urge to go into the booth to say hi is thankfully outvoted by my desire to see her succeed and I don't want to be a distraction.

The elevator ride down to the parking garage feels different today. Usually by this time, my hands are already starting to shake, dreading the quiet drive home. But watching Shelly absolutely excel at moderating has left me with an unexpected lightness.

"I'll make sure she gets back home safe," Ashlyn says in a text message. Another text bubble shows she it typing more and after what feels too long it comes through. "She did amazing today. The lead moderator wants her back tomorrow but I told him that it was a one time thing. He was disappointed.."

"Good. That's really good." I can't help but smile. "Let her know she's welcome to come back as often as she wants." I reply.

The elevator opens and I slide behind the wheel of my Lexus again. I've grown to almost hate this car because I associate it with panic episodes. It should be hitting me right about now - the silence, the emptiness, the crushing weight of going home to nothing but memories. I brace for it, waiting for that familiar vice grip around my chest.

But it doesn't come.

There's still anxiety lurking at the edges, like a shadow in my peripheral vision. But it feels... manageable. Different. Instead of spiraling into thoughts of Liv and Des, my mind keeps drifting back to Shelly's determined expression as she moderated the stream, completely in her element.

I start the car, and for the first time in years, I don't immediately reach for the radio to drown out my thoughts. The quiet feels almost peaceful.

I end up flicking on the radio anyway, but this time it's different. No desperate grab for noise to drown out the demons - just a real desire to hear some music. My classic rock playlist hits with "More Than a Feeling" by Boston, and I find myself actually enjoying it, drumming my fingers on the steering wheel as I navigate through evening traffic.

The drive home passes in a blur of good tunes and surprisingly peaceful thoughts. Before I know it, I'm pulling into my designated spot in the parking garage. As I step off the elevator onto my floor, I nearly collide with Alicia, who's juggling her purse and a bag for dry cleaning.

"Whoa there, Mr. Ebin!" She steadies herself, giving me that motherly look she's perfected over the years. Then her eyes narrow suspiciously. "Hold on a minute... you're smiling. Actually smiling. Are you feeling alright? Should I call a doctor?"

I can't help but laugh. "I'm fine, Ali. Just had a good day at work."

"Uh-huh." She shifts the laundry to her hip, studying me

like I'm one of her grandkids trying to hide a secret. "You sure you're not coming down with something? Because I haven't seen you this chipper in years..." She trails off, probably catching herself before mentioning Liv.

"Really, I'm good. Promise." I reach out and take the dry cleaning bag from her so I can help her back to her car, but she smacks my hand away.

"Well, whatever's got you in such a good mood, keep it up." She pats my cheek like she used to when I first hired her. "It's nice to see some light back in those eyes of yours." And with that she is on the elevator and headed down.

I step into my apartment, and just like in the car, the silence doesn't feel like it's trying to swallow me whole. My footsteps echo slightly as I cross to the master closet, but they don't carry that usual weight of dread. It's... different. Almost peaceful.

I'm putting my clothes and briefcase away when I notice the stack of Liv's tarot cards I dropped and then placed next to my watches a day or two ago, the deck's fur wrapping lying open like a wound. I start gathering them up, and there it is again - The Lovers card that had caught my eye when I picked them up. But then I remember there was another card stuck to its back.

The Ace of Cups.

My hands shake slightly as I separate them. I remember Liv's excitement when Des gave her these cards, how she'd spend hours reading about their meanings. The little guidebook should still be...yes, there it is, nestled at the bottom of the fur wrap.

I flip through the pages until I find the Ace of Cups description. My heart starts pounding as I read:

"The Ace of Cups represents new beginnings of the heart, emotional fulfillment, and a spark of new deep spiritual connections. It heralds the potential birth of new relationships, creative inspiration, and inner peace. When this card appears, it suggests opening yourself to love and letting joy back into your life."

The book trembles in my hands. Both cards - The Lovers and the Ace of Cups - falling out together...

"Liv?" My voice sounds strange in the quiet room. "Are you... reaching out to me? Is this permission?"

The silence that follows feels different somehow. Not empty, but expectant. Like the pause between heartbeats.

Chapter 17: Ramen & Rock Stars

Shelly

I'M STANDING IN HEIDI'S kitchen, flipping through a stack of junk mail when a coffee maker catches my eye. Twenty-five bucks - not bad. It's basic as hell compared to the one that sits unused on Heidi's counter, but it'll do until she can replace the fancy one that she couldn't get to taste right anymore.

A soft knock at the door makes me jump. Connor, being thoughtful as always, clearly remembers that Heidi would most likely be asleep right now. My face flushes when I see him standing there in casual clothes - Levi's jeans, Vans that look well worn, and holy shit, is that a Nightfallen hoodie?

I move in for a hug before I can overthink it, then immediately start second-guessing myself. Are we there yet? Is this weird? But his arms wrap around me tight and sure, and I sudden realize I've been holding my breath. His hoodie is soft against my cheek, and his beard smells like sweet ginger.

"I didn't know you were into The Nightfallen, I love them!"

I say when we pull apart, gesturing at his hoodie. Their logo sprawls across his chest in that signature creepy-elegant font I love so much.

A grin spreads across his face. "Actually, then I've got some news you might be interested in." He holds up his hand when I open my mouth to ask. "But first, I think we both need some coffee in our system before we unpack that."

Connor holds the car door open for me, and I feel my cheeks heat up. I can't remember the last time someone did that - actually, I'm sure no one ever has. The leather seat is butter-soft against my legs as I slide in.

As we pull away from Heidi's, "Take On Me" starts playing and Connor immediately launches into the chorus. His voice isn't half bad, and there's something adorably dorky about watching this successful CEO belt out A-ha like he's alone in the shower. He seems different today. Which is probably weird of me to think since I barely know him, but still. He seems more…open. When the next verse hits, I surprise my-self by joining in. Connor shoots me a delighted grin that makes my stomach do weird things.

"You know this one?" he asks during the instrumental break.

"Who doesn't?" I laugh, then immediately catch myself. Right, people my age probably don't.

We pull into the Books and Beans drive-thru, and Connor turns down the music. "So what's your actual favorite? I know you like the White Chocolate Mocha, but is that going to be your go-to now?"

"Caramel Macchiato, extra shot," I admit. "The White

Chocolate is good too though."

He orders for both of us, and when we reach the window, Jenny's familiar face appears. Her eyes go wide when she spots me in the passenger seat, and she breaks into this huge knowing smile that makes me want to sink through the floor.

As we pull away with our drinks, Connor asks, "Alright, where to for food? Sky's the limit."

I take a sip of my perfectly made macchiato and consider. "Um...you really don't have to-"

He interrupts me with a wage of his finger. "Shelly, let me take you to dinner. Please."

It is easy to see that he got to have some experience as a father since I feel a little scolded. "I've always wanted to try ramen."

Connor's whole face lights up at my ramen confession. "Oh, you're in for a treat. I know exactly where to take you."

The music keeps playing as we drive - some 80s mix that has him humming along and occasionally singing bits of chorus. It strikes me that he's not playing it to cover awkward silence like most people would. He's just... comfortable. The thought makes me smile into my coffee.

I watch the city slide by, familiar streets looking different somehow from inside his fancy car. The leather seat cradles me like it costs more than everything I own (which, let's be real, it probably does). When we pull up to a spot between two cars, Connor executes this perfect parallel parking job that makes me feel like I'm watching some kind of automotive ballet.

I reach for the door handle, but he holds up a finger. "Ah ah

- don't touch that." Before I can protest, he's out and around to my side, pulling the door open with a flourish.

"You really don't have to do that," I mumble, feeling my cheeks heat up.

He raises an eyebrow at me, his expression deadly serious. "Are you telling me my father raised me to be the wrong kind of gentleman?"

I start to stammer an apology until I catch the way his lips are twitching, fighting back a smirk. The tension breaks and I find myself snickering, shaking my head as I step out onto the sidewalk.

The storefront is tiny, wedged between a Korean BBQ place and what looks like an antique shop. The only English I can make out is "RAMEN" in block letters - everything else is in Japanese characters that might as well be abstract art to me.

Connor holds the door (again) and warm, savory smells hit me like a wall. My mouth starts watering instantly. A woman in a traditional-looking dress greets us with a bow, and to my complete surprise, Connor starts speaking to her in fluid Japanese. His accent sounds perfect to my untrained ear, and they share a brief laugh about something I don't under-stand.

"You speak Japanese?" I whisper as we follow her through the narrow restaurant.

He grins. "Video game industry. Plus, I spent some time there developing our Asian market presence." He says it ca-sually, like knowing multiple languages is no big deal.

The hostess leads us to what looks like a private booth sectioned off by delicate paper walls. Connor smoothly slips off his shoes before stepping up onto the raised platform, and I quickly follow suit, grateful I remembered to wear matching socks today.

Inside, there's a low wooden table surrounded by plush cushions on the floor. I watch Connor fold himself down onto one before attempting it myself, trying not to look completely graceless in comparison. The cushion is surprisingly comfortable once I get settled.

"I feel like I should be wearing a kimono or something," I admit, looking around at the traditional décor.

"That is an option." He says with a straight face.

My eyes go wide and he breaks a smile. He's teasing me…I surprised to find that I kind of like it. For some reason it feels…nice.

"You're doing fine," Connor assures me. "Though I should warn you - the chopsticks here are the really smooth kind that like to slip out of your fingers at the worst possible moment. No judgment if you need a fork. Okay, maybe a little judgement."

I stare at the menu, my eyes darting between unfamiliar Japanese terms. Each description sounds amazing, but also intimidating. I've never had proper ramen before - what if I pick wrong?

Connor must sense my hesitation because he offers, "I could order for you if you'd like?"

"No," I say, maybe a bit too quickly. Years of other people making choices for me have left their mark. "I want to try ordering myself."

When the waitress returns, Connor orders spicy chicken ramen in Japanese. I point to the tonkotsu bowl on the menu, careful to pronounce it exactly like I heard the couple at the next table say it.

"Excellent choice," Connor says after she leaves. "The pork here is incredible."

The waitress brings us a pot of green tea almost immediately, and I can't contain myself anymore. "So what's this news about The Nightfallen?"

Connor's eyes light up with amusement at my barely-contained excitement. "Well, I've been asked to present the Game of the Year award at the People's Video Game Awards next month." He pauses, clearly enjoying the build-up. "Alongside Dahlia Nightfall."

"Holy shit!" I blurt out, then clap my hand over my mouth. "Sorry, holy shit!" I say in a lower voice. "You're going to be on stage with Dahlia?"

He chuckles. "Actually, I already know her fairly well. She does the voice work for the Seidr Witch in Rune Beast."

My jaw drops. "The witch is Dahlia?"

Connor nods and then continues, "The Nightfallen also provide about half of the soundtrack. Plus some original pieces specifically for certain scenes."

I'm practically vibrating in my seat. The Nightfallen got me through some of my darkest nights in foster care, and now I'm sitting across from someone who actually knows them. Who works with them. It feels surreal.

"What's she like?" I ask, still trying to process that Connor actually knows Dahlia Nightfall. The woman whose voice helped me survive countless nights in foster homes, whose lyrics felt like they were written just for me.

Connor smiles, taking a sip of his tea. "Why don't you find out for yourself? Be my plus one to the PVGAs?"

I freeze, my teacup halfway to my lips. "What?"

"Come with me to the People's Video Game Awards. You can meet Dahlia in person."

"I..." My mind starts racing, anxiety flooding in. "That's ... I mean... there'll be so many people there, and I won't know anyone, and what would I even wear? Surely there is someone else you should take. I don't own any clothes, especially something nice enough for that, and everyone will be looking at-"

The gentle pressure of Connor's hand on mine stops my spiral cold. His palm is warm against my skin, and I feel heat rush to my cheeks as I look down at where we're connected.

"Hey," he says softly, "you'll know me. That's all that matters. And I'm either going with you or by myself." He squeezes my hand lightly. "As for clothes? It's the People's Video Game Awards, not the Oscars. Half the people there show up in jeans and t-shirts."

I stare at our hands, his larger one still covering mine. The contact feels... grounding. Safe. Like when he held me after the attack, but different somehow.

"You really want me to go with you?" I ask quietly, hardly daring to believe it.

"I really do."

I turn my hand over, letting my fingers slide between his. My heart's fucking fluttering like a damn butterfly again as I peek up at his face through my lashes. He's watching me with those gentle eyes, and for a moment I let myself believe this is real - that someone like him could actually want someone like me around.

But the doubt of reality crashes back in. He's probably just being nice, taking pity on the homeless girl who reminds him of his dead wife. The thought stings, but I force myself to remember where I came from. People like me don't just get invited to things like fancy award shows without ulterior motives.

Still... his hand feels so warm against mine. Safe. Like maybe I could trust this, trust him.

"Okay," I whisper, surprising myself. "I'll go with you."

The smile that breaks across his face is like a sunrise on my skin, and for a second I forget to breathe again. Before either of us can say anything else, the paper door slides open with a soft whoosh. We jerk our hands apart like guilty kids as the waitress appears with two steaming bowls of ramen.

The rich, savory smell hits me immediately, making my mouth water. The broth is cloudy and perfect-looking, with thin slices of pork arranged artfully on top alongside a soft-boiled egg that looks like it belongs in a food magazine.

I catch Connor watching my reaction out of the corner of my eye, but I'm too mesmerized by the food to feel self-conscious about it. This is about as far from cup noodles as you can get.

I take my first bite of ramen and can't help the moan that escapes my lips. The broth is rich and complex, the noodles perfectly chewy, and the pork melts in my mouth. It's only after the sound leaves my throat that I realize how... suggestive it might have sounded.

Before I can die of embarrassment, Connor makes an almost identical noise of appreciation as he tastes his spicy chicken ramen. The deep, satisfied sound sends an unexpected shiver down my spine, and I immediately choke on my next sip of broth.

"You okay?" Connor asks, concern crossing his features.

I clear my throat, trying to will away the blush I can feel creeping up my neck. "Yeah, just... went down the wrong way."

We eat in comfortable silence for a few minutes before Connor asks, "So how was the moderator job yesterday?"

"It was actually really fun," I say, carefully maneuvering another bite with my chopsticks. "Ashlyn showed me how to filter comments and keep the chat civil. The streamer was super nice too."

When we finish, Connor insists on paying despite my protests. I don't have much but I could have at least paid for my own after yesterday's work. Back at his car, he opens my door again (I'm starting to think this is just who he is), and as soon as we're settled, the opening riffs of The Nightfallen's "Midnight's Pitch Embrace" fill the car.

"I thought you might appreciate this playlist on our way to find you a laptop," he says with a smile, pulling into traffic as Dahlia's haunting vocals begin.

I sink into the leather seat, letting the familiar music wash over me. Between the amazing food in my belly and one of my favorite bands playing, I almost forget we're headed to a potentially sketchy computer sale. Almost.

I hop out of Connor's car before he can rush around to get my door, feeling a little surge of victory. His mock-offended expression makes me grin.

"Brat," he says, but his eyes are twinkling with amusement. Something about the way he teases me makes me feel warm inside, like I'm in on some private joke rather than being the butt of one.

The computer store looks like a tornado hit it. Parts and cables are strewn everywhere, with desperate-looking people pawing through boxes. My heart sinks as I spot the nearly empty laptop section.

We check out the few remaining options, but Connor keeps shaking his head. "This one's processor is from 2010 - it would struggle to load YouTube." He points to another. "And that one's running Windows Vista. I didn't even know that still existed."

My hopes are fading fast when Connor suddenly grabs my arm. "Shelly, come here - quick!"

He's crouched by a laptop that's plugged into a power strip, his fingers flying over the keyboard as he checks something. It looks old but well-maintained, with a $175 price tag stuck to the lid.

"This is incredible," he whispers, eyes scanning the screen. "Someone's upgraded the CPU and GPU. This model... it's just like the one I learned to code games on years ago." He looks up at me, excitement written all over his face. "Shelly, this machine is worth at least three times this price with the upgrades that are in it. They must not have been paying attention when they priced it."

"Should I get it?" I ask, practically bouncing on my toes.

"Absolutely. This is exactly what you need." Connor's enthusiasm matches mine as I count out the money from yesterday's moderating work.

While I'm paying, Connor wanders off to browse. He returns with an old game case, his eyes lit up like he's found buried treasure. After buying it, he hands it to me - Critical Chaos in Chains.

"Your first ever pride and joy?" I remember him mentioning games he'd made before.

"Yep. First award winner too." He grins. "Want to try it?"

"I've never really played many video games. I didn't get many opportunities," I admit, turning the case over in my hands. "But I'll give it a go."

"Wait - you said you learned coding on a laptop like this?" I ask as we head to his car. "You really didn't go to school for any of this?"

Connor shakes his head. "Nope. Self-taught. Sometimes the best way to learn is by doing or something. I don't know, insert your own inspiring quote here." He chuckles

The drive back is comfortable, filled with more of The Nightfallen's music. When we reach Heidi's apartment, Connor walks me to the door. This time when we hug goodbye, there's none of the awkwardness from before. His arms feel warm and safe around me.

"Thank you," I say softly as we pull apart.

"One more thing," he says. "Would you let me take you shopping for some new clothes for the PVGAs? Nothing fancy, just... new?"

The old me would have hesitated, would have worried about owing him. But something's shifted between us, and I find myself nodding without a second thought. "Yes, I'd like that."

Chapter 18: Voidmancer's Secret

Connor

T HE OFFICE CHAIR CREAKS as I lean back, watching the last light of day paint shadows across my desk. For once, the usual weight of grief isn't crushing my chest as my workday winds to a close. Even Ashlyn's relentless interrogation about yesterday's shopping trip with Shelly couldn't dampen my mood.

"So you helped her pick out a laptop?" Ashlyn had practically bounced in place. "And?"

"And nothing. We talked tech, grabbed coffee and ramen. She loves The Nightfallen. Normal friend stuff." I'd tried to focus on my monitor, but Ashlyn wasn't having it.

"Friend stuff. Right." Her knowing smile had been insufferable.

I mumble the next part knowing the over the top reaction I am going to get but figure it is only a matter of time before she finds out anyway. Afterall she will be the one to contact the People's Video Game Award Committee with my plus one. "She's going to the PVGAs with me."

"She's what?" Ashlyn's shriek could probably shatter glass. Before I can brace myself, she launches across my desk like an overexcited labrador, nearly knocking over my coffee in her rush to hug me.

"Shit, Ash—" I grunt as she squeezes the air from my lungs. For someone so professionally composed most of the time, she has these moments of pure chaos that remind me why Liv loved her so much.

"Connor, this is huge!" She pulls back, hands on my shoulders, eyes bright with unshed tears. "Do you know how long I've waited to see you actually trying to live again instead of just... existing?"

I flick at my wrist. "It's not—we're just friends. She likes The Nightfallen, and I get a plus one. That's all."

"Oh, shut up," Ashlyn says, but her smile is gentle. "I don't care if you're 'just friends' or something more or whatever. You're engaging with life again. You're letting someone new matter to you. That's what Liv would have wanted."

The mention of Olivia doesn't hurt as much as it usually does. Maybe because for once, I'm not drowning in guilt about feeling something other than grief.

"She would have liked Shelly I think," She says quietly. "They both have that same way of seeing right through bullshit. Ashlyn wipes at her eyes, trying not to smear her mascara. " And that quiet strength thing? Total Liv energy." She squeezes my shoulder one more time. "I'm just... I'm really happy for you, Connor. Whatever this turns out to be."

Now, sliding into my car, I notice something different -

the silence doesn't feel like it's trying to strangle me. Just yesterday it had subsided, hiding under the surface, but right now it is gone. I'm out of the garage and at a stop light when I pull out my phone, thumb hovering over Shelly's number. The guilt that usually accompanies pursuing happiness is there, but muted. Images of Liv and Des float through my mind as I dial, more like cherished photographs than the usual gut-punching memories.

The phone rings twice before Shelly's voice comes through, slightly breathless. "Connor?"

In the background, I hear the unmistakable music from Critical Chaos in Chains. A smile tugs at my lips as the light turns green. "Playing CCC, huh?"

"Oh my god, yes! I can't believe you did this to me! The fighting is insane!" Her enthusiasm radiates through the phone, making me chuckle. "I just beat the Crimson Archon, but these void puzzles are killing me."

The fact that she's playing one of my games - and actually enjoying it - creates a warm feeling in my chest that I'm not quite ready to examine too closely.

"Need any hints?" I ask, turning onto the street that leads to the academy.

"Absolutely not. I'm doing this myself, even if it takes all night."

"When did you start playing?" I ask, pulling into the Knuckledraggers parking lot. The familiar sight of people filing in for evening classes brings a sense of routine normalcy that grounds me.

"Pretty much the second I got the laptop set up last night,"

Shelly admits. There's a pause and the distinct sound of her character dying. "Dammit! These void things are evil."

I bite back a laugh. "You've been playing since last night?"

"Well..." She draws out the word like a guilty confession. "I made myself take breaks to watch some Excel tutorials. You know, responsible adult stuff for the new job? Then I'd take a power nap and jump right back in."

"Excel tutorials and CCC? Living the dream there." I can't help but grin, remembering my own marathon gaming sessions when I was younger. Before I became the guy who makes them instead of just playing them.

"This is entirely your fault," she declares. Another death sound effect comes through the phone. "You just had to mention it was one of your first games, didn't you? Now I'm completely addicted. I need to know how it ends!"

"My fault? I didn't force you to download it."

"You practically dared me with all that 'best new developer award' humble bragging yesterday." Her mock accusation carries a heat that makes me smile wider. "Besides, the story is actually really good. I need to know if the Voidmancer actually betrayed the Council or if he was framed."

"No spoilers from me," I say, killing the engine. "You'll have to figure that out yourself."

"Evil. You're evil, Connor Ebin."

"I'll see you tomorrow, Shelly. Happy gaming." I end the call, still grinning at her enthusiasm for CCC. It's been years since I've thought about that game without the weight of memories crushing me. Olivia had helped me a lot with the story development on that one.

Inside Knuckledraggers, the familiar scent of sweat and determination fills my lungs. Professor Armando spots me from across the mat, his weathered face breaking into a warm smile.

"Connor! Ready to work today?" He claps me on the shoulder as I bow onto the mat.

"Always, Professor."

The class flows like water, techniques melding into drills until we hit the sparring rounds. Marcus, one of our resident black belts, catches my eye with a questioning look. We've had some epic battles lately, and I can tell he's itching for another go.

"Best three out of five?" he asks, adjusting his belt.

I nod, dropping my center of gravity low as we begin. The first round goes to him - a slick arm bar that I should have seen coming. I take the second with a darce choke that would have made Des proud. She always loved watching that technique. I admittedly probably only secured that one because I am stronger than Marcus.

Back and forth we go, neither giving quarter. Third round, I catch him in a twister. Fourth round, he returns the favor with a sweep to mount that I can't recover from and sinks a collar choke that I am not aware he's working until it's too late. He takes the final and fifth round with a heel lock that I had no hope of escaping.

"Solid rolling," Marcus pants, helping me up. "That twister was brutal."

"I still have no idea how you make yourself so damn heavy from the mount." I reply, both of us grinning like idiots despite the exhaustion.

Professor Armando calls us all to line up, but motions for me to stay forward. He holds up a fresh brown belt stripe, and my eyes go wide.

"Connor," he says, his Portuguese accent thick with pride, "this is your fourth stripe. Next promotion will be your black belt test and that is all you." The other students applaud.

As he ties the stripe onto my belt, I feel Des's presence so strongly it almost knocks me over. She would have been bouncing off the walls at this moment. The thought brings a smile instead of tears for once.

Professor Armando wraps up the remaining promotions - two white belts getting their first stripe, a blue belt moving up to purple. The usual mix of pride and nostalgia washes over me as I watch these milestones that Des would have hit by now.

After class, Marcus and a few others crowd around, offering congratulations with that particular BJJ blend of respect and casual brotherhood. I'm stuffing my gi into my gym bag when a familiar voice cuts through the post-class chatter.

"Mr. Ebin! Mr. Ebin!"

Before I can fully turn, Krista crashes into me with the kind of full-force hug that only pre-teens can deliver. Her dark curls bounce as she pulls back, beaming up at me with that same infectious energy Des always had.

"Congratulations on your stripe! Are you gonna test for black belt soon? Des always said you'd get there!"

The mention of Des doesn't hurt like it used to. "Thanks, kiddo. Still got some work to do before that test, but I'll get there."

Krista's eyes suddenly light up with mischief. "Hey, I saw you and your new girlfriend going into the ramen shop yesterday! She's really pretty!"

My breath catches for a moment. There's no judgment in Krista's voice, just genuine matter of fact happiness. One of Des's best friends, practically accepting… what? The thought of me moving on?

"Oh, uh, Shelly's just a friend," I manage to stammer out.

Krista gives me that patented pre-teen 'adults are so clueless' look. "Are you sure? Because you guys looked pretty close when-"

"Krista! Time to go, honey!" Her mom calls from the door, giving me a friendly wave.

Krista bounces away before I can respond, leaving me standing there with her words echoing in my head. Even Des's closest friend think it's okay for me to…

I shake my head, trying to focus on packing up my gear. But Krista's innocent observation has stirred something I'm still unsure if I'm fully ready to examine.

The drive home from Knuckledraggers feels different tonight. Maybe it's the new stripe on my belt, or maybe it's just everything else shifting in my life lately. I pull into my parking spot and grab my phone, knowing Ashlyn's probably still up with a glass of wine in hand and watching some romcom. "Please tell me you're not calling about work. I'm relaxing."

"Actually…" I lean back in my seat, not quite ready to face my empty apartment. "I need to change plans for tomorrow.

Taking the full day instead of just the afternoon."

"Connor?" Her voice shifts from playful to concerned. "Everything okay?"

"Yeah, I just..." I flick at my wrist. "I need to visit the girls in the morning. Before taking Shelly shopping."

There's a pause, and I can practically see Ashlyn's expression softening through the phone. "Of course. Do you want company? I can move some meetings around-"

"No, I think I need to this conversation alone." I close my eyes, seeing Des's bright smile, Liv's knowing gaze. "It's been a few months since I've been there, and with everything changing..."

"They'd be happy for you, Connor." Ashlyn's voice is gentle. "Both of them."

"Well." My throat tightens. "That's what I'm unsure of."

"Connor…" I can tell she wants to argue with me but she holds it back. "Take all the time you need tomorrow. I'll handle anything that comes up."

"Thanks, Ash."

After hanging up, I sit in my car for a few more minutes, letting the quiet wrap around me.

Chapter 19: Cherry Blossoms & Cat Ears

Connor

THE MORNING AIR BITES at my face as I juggle the drinks from Books and Beans. Jenny gave me that look again when I ordered Liv's ridiculous caramel macchiato with extra whip and Des's hot chocolate with rainbow marshmallows. She knows where I'm headed.

The Pioneer Cemetery gates creak open, and I follow the familiar path past aging headstones and fresh flowers. My feet know the way by heart and I could get there blindfolded. They lead me to the black granite markers under the old oak tree. The bench I had installed faces them perfectly - close enough to feel present, far enough that the weight of their names doesn't crush me.

I set Liv's coffee on my left, Des's cocoa on my right, just like when they used to sit with me on movie nights. The drinks steam in the cool morning air, sending ghostly wisps skyward.

"Hey, girls." My voice cracks. "I miss you. Dammit...so

much."

The wind rustles through the oak leaves, and I can almost hear Des's giggle, feel Liv's hand on my shoulder.

"Rune Beast is coming along well. I'll be finishing the mo-cap scenes this Friday. I hate that damn suit but I really enjoy the work and I'm glad I insisted on being the one to do it. Ashlyn says hi."

I pause for a minute and gather some courage. "Things are... changing. I met someone. Well, not met like that, but..." I run my hands over my face. "She reminds me of both of you. Sometimes when she smiles, it's like seeing echoes of you both."

Tears start falling, and I don't bother wiping them away. "Liv, baby... those tarot cards you loved so much. The ones Des got you for your birthday. They fell the other day, but only two cards came out. The Lovers and the Ace of Cups."

My voice drops to a whisper. "Was that you? Are you trying to tell me something? Because I don't know if I can... if I should..."

The tears come harder now, and I grip the edge of the bench until my knuckles turn white. "I don't want to forget you. I don't want to feel like I'm trying to fill the hole left in me. I just... I don't want to hurt anymore."

I let out a heavy sigh, feeling like each word I've spoken is a betrayal of what we had. What we still have, even if they're gone. The thought makes my chest tighten.

I let out a bitter chuckle. "This is the most cliche thing I've ever done. Sitting here, asking for a sign like I'm in some cheesy cable Christmas movie."

I start to flick my wrist and stop. I don't need to do that anymore. "But here I am anyway. If you're listening... if you can... just let me know what to do. Because I'm lost here. Completely fucking lost." I wince at those last words. "Sorry Des."

She hated when I said fuck.

The deep bellow of a ship's horn cuts through my melancholy. I turn toward the sound, and for a moment, I'm transported back in time.

"Daddy, daddy! Look at the big boat!" Des would bounce on her toes, pointing at every vessel that passed through the waters around Seattle. She knew the difference between container ships and cruise liners by the time she was six, proudly explaining it to anyone who'd listen.

I rise from the bench and walk to the fence overlooking Possession Sound. The massive container ship cuts through the water with surprising grace for something so enormous. Des used to make up stories about where each ship was going, what treasures they might be carrying.

"That one's full of unicorn food," I whisper, mimicking her excited voice. "No, daddy, it's carrying dragon eggs! They have to keep them cold or they'll all hatch!"

The morning sun catches on the water, creating that sparkle effect she loved so much. "Look, daddy! The mermaids are saying hello!"

I grip the fence, letting the cool metal ground me as I watch the ship's steady progress. Just a few weeks ago memories like this one would have broken me. Now I feel like I'm able to enjoy the pleasant parts of them without the overwhelming weight of grief. They still ache, but they're starting to feel more like a warm embrace than a stranglehold.

The ship sounds its horn again as it passes beneath the bridge, and I can almost hear Des's delighted squeal echoing across the water.

I turn back toward their graves, ready to collect the untouched drinks, when something catches my eye. Behind Liv's headstone, barely visible, is a splash of green I've never noticed before. My heart skips as I move closer.

There it is. The cherry blossom sapling I planted three years ago has finally taken root. It's tiny, hardly tall enough to peek over the black granite, but it's alive. Really alive and I cannot fathom how after all this time.

I drop to my knees, careful not to disturb the tender shoots. "You stubborn little thing," I whisper, gently touching one of its delicate leaves. "Three years. How?"

Liv and I fell in love with cherry blossoms on our honeymoon in Japan. When we got back she'd drag me to the University of Washington campus every spring to see them in bloom. After Des was born we'd always take her with. When she was old enough she'd go off skipping ahead of us throwing handfuls of fallen petals in the air. The day I buried them, I promised I'd bring their favorite flowers here somehow.

A warm breeze rustles through the little sapling's leaves, and suddenly I'm crying again – but these tears feel different. Like release rather than grief.

"Okay," I say softly, looking between their headstones and the determined little tree. "Okay, okay. I'll try." I take a deep breath, "I'm scared, but I'll see where this thread leads."

Shelly

I blink awake, fragments of my dream about CCC still dancing behind my eyelids. The last thing I remember is trying to figure out how to beat that damn frost giant without losing any of my companions. Even in my dreams, I can't stop playing Connor's game.

Something feels odd this morning. I actually slept through the night without jerking awake at every little noise. Living on the streets teaches you to sleep with one eye open, but here in Heidi's apartment, I'm starting to let my guard down.

Speaking of Heidi, as I swing my legs off the couch and rub my eyes I notice a note on the coffee table in front of me:

"Had another rough night at work. Need some good sleep. I'm off tonight though, so we'll catch up later! - H"

I can't believe I didn't hear her come in. A month ago, a mouse farting three blocks away would have had me bolt upright, ready to run. Now I'm sleeping through Heidi coming home from work? It's... nice. Scary nice.

My hand traces the soft blanket I'm wrapped in - another luxury I'm still getting used to. The morning sun filters through the half-drawn blinds, casting warm stripes across the living room. Everything feels safe, solid. Real.

I stretch and yawn, feeling more rested than I have in... well, longer than I can remember. No more concrete pillows or cardboard mattresses. No more watching over my shoulder every second. Just actual, honest-to-goodness sleep.

It's kind of terrifying how quickly I'm adapting to this. How easy it is to let myself feel comfortable after all this time. Part of me wants to fight it, to stay sharp and ready for when it all falls apart. But maybe... maybe this time things will be different or maybe I'm just tired of worrying about it all.

I tiptoe past Heidi's room, though I know she sleeps like the dead after work. The bathroom feels like a sanctuary as I slip inside and turn on the shower, waiting for the water to warm up. Steam begins to fill the small space, and I catch my reflection in the mirror – cheeks flushed with anticipation.

God, I'm being ridiculous. Connor's just being nice. He's successful, mature, established... everything I'm not. What would he need me in his life for? I spend a moment worrying that I am a replacement for what he lost, but my heart reminds me that Connor doesn't feel like that kind of person to me. My stomach does this weird flip-flop thing whenever I think about him picking me up soon.

The water hits my skin and I close my eyes, letting myself enjoy this simple luxury that still feels so alien. Sometimes I still can't believe this is my life now.

After probably staying under the spray too long (sorry, Heidi's water bill), I wrap myself in a towel and face my limited wardrobe options. The same jeans and shirt from two days ago mock me from their folded place on the counter. They're clean enough, I guess – I threw them and the other two items I've borrowed from Heidi in the wash yesterday – but wearing the same outfit again makes me feel weak with embarrassment.

Back in the bathroom, I run Heidi's brush through my auburn waves, trying to tame them into something presentable. My reflection stares back at me, and I catch myself actually smiling. When was the last time I did that while looking in a mirror?

The age gap between Connor and me keeps nagging at my thoughts. He's got to be in his early forties, and here I am, barely out of my teens. But it's not like that, right? He's just being kind. Helping out some homeless girl who reminds him...I stop myself from finishing that thought.

Still... the way he looks at me sometimes...

I shake my head at my reflection. No, Shelly. You owe it to yourself to see where this goes. I tell myself those words over and over again like they're a mantra.

My leg bounces up and down as I watch the clock tick by with agonizing slowness. CCC is right there on my laptop, tempting me with its endless possibilities and that damn frost giant I still need to figure out. But I know better - one more quest and I'll be so deep in the game Connor will have to drag me out kicking and screaming.

Twenty-eight minutes. Twenty-seven. I swear time is moving backwards.

My laptop dings and I nearly jump out of my skin, but it's just an e-mail notification from one of those job searches I did. I'm already employed now - sort of - but I can't bring myself to delete the few responses I've gotten. Not yet.

The soft knock at the door makes my heart skip, and I'm on my feet before I realize I'm moving. Connor's standing there with that gentle smile of his, and before I can overthink it, I step into his offered hug. He smells so damn good - it has to be that beard oil I noticed before.

As we get off the elevator to the parking garage I break away first, practically skipping to his car. The handle doesn't budge when I try it, and I throw an exaggerated glare over my shoulder. He's standing there with that infuriating grin, key fob in hand, clearly enjoying this little game.

The lock clicks and he reaches past me to open the door. I can't help but smirk as I say, "Thank you," with just a hint of playful sass in my voice.

"Please," he says, his tone warm but serious, "let me do this for you from now on. It's not taking anything away from you - it's just me being a gentleman and trying to do some-thing for you. Let me be old fashioned while the rest of the world screams at these little kindnesses to stop."

Something in his voice makes my sass evaporate but I take it for what it is, sweetness and not the rebuke a lot of woman would feel it was. I nod, suddenly shy and red cheeked. "Okay."

The car's interior wraps around me like a cocoon, the leather seats still carrying a hint of Connor's scent. The heater immediately warms me and I think about how won-derful this would have been at night before Heidi took me in.

Some 80's song I don't recognize plays softly through the speakers - something about dancing in the dark. Connor's fingers tap along with the beat on the steering wheel as we cruise toward the mall.

"So," he says, glancing over at me with that playful glint in his eye that makes my stomach do somersaults. "Want to make a bet?"

I turn in my seat slightly, intrigued. "What kind of bet?"

"A riddle," he says. "If you can't solve it, you have to let me take care of you today at the mall. No arguments about prices, no trying to talk me down to cheaper options. Just let me be me."

My core constricts at the thought of him spending money on me, but I'm also curious. "And if I get it right?"

"What do you want?"

What I want is for him to tell me if this thing between us is real or if I'm just seeing what I hope to see. If these moments mean as much to him as they do to me, or if I'm just someone filling a hole from his past.

But I can't say that. Instead, I blurt out, "If I win, we both have to get piercings at the mall."

His laugh fills the car, deep and genuine. "You're on, Little Lysa."

He just called me by one of the love interests in CCC. Little Lysa is a short, small and gothic looking pixie with a spunky attitude. I wouldn't say I was goth but the rest of it… my heart quivers at the nickname. I'm almost more caught off guard that I don't feel a hint of embarrassment at the comparison.

"So, what's the riddle, Quinn?" I return the nickname exchange with one of the other romance options from CCC.

Quinn was a disgraced knight that fell from the grace of his king for refusing to follow an order that would have killed many innocent people. He turned to magic instead of hand to hand combat after that and became a very shadowy and mysterious figure.

He grins wide at me and I think he even shows a hint of a blush himself.

"Alright," Connor says, drumming his fingers on the steering wheel. "Here's your riddle: I have cities, but no houses. I have mountains, but no trees. I have water, but no fish. I have roads, but no cars. What am I?"

I bite my lower lip, considering. The heat from the car's vents warms my face as I think, watching the city scroll past the window. Cities without houses... mountains without trees... I'm about to give up and my mind drifts to CCC for a moment, thinking about the various maps I've been studying to find all the hidden locations.

Wait. Maps.

"A map!" I exclaim, turning to face him with a triumphant grin. "The answer is a map!"

Connor's playful glare makes me giggle. He dramatically covers his chest with one hand while keeping the other on the wheel. "Oh god, please tell me we're not getting nipple piercings. I've seen how those heal and I am not ready for that kind of commitment."

I roll my eyes, still giddy from solving the riddle. "Relax, you big baby. I'm getting my nostril done, and I'll be nice and let you just get your ear done."

"Just the ear?" He sounds almost relieved as he drops his

hand from his chest. "I can handle that. Though I have to say, I'm a little disappointed you solved it. I had plans for spoiling you today."

"Too bad," I sing-song, feeling bold. "A bet's a bet, Quinn."

He chuckles and shakes his head. "That it is, Little Lysa. That it is."

The automatic doors of the mall whoosh open, and I let Connor guide me through with a gentle hand at the small of my back. His chivalry should annoy me - I've taken care of myself for so long - but there's something disarmingly genuine about it.

"Piercing time!" I practically skip toward the jewelry shop, partly to hide how his touch affects me. "And you're going first."

Connor trails behind me, eyeing the shop's display window with mock trepidation. "You're enjoying this way too much."

Inside, I watch as he browses the selection of earrings, finally settling on a black titanium hoop with a matching ball. "Very edgy," I tease. "Sure you don't need me to hold your hand?"

He chuckles, settling into the piercer's chair. "I think I can manage. I've had worse."

The piercer works quickly and efficiently, and Connor doesn't even flinch. Show-off.

My turn comes, and I pick out a small stud with what looks like an emerald. It reminds me of Connor's eyes when he laughs, though I'd never admit that out loud.

The needle going through my nostril makes my eyes water

instantly. Connor's there with a tissue before I can even reach up, gently dabbing at the tears.

"Such a gentleman," I manage through a giggle, trying to ignore how close his face is to mine as he checks the piercing.

At the counter, I pull out my wallet before Connor can reach for his. Nearly the last of my cash goes to cover both piercings - it feels right somehow, since this was my idea. Besides, I won the bet fair and square.

"There," I say, touching my nose gently. "Now we're both properly decorated."

I catch Connor's reflection in the jewelry store window as I check my nose one last time for any signs of bleeding. The way he's looking at me... it's not the careful but warm gaze I'm used to from him. There's something softer and more open there, something that makes me feel light and warm, like I'm on a roller coaster that just dropped.

He doesn't realize I can see him, which makes it even more genuine. His eyes are praising, almost reverent, and there's the ghost of a smile playing at the corners of his mouth. It's the kind of look that makes me feel seen - really seen - for the first time in forever.

The piercing throbs slightly as I lower my hand, but I barely notice it. That look... it gives me the courage to turn around and face him.

"Hey," I say, fidgeting with the hem of my shirt. "Since you were such a good sport about the piercing, maybe... maybe we could do your end of the bet too? If you still want to, I mean."

The words tumble out before I can overthink them, and I

watch his expression shift from surprise to that warm smile and my stomach starts performing backflips again.

My heart hammers against my ribs as Connor reaches for my hand. His fingers intertwine with mine. His hand is warm, strong, and I can feel the slight roughness from his jiu jitsu training against my palm. I keep waiting for him to let go, for this moment to shatter like every other good thing in my life, but his grip stays steady.

Play it cool, Shelly. Don't make this weird.

But my body has other ideas. Before I can stop myself, I'm pressing closer, wrapping my other hand around his arm like I've seen couples do in those rom-coms I used to watch late at night when I couldn't sleep at some of my foster homes. His bicep is firm under my touch, and I catch a stronger whiff of that intoxicating beard oil.

Connor squeezes my hand tighter in response, and oh god, I'm actually melting. My knees feel wobbly, and my chest is so light I might float away if he wasn't anchoring me here. This can't be real. But it is - his warmth, his scent, the way he's looking down at me with those soulful eyes that crinkle at the corners when he smiles.

"Get ready to be pampered," he says, his voice soft but playful. "No arguments."

I want to make a playfully sarcastic remark but I'm too busy trying to remember how to breathe. This isn't pity or obligation - the way he's holding my hand, guiding me through the mall like I'm something precious... he actually likes me. Really likes me.

Be cool, I tell myself again. My heart might as well be in

gymnastics training with the number of somersaults he is making it perform. But who am I kidding? Cool flew out the window the moment he took my hand.

I can't help grinning as we approach Hot Topic's storefront, the familiar mix of anime, band merch, and pop culture memorabilia visible through the entrance. Connor catches my expression and smirks.

"Let me guess - because I'm nineteen, you assumed this would be my first pick?" I tease, nudging him with my elbow.

"Maybe, I mean I still get things from here some times too. So…" he admits, rubbing the back of his neck.

"Well…" I draw out the word, watching his face. "You're absolutely right. I love this place."

His laugh echoes through the mall corridor as I pull him inside. The familiar scent of plastic and new t-shirts hits me, along with the heavy bass line of some metal song playing overhead. It feels like coming home, in a weird way.

My eyes catch on a Gojira shirt similar to my worn-out one, but the price tag makes me wince. I start to move away, but Connor's hand on my shoulder stops me.

"Ah-ah," he says, reaching for the hanger. "We had a deal."

"But-"

"No buts. What size?"

I bite my lip. "Small."

He places it over his arm and before I know it I've added a few band shirts, some cute knee-high socks with lightning bolts, leggings with little skulls, and a hoodie with cat ears that I couldn't resist touching. Every time I try to check a price tag or put something back, he gives me this look that's both stern and playful.

"You're impossible," I mutter, but can't keep the smile off my face.

"Part of my charm," he replies, steering me toward the fitting rooms. "Now go try these on before I find more things you're pretending not to want."

I stick my tongue out at him but take the pile of clothes. My heart feels like it might burst - not just from the gifts, but from how natural this feels. Like we've been doing this forever. I feel like I underwent some strange transformation from the time I left Heidi's apartment to the time we walked into the mall. Like the girl that's been hidden and protected behind my own constructed walls for all these years has been set free and been given permission to feel safe and become a woman.

I step out of the fitting room in the cat ear hoodie paired with the skull print leggings. The mirror shows someone I barely recognize - someone who looks... cute? The hoodie is soft and oversized, falling just past my hips, while the leggings hug my thighs in ways my ratty jeans never did.

"What do you think?" I ask, giving a little twirl that makes the hoodie's tail swing. Yes, it has a tail. No, I'm not ashamed of how much I love it.

Connor's looking at me with this expression I can't quite read. His eyes are soft, but there's something else there too. "The hoodie's really cute on you," he says, his voice a bit rougher than usual. "And the, uh, the leggings look good too."

I tug at the hem of the hoodie, suddenly self-conscious.

"Yeah? Not too childish with the ears?"

He shakes his head, and is that... is he blushing? The tips of his ears are definitely pink. "No, not childish at all. It's..." He clears his throat, running a hand through his hair. "I'm gonna go look at some band shirts while you finish up. Take your time."

Before I can respond, he's turning on his heel and practically power-walking toward the t-shirt wall. I watch him go, feeling my own cheeks heat up as I realize what just happened. Those leggings must look better than I thought.

I duck back into the fitting room, pressing my hands to my burning face and trying not to grin like an idiot. Connor Ebin, CEO of Eldritch Magic Games, just got flustered looking at me in cat ears and leggings.

Maybe I should get both.

I step out of the fitting room in my old clothes, clutching my chosen items like precious cargo - the cat ear hoodie, skull leggings, and that beautiful new Gojira shirt that isn't held together by safety pins and hope as well as a few other things.

Connor's waiting by the counter, and before I can say anything, he's holding out another hoodie and shirt combo. My heart actually stops for a second when I recognize The Nightfallen's logo sprawled across both pieces.

"I saw you eyeing these earlier," he says with that knowing smile of his. "Thought you might want the set."

I reach out to touch the fabric reverently. "You're going to spoil me."

"That's kind of the point, Shelly."

He's got his own picks too - a Skyrim shirt with some symbol I don't recognize (mental note: study up on Skyrim so I don't expose myself as a gaming fraud), and another that reads 'I need coffee before your bullshit' which is so perfectly Connor it makes me grin. There's also a Fallout mug designed like a Pip-Boy sitting on the counter.

"What's with the symbol?" I ask, pointing to the Skyrim shirt.

"It's the Companions insignia," he explains, looking pleased that I asked. "They're actually one of the more complex factions in the game. Reminds me a bit of the Moon Fangs in CCC, actually."

I try to hide my smile at how his eyes light up when he talks about games. It's like watching a kid show off their favorite toy, except he's literally made some of these toys himself.

I eye the growing pile of clothes, "Are you sure about all this? It's... a lot."

He just gives me that look again - the one that brooks no argument - and starts placing everything on the counter.

While Connor's at the register, I spot a small clearance rack tucked away in the corner. My mind wanders when I see the matching bra and panty sets - simple cotton things in black and dark purple, nothing fancy, but they actually look my size. Unlike Heidi's hand-me-downs that keep sliding off my hips at inconvenient moments.

I glance over at Connor, still occupied with the cashier, and quickly check the prices. They're marked down enough that I can afford both sets with my remaining cash. Next to them, a leather bracelet catches my eye - just a simple braided band with two silver beads. Something about it feels right, like it's meant to be a reminder of today and I need him to have it.

"Hey," I call out to Connor as he finishes up. "I need to grab something real quick. It's a surprise, so... wait outside?"

He raises an eyebrow but doesn't question it, gathering our bags and heading toward the entrance. I clutch my selections close to my chest, face already warming as I approach the counter.

"Can you bag these separately?" I whisper to the cashier, a girl about my age with pink and red hair.

She nods, understanding in her eyes as she starts scanning the underwear. I'm just finishing up the transaction when The Nightfallen's newest song ends overhead.

"Oh my god," the cashier suddenly exclaims, way too loud as she is clearly used to talking over the music that at the moment does not exist. "Your dad is so cool! My parents would never buy me band merch!"

My stomach drops through the floor. I can see Connor in my peripheral vision, pretending to be fascinated by something across the mall. The few other customers in the store are looking between us now, probably noting our similar cheek coloring and drawing their own conclusions.

I stuff my bags under my arm, wishing I could disappear into the cat ear hoodie I'm not even wearing yet.

I hurry out of Hot Topic, my face still burning from the cashier's comment. Connor's waiting just outside, pretending to be fascinated by a directory map like he doesn't know this mall by heart.

"Hey," I say, fidgeting with the small paper bag the bracelet is in. "Hold out your hand."

He raises an eyebrow but complies, extending his right hand palm-up. I pull out the braided leather bracelet, suddenly nervous. What if it's too simple? What if he thinks it's childish?

But as I wrap it around his wrist, fastening the clasp, his whole face lights up. It's like watching the sun break through clouds - his eyes go wide, and this wholesome, unguarded smile spreads across his features.

"Shelly, this is..." He turns his wrist, admiring how the silver beads catch the light. "Thank you."

Before I can respond, he pulls me into a tight hug. His beard tickles my temple, and I catch that familiar mix of lavender and ginger again. I think I'm obsessed with it. I melt into the embrace, wrapping my arms around his waist.

When we pull apart, I loop my arm through his again, grinning mischievously. "Where to now, daddy?"

Connor makes this amazing strangled sound, somewhere between a laugh and a cough. For a split second, I freeze - oh god, why did I say that? How the fuck did that slip out? What if I've gone too far? What if I've made him think about his daughter? "Shit, I was just trying to tease you because of what the cashier said. I wasn't think-"

But then he's laughing for real, deep and authentic. "You're terrible," he says, squeezing my hand. "And it's absolutely fine. I needed that laugh."

"So," Connor says, steering us toward the mall's central plaza, "you've got three options here - massage, chocolate shop, or hair salon. Though I have to say, your hair's pretty perfect as is."

I tense at the mention of a massage. The thought of a stranger's hands on me makes my skin crawl, memories of unwanted touches flickering at the edges of my mind. "No massage," I say quickly, then soften my tone. "But chocolate sounds amazing."

My mind drifts to a rare happy memory from my foster care days. "You know, when I was ten, one of my foster families got me this chocolate frog filled with caramel. It was the first time I'd ever had anything like that." I can still taste it, the way the chocolate shell cracked perfectly, revealing that golden center. "I saved half of it for three days, just taking tiny nibbles."

Connor's eyes light up. "I know exactly where to get those. Come on."

Twenty minutes later, I'm clutching a box of twelve chocolate frogs, still warm from being freshly made. My inner ten-year-old is practically vibrating with joy.

"And..." I bite my lip, glancing toward the salon. "If you're still insisting on spoiling me - which you really don't have to - maybe we could do the hair thing? Just a wash and trim, and..." I touch my bangs self-consciously. "Maybe a silver highlight strip here? Like Little Lysa. Nothing crazy."

The way Connor beams at me makes me throb all over. "Of course. Whatever you want, Little Lysa."

We're halfway to the salon when Connor suddenly stops dead in his tracks, nearly causing me to stumble. I follow his gaze to a toy store window display where an enormous Battle for Helm's Deep Lego set dominates the space, complete with tiny plastic Rohirrim defenders and a sea of Uruk-hai.

"No way," I breathe, watching Connor's face light up like he just won on a scratch off ticket. "You're into Legos?"

He doesn't even try to play it cool. "Are you kidding? This is the collector's edition. Look at the detail on those fortress walls!" He presses closer to the glass, pointing out features I can barely distinguish. "They even included the culvert where Saruman's forces plant the explosives."

I can't help but grin at his enthusiasm. "You know," I say, affecting a casual tone, "Return of the King was definitely the better movie though."

Connor turns to me slowly, one eyebrow raised. "I'm sorry, what was that?"

"You heard me. Two Towers is great and all, but Return of the King? Epic battles, ghost armies, Eowyn being a total badass..." I tick off points on my fingers, trying not to laugh at his increasingly scandalized expression.

"Nobody tosses a dwarf," he says gravely, taking a menacing step toward me. "But I might make an exception if you don't take that back."

I dance backward, giggling. "Make me, Quinn. The beacons are lit! Return of the King calls for aid!"

"And Two Towers will answer!" He lunges playfully, and I dodge behind a mall bench, still laughing.

"Face it," I tease, "you just like Two Towers better because of the Legos."

"That's it." He makes another grab for me, but I slip away again. "Just wait until we get to that salon, Little Lysa. I'm telling them to dye your whole head Gollum-gray."

The salon chair spins so I face the mirror, and I can't help sneaking glances at Connor's reflection. He's lounging in one of the waiting chairs, alternating between scrolling through his phone and making these ridiculous faces every time someone walks past with a questionable hair choice. When a guy struts by with what can only be described as a neon green half mullet, Connor's eyebrows shoot up so high they nearly disappear into his hairline. I have to bite my lip to keep from laughing out loud.

The stylist works quickly, and I watch as she weaves in the silver highlight. It's subtle but striking against my auburn waves, exactly what I'd hoped for. When she's done, I stand up, running my fingers through my freshly cut hair.

"What do you think?" I ask, turning to Connor.

He steps closer, and my breath catches as his fingers thread through my hair, lingering on the silver strand and then pushing in over my ear. "It suits you," he says softly. "Beautiful."

My heart returns to the gymnastics class, and I no longer feel foolish about it. I grab his arm before my knees can betray me. As we walk to his car, I catch him tilting his head slightly, and realize he's sneaking subtle sniffs of my freshly washed hair. The thought makes me feel warm all over, and I press closer to his side, trying to hide my ridiculous grin.

I probably look like a lovesick teenager. Fuck, technically I am. For once in my life, everything feels perfect.

"Coffee?" He asks me, already knowing the answer.

Chapter 20: Coffee Shop Confessions

Connor

THE LATE AFTERNOON SUN filters through Books and Beans' front windows, casting long shadows across us as we sit in the same chairs as when we first met. Shelly is fidgeting with the new silver streak in her hair - seemingly in deep thought.

I catch myself playing with my bracelet that Shelly gifted me. I have always been blown away by sweet gestures toward me, no matter how small some may thInk them.

Shelly looks radiant, practically glowing from our afternoon of pampering and shopping. She couldn't help herself and put the cat ear hoodie on the moment we pulled in here. Seeing her truly happy like this takes my breath away. But now her expression shifts, growing more serious as she seems to wrestle with something internal.

"What were they like? Your wife and daughter?" The question comes out soft, hesitant.

My body stiffens instantly. I've talked about them before,

but usually in fragments, pieces scattered through other conversations. Never head-on like this. The direct question puts a twist in my stomach, and I have to take a steadying breath.

I look down at my coffee cup, buying time while I gather my thoughts. How do you compress the essence of the two people who were your whole world into mere words? How do you describe the way Des's laugh could light up an entire room, or how Liv knew exactly when to hold me and when to let me fight through things on my own?

"Liv, Olivia, was..." I start, then pause, realizing my voice is shakier than I'd like. "She was my foundation. The kind of person who'd dance around our apartment to our favorite '80s rock while baking cookies at midnight. And Desiree, Des..." A smile breaks through despite the ache. "Des was pure energy. She'd drag me to jiu-jitsu class even when I was dead tired, then fall asleep on the couch still in her gi."

I find myself sharing memories I usually keep locked away. "Liv had this thing about tarot cards - she liked to dabble in Wicca, she also loved the styles of artwork. Des got her this beautiful deck for her last birthday..." My voice catches. "And Des, she was fearless. She'd climb anything she could reach, give me heart attacks daily. But she was also so gentle. Found a hurt bird once and insisted we nurse it back to health."

A warm hand slides over mine, and I look down to see Shelly's fingers intertwining with my own. The touch should trigger my usual spiral of guilt, but instead, I feel... calm. Present.

"They sound wonderful," Shelly says softly. "I wish I could have met them."

I squeeze her hand gently before I redirect the conversation and my emotions overwhelm me. "What about you? Any good memories from foster - from before?"

She's quiet for a moment, considering. "There was this one home, when I was twelve. The mom taught me how to braid hair. And another family had this huge garden - they let me grow my own tomatoes for a little while before their biological son wanted a tree house in that spot." A shadow crosses her face. "But mostly it's just... a blur. It felt like most families just wanted the check from the state."

"That must have been awful," I say, feeling a surge of protective anger. "Being treated like a transaction instead of a person."

Shelly shrugs, but I can see the hurt in her eyes. "You get used to it. Learn not to expect anything else."

"You shouldn't have had to get used to that," I tell her firmly.

Shelly's eyes meet mine, that familiar mix of vulnerability and strength I've come to recognize shining in them. "Thank you for today. I'm... I'm not used to people trying to take care of me without wanting something in return."

The words hit me like a punch to the gut. I lean forward slightly, running my thumb across the rim of my bracelet. "That's not entirely true, you know. You've helped me more than you realize." I pause, gathering my thoughts. "I built these walls after losing Liv and Des. Turned my whole life into work and routine. You've helped me start breaking out of that shell. I needed that. So I did get something in return."

Something shifts in the air between us, a weight and lightness all at once. Shelly opens her mouth to respond, but before she can, Jenny appears with fresh coffees and a plate of Danishes.

"Good to see you both smiling so much," Jenny says, setting everything down with a knowing grin. "You two are becoming my favorite regulars."

I feel heat creep up my neck, and notice Shelly's cheeks flush pink. Neither of us seems to know quite how to respond. Whatever this thing between us - friendship, connection, possibility - it's still too new, too undefined to put into words. I know on my part their is still some fear.

Jenny seems to sense our awkwardness and backs away with a small wave, leaving us to navigate this moment on our own.

The conversation drifts into comfortable silence before Shelly speaks up again. "Do you have any other family?"

I shake my head, running my finger along the rim of my coffee cup. "Only child. Lost my parents about eight years ago - carbon monoxide leak while they were sleeping." The memory still stings, but differently than losing Liv and Des. More of a dull ache than a sharp pain. "They had one of those old furnaces. The kind that should've been replaced years before. My father always refused to let me help them with money."

Shelly's hand finds mine again, and I give her a small smile. "Actually, when it happened, we were developing Tales of Fallen Embers. Built this whole mausoleum area in the game for them. Hidden little tribute that most players probably just run past."

"That's beautiful, Connor. In-laws?" she says softly, then looks down at her coffee.

"Olivia's parents live in Ireland. They were never crazy about me, so after she and Des died…the funeral was the last time I had any contact with them."

"I tried looking for my birth mother when I aged out. Turns out she had her records sealed. Means there is no way I can get access because she never wanted me to find her." She lets out a bitter laugh. "So I don't even know if I have siblings out there somewhere. Could walk past them on the street and never know it."

The vulnerability in her voice hurts. I've at least had the closure of knowing my family, of having memories to hold onto. Shelly's been denied even that basic connection.

"That must be hard," I say, knowing the words are inadequate but needing to acknowledge her pain somehow. "Not knowing."

She shrugs, but I can see the hurt in her eyes. "Can't miss what you never had, right?"

We both know that's not true, but I let the lie stand. Sometimes pretending to be okay is the only way to get through the day. I learned that lesson well enough after losing Liv and Des.

"Oh shit, hang on," I say, suddenly remembering the bag in my trunk. "I'll be right back."

I practically jog to the parking lot, feeling like an excited kid about to give someone their birthday present. The evening air has cooled considerably, and I take a deep breath to steady my nerves before popping the truck and grabbing the small bag.

Back inside, Shelly's eyebrows raise as I approach with the hidden package behind my back.

"Now remember," I say, trying to keep my voice casual, "you agreed to let me pamper you today." I look at my watch. "Look, it's still today. If you have to, consider it an early Christmas present."

Her eyes narrow suspiciously. "What are you hiding?"

"First agree that the deal still stands."

"Connor..." She draws out my name like a warning.

"Just agree," I insist, fighting back a grin.

She lets out an exaggerated sigh. "Fine. I agree. Now what are you up to?"

I pull the phone from behind my back and set it on the table. Her eyes go wide as she realizes what it is.

"Connor, no. This is way too-"

"Ah!" I hold up a finger. "No complaints, remember? You agreed."

She picks it up with trembling hands. "But this is... I can't..."

"You need a phone," I say firmly. "It's already programmed you just need to put your own information in. I don't like the idea of you being out there with no way to call for help if you need it. And relying on Heidi's landline isn't practical."

She stares at the phone for a long moment, then looks up at me with green glistening eyes that somehow manage to be both fierce and vulnerable at the same time.

Her gaze falls to the floor. "You're too nice to me," she whispers.

"I'm exactly as nice as you deserve," I counter, reaching over to squeeze her hand.

I see Shelly's body start to tremble before I see the tears. She's fighting them hard, pressing her lips together in a tight line, but they're winning the battle. Without a word, she gets up and practically climbs into my seat right beside me. There is barely enough room for both of us.

My arm moves around her automatically, pulling her closer as she tucks herself against my side. The scent of the salon shampoo - something floral and sweet - fills my senses and I can't help but wonder is the stylist tries to match the scent to a client's personality.

"I don't want people to see me cry," she whispers, her voice catching.

Looking down at her, my chest constricts. I lean over and press a gentle kiss to the top of her head, tightening my arm around her. "I care about you, Shelly. I need you to try and understand how valuable you are as a person. Can you do that for me?"

She sniffles quietly, her hand disappearing into the pockets of her new hoodie. "I'll try," she murmurs, then looks up at me, her eyes still wet with tears. "But only if you do the same."

The words hit me harder than I expect, bringing a lump to my throat. She can see it in me. She recognizes that same struggle for self-worth that I've been wrestling with since losing Liv and Des.

The comfortable weight of Shelly against my shoulder feels right somehow, like we've done this a hundred times before. Neither of us speaks - we don't need to. The coffee shop's ambient noise fades into the background as we simply exist in this moment together. I look at the all too familiar seat she sat in across from me, now empty, and smile to old memories of who used to sit there years ago.

When our cups are empty, we exchange a look and wordlessly gather our things. The drive to Heidi's apartment passes in the same peaceful silence, broken only by the soft hum of the engine and occasional city sounds that filter through the windows.

Walking her to the door, I can't help but marvel at how natural this feels. Most people can't handle silence - myself included for the last five years. So many people have to fill silence with nervous chatter or constant activity. But Shelly gets it. She understands that sometimes just being present is enough.

She fumbles with her keys for a moment before getting the door open, then turns and wraps her arms around me in a tight hug. I press a gentle kiss to her cheek, breathing in that floral shampoo scent again.

"Thank you for letting me take care of you today," I murmur.

As I start to pull back, my new earring - her gift from earlier - catches in her hair. We both laugh as I carefully untangle it.

"And thank you for this," I add, touching the small black hoop. "Never thought this would be the age I would start getting piercings, but I kind of love it."

"Welcome, Quinn." She says softly.

She gives me one last quick squeeze before stepping back into her apartment. As the door closes behind her, I find myself grinning like an idiot. Today has been... incredible. Perfect, even. The kind of day I'd forgotten was possible.

Shelly

I press my back against the apartment door, clutching my shopping bags to my chest like they might disappear if I loosen my grip. The whole afternoon on into the evening feels surreal - like one of those dreams where everything's too perfect and you're just waiting to wake up.

Moving to what's become my command center (aka Heidi's couch), I set down my haul and fish out the chocolate frogs. Two more won't hurt, right? The chocolate melts on my tongue, and I let myself savor it instead of wolfing it down like I usually do with food. The caramel is heaven.

My new phone feels weird in my pocket - heavy with possibility. I pull it out and start the setup process, linking my old email and choosing a passcode. When the time pops up on screen, something clicks in my brain. Heidi should definitely be awake by now.

"Heidi?" I call out, but the apartment stays quiet.

The bathroom looks different than when I left - towels moved, shower curtain adjusted. She's definitely been up and around. I pad over to her bedroom door and knock softly. Nothing.

When I ease the door open, I'm struck by how different it looks. The usual chaos of clothes and makeup is gone, replaced by an almost surgical tidiness. Her bed's made (weird for Heidi), and the usual clutter is nowhere to be seen. Maybe she woke up and decided to do some stress cleaning? Or went shopping since I wasn't here?

But something feels off about the whole thing. Like when you come home and all your furniture's been moved an inch to the left - you can't quite put your finger on what's wrong, but you know something is.

My stomach sinks when I spot the note on the kitchen counter. Heidi's usually messy scrawl is weirdly neat, like she took extra time with it. I read it twice, then a third time, trying to parse what feels wrong about the whole thing.

'Shell, I'm going to be gone for several days on a trip with a client. I left some cash in the drawer by the fridge. Could you restock the pantry while I'm gone? See you soon. Be careful. -H'

A client trip? Since when does Heidi do overnight bookings? This doesn't seem like her at all. I mean she said she has had repeat clients ask for her cell and she always refused. Now she's going on a getaway with one?

I grab the kitchen phone and call her, figuring she won't answer a call from my cell since she doesn't know the number. Straight to voicemail. I try again from my cell and get the same thing but this time I leave a voicemail so she knows who the number belongs to.

"Hey Heidi, it's me," I say after the beep, forcing a laugh into my voice. "Got some news - Connor hooked me up with a phone today. And before you get any ideas, no, he's not my sugar daddy or anything. Though he did take me shopping and..." I trail off, remembering the way he insisted on taking care of me. "Okay, so maybe it sounds a little sugar daddy-ish when I say it out loud, but I swear it's not like that."

The fake cheerfulness in my voice fades as I continue: "I miss you. Hope you're okay wherever you are. Please call me back when you can? You've got me a little worried."

I hang up and stare at the drawer next to the fridge. Inside, there's a neat stack of twenties - way more than needed for restocking the pantry. Three hundred dollars. How much does she think I'm going to eat while she's gone? My fingers brush against something else in the drawer - a few folded pieces of paper with what looks like multiple failed drafts of the note she left me. I look through them carefully and see that they are all in her handwriting just some more rushed than others.

The money feels wrong in my hand. Everything about this feels wrong. I try to wrap head around it all - wondering what the hell I can do about it. If I call the police what am I going to say, 'Hello, my friend is acting really weird and said she was going on a trip. By the way, I think cocaine is involved.'

That would turn out wonderfully. I could call Connor or Ashlyn but it's not going to do anything but worry them. I have no idea where she could have gone so I can't even begin to try and look for her.

I need to stop obsessing over this. Heidi's an adult - she can take care of herself.

Standing in front of Heidi's full-length mirror, I admire how the new silver highlight in my bangs catches the LEDs in Heidi's room.

I peel off the cat ear hoodie and Heidi's borrowed clothes, letting them fall in a heap by my feet. I try on one of my new bra and panty sets. They feel decadent against my skin - smooth cotton, nothing crazy. The deep purple set makes my eyes pop, and feels like a second skin. Which is something I have never been able to say about a bra in my life.

Turning sideways in the mirror, I run my hands over my ribs. They don't stick out quite as sharply as they did a few weeks ago. Hell, I can honestly barely make them out. Regular meals, frequent bathing and not sleeping in the cold have done wonders. My skin looks better too - clearer and warmer, with a hint of color instead of that sort of pale cast I'd gotten used to seeing.

Maybe it's all in my head, but I swear my breasts look fuller, fitting perfectly into the B-cup instead of swimming in it like before. The panties hug my hips just right, making me feel... pretty. Sexy even. It's been so long since I've felt either of those things.

I do another slow spin. My freckles stand out against my skin, but not in that harsh way they used to when I was malnourished. Now they look almost cute, scattered across my chest and shoulders like constellations.

For the first time in forever, I actually like what I see in the mirror. I look… healthy. Like a normal young woman instead of someone just trying to survive.

I pull on the skull leggings and eye the one pair of jeans for the next mini fashion show. Pulling the Nightfallen shirt over my head blows my mind. It fits perfectly. It might be my favorite. Okay, no, the cat ear hoodie is my favorite.

I think about how Connor looked at me when I came out of the dressing room in this thing and spun so the tail swooshed out. I had been a little afraid he would think it was childish, but he hadn't. In fact, he seemed to really like it. Then I remembered all the people I ran into at Eldritch Magic and how many headsets I saw people wearing with car ears, horns and all sorts of decorations on them as well as a hell of a lot of other things that many people would find immature. I snicker at myself because this hoodie is probably one of the least weird things he's seen on someone. The gaming industry seems very excepting of embracing your inner child. Hell, he loves Legos.

For a moment, I let myself indulge in a fantasy - Connor standing behind me, his strong arms wrapped around my waist, his smile reflected in the mirror beside mine. I shake my head, trying to dislodge the thought. Then I get a little perturbed with myself. Every time I start to think about him like that my gut reaction to to fight it. No more. From now on I just let it flow and if it happens then great. If it doesn't…I'll live.

My new laptop beckons from the coffee table. Time to dive back into CCC and forget about everything else for a while.

As I'm settling in, my phone chirps with a notification about adding contacts. Right - blank slate.

I attach Heidi's name to her number first, since I already dialed it. Then Connor's and Ashlyn's. It feels weird having actual contacts instead of just memorizing numbers. Good weird though.

I text Ashlyn first just to let her know I now have a phone. Then I text Connor, 'Phone's all set up!'

His response comes quick - a photo of me at the salon, caught mid-laugh while the stylist was working her magic. I didn't even notice him taking it. The only reason this man is single is because his love was taken from him. There is no other reason in the world he could be.

I respond with a laughing emoji and then he tells me to text or call anytime. He sends me a picture of himself holding the phone so I can see he is playing some video game I have never seen. I heart the image and tell myself that it was a normal reaction to the picture and then follow it up by sending a pic of the Critical Chaos in Chains menu screen.

Another buzz: Ashlyn asking how the shopping went. I smile, still not quite used to having people actually care about my day.

I stare at Ashlyn's text, fingers hovering over the keyboard. I'm a little surprised by her asking about the shopping trip. I suppose more so because that meant Connor had talked to her about it. That means he talks about me when I'm not around. There goes that giddy feeling again.

'Shopping was amazing,' I type. 'Connor got me this super cute cat ear hoodie and some new clothes for the awards show. Plus a phone obviously lol.'

Her response pops up instantly: 'Girl, don't you dare give me the cliff notes version! I want ALL the details. And I mean ALL of them.'

Before I can respond, another message appears: 'You might not believe this, but I don't actually have many female friends. Most women at work keep their distance because of my position, and outside... well, let's just say I could use some girl talk that isn't about quarterly projections and how many pixels are in a characters tits.'

I smile at my phone, warmth spreading through my chest. 'You sure? Because there's kind of a lot...'

'Spill it! And don't worry - whatever you tell me stays between us. Connor won't hear a word. Scout's honor!' Ashlyn threw in a zippered mouth emoji for reassurances.

It's tempting. Really tempting. Having someone to talk to about all this who actually knows Connor, who might understand why I'm so confused about everything...

'Well,' I type, 'first he bet I wouldn't be able to solve a riddle and I said if I did we had to get piercings. So I am the reason he now has his ear pierced.'

The words start flowing easier after that. I tell her about the shopping spree, about how Connor seemed to know exactly what stores I'd like without me having to say anything. About how he made sure I got the caramel filled chocolate frogs when I talked about them. About how natural it felt spending time with him. I told her pretty much everything except the girl at Hot Topic thinking he was my dad.

She sends me a gif of someone looking quite serious and

then laughing until they fall over - a direct reply to the message about the piercing. Then she tells me that is how Connor is when he cares for someone. She then says it was good that I asked about Olivia and Desiree and that she is really glad he opened up about them because they were very special and the more people that know that the better.

My phone nearly slips from my trembling fingers as I read Ashlyn's next message: 'Actually, speaking of work... are you busy tomorrow?'

'Just grocery shopping,' I type back, already wondering if I should mention the weird situation with Heidi.

'Perfect! Listen, we had someone cancel last minute for a really important position tomorrow. Family emergency. Would you be interested in making $3500 for the day?'

The phone actually does slip this time, bouncing off my nose before landing on my chest. Three thousand five hundred dollars? For one day? I snatch the phone back up, my thumbs hovering over the keyboard.

I start typing 'Are you sure?' but delete it.

'What kind of position?' Delete.

'There has to be someone better qualified...' Delete.

'Is this legal?' Delete.

Finally, I manage: 'Ashlyn, I appreciate it but there has to be someone more qualified for whatever this is.'

Her response is immediate: 'Please? Consider it a personal favor to me. I promise it'll be worth it. Just trust me on this one.'

My heart's on it's way to becoming an Olympian at this point as I read her next message: 'Like last time, I'll pick you up on the way in. How do you feel about motion capture work…with Connor?' She throws a winky face emoji at the end to sweeten the message. As if three thousand five hundred dollars wasn't sweet enough.

I stare at my screen, mind racing and my heart feels like I am running a marathon. Motion capture with Connor? I absolutely want to do that. I flash back to the night we met at the Books and Beans and the…revealing suit he wore in the promo video for Rune Beast that they played on the TV. I'm not entirely sure I can be around him while he is that…exposed.

But before my mind can talk me out of it, my fingers type 'Okay, What time?'

The phone rings in my hand and surprises me to the point I nearly drop it again. Ashlyn is calling now? I hit 'Accept.'

Her voice comes over the speaker, pleasant but guarded. "Let me give you the full details before you commit."

Chapter 21: Captured Chemistry

Connor

TODAY IS THE FINAL shooting for our Rune Beast game. Maddison Ball and I will have to get a little more intimate this morning. The scenes are more romantic and passionate than raunchy, thankfully. Also, thankfully, there are only a handful that we need to record together and the animation and cinematics team can handle the rest.

The mo-cap suit sits next to me like a deflated black fabric mannequin, mocking me. I've done this dozens of times, but I still get that twinge of dread every time I have to squeeze into this thing. It's like trying to put on a condom made for your entire body - not exactly a confidence-boosting experience.

At least I came prepared today, I hope. I brought a jock strap in hopes it'll lessen my… outline. It's a bit uncomfortable, but it beats having my junk mapped in high-definition for the entire animation team to see. Last time, Ashlyn couldn't look me in the eye for a week after reviewing the raw footage and Manu kept sending me long john donuts everyone morning while laughing. Something about "excessive detail in the groin region during combat rolls."

I strip down to my compression shorts in the men's green room, carefully positioning the 'cradle' of the jock strap. It pinches and makes me wince. "The things I do for art," I mutter, reaching for the suit.

Getting into this thing is always a dance. Left leg first, wiggling and shimmying like I'm trying to escape a straight jacket in reverse. The material clings everywhere, showing off everything I am proud of and everything I am self conscious about. Thank god for the gym and the jock - though now I look like I'm smuggling a small animal.

The reflective markers dotting the suit catch the bright lights as I adjust everything into place. Each one will help translate my movements into Rune Beast's fluid animations. It's worth the discomfort, I remind myself. The players deserve that level of authenticity.

I catch my reflection in the mirror and can't help but snort. Here I am, CEO of Eldritch Magic Games, trussed up like a BDSM ninja. If only the rest of the team could see me now. Except they don't need to. The original footage I shot before anyone bothered to tell me how 'proud' I should be was on our main website. They had all seen it. At least the team's used to it by now - though I still catch the occasional stifled laugh when I have to do the these more intimate scenes.

In truth, I did this to myself. When we were writing Rune Beast I had done everything in the industry, even some minor voice work. But I had never done the motion capture and at the time I was really struggling to keep my myself from losing it anytime I had a moment of silence. I may have used my power as Owner and CEO to give myself the voice and animation spot. Aimi had thankfully not fought me on it, but at the time I think it was because we were paying her almost double what she made at her former game studio. She later told me that she thought I had done this kind of work before, which I took as a great compliment.

Time to head to the capture stage. I grab my water bottle and take a deep breath. Another day of being digitally naked in front of my employees. At least this time my dignity's somewhat protected.

I push through the capture stage door, immediately noticing how empty the usually bustling space feels. The familiar gray and green walls stretch around me, a few props scattered strategically along the edges, but the usual crowd of techs and assistants is conspicuously absent. My footsteps echo more than they should.

Something's off.

The control room door swings open, and Ashlyn emerges with Aimi. They're both wearing those carefully neutral expressions that set off warning bells in my head. You don't run a gaming company for fifteen years without learning to read people's faces.

"Where is everyone?" I ask, scanning the room again. Normally we'd have at least twelve people for a capture session - techs, calibration specialists, the works.

Aimi clasps her hands in front of her, all business. "Given the intimate nature of today's scenes, we felt it more appropriate to maintain a skeleton crew for you and the actress. Everything has already been adjusted and set up."

My eyebrow shoots up. "The actress?"

It's not like Aimi to be so formal - she's always called Maddison by name. Hell, they went to dinner together last week to discuss the Seidr Witch's character motivations for these scenes. Something about this whole setup feels orchestrated, like walking onto a stage where everyone knows their lines except me.

I glance between them, catching the ghost of a smile trying to escape the corner of Ashlyn's mouth. They're up to something, these two. The question is what?

Ashlyn is trying not to smirk mischievously but she can't help herself. "Maddison had to pull out last minute, family emergency." She throws her hands up, knowing I am going to freak because of the deadline to get this done today.

"But I found a suitable replacement." She goes to open the door to the women's green room and my heart stops dead. Shelly.

My brain short-circuits, mouth going dry as I stare at Shelly standing there in a motion capture suit identical to mine. The markers catch the light as she shifts nervously, but there's a determined set to her jaw that I wasn't expecting.

"What... how..." I manage to stammer, looking between Ashlyn and Shelly. This has to be some kind of elaborate joke.

Ashlyn's smirk grows wider. "Surprise!"

I drag my eyes back to Shelly, trying to maintain professional composure despite the fact that my heart is doing backflips. "Did Ashlyn put you up to this? Because if you're uncomfortable-"

"She offered me a really well-paying job," Shelly cuts in, her voice steadier than I expected. "She ran me through everything last night, so I agreed." She shrugs, the motion capture markers bobbing. "And this morning she told me I can change my mind at any point." Her eyes meet mine. "I'm good, Connor. Promise."

There's something in that look that makes my entire body want to tense up and relax at the same time. Trust. She trusts me. After everything she's been through, after all the people who've let her down, after that asshole in the alley, she's standing here in this ridiculous skin tight suit because she trusts me enough to do this.

I have to swallow hard before I can speak. "You're sure about this?"

Shelly nods, a slight blush creeping across her cheeks, but her eyes remain steady and determined. I catch Ashlyn's self-satisfied smirk and shoot her a look that could curdle milk. She knows exactly what she's doing, and right now I'm not sure whether to thank her or fire her.

"Ashlyn. A word?" I gesture toward the corner of the studio, fighting to unclench my jaw.

Once we're out of earshot, I lean in close. "Are you insane? She's not ready for something like this. Hell, after everything that happened the other night-"

"I ran her through the whole process last night. Twice," Ashlyn cuts me off, her voice low but firm. "Every detail, every position, every possibility. I gave her multiple chances to back out." She touches my arm lightly. "Connor, she was adamant. Actually got annoyed with me for continuing to ask so many times if she was sure."

I glance back at Shelly, who's talking quietly with Aimi about something technical. The motion capture suit highlights every curve of her body, but it's the confident set of her shoulders that catches my attention. Where did this boldness come from?

"She trusts you completely," Ashlyn continues softly. "And honestly? That's huge for someone with her background. Don't underestimate her strength just because you want to protect her."

The words hit home harder than I'd like to admit. I run a hand over my face, feeling the tension in my jaw slowly release. "If she shows any sign of discomfort-"

"We'll stop immediately," Ashlyn promises. "But I don't think we'll need to."

I walk back to where Shelly and Aimi are standing, trying to keep my professional demeanor intact despite the circus of emotions running wild in my chest. The motion capture suit suddenly feels about ten degrees warmer than it did a minute ago.

"Are you absolutely certain about this?" I ask Shelly, keeping my voice gentle. "There's no pressure. We can figure something else out if-"

"Yes, I'm nervous," she admits, fidgeting with one of the markers on her wrist, "but only because I've never done motion capture before. I don't want to mess up your game. But if you or Ashlyn ask me again if I am sure, I'm going to lose my mind. I can make my own damn decisions."

Her earnest and firm response makes my heart jolt with pride. Before I can respond, Aimi steps between us, all business.

"Let me be clear about expectations," she says, glancing between us. "While these scenes are intimate, we don't need much physical contact. No kissing, and no heavy touching are needed - we can add all that in post. If you're both feeling it then go for it but only if you both are. We just need natural movement patterns to work from." She demonstrates with her hands, showing how we should maintain light touch for the most part while mimicking intimate gestures.

I nod, grateful for Aimi's professional tone. "Understood."

Turning to Shelly, I meet her eyes directly. "Please tell me immediately if anything makes you uncomfortable. We can stop or adjust at any time. This needs to feel safe for you."

The small smile she gives me in response does dangerous things to my ability to maintain professional distance. "Stop. I trust you, Quinn."

The nickname hits me like a punch to the solar plexus, but in the best possible way. She must be feeling comfortable. I have to clear my throat before I can speak again. At least it is only the four of us here. That is until I see Manu sneak in behind Aimi and Ashlyn in the control room.

Aimi claps her hands together. "Alright, first scene is relatively simple. The Rune Beast comes in from stage left, picks up the Witch, and places her on the table. The intimacy builds gradually - we're focusing on the tenderness here, not raw passion."

I nod, trying to stay professional despite the sudden dryness in my mouth. This is just another motion capture session. Just another day at work. Right.

"Connor, you'll lift Shelly there," Aimi continues, gesturing to a spot near the prop table. "Shelly, when he lifts you, just let your arms naturally find their way around his neck. We want fluid, natural movements."

Shelly nods, her markers catching the light as she moves into position. I can see her pulse fluttering at her throat, but her eyes remain steady when they meet mine.

"Ready?" I ask softly.

"Ready," she whispers back.

"And... action!" Aimi calls.

I move forward, lifting Shelly as if she weighs nothing. Her arms slide around my neck exactly as choreographed, but there's nothing choreographed about the small gasp she makes when I do. Her legs wrap around my waist instinctively and I carry her to the table, trying to focus on my marks and not how perfectly she fits against me.

Following Aimi's direction, I lean in to simulate kissing Shelly's neck, keeping a careful distance. But my breath must tickle her flesh because she shivers in my arms, her fingers tightening slightly where they rest against my shoulders.

"Perfect!" Aimi calls from somewhere behind us. "Hold that position while we check the markers."

I remain frozen, hyperaware of every point where Shelly's body connects with mine through the thin material of our suits. Her pulse races beneath my hovering lips, matching the thundering of my own heart.

"Perfect!" Aimi says, and I can hear the slight surprise in

her tone. "Let's do two more just to be sure," Aimi calls out. "Same marks, same energy."

I set Shelly down gently between takes, careful to maintain professional distance while still staying in character. Her eyes meet mine briefly, and I catch a small smile that makes my…well, the jock strap becomes a little more uncomfortable.

The second take flows more naturally. The initial nervousness has faded, replaced by a comfortable rhythm. Shelly's movements are more fluid now, her arms finding their way around my neck with practiced ease. When I lift her, she moves with me like we've done this a hundred times.

By the third take, we're practically reading each other's minds. The hesitation is gone completely. Each motion feels organic, natural. I barely have to think about my marks anymore - we just flow together like water.

"Beautiful work, you two," Aimi approaches after calling cut. "Now for the next sequence. Connor, you'll guide Shelly to lie back on the table. Then you'll climb up, positioning yourself above her. Remember - we're capturing the anticipation here, the buildup of tension. So take your time, go slower than you think you need to."

Before we take our positions, I catch Shelly's eyes. "Hey," I say softly, making sure only she can hear me. "I need you to promise me, If anything - anything at all - makes you uncomfortable, tell me immediately. I…" I swallow hard, surprised by the intensity of emotion in my voice. "I never want you to be afraid of me. Ever."

She narrows her eyes and smacks my arm. "I said stop

doing that. I know how to use my own voice." I must look rebuked because the look she gives me changes to one so full of trust it almost hurts. She nods, reaching out to squeeze my hand briefly. "I promise, Connor, I'm fine." she whispers.

I can hear Manu whispering something to Ashlyn in the control room, followed by what sounds suspiciously like a smack and an "ow!" But I keep my focus on Shelly, trusting that she is fully comfortable now. Which I am thankful for because I feel a little looser now.

"Ready when you are," Aimi calls out, positioning herself behind the monitors.

I place my hand gently in the center of Shelly's chest, feeling her heartbeat racing beneath my palm. Following the choreography, I guide her back onto the table with careful precision, trying to maintain professional detachment despite how natural this feels.

A scripted growl rumbles from my throat as I move over her - low and gentle, just as I practiced in previous mocap sessions. But Shelly's reaction catches me off guard. She shudders beneath me, a small involuntary movement that makes the markers on her suit shakes a little. When she realizes what she's done, a blush spreads across her cheeks and she squirms slightly, adjusting her position.

I hover above her, lowering my face near hers as directed, maintaining the careful distance Aimi specified. The professional part of my brain catalogs angles and positions, making sure we're hitting our marks correctly. But there's another part - one I'm trying desperately to ignore - that notices how perfectly we move together.

"Cut!" Aimi calls out. "That was incredibly organic, guys. Let's get a couple more takes so we can splice pieces of them together if needed."

We reset and run through it four more times. The final take feels different somehow - more fluid. Shelly arches her back in an unscripted movement that I can't help but register, I'm focusing less on angles and performance and I find myself just being present in the moment.

"Perfect!" Aimi sounds pleased. "That last one was exactly what we needed. The improvised back arch really sold it, Shelly. Excellent instincts."

I blink, almost like I forgot where I was. I'm keenly aware that the jock strap is… I start trying to think about anything else, puppies. Yes, puppies. Shelly is really blushing now.

Aimi acts as the intimacy coordinator and checks on us both to make sure were are still comfortable and ready to continue. We both agree that we are good to move on.

I remain in a crawling position above Shelly and get ready for her to essentially sweep me to one side and come out on top of me.

"For this sequence, Shelly, you'll need to roll Connor over and straddle his position. Remember, fluid movements, keep the markers visible."

"Ready?" I ask, glancing up at Shelly.

She nods, determination written across her face. On Aimi's mark, Shelly attempts to roll me over. There's a moment of resistance - I'm not exactly light, and years of jiu jitsu have made me pretty solid. It doesn't help that I am feeling very distracted. Instead of the smooth motion we're going for, we both end up toppling sideways in an ungraceful heap.

"Oh god, I'm so sorry!" Shelly squeaks, but she's already giggling.

I can't help but laugh too, the tension of the previous scenes breaking. "My fault - I should've gone with the movement far more than I did."

"Cut!" Aimi calls, but she's chuckling too. "Let's reset and try that again. Connor, maybe help with the roll this time?"

We untangle ourselves and return to starting positions. This time, when Shelly initiates the move, I work with her momentum. The roll is smooth, natural, and suddenly she's above me, the fabric of our suits getting hotter. I am beyond thankful that I wore the jock strap is doing what little it can today because I am… praying to the god of puppies to help me become less than half flaccid. This was never a problem with Maddison. I should feel extremely unprofessional right now.

It doesn't help when she repositions her weight and suddenly freezes. I know instantly that she has felt it. Her face is redder than a crayon and she turns to look away form me.

I start to freak out, "I'm so sorry." I whisper so hopefully only she can hear me. I am beyond embarrassed and starting to be extremely ashamed.

Shelly squeezes my arm and starts to speak but Aimi cuts in on the control room mic quickly.

"Perfect!" Aimi calls out. "Hold that pose while we check the markers again."

I focus on keeping my breathing steady, trying to think about anything else - bug fixes, deadline schedules, that weird noise my car's been making lately. Anything but how right this feels.

Shelly is looking down at me with a nervous but eager smile and I get the feeling she really is enjoying this. The motion capture I mean.

The next few scenes have gone incredibly smooth - almost too smooth. Shelly and I have found a rhythm that makes everything feel natural, which is both amazing and terrifying. Each scene flows into the next like we've been doing this for years instead of hours. The familiarity that we seem to have transitioned into has also made my prayer to the god of puppies seem answered. I am no longer threatening to tear through the suit, I'm still very much a mix of professionalism and… I'll say enticed, but it is no longer interfering in any-way.

"Final sequence," Aimi calls out. "Connor, you'll approach from behind, wrap your arms around her waist and shoulder, pause at the neck, then spin and hold for the kiss."

We run through it once for practice, marking our positions. Even the practice feels charged, electric. When we reset for the actual take, my hands are practically trembling as I wrap them around Shelly's waist and shoulder.

I pause at her neck, breathing in the light scent of her. The script calls for hesitation here, but it's not acting anymore. My heart is pounding so hard I wonder if the motion capture markers can pick it up.

When I spin her around, pulling her close, something shifts. The air between us feels thick, heavy with possibility. We're supposed to stop here, maintain that careful distance of a few inches we've kept all day.

But we don't.

I'm not sure who moves into it first - maybe we both do. Our lips meet in the middle, soft and tentative at first. A shudder runs through my entire body as Shelly lets out a small whimper that shoots straight through me. Our mouths open and our lips dance for a few seconds more before they part.

There's silence from the control room and we break the kiss before we hear a belated, "Cut!" Aimi's voice breaks through the fog around us.

We slowly pull ourselves apart, both breathing heavily and nervous. "Was that okay?" we ask simultaneously, then laugh nervously at the jinx.

The silence in the control room turns to an eruption of applause as Aimi, Ashlyn, and Manu emerge, all wearing varying degrees of surprised smiles.

"That was..." Aimi shakes her head, grinning. "That was absolutely perfect. The most organic performance I've seen in a while. We couldn't have scripted it better."

I sink into the nearest chair, grateful for the sturdy support and even more grateful for the little assistance the jock strap contributes to hiding the pulsing I am feeling. My heart's still racing, and every inch of me feels like a lightning storm. There is life I haven't felt in...

Ashlyn practically bounces over to Shelly, her face lit up like Christmas morning. "You were amazing! Come on, let's get you changed." She grabs Shelly's hand and practically jogs her toward the women's green room, leaving me to deal with Manu's knowing looks.

"So..." Manu drawls, leaning against the wall. "How long do you think you'll need that chair? Should I grab you an ice pack? Maybe some loose-fitting pants?"

I glare at him as Aimi disappears back into the control room, presumably to review the footage. "You're a fucking ass, you know that?"

"Maybe," he snickers. "But you keep me around because of my charming personality so I'm not worried."

"Right," I say with dripping sarcasm, thought there isn't much energy put into the words. The lingering effect of that kiss has left me too stunned to summon genuine outrage.

"Jokes aside, you did well though, Connor. It's going to translate perfectly into the game." Manu remarks in earnest. But he still slides closer with that infuriating grin plastered across his face. "Ass and titties."

"You prick."

Chapter 22: Protective Measures

Shelly

I'M FLOATING, LITERALLY BUZZING with energy as Ashlyn pulls me into the green room. My heart's racing so fast I can barely get the words out, but they tumble from my lips anyway.

"Was it okay? Did the movements look natural? Did I hit the marks right? The kiss - oh god, should I not have-"

Ashlyn's laugh cuts through my rambling. "Breathe, honey. Just breathe." She guides me to sit on one of the plush chairs. "You were perfect. And Connor?" She wiggles her eyebrows. "I haven't seen him that focused in years."

"Really?" My voice comes out squeaky, and I clear my throat. "I mean, I was worried about messing up the whole scene..."

"Trust me, that was exactly what we needed." Ashlyn's smile turns mischievous. "Though, between us ladies, I have to say, you seemed pretty... invested in the performance."

"What do you mean?" I fidget with the sleeve of the mo-cap

suit.

"Shelly..." She glances down meaningfully. "Don't freak out on me okay? You did wear the protective underwear under the suit, right?"

"Of course! You told me it was required-"

"Huh." Ashlyn looks genuinely puzzled. "That's interesting, because usually those things prevent..." She gestures vaguely at my lower half.

I look down and notice the wet spot forming between my legs. My face ignites with heat so intense I'm sure I'm glowing red. Without another word, I bolt for the bathroom, mortification following me like a shadow.

Behind the closed door, I press my burning face into my hands. Oh god. Oh god oh god oh god.

I hear Ashlyn's gentle laughter through the bathroom door, which somehow makes this whole situation both better and worse.

"Sweetie, come out. I promise no one else noticed. I just happened to see it while I had my head done checking my phone. If anyone else in there had seen we would have known. Not because they would brought attention to it but because it would have been obvious they were trying not to."

Cracking the door open, I peek out. "This is the most embarrassing...you swear you don't think anyone else saw?"

"Cross my heart. It was barely noticeable - like a dime-sized spot at the time. That's why I rushed you back here." She gives me a warm smile. "Want me to step out while you change?"

I nod gratefully, and she slips out of the green room.

I'm wrestling with the mo-cap suit, peeling it off layer by layer, feeling like I'm shedding a second skin. The thing is a beast, all clingy and unforgiving, but I manage to wriggle free, a little victory dance playing in my head.

As I strip off the protective underwear, I can't help but notice the dampness—a glaring reminder of every shot of the day. The kiss, especially. It was just acting, I tell myself, but my body's reaction tells a different story, one that's etched in a blush spreading across my cheeks. No, Shelly. I tell myself. You said you would stop lying to yourself. You meant every second of that kiss.

I clean up quickly, splashing water on my face, trying to regain some semblance of composure. I slip back into my clothes, the familiar fabric a comforting embrace. Jeans, a band tee, my new Nightfallen hoodie—it's like donning armor against the vulnerability of my open want.

With a deep breath, I give myself a once-over in the mirror. I look... normal. Like I haven't just spent hours pretending to be a video game character caught in a steamy embrace with a man who cares for me, in one way or another.

"Ashlyn," I call out, my voice steadier than I feel. "You can come back in."

The door swings open, and Ashlyn steps inside, her eyes scanning me for any signs of lingering embarrassment. She's like what I imagine an older sister would have been like, always looking out for me but perfectly fine teasing me.

"Feeling better?" she asks, her tone gentle.

I nod, mustering up a smile. "Yeah, I'm good. Thanks for... you know, keeping it under wraps."

She chuckles, waving away my thanks. "Honey, when it comes to work-related wardrobe malfunctions, we've all been there. Besides," she adds with a wink, "it's not every day we get to see the stoic Mr. Ebin so... flustered."

I groan, burying my face in my hands. "Don't remind me. I can't believe I let that happen. What must he think of me?"

Ashlyn's hand lands on my shoulder, squeezing reassuringly. "He thinks you acted like a professional and did an amazing job today. It's going to make for one hell of a game cutscene. And for what it's worth, I think you two have real chemistry. He likes you Shelly. I can see it. I think he's just trying to fully admit it to himself and he needs time to process that."

Her words should comfort me, but they only stir the whirlpool of emotions churning in my stomach. Chemistry? With Connor? She thinks he likes me? The thought is both thrilling and terrifying.

"Thanks, Ashlyn," I mumble, still not entirely convinced. "Is this… am I being foolish? Could this actually work?"

She tilts her head with a warm but concerned smile starting to spread on her face. "Just ask him, Shelly."

I look down at my feet and rub my arm nervously. I probably look ridiculous right now. I'm reminded of the girls in different anime that stand like this when they're unsure and abashed. Ashlyn stops me from spiraling, "Come on, let's get out of here. You deserve a break after today's performance."

I stop at the door before we leave. "Ashlyn, did you ask me to do this because you expected something to happen?"

She raises her eyebrow. "Me? Give some friends of mine a

helping push? Never."

I follow Ashlyn out of the green room on shaky legs, when I see Connor standing there alone, everyone else already gone. Ashlyn chirps a quick "bye" and practically skips away, leaving us in awkward silence.

The fluorescent lights dim overhead as I shuffle towards him, trying to find my voice. He's changed back into his CEO suit, as I call it, that makes my mouth go dry.

"So..." I tuck the silver strand of my hair behind my ear, fighting the urge to run away. "How... how did I do?"

Connor shifts his weight from one foot to the other, his expression unreadable. There's something in his eyes though - something that makes my stomach twist into knots. He opens his mouth, then closes it again, running his tongue over his bottom lip like he's trying to taste the words before speaking them.

The silence stretches between us, heavy with unspoken things. I've never seen him look so uncertain before, not even during our late-night conversation at Books and Beans. I feel like he always knows exactly what to say, but right now he looks like someone trying to defuse a bomb with trembling hands.

I wrap my arms around myself, suddenly feeling very small. "That bad, huh?"

My heart skips as Connor quickly jumps in. "No! God no, you were... you were amazing actually." His voice carries that gentle authority I've come to know, but there's something else there too - a slight tremor I've never heard before. "You shocked me with how good you were."

I'm still processing his words when he steps closer, taking my hand in his. The touch sends electricity shooting up my arm, and I fight the urge to gasp. His palm is warm against mine, the callouses strangely comforting to me.

The silence stretches between us again, and anxiety creeps in. Maybe I read this wrong. Maybe he's trying to figure out how to let me down easy, tell me it was too much. I start to pull my hand back, but his fingers tighten around mine, not letting go.

"You make me nervous," he blurts out.

The words hang in the air between us, and I freeze. Connor Ebin - CEO, BJJ brown belt, the man who just hours ago performed intimate scenes with me without breaking character - is nervous because of me? Little homeless Shelly who, until recently, was sleeping behind dumpsters?

My mouth goes dry as I stare at our joined hands, unable to look up at his face. The lights overhead buzzing like a steady drone, matching the humming in my veins.

I take another step closer, my heart thundering in my chest. This isn't me - I'm not the brave one, not the one who pushes for answers. But something about the vulnerability in his eyes pulls the words from me.

"Talk to me, Connor. Please. I need to know."

His eyes glisten with unshed tears, and my chest aches at the sight. Connor - my strong, confident Connor - looking so raw and exposed makes me want to wrap my arms around him and never let go. Did I just call him mine?

"You make me feel again," he whispers, his voice rough. "And it terrifies me. I keep trying to put you in these neat little boxes in my head - friend, someone to protect, someone to..." He trails off, swallowing hard. "But none of them fit quite right, and I don't know what to do with that."

My fingers tighten around his, anchoring us both. He continues, words tumbling out like he can't hold them back anymore.

"Yesterday at the mall, watching you get excited over the cat ear hoodie, seeing your face light up over that stupid fantasy Lego set I wanted... I had to admit to myself that I care about you. Deeply." He lets out a shaky breath. "But I don't know what that means yet, or what I'm ready for it to mean."

The confession hangs between us, heavy with possibility. I feel dizzy with the weight of it, with the knowledge that this man who means so much to me is struggling with the same confusing feelings I am.

"And that scares you?" I ask softly, though I already know the answer.

He nods, a tear finally breaking free and rolling down his cheek. "More than anything." He pauses for the briefest of moments before taking a half step closer, "That kiss…it was lightning throughout my whole body. I just I needed to tell you all of this or I wasn't going to be able to look at you again." He looks up from our hands and meets my eyes.

My lips grow dry as I struggle to find the right words. "I'm scared too," I whisper, watching his thumb absentmindedly trace circles on the back of my hand. "At first, I was terrified you only saw them when you looked at me. Olivia and Des." The names feel sacred on my tongue. "But yesterday at the mall, the way you looked at me when I was geeking out over that Nightfallen shirt... how you took that picture of me at the salon when I wasn't paying attention. That wasn't about them. That was just... us."

I take a shaky breath, fighting back my own tears. "You make me want to open up, to let someone in, and that terrifies me more than any night I spent on the streets." A bitter laugh escapes me. "And there's this voice in my head, this stupid little voice that keeps telling me you're going to realize I'm just some sad girl you took pity on. Like those fairy tales where the peasant girl gets to dance with the king, but midnight always comes eventually."

His hand tightens around mine, and I force myself to continue. "I know you're not like that. I know it here," I tap my chest with my free hand. "But knowing something and believing it are different things, you know?"

"Every time you do something kind for me, every time you look at me like... like you're looking at me right now, I keep waiting for the other shoe to drop. Because good things don't happen to girls like me. They just don't."

My whole body trembles as Connor pulls me against him, his arms wrapping around me like a shield against everything that's broken in both our lives. I press my face into his chest, letting my tears soak into his expensive suit while his own fall into my hair. The familiar scent of his beard mingles with the salt of our shared grief and hope.

I push myself harder against him when his lips press against my scalp, seeking more of his warmth, more of this feeling of safety I've never known before. His chest rumbles as he speaks, voice low and thick with emotion.

"Maybe we're all of those things, Little Lysa," he whispers against my hair, using that nickname that makes my heart skip. "The broken parts, the healing parts, the scared parts... and maybe that's okay."

I grip the back of his suit jacket, fingers curling into the fabric like I'm afraid he'll disappear if I let go. "What if-"

"Shh," he cuts me off gently. "What if we try something different? What if we take this slow, see where it leads us?" His arms tighten around me. "Instead of listening to all those voices telling us what we shouldn't feel - what we're afraid of, what if we just... focus on the good voices and trust in each other?"

I nod against his chest, unable to form words around the lump in my throat. He's right. We're both so caught up in what could go wrong, we're afraid to see what could go right.

"The good things," I manage to whisper. "Like how safe I feel right now."

His breath catches, and I feel him press another kiss to my head. "How needed I feel."

When we finally separate we look at each other, and we are both an utter mess. "Is this what they call ugly crying?" He asks me with a smirk.

I laugh and snort, making a terrible sound that makes us both chuckle more.

"Don't act like you're so old you don't know what ugly crying is." I tease.

"Can I drive you home?"

As we walk out of the office, I am extremely thankful that

the lights are dimming for the end of the day because our faces are red nightmares. He holds my hand and I lean into him like I did yesterday at the mall.

There aren't many people still in the building but those that are spare us a glance, no doubt wondering if the boss finally moved on. I realize I hate that term, 'moved on.' I don't think anyone that loses the closet person or people to them ever moves on. They just learn to live with it.

The drive back to Heidi's apartment is quiet, other than the rain that starts pelting the car windows. He still holds my hand as he drives us in silence. When he walks me to the door I see him struggling again with how to tell me good-bye, like when he wasn't sure if he should hug me.

I want so badly for him to kiss me, but if he does I know we are both just going to start 'ugly crying' again. He hugs me like a bear, the pressure of it comforting to my core.

"Shelly…" His whisper like a breeze against my skin.

Breathlessly I plead with him, "Please kiss me."

I look up at Connor, my whole body shaking. Standing on my tiptoes, I reach for him as he bends down to meet me. Even with both of us adjusting, there's still this adorable height difference that makes my soul tingle.

His lips meet mine with a gentleness that makes my knees weak. It's not the desperate, heated kiss from our scene earlier - this is something else entirely. Something real. His beard tickles my chin as he deepens the kiss slightly, and I feel his hand cup my face with such tenderness it makes my chest ache.

For several perfect seconds, the world narrows down to

just this - the soft press of his lips, the warmth of his palm against my cheek, the steady beating of his heart under my hand that's somehow found its way to his chest.

When we finally part, I brace myself for another emotional overflow, but surprisingly, the tears don't come. Instead, there's this warm certainty settling in my bones, like puzzle pieces clicking into place.

"Goodnight, Shelly," he whispers, his thumb brushing my cheek one last time.

"Goodnight, Connor," I manage to reply, my voice steadier than I expect.

I slip inside and close the door, leaning back against it as my legs threaten to give out. And just like that, I know - with a clarity that should probably terrify me but instead feels like the comfort of a warm blanket - I'm in love with Connor Ebin.

Chapter 23: Systems Always Fail

Shelly

I'M SITTING CROSS-LEGGED ON Heidi's couch, sipping my caramel macchiato and trying not to think about how Connor's been secretly taking care of me even before we really knew each other. The warmth from the coffee cup spreads through my fingers as I double-check all my software installations one last time.

"He what?" I'd asked Jenny this morning, nearly dropping my coffee when she told me about Connor's standing order to cover my tab.

"Oh yeah, that first night you guys sat in the alcove over there," Jenny had said with a knowing smile. "Right after you left."

I touch my lips, still feeling the ghost of last night's kiss, and try to focus on my screen. The Excel tutorials I've been binging have my head spinning with formulas and tables, but at least I feel somewhat prepared for my first official day with Flex Data Flight Solutions, 'We make your data take flight.' I'm still not entirely sure how that conveys the logging of information onto a server.

My new phone buzzes - still weird having one of those - and I see a good luck text from Connor. My stomach does that flippy thing it's been doing every time I see or hear from him. It would be annoying if I didn't admit my feelings for him to myself last night. I type and delete about five responses before settling on a simple "Thank you." With a heart emoji. Before last night I would have agonized about that heart and hitting send for hours, maybe days.

The clock on my laptop shows 7:45 AM. Fifteen minutes until I need to log on for my first day. I take another sip of the macchiato, wondering if Connor remembered it was my favorite or if Jenny just makes really good guesses. Still no word from Heidi, but I'm trying not to spiral about that right now. One crisis at a time and I can't afford to mess up anything on my first day.

I close my eyes and take a deep breath, centering myself. New job. New phone. New... whatever this is with Connor. It's more hope than I've had in years, and for once, I'm not waiting for the other shoe to drop.

I am a few hours into my work when I peek at the productivity clock that Flex Data Flight Solutions had built into the software. Sitting in the upper left corner of my screen its tells me that I'm at 247% of expected output for minutes clocked. The data entry is mind-numbingly simple, just transferring information from scanned physical copies to different spreadsheets while occasionally checking for specific keywords and tags that tell me they need to go into two different folders. My Excel tutorials were definitely overkill for this.

My fingers tap rhythmically on the keyboard as I think back to moderating for Eldritch Magic's stream. That had been exciting - watching chat fly by, catching trolls, engaging with viewers who were genuinely passionate about gaming. Wondering if Connor peaking at me through my pod's window had made the whole experience more engaging. Though I'm pretty sure he thought I hadn't noticed him checking on me.

I glance at the clock again - only 11:30 AM. The morning has crawled by like a snail on sedatives. I've already completed what should have been a full day's work, according to the orientation materials. Part of me wonders if there's something wrong with their metrics, but another part knows this just isn't challenging. I begin to wonder if I am some sort of computer savant.

Opening another batch of data, I let my mind drift to yesterday's mo-cap session. Now that was interesting work. Challenging. Terrifying. Exhilarating. Even if it did end with me practically flooding the green room while trying not to die of embarrassment. More than just my cheeks flush at the memory.

The monotonous clicking of my keyboard brings me back to reality. At least this job is steady income, even if it's about as stimulating as watching paint dry in slow motion. I pull up another spreadsheet and sigh. Four more hours to go.

The landline's shrill ring barely registers through my data entry trance. My fingers keep moving across the keyboard, muscle memory taking over as I mechanically input numbers and dates. The answering machine clicks on after four rings, and I'm vaguely aware of Heidi's cheerful outgoing message playing in the background.

"This message is for Michelle Lockhart. This is Assistant District Attorney Caroline Weber with the King County Prosecutor's Office, and I'm calling regarding-"

My heart stops. I lunge for the phone, nearly knocking over my laptop in the process. Oh god, Heidi. Please don't be dead in a ditch somewhere.

"Hello?" I interrupt, my voice cracking. "This is Michelle Lockhart."

My hand trembles as I grip the receiver, and I can feel my pulse thundering in my ears. The productivity clock on my screen begins to slow to a halt, completely oblivious to how my world might be about to shatter. Again.

My knees give out and I sink into Heidi's plush armchair, the phone pressed tight against my ear as the ADA's words wash over me like ice water.

"I'm sorry, what?" I manage to whisper, though I heard her perfectly the first time. Cashless sympathy bond. Misdemeanor. Minor injuries. The words bounce around my skull like pinballs, each one striking a new nerve.

"The judge felt that since there was no... penetration," ADA Weber's voice softens slightly on that word, "and your physical injuries were classified as minor, the assault charge would be reduced. I want to be clear - I fought for stronger charges, but-"

"He's out?" My voice sounds strange to my own ears, higher and thinner than usual. "Right now?"

"Yes. I wanted you to be aware so you can take appropriate precautions. If you see him or he attempts to contact you in any way, call 911 immediately."

I nod numbly, then realize she can't see me. "Okay," I mumble.

The call ends with more legal terminology and promises to keep me updated, but I'm barely listening. My eyes dart to the windows, suddenly aware of how exposed I feel. The productivity clock on my screen continues its meaningless count backward as my world tilts sideways.

I should call Connor. Or Ashlyn. Someone. Anyone. But my fingers won't move, and my throat feels too tight to speak. Instead, I sit frozen in Heidi's chair, staring at nothing, as the reality sinks in that the system has failed me. Again.

Minor injuries. I look down at my hands, remembering how they scraped against the concrete when Bertrand pushed me down. How my shoulder ached for days from him yanking my arm. The nightmares that still wake me up in cold sweats.

Minor injuries.

I can't stop moving. My feet trace endless circles through Heidi's apartment as my hands shake with a cocktail of fear and rage that makes me want to scream or throw things or both. I instinctively grab a kitchen knife. It feels both comforting and terrifying in my sweaty grip. It's one of those fancy chef's knives with the heavy handle - the kind that could do some real damage.

I'll kill him. If I see him I'll fucking kill him.

I push open Heidi's bedroom door, needing more space to move around. The knife feels awkward now, out of place.

I set it down on the small table by her door, trying not to notice how bizarre it looks next to her collection of colorful sex toys. Any other time I'd probably laugh at the absurd juxtaposition.

My hands are trembling so bad I can barely unlock my phone. I hit Connor's number and press the phone to my ear, my heart hammering against my ribs.

"Connor?" My voice comes out high and tight. "I'm sorry, I know you're probably busy, but Bertrand's out. They let him out. The ADA just called and said something about cashless bond and minor injuries and-" The words tumble out in a panicked rush. "I'm sorry, I shouldn't ask you to come over, I just-"

Connor cuts me off, his voice firm but gentle. "I'm already walking out of my apartment. I'll be there in twenty minutes, okay? Just stay on the phone with me."

The steel in his voice makes some of the tension leak out of my shoulders. I sink down onto the edge of Heidi's bed, clutching the phone like a lifeline.

Chapter 24: Reach For Me

Connor

THE SPEEDOMETER EDGES PAST sixty-five in a forty mile per hour zone, but I couldn't give less of a shit right now. My knuckles are white against the steering wheel as I weave through traffic.

"Fucking cashless bail," I mutter in my own head, flicking my turn signal and cutting across two lanes. Some asshole in a Prius honks at me. I ignore him. On the other end of the phone Shelly is near tears and saying she knows she's being irrational, Bertrand doesn't know where she lives and he can't find her. I tell her to just keep talking to me and stay calm.

The image of Shelly's terrified face when I ran back to her that night flashes before my eyes, and my jaw clenches so hard it hurts. The satisfying crunch his nose made under my fist wasn't enough punishment. Not nearly enough.

As I pull into Heidi's apartment complex I hang up the call, tires squealing slightly as I take the corner. The security gate is open - thank fuck - and I barely remember to put the car in park before I'm out and running to the elevator. The elevator is taking too long so I bolt up the stairwell. My shoes make a scrapping sound like I'm running on trail gravel with the amount of friction I'm creating on the concrete stairs.

My hand is already raised to knock when I hear sobbing through the door. That sound - Christ, it's like a knife in my chest. It reminds me too much of Des after her nightmares, of Liv when we lost the first pregnancy.

"Shelly?" I call out, keeping my voice gentle despite the adrenaline still coursing through me. "It's Connor. I'm here."

The crying stops abruptly, followed by the sound of rapid footsteps from inside.

Its only then that I notice three men at the end of the hallway. Like an animal, the instinct in my brain screams to me that the situation isn't right. The men aren't going into or out of an apartment. They're just standing there trying to look like they aren't paying any attention in my direction. I silently curse myself for being in such a hurry that I didn't pay attention to my surroundings.

The door flies open, and I catch a glimpse of Shelly's tear-streaked face before movement in my peripheral vision kicks my instincts into overdrive. The three men from the hallway are charging.

"Lock the door!" Without enough time to enter and close the door from the inside, I pull the door closed and whirl to face the incoming threat. "Call 911!"

Two bodies hit me like linebackers, driving me back from the door. My brown belt training kicks in - I manage to keep my feet, sprawling to avoid being taken down completely. One guy's wearing a leather jacket that my fingers slip right off of. The other has a grip on my shirt, fabric ripping.

A sickening crack and Shelly's scream pierce the air as the third attacker kicks in the door. My heart stops - but I can't get to her. Not yet. These fuckers have made sure of that.

I drive an elbow into Leather Jacket's temple, and he staggers. But his buddy uses the moment to hook my leg. I'm going down, but I make sure to drag him with me. We hit the hallway floor hard enough to knock the wind from both of us.

The sound of breaking glass comes from inside the apartment. Shelly screams again.

I roar with a primal growl, thrashing against the weight of both men trying to pin me. One of them gets a solid punch to my ribs and then a shot at the back of my head as I shift my weight and roll to get up. The strike makes my vision blur. But all I can think about is Shelly alone in there with the third guy.

I buck hard, managing to create enough space to slam my head back into someone's nose. There's a satisfying wet crack and a howl of pain. But the other one still has me locked down, and I can hear things being knocked over inside the apartment.

I drive my elbow into the guy's throat, feeling his windpipe compress under the pressure. His eyes go wide as he starts making desperate wheezing sounds. One problem down.

The burning sensation hits before I register what's happened. My back erupts in white-hot agony, and suddenly breathing becomes a monumental task. The metallic scent of blood fills my nostrils - my blood.

Survival drives me onward. I push away, rolling to my feet despite the fire spreading through my torso. The knife-wielding bastard slashes at me again, but adrenaline makes everything crystal clear, like I'm watching in slow motion.

I catch his wrist mid-swing. The momentum carries through as I yank down hard, then wrench his arm backward. He loses balance, toppling forward onto his stomach and dropping the knife that goes sliding several feet down the hallway. Without hesitation, I drop my knee into his back, securing his arm behind him.

One sharp upward wrench and the satisfying series of pops tells me his shoulder just went to shit. His scream echoes through the hallway, but I barely hear it over the pounding in my head and the wheezing in my breathing.

Without fully thinking anything through, my drive to get to Shelly overriding everything, I turn and run into the apartment. I curse myself for leaving the knife where it fell from the prick's hand.

Shelly

I recoil quickly from the door, narrowly missing what would have flung me to the floor. A stout man, nearly Connor's size, barrels into the apartment and grabs me by the shirt collar. Fear of what happened to me the other night sends my fists into the man's face frantically.

My head snaps back as his own connects with my jaw. The world spins, and I taste copper in my mouth. Through the ringing in my ears, I hear grunting and thumping from the hallway. Connor. Please be okay.

He pulls a gun from his waistband. "Where the fuck is Heidi?" The stout man's breath reeks of cigarettes as he screams in my face, his meaty fingers twisting my shirt.

"I don't know!" My voice cracks. "She left a few days ago, just said she was going on a trip with a client. Please!"

The man's face contorts with rage. "That bitch!" He slams me against the wall, and stars dance across my vision. "She took our coke, didn't she? Ran off with that piece of shit boyfriend?"

My mind flashes to the baggie I found in her drawer. Oh god. Oh god. This is what that was about.

"I didn't even know she had a boyfriend, I swear I don't—" The words die in my throat as cold metal presses against my temple. The gun's barrel trembles slightly against my skin, and I can't stop the sob that escapes me.

Tears blur my vision as I think of Connor fighting outside. I can still hear the struggle, but it sounds far away now, like I'm underwater. The pressure of the gun barrel becomes my whole world.

"Please," I whisper. "I really don't know where she is."

"Wrong answer," he snarls, and I hear the click of the safety being released.

The man's fingers dig into my shirt as he drags me into Heidi's room, my feet stumbling to keep up. The gun never wavers from my direction, and my heart feels like it might explode from my chest.

"Where are the fucking bricks?" he screams, yanking me around like a rag doll. "Tell me where that bitch kept them!"

"I don't know!" My voice comes out high and desperate. "I just moved in, I barely know her!"

He shoves me hard, and I fall backward, my hip connecting painfully with the floor near the foot of Heidi's bed. The gun stays trained on me while he tears through her closet, throwing clothes and shoes everywhere.

Movement at the doorway catches my eye, and relief floods through me as I spot Connor. He's pressed against the wall just outside the frame, careful to stay hidden. His phone sits on the floor near his feet, screen glowing with an active call. My mind races – he must have dialed 911.

The man's back is to the door as he continues ransacking the closet, and while he isn't looking in my direction his gun remains steady, pointed right at my chest. Connor's eyes lock with mine, and I can see him assessing the situation, his jaw tight with tension.

"Wait," I say, trying to keep my voice from shaking. "H eidi... she always told me to stay away from her bed. Like, really insisted on it. Maybe..." I swallow hard. "Maybe she hid whatever you're looking for under there?"

The man's eyes narrow at me, considering my words. "If

you're lying..." He leaves the threat hanging as he moves toward the bed, gun still trained in my direction.

My heart pounds so hard I can barely hear anything else. I watch as he crouches down, reaching beneath the bed frame with his free hand. That's when Connor strikes.

It happens so fast – Connor's arms wrapping around the man's gun hand, their bodies crash to the floor. I should move. I need to move. But my legs won't work, like they're cemented to the spot.

"Run!" Connor's voice cracks through the air like a whip, but I'm frozen, watching them struggle.

The gunshot is deafening in the small room. My ears ring as I watch red bloom across Connor's shirt, spreading like spilled wine. Oh god. No. Please no.

Connor goes slack for a moment, his body sagging against the intruder, and another shot tears through the air. The sound pierces my skull like a physical thing, making my stomach lurch. But instead of falling, Connor seems to surge back to life, his muscles bunching beneath his blood-soaked shirt as he wrestles with renewed desperation. The way he moves reminds me of a wounded animal - all raw instinct and fury. I can see his jaw clenched tight, the tendons in his neck straining as he fights.

Through my terror-fogged brain, I spot the kitchen knife I'd left on Heidi's side table earlier. My fingers close around the handle just as the man starts to use Connor's weakening state of blood loss to roll on top of him. The carpet around them is beginning to look like someone spilled red paint.

I don't think. I just move.

The knife plunges into the man's back. He whirls around with shocking speed, and pain explodes through my head as the gun slams into my my temple. The world spins as I crash into the wall.

Through blurring vision, I see Connor grapple the bastard in a better hold and wrench the gun away. Three shots ring out in rapid succession. Two to the chest and the man goes limp. Connor nearly falls over but then steadies himself and presses the barrel to the man's head. Another shot point blank to his head.

Connor's eyes find mine, his hand reaching out. Then he crumples to the floor, motionless.

"Connor?" My voice sounds far away as I crawl toward him, reaching for his outstretched hand. Everything starts to fade, darkness creeping in at the edges of my vision until there's nothing left at all. I never told him.

Chapter 25: Tough Girl, Clever Girl

Shelly

THE STEADY BEEP OF monitors pulls me from darkness. My head throbs like someone's using it for drum practice, and my mouth feels stuffed with cotton. Antiseptic smell hits my nose – hospital. Right.

Ashlyn sits beside my bed, mascara tracking down her cheeks. The sight of her tears makes my stomach clench as fragments of memory flash through my mind: The ER, bright lights stabbing my eyes, voices telling me to stay awake. So many people rushing around.

Then I remember – Connor's blood-soaked shirt, his body going limp, reaching for his hand as everything went dark. The memory of them wheeling his motionless body out of the ER hits me like a physical blow. They were yelling something about the OR, moving so fast I could barely track them through my own swimming vision.

His face had been so pale, almost gray, and his usually perfect salt-and-pepper beard was matted with dark crimson. The whole time, I kept thinking how wrong it looked – Connor's always so put together, so in control. Not like this. Never like this. I remember fighting to get out of the bed and trying to follow them, my legs giving out as a nurse caught me, voices floating around my head about shock and blood pressure.

"Connor?" My voice comes out as a croak. When Ashlyn just continues crying, panic claws up my throat. "Where is he? Please, is he alive?"

The monitors start beeping faster as my heart rate spikes. I try to sit up but everything spins, making me fall back against the pillows.

"Ashlyn, please," I beg, my own tears starting to fall. "I need to know if he's okay. Tell me he's alive."

The room tilts as I try to push myself up again. My head pounds with each heartbeat, and the damn lights above make everything too sharp, too harsh.

Ashlyn finally notices I'm awake and rushes to my side, her hands gentle as she tries to keep me from getting up. "Shelly, honey, you need to stay still. You have a very bad concussion."

"Connor," I croak again, gripping her arm. "Please, just tell me if he's okay."

She wipes at her face, smearing what's left of her makeup. "He's in the ICU. They took him into surgery as soon as he arrived, but..." She swallows hard. "That's all they'll tell us. Manu and I have been trying to get more information, but since we're not family..."

The words hit me like another blow. Not family. Just like

always, just like every other time in my life, being alone means being shut out. But this time it's different – this time it's Connor.

"I have to see him." I start pulling at the IV in my arm. "Now. I need to see him right now."

"Shelly, stop-"

"No, you don't understand." My voice breaks as tears start falling faster. "I have to tell him. He needs to know that I love him. He can't..." A sob catches in my throat. "He can't leave without knowing that. Please, Ashlyn. Please help me see him."

Ashlyn's arms wrap around me as we both break down. Within seconds I have her blouse covered in snot and tears. I'm pawing at her like a kitten trying not to fall to the ground after climbing too high.

"He knows, sweetie," she whispers, stroking my hair. "Trust me, Connor knows."

I shake my head against her shoulder. "Not the same. I need to tell him myself. I need him to hear it from me."

The monitors keep their steady rhythm, mocking me with each beep. How can machines be so calm when everything's falling apart?

A soft knock draws our attention. Manu stands in the door-way, his usually pristine polo wrinkled and his hair a mess from lack of sleep and running his hands through it. The look on his face makes my heart sink.

"Still nothing," he says, his voice rough. "They won't tell me shit. I've tried everything, even bribery."

"Please keep trying," I beg. "There has to be some way-"

"I will," he cuts me off gently. "I promise."

Time crawls by each hellish minute feeling like thirty. Every footstep in the hallway makes me tense, hoping for news. Instead, I see a familiar face – Sergeant Wesley from last week's case with Bertrand. She looks different in plain clothes instead of her uniform.

"Hello again, Ms. Lockhart," she says, pulling out a small notebook. "I know this isn't the best timing, but I need to get as much information I can from you about what happened at the apartment while it's still fresh. Two of the men were deceased when we arrived on scene but a third got away. We have surveillance footage that shows him fleeing the apartments but we don't have any idea where to look. We're trying to track him with footage from the surrounding area. But anything else you could tell us might be helpful in knowing where he is going or who he might reach out to."

My fingers twist in the hospital blanket. The last thing I want to do is relive those moments, but if it helps catch those men, helps protect Connor...

"Okay," I whisper. "Where should I start?"

"The man that got away, can you give me any descriptive details about him? Let's start from there."

"I didn't get a look at the men in the hallway. It all happened so fast. Connor shut the door before I could see them…I didn't lock the door in time. He yelled for me to but I wasn't fast enough." My voice shakes and Ashlyn puts her hand on my leg to try and calm me. I take a deep breath. "Maybe six feet tall. A little fat? I'm not sure."

Sergeant Wesley nods, clearly wishing I could tell her

more. "Okay, let's move on to everything that happened. Start from the door."

I force myself to continue, detailing everything I can remember about their appearances, their voices, how they moved and the attack that ensued. Ashlyn sits on the side of my bed and grips my arm tight with a thankful nod when I mention stabbing the one that shot Connor. Then I start to backtrack to the things with Heidi that I found concerning. I hesitate briefly before mentioning the cocaine I found in her drawer.

"I should have said something sooner," I admit, twisting the blanket between my fingers. "Maybe if I had..."

Sergeant Wesley makes notes, her face neutral. "This helps establish the drug connection we were assuming. The two bodies we identified have gang ties. We'll look into Ms. Mason's recent activities."

As she closes her notebook, panic grips me. "Wait! Please – can you tell me anything about Connor?"

She pauses, sympathy crossing her features. "I can only say he's in the ICU, critical but stable. All these damn privacy laws prevent me from sharing more until he can authorize visitors himself. I honestly shouldn't be telling you what I already have."

"What if..." My heart races. "What if I was his girlfriend? Would that help?"

She shakes her head. "Not right now. Only spouse or immediate family."

The monitors beep faster as frustration and fear overwhelm me. My pulse pounds in my ears, matching the frantic rhythm of the medical equipment. "This is ridiculous!" I snap, tears threatening again. My hands clench into fists at my sides as desperation claws through my chest. "What about – what if I was his daughter?" My voice cracks on the last word, thinking of Desiree and apologizing to her as I say it. "Would that work?"

The words come out desperate and angry. I know it's absurd, but with our age difference and after what happened at the mall with that store clerk... But I'm grasping at anything that might get me to his side.

Sergeant Wesley's dark eyes soften as she looks at me. I can see the conflict playing across her features – she wants to help, but there are rules. There are always rules.

"That's quite clever," she says gently. "And I appreciate how desperately you want to see him but..."

Ashlyn steps forward, her heels clicking on the linoleum floor. "I can vouch for her. If it helps take some of the legal pressure off you, Sergeant." Her voice carries that professional authority she uses in meetings, but there's an edge of pleading underneath as she wipes more tears away. "If we both swear by it then surely you can't get in any trouble if they find out it's not true."

I hold my breath as Sergeant Wesley considers this, her fingers tapping thoughtfully against her notebook. For a moment, hope flutters in my chest – maybe this ridiculous plan will actually work. Maybe I'll get to see him.

But then she shakes her head, and that hope crashes down around me. "You're a tough and resourceful woman, Michelle," she says, using my first name for the first time. "I'll see what I can do, but I make no guarantees."

I nod at Sergeant Wesley, grateful for even that small promise to try. As she leaves, the weight of everything crashes over me again. Ashlyn perches on the edge of my hospital bed, and I practically collapse into her arms as fresh tears start falling.

"I can't lose him," I choke out between sobs. "Not when I just found him."

Ashlyn's arms tighten around me as she starts crying too. Her designer blouse is probably ruined between our combined tears and my hospital-grade snot. "Connor's strong," she manages through her own tears. "He's the most stubborn man I've ever met. If anyone can..."

I press my face into her shoulder, trying to muffle the ugly crying sounds I'm making. It's strange – a couple of weeks ago I was alone on the streets, and now I'm crying in the arms of a woman I barely know, both of us terrified of losing the same person. The same wonderful, ridiculous man who has been a beacon of love in both our lives.

"He saved me," I whisper. "From Bertrand, from being homeless, from being alone. And now he might die because I got pulled into Heidi's mess."

"Stop that," Ashlyn says firmly, though her voice is still thick with tears. "Connor made his own choices. He chose to help you because that's who he is. That's why Liv fell for him. That's why we all love him."

The mention of Olivia makes me cry harder. What would she think of all this? Of me? Of her husband getting shot trying to protect some homeless girl who's young enough to be one of their own daughters?

Ashlyn rocks me gently, like I'm a child. No, a friend - a real friend. I just want to know he's okay. I just want to see those kind eyes again, hear that gentle voice, feel safe in his presence one more time.

"Please," I whisper, though I'm not sure who I'm talking to – some god, Olivia's spirit, the universe itself. "Please let him be okay."

Chapter 26: Not Until You're Whole Again

⬥

Connor

EVERYTHING FEELS LIKE IT'S underwater. The steady beep of machines filters through something around my head, distant and muffled. My throat burns around the breathing tube - an unwelcome intrusion that makes me want to gag, but I can't even manage that.

Shelly.

Her name pulses through my mind with each heartbeat. I need to know if she's okay. The call button has to be right there, probably just inches from my hand, but my body won't respond. My eyelids are lead weights, refusing to lift more than flickering glimpses of the dim light cast by what I assume are a plethora of machines keeping me alive.

Images flash behind my closed eyes: Three men in the hallway. The door. Shelly's terrified face as that bastard pushed into the apartment. The cold steel of the knife stabbing into my back, followed by the white-hot punch of bullets tearing through me. Shelly lunging to my aid with a kitchen knife, fierce and desperate. The gun in my hand, one final shot...

Shelly.

The sedatives pull me under again, but her name stays with me, a prayer I can't voice around the tube forcing air into my lungs. I drift in and out, catching fragments of hushed voices and more damned beeping. Each time I surface, I try to move, to signal someone, anyone. But my body remains frustratingly still, weighted down by drugs and trauma.

Shelly.

Please let her be alive. Please let her be safe. The thought circles endlessly as consciousness slips away again. I promised her I'd protect her. After everything she's been through, she trusted me to keep her safe. And now I'm trapped here, unable to even ask if she survived.

The darkness pulls me under once more, but her name follows me down.

Shelly...

I feel suddenly warm. I'm still in this prison of a bed, but I have use of my arms and there's no tube in my throat anymore. My eyes are still sluggish and my mouth still dry but there is a soft light in the room and a cloudy haze at the edges of my vision. The warmth explodes when I see them enter my room.

My heart monitor spikes as they enter, ethereal and solid all at once. Liv's auburn hair catches the dim light like a halo, and Des... god, Des looks exactly as she did that last morning, freckles dancing across her nose as she grins and skips toward my bed.

I try to lift myself up, but my legs won't move beneath the hospital sheets. My mouth opens but no sound emerges - whether from emotion or injury, I'm not sure. Tears blur my vision as Des climbs onto the bed with the casual grace only an eight-year-old can manage, tucking herself under my arm like she used to during our weekend movie marathons.

Liv approaches with that smile that always made my knees weak, the one that says she knows exactly what I'm thinking. She leans down, and I feel the ghost of her lips against mine - not quite solid, not quite air. The scent of her favorite lavender shampoo washes over me, and for a moment I'm home again, all those years ago. I want to fall apart but I can't even manage that.

She settles onto the edge of the bed, facing me, her hand hovering just above mine. Des snuggles closer, and I swear I can feel the warmth of her small body against my side. The familiarity of it breaks something in me, and the tears flow freely now.

They're here. They're actually here. Whether this is a dream, a hallucination, or something else entirely, I don't care. My girls are here with me, and for the first time since losing them, the hole in my chest is gone. Completely.

Liv's eyes meet mine with that penetrating gaze she always used when I was being particularly stubborn about something. "Why have you been torturing the man I love so much?"

I become keenly aware that while I am speaking to them my mouth is not moving.

I should have been there. If I hadn't stayed late at the office that night, you wouldn't have had to pick up Des from Knuck-ledraggers. It should have been me driving.

Des squeezes closer to my side, her small hand finding mine. The guilt crashes over me in waves - familiar, crushing waves that have been drowning me for years. *I can't forgive myself... if I try and fully move on... I'm afraid I'll lose what little I have left of you both.*

"Oh, Connor." Liv's voice carries that gentle exasperation she reserved for when I was being ridiculous. "You can't blame yourself for what happened. That truck driver had a stroke - it wasn't anyone's fault." Her almost-solid hand hovers over my cheek. "But this isn't living, my love. Locking yourself away from the world, from the possibility of new love... that's not what we want for you."

*I miss you both so much it physically hurts. Some days I think I might just…*The monitor beeps faster as emotion tightens my chest. *Every single day…*

"We know," Liv says softly. "But punishing yourself won't bring us back. And it's killing us to watch you suffer like this."

Des nods against my shoulder, her voice small but clear. "We want you to be happy again, Daddy. I don't like when you cry. It hurts."

I feel like my body is beginning to convulse, racking with a sob that can't escape my paralyzed body.

I am trying to… I don't want to say the words 'move on.' They feel wrong, so very wrong. *I'm terrified I'll lose a piece of the love I have for you both. That somehow I'll forget parts of you both. I don't want that. It's why I'm holding myself…*

I look down at my lap feeling shame wash over me.

"Why is your solution to holding onto us to slowly destroy the soul of the man we love?" My throat constricts at Liv's words, the truth of them hitting harder than those bullets ever could. She leans closer, and I swear I can feel her breath against my cheek. "Do you think we want to watch your spirit decay? The husband and father we love becoming a hollow shell?"

I want to look away, but I can't. Not from those piercing green eyes that always saw straight through my bullshit. The monitor beside me picks up speed, matching the rapid beating of my heart and I can hear frantic foot falls in the room, but I see nothing but my girls.

Des shifts against my side and sits on her knees, her small voice cutting through the tension. "I think Shelly's nice, Daddy. She makes you smile like Mommy used to."

The simple observation from my little girl hits me like a kick below the belt Because she's right - Shelly does make me smile. Really smile, not the practiced CEO version I've perfected over the years for people that I have to play nice with.

Liv's expression softens, and she places her almost-there hand over my heart. "Things are different now, my love. I'm not there with you anymore, and that's okay. I'm willing to share a piece of your heart with someone else." Her voice catches slightly. "But I can't bear watching you kill your soul with grief any longer. I won't."

The truth of her words settles into my bones. All these years, I've been so focused on holding onto them that I've been letting the best parts of myself - the parts they loved most - slowly die. And they've had to watch it happen, powerless to stop me.

I'm sorry, I manage to think through the tightness in my chest. *I'm so sorry and now I think it's too late. I think I'm dying. But…then I can be with my girls.*

Des shakes her head vigorously, her braided hair swaying. "No, Daddy. You have to get better first. You have to be whole again before you can come back to us."

The familiar steel enters Liv's voice - the tone that always meant the discussion was over. "My husband never gave up on anything in his life until we died. I will not allow you to come back to us until you've healed that wonderful soul." I swear I feel her hand press against my chest this time. "You need her to become who you were before. And that sweet, kind, fierce young woman needs you. "

I miss you both so damn much. The thought comes unbidden, raw and honest.

"We miss you too, Connor," Liv whispers. "But we've been trying to show you the way forward."

Suddenly everything clicks into place, hitting me with the force of revelation. Shelly sitting in Liv's usual seat at Books and Beans when we first met. "Hot Blooded" playing on the radio - the song Liv always demanded we blast with the windows down - which let me hear Shelly's cry for help. The tarot cards falling just so. My apartment building finally fixing the dent in the gym wall Liv made with an errant slam ball. Even my dream, where Liv's face morphed into Shelly's…

Liv's eyes sparkle with that familiar mischief. "Oh no, I

didn't do the dream face-switch thing. That was all you, dear." She winks. "Though I approve of your subconscious's choice. My hips are nicer though." She teasing me, even now.

"When you come back to us you have to read it to me again." My little Desiree holds up the book I used to read her at least three times a week, 'Mommy Fox and Tiny Fox Adventures.' It's a series of short stories with a mommy and baby fox in the woods of a fairy tale land. It's the reason for the fox tattoo on my arm. Des in particular had loved when I got it done. She liked to trace it with her fingers, just like she was doing now.

Des leans over, her small arms wrapping around my neck as she places a kiss on my cheek. The sensation is solid this time. "I love you, Daddy," she whispers, and my heart constricts at the sound of those words I've missed so desperately.

Liv stands, graceful as ever, and leans down to press her lips against mine. The ghost of our last kiss mingles with this one, and I feel tears sliding down my cheeks. Her hand presses against my chest, and sudden warmth blooms beneath my sternum, spreading outward like sunlight breaking through storm clouds.

In the distance I hear the ever present beeping machines calm their song.

"Take care of her, Connor," Liv says softly. "And please, for me, for us, let her take care of you." Her eyes shine with unshed tears and that fierce love I remember so well. "Let Shelly help make you whole again."

They begin to fade, Des's small hand waving goodbye as

Liv gives me one last knowing smile. The warmth in my chest pulses once, strong and sure, and then darkness claims me once more.

The fog is lighter now, more like morning mist than the thick soup of earlier. I feel a gentle pressure around my right hand, warm and real in a way my visit with Liv and Des wasn't. My eyelids cooperate this time, lifting enough to make out the figure beside my bed.

Shelly.

She's alive. She's alive! She's in a wheelchair, looking pale and bruised but beautifully, wonderfully alive. Her hand clasps mine, and I want to squeeze back but my muscles won't quite obey my pleas yet. The sight of her breaks down what is left of the walls I've built. Walls she has been chipping away at and that Liv and Des gave me permission tear down.

I've been such a fool. All this time spent building walls, rationalizing away what I feel for her as friendship or protective instinct or misplaced grief. But seeing her here, the moisture in her eyes and her face an absolute mess but still so damn beautiful, I can't deny it anymore. I don't want to.

I'm in love with her.

The realization doesn't come with any guilt. My wife and daughter exonerated me of that crime. Instead, I feel the warmth from my dream-visit spread through my chest again. Liv was right - I've been slowly killing myself with grief, and in doing so, I've been dishonoring everything she and Des loved about me.

I want to tell Shelly everything. How she makes me feel alive again. How her smile lights up rooms I thought would stay dark forever. How watching her open up fills me with more joy than I've felt in years. How seeing her fight through her own trauma with such grace inspires me to be better, to be whole again.

But the breathing tube is still in place, and my body isn't quite ready to cooperate. So I focus all my energy on my hand, willing my fingers to move, to give her the smallest squeeze to let her know I'm here. To let her know everything has changed.

Chapter 27: Heart Tracing

Shelly

T HE NURSE WHEELS ME into Connor's room, following Sergeant Wesley's lead. I caught their shared glance, the silent understanding passing between them about my supposed relation to Connor. Right now, I don't care about the lie - I just need to see him.

My breath catches in my throat as we enter. The steady beeping of monitors fills the sterile air, but it's the tubes - so many tubes and drains - that make my stomach lurch. Two snake from his chest, three more from his abdomen, another down his throat, and IV lines everywhere. Each one represents how close I came to losing him and how likely that I might still.

The nurse starts explaining each machine in a gentle, practiced voice. "This one monitors his heart rate, this maintains his breathing..." But her words blur together as I stare at Connor's still form, watching his chest rise and fall with mechanical precision.

Sergeant Wesley pushes my wheelchair closer to the bed. My hands tremble as I reach for Connor's. His skin feels cool against mine, but there's still strength in those fingers that held mine while we walked at the mall, that guided me through motion capture scenes just yesterday and held me at the Books and Beans when his kindness made me cry.

Movement catches my eye - Connor's eyelids flutter, then slowly open. His gaze finds mine, clouded but present. His fingers tighten ever so slightly around my hand, and suddenly breathing becomes easier. He's here. He's still here.

The doctor's footsteps make me turn from Connor's face. He's younger than I expected, maybe early thirties, with scholarly eyes behind wire-rimmed glasses. His white coat is crisp, but there are coffee stains on his sleeve.

"I'm Dr. Martinez. And you are...?" He glances between me and Sergeant Wesley.

"I'm his daughter," I say, the lie coming easier now that I've practiced it in my head on the way in here, prepared to give an Oscar worthy performance if I had to. My fingers tighten around Connor's hand, seeking forgiveness for the deception.

Dr. Martinez nods, consulting his tablet. "Your father's injuries are severe. The stab wound in his back punctured one lung, and he took gunshot wounds to both his other lung and liver." He gestures to the various tubes. "These chest tubes are preventing blood from collecting in his lungs, and these drains here are removing excess fluid from his abdomen where we had to go in surgically to repair the damage."

My vision blurs as I process this. Connor got these injuries protecting me. The doctor continues, his voice gentle but clinical.

"He lost a significant amount of blood, but we've managed to stabilize his labs for now." He looks directly at me. "We're guardedly optimistic, but I need you to understand that with injuries this severe, things can turn quickly."

I nod, unable to speak past the lump in my throat. Connor's hand twitches in mine, and I look to see his eyes are open again, watching me. Even through the haze of sedation, I can see concern there - for me, of course. Even now, he's worried about me instead of himself.

"Could... could I have a moment alone with him?" My voice cracks as I look at Dr. Martinez, and Sergeant Wesley. They exchange glances before nodding, and the nurse follows them out, pulling the door closed behind her.

The steady beep of the heart monitor feels deafening in the sudden quiet, each electronic pulse marking another precious second he's still with me. I squeeze Connor's hand gently, feeling his calloused palms against mine, searching his face for any sign of recognition through the medically induced haze I know he must be in. His eyes, though glazed, still hold that familiar spark that makes my chest ache. "Can you understand me?" I whisper, my voice barely louder than the rhythmic monitoring equipment. He blinks twice, deliberately, and my heart skips. It's such a small gesture, but right now it means everything.

"I need to tell you," I start, trying to keep my voice steady. "And I know the timing is awful, and maybe this isn't fair, but..." The tears that have already been falling begin to pour forward like a burst damn no longer simply leaking. "I'm in love with you, Connor. I think I have been since that first night at Books and Beans when you pretended to know me just to help me. I know that sounds rushed and crazy, probably even childish. But I knew it for sure when you held me after the motion capture scenes and then I fully admitted it to myself when you kissed me good night." I'm sobbing so hard now I can barely breathe, and I try to swallow back the the panic that is threatening to follow. "Please fight. Please stay. I don't want to lose you. Not when I just found you. I want to make you smile and laugh. I want you to hold me. I want to try and heal what you think is broken inside you."

My tears are soaking my entire face now and I can feel snot and saliva starting to drip from how forceful I am crying. I lean forward, resting my face against his lap. The fabric of his hospital gown is scratchy against my wet cheeks, but I barely register the texture. I feel so stupid crying like this, certain that it would be better for him if I was strong right now. But the sobs keep coming, shaking my shoulders, and part of me wants to run away and hide from the pain. Then I feel him - his hand, trembling with effort, lifting to touch my cheek. My breath shudders at the contact. His fingers are cool against my skin and he pets me slowly, the way you might comfort a frightened animal. Then I feel him tap at my cheeks with his finger, gentle but deliberate, and I freeze all movement when he starts to trace something. I hold perfectly still, afraid that if I move, I'll miss whatever he's trying to tell me.

My breath catches as I realize what he's writing: 'I LUV U'

The tears come harder now, but they're different - relief

and joy mixing with the fear that still grips my chest.

I sob even harder as his other hand moves and he rests it over my head, running his fingers through my hair with very small movements. Each gentle stroke sends tingles down my spine, and I search for the scent of his beard oil but I can't smell it. The smell that has grown synonymous with the man I love is gone and I find it increases my fear of losing him. As though it is a portent to losing him.

But his touch calms me in a way only he has ever made me experience, melting away the years of a defensive fortress I've built around myself. I reach up to place my trembling hand on his chest, feeling his steady heartbeat beneath my palm. I keep whispering to him that I love him over and over again, my voice breaking with emotion each time, but I can't stop myself - it's like my mind can no longer keep inside the number of times I have felt it or wanted to say it and held it back.

I feel myself falling asleep in his lap and hear Dr. Martinez tell someone I can stay for a bit longer and that they are going to decrease Connor's sedation tomorrow. I smile and hope he will be awake enough to tell them Ashlyn and Manu can visit. They need to see their friend - family, whether related or not, they are his family. The steady beep of the monitors has become a comforting lullaby, and my fingers trace lazy patterns on Connor's arm where it rests beside me. I know they're all worried sick about him, especially Manu who's probably driving everyone crazy with his constant calls to check on Connor's status. Family isn't always about blood - it's about who stays by your side through the darkest moments, and these people have earned that title many times over for Connor.

Chapter 28: Story Time with Ashlyn

Shelly

TWO WEEKS. IT FEELS like both an eternity and a blink since that night. I'm curled up in Connor's hospital room, watching him sleep peacefully without all the tubes and wires that used to terrify me. My own discharge came quickly - a moderate concussion and some bruising - but these walls have become my second home since then. He had a few scary moments while getting to where he is at now. He ended up with a third chest tube. Dr Martinez said his other lung collapsed. A few days after that his blood pressure just mysteriously bottomed out and he ended up with even more IV lines and medications that might as well have been in Latin to my ears.

Ashlyn's guest room has been a godsend. She fusses over me like a mother hen, though I suspect it's partly to keep her mind off worrying about Connor. The headaches from the concussion lasted a week, each throb a reminder of that night, but they've finally subsided.

Sergeant Wesley's updates kept coming, each one more surreal than the last. Bertrand's body turned up behind some dumpster - heroin overdose. I have no shame in admitting that I celebrated that news. The third attacker who ran? Got himself killed in a shootout with police when they cornered him outside of Seattle. But the real kicker was about Heidi. LAX security caught her and some boyfriend I never knew existed trying to flee to Ecuador with $320,000. Non-extradition country, Sergeant Wesley explained. Turns out my former foster sister was deeper into the drug scene than I'd imagined.

My thoughts on Heidi are conflicted. On one hand she took me in and gave me a place to stay, a warm couch, food and safety. On the other hand her decision to run away with drug money got me assaulted and Connor nearly killed. I told Ashlyn that I hope I never see her again because I don't want to deal with the conflicting emotions of gratitude and rage I feel toward her.

I reach out and trace my fingers along Connor's arm, careful to avoid the healing wounds. The monitors still beep steadily, but they're more of a comfort now than a source of anxiety. The doctors say he's doing well, though they want to keep monitoring him a bit longer. It's strange - all those years of having no one, and now I find myself surrounded by people who care. Ashlyn, Manu, even Sergeant Wesley checking in regularly.

I watch Connor's chest rise and fall, no longer needing assistance from machines. Each breath feels like a gift. He has trouble sleeping and they are still giving him medication to help with that. Visiting hours are nearly over. Ashlyn went to get the valet to pull her car around and I told her I would be down in a few minutes. Connor and I haven't had much alone time and when we have I still pretend to be his daughter just to avoid any issues, mostly just to make sure I don't get Sergeant Wesley or any of Connor's nurses from the first few days into trouble for allowing me in before he could consent. I've still managed to steal a few kisses without anyone seeing and thinking there's a strange family dynamic they need to be worried about.

Satisfied that Connor is in a deep sleep now, I kiss his cheek and forehead while whispering to him that I love him and can't wait for him to be out of here. I peel myself away as quietly as possible to make sure I don't wake him and wave to his nurse at the desk.

I slide into Ashlyn's Tesla, still getting used to how quiet these things are. My phone buzzes against my hip and I fish it out, expecting another text from Manu about Connor's dinner preferences for when he's released. I asked him to give me some ideas because I wanted to make sure I took care of his food for at least a few days, until he could forcefully tell me I didn't need to take care of him.

Instead, it's an email from Flex Data Flight Solutions. I feel a pit in my stomach as I scan the first few lines. "Due to your extended absence... company policy... termination effective immediately."

"Well shit," I mutter, showing Ashlyn the screen. "Guess I'm officially unemployed."

To my surprise, she bursts out laughing. "Fuck that place,"

she says, pulling out of the hospital parking garage. "Their loss. Besides, we've got an open moderator position at Eldritch that I was waiting to offer you at just the right moment. Full benefits, better pay, and you already know half the team."

My heart skips. "Are you serious?"

"Dead serious. One of the girls left early for maternity leave and informed us she was going to stay home after the baby was born, so we have an open spot. You've already proven you can handle the work, and honestly? We need someone who actually gives a damn about gaming culture and Connor told me you have gotten sucked into it quite willingly. I also loved how focused you looked while you were doing it."

I knew he was watching me through that little window!

A few months ago, I would have refused the offer. Would have insisted on finding my own way, proving I could make it without help. But looking at Ashlyn's genuine smile, I realize something has shifted inside me. These people - Connor, Ashlyn, Manu - they're not trying to trap me or use me. They actually care and I need to start acting like I know that.

"I'd love that," I say, feeling a warmth spread through my chest. "Thank you."

"Perfect! We can head to the office tomorrow morning and get your paperwork started." Ashlyn grins. "Plus, you'll get to see Connor more once he's back at work."

I blush, remembering those stolen kisses in his hospital room. "That's just a bonus," I say, but I can't hide my smile.

The door to Ashlyn's apartment clicks shut behind us and I kick off my shoes, already feeling at home in this space after two weeks. My eyes drift, as they always have since I started staying here, to the family photo on the wall - Connor, Olivia, and little Desiree at what looks like a company picnic. The resemblance still catches me off guard sometimes. Same auburn hair, same angular features, even similar builds, although Olivia was fuller in the hips and breasts than I am.

The first time I saw the picture I was speechless. Had I not come to know the man Connor is I would have definitely thought he was searching for their ghosts within me. Thankfully I know just how genuine of a man he is. He would never disrespect me or their memory to hold on what he lost.

"Want some tea?" Ashlyn calls from the kitchen. "I got that orange blend you liked."

"Sure," I say, still studying the photo. Olivia's smile is radiant, genuine. The kind that reaches her eyes and makes them sparkle. Desiree has her mother's freckles, scattered across her nose and cheeks just like mine.

"You know," I say, keeping my tone light, "maybe Olivia was secretly my mother. Would explain the uncanny resemblance."

Ashlyn chokes on her drink, sputtering and coughing. "Oh god, no - absolutely not possible," she manages between coughs. "I knew Liv since college. Trust me, if she'd had a secret baby, I would've known. She couldn't keep a secret to save her life."

I can't help but laugh at her panicked expression. "Ashlyn, I'm kidding. Just trying to lighten the mood."

She visibly relaxes, though her eyes still look a bit wild. "Don't even joke about that. I mean, I know you've wondered if the resemblance was why..."

"I did at first," I admit. "But I know that's not why Connor helped me. He's just... genuinely kind. Even if I looked nothing like them, I think he still would have stepped in that night."

I fidget with my tea mug, the warmth seeping into my palms as I gather my courage. The question has been nagging at me since I moved in here.

"Ashlyn?" My voice comes out smaller than intended. "Does it... bother you that I'm staying here? I mean, considering everything with Connor?"

She looks up from her phone, brow furrowed. "Why would it bother me?"

"Because you were Olivia's best friend, and now I'm..." I trail off, realizing I don't know how to finish that sentence. "Actually, I don't even know what I am. Are Connor and I officially together? We haven't really had that conversation yet, what with him being in the hospital and everything."

Ashlyn sets her phone down and turns to face me fully. "First off, you're staying here because I want you to. Period. And as for you and Connor..." She pauses, choosing her words carefully. "I loved Olivia like a sister. Still do. But I also love Connor, and I've watched him slowly dying inside for years. Then you show up, and suddenly he's alive again. You think that bothers me?"

"But-"

"No buts." She reaches across the couch and grabs my hand. "Look, I know it might seem weird that Olivia's best friend is rooting for her husband to move on with someone else. But Liv would have wanted this. She would have kicked his ass for spending so long drowning in grief."

I squeeze her hand, feeling tears prick at the corners of my eyes. "Thank you. That means more than you know."

"Besides," she adds with a mischievous grin, "after that mo-cap session, I think it's pretty clear where you two stand."

I groan and bury my face in a throw pillow, my cheeks burning hot. "We are never speaking of that again!"

Ashlyn laughs and snorts. "I can't agree to that. It makes you turn a shade of red that I find very amusing."

I laugh at her teasing even though this particular teasing is indeed making my face turn that shade of red she apparently finds hilarious. My hand runs through my hair as I look into my tea cup. "I was afraid at first that you might just think I was a young girl with daddy issues looking for someone to take care of her."

Ashlyn snickers and then looks at me with a smirk, "Shelly, you definitely have daddy issues."

My mouth drops open in shock.

She rolls her eyes at me with a mocking sigh. "I don't mean it in a bad way, Shelly. You never had any semblance of stable parental figures. Anyone would have daddy issues after that. I just mean that you finally have someone in your life that loves you and is going to take care of you whether you want him to or not. Every girl should have that growing up. Someone that takes care of them and makes sure they feel protected and loved. Hell, I've got daddy issues. My bastard of a father left my mother and I when I was nine. I spent a lot of time seeking approval from older men. Only difference between us, Shelly, is that you aren't seeking anyone's approval. You are just being you."

My shock turns to understanding. When she puts it that way I makes more sense and doesn't feel weird.

"But you definitely have daddy issues." She glances at me side-eyed while sipping her tea. "But that's not any of my business." It reminds me of that meme that went around the internet for awhile.

I curl my legs under me on the couch, cradling the warm mug in my lap. The orange tea's aroma fills the space between us, and for a moment, I'm struck by how comfortable this feels. Like those TV shows where sisters hang out and talk about life.

"Hey Ashlyn?" I take a small sip of tea. "Would you... would you tell me about them? Liv and Des? Something happy or funny? I mean, only if you want to."

Ashlyn's face lights up, and she settles deeper into the couch. "Oh god, where do I even start? Okay, so there was this one time Liv tried to surprise Connor with homemade bread. She was amazing at baking, but for some reason, bread was her nemesis."

She laughs, shaking her head. "She forgot the yeast, and this dense brick of dough just sat there, refusing to rise. Des kept poking it, saying 'Mommy, I think it's dead.' But Liv was determined. She baked it anyway, and when Connor got home, she presented it to him like it was a masterpiece."

I find myself grinning, picturing the scene.

"Connor, bless him, took one bite and tried so hard not to react. But Des just burst out laughing and said, 'Daddy's face looks like when I eat broccoli!' They ended up ordering pizza and Desiree used the bread as a doorstop for like a month."

Ashlyn wipes a tear from her eye, still chuckling. "And Des - that kid was something else. She used to insist on wearing her BJJ gi everywhere. Grocery shopping, restaurants, didn't matter. She'd tell everyone she was a shinobi princess."

The image of a little girl in a martial arts uniform declaring herself royalty makes my heart ache in the best way. These aren't just stories - they're pieces of the people Connor loved, still loves. And somehow, hearing about them doesn't hurt like I thought it might. Instead, it feels like being let in on a precious secret. Feels like somewhere out there they are accepting me into their family.

Chapter 29: A Work of Art

✦ ⬥ ◆ ⬥ ✦

Connor

THE HOSPITAL CHAIR ISN'T exactly comfortable, but it looks like a luxury recliner compared to lying in that bed staring at the ceiling. My own flannel pajama pants and soft cotton tank top feel like luxury items after two weeks of that drafty hospital gown showing my ass to everyone who walked in.

"I've got it," I wave off Manu and Sarah, my nurse, as they hover nearby. They've had me doing laps around the unit floor the last few days to get my lungs back into shape. The walking's getting easier, even if my lungs still burn a bit. Progress is progress.

Sergeant Wesley stands near the window as I carefully sit down, her notepad ready. I called her this morning when the fog finally lifted enough to give a proper statement. She's been patient, letting me get my bearings back before diving into the details.

"Take your time, Mr. Ebin," she says, her voice carrying

that same steady calm from the night with Bertrand. "Start wherever you feel comfortable."

I take a careful breath, mindful of the healing wounds. The skin still pulls when I take deep breaths sometimes. "I got the call from Shelly about Bertrand getting out on a cashless bail. She was terrified." The memory of her voice trembling through the phone makes my jaw clench. "When I got to the apartment, I noticed three men at the end of the hallway. Something felt off about them, but I noticed it too late."

Manu shifts his weight, arms crossed. He's heard bits and pieces but this is the first time I'm telling the whole story.

"I tried to get Shelly to lock the door, but it happened too fast. Two of them came at me while the third—" I pause, remembering the sound of that door being kicked in. "The third got to Shelly."

The image of her being struck floods back, along with the helpless rage I felt while wrestling with the other two. My hand automatically moves to my side where the bullet wounds are started to turn a calm pink.

"I fought with the two men outside and from what I've been told collapsed the windpipe of one and killed him. The other stabbed me and I wrestled with him and broke his arm. I ran into the apartment and dialed 911 on my phone and set it down, hoping the dispatcher would hear the commotion and track the call."

"Shelly was brilliant," I continue, shifting in the chair to ease the pressure on my side. "She saw me put the phone down and understood what I was doing. When the guy had her at gunpoint, she came up with this story about Heidi telling her to stay away from the bed. Made him think there might be drugs hidden there."

I pause, remembering how everything slowed down in that moment. "When he bent to look under the bed, I took my shot. I had control of the his gun hand for awhile but he moved in a way that made the muscles where I got stabbed feel like they were tearing and I lost my grip. That's when he shot me." My hand wipes sweat from my brow. "I must have been losing blood fast, could feel myself getting weaker by the second."

Sergeant Wesley nods, her pen moving steadily across the notepad.

"That's when Shelly..." I have to take a breath, the memory still raw. "She saved my life. While I was struggling with him, she grabbed a knife and stabbed him multiple times. He hit her with the gun, but it gave me the opening I needed. I managed to get the weapon and put him down."

I look directly at Sergeant Wesley. "If Shelly hadn't acted when she did, I wouldn't be here giving this statement. My vision was going dark fast, and he would've finished me off. She's the real hero in all this."

Manu makes a small noise of agreement from his corner. "You saved each other Connor."

"The last thing I remember was trying to reach for her," I say quietly. "Then everything went black."

Sergeant Wesley tucks her notepad away with a satisfied nod. "Everything matches Ms. Lockhart's statement perfect-ly. With all three assailants deceased, this is really just cross-ing t's and dotting i's." She adjusts her uniform collar. "And of course, Ms. Lockhart has been cleared of any involvement or knowledge regarding the cocaine situation."

Relief washes over me. I never doubted Shelly's innocence, but it's good to have it officially confirmed that the authorities know it as well.

"Thank you, Sergeant Wesley," I say, genuinely grateful for her handling of everything, including the whole 'daughter' situation that apparently got Shelly access to my room.

As Sergeant Wesley heads out, Ashlyn sweeps in like a caffeinated whirlwind, pressing a quick kiss to my cheek before distributing coffee cups to Manu and me. The familiar scent of Books and Beans' signature roast hits my nose, and I could almost cry from the simple pleasure of it after weeks of hospital food and IV drips.

"You're a doll," I tell her, carefully wrapping my hands around the warm cup.

"Don't I know it," she grins, perching on the arm of my chair. "And you look significantly less corpse-like than last week. The color's coming back to your face."

Manu takes a long sip of his coffee. "That's because he's finally stopped trying to be a hero and started actually resting like the doctors ordered."

I roll my eyes at him, but there's no heat in it. They've both been here nearly every day, making sure I don't push myself too hard in my recovery. Between them and Shelly, I couldn't ask for better people in my corner.

"To be clear, it was the work on my lungs, not the doctors I was listening to." I say with dripping sarcasm.

"Speaking of work," Ashlyn says, setting her coffee aside

and pulling out her laptop, "everything's still on track with Rune Beast. The team's been crushing it while you've been playing invalid."

Manu nods. "The beta feedback has been incredible. We're actually ahead of schedule on the final polish pass and ending the beta in two days."

"But this..." Ashlyn turns her laptop toward me, "this is what you need to see."

The familiar opening notes of The Nightfallen's original theme for the Seidr Witch fill the small hospital room as the cutscene begins to play. My breath catches slightly as I watch the finished version of the Rune Beast and Seidr Witch romance sequences we captured.

We're both replaced with the CGI representations of the aforementioned characters but the way Shelly and I moved together on screen is... perfect. There's an intimacy, a connection that transcends the digital characters. Every gesture, every subtle movement carries meaning. The way the Witch's hand traces the Rune Beast's chest, how he pulls her close – it's all there, preserved in stunning detail.

Heat rises to my face as I remember every detail of filming the scenes with her. The nervous energy, the initial awkwardness melting away into something natural and honest. How everything else seemed to fade until it was just us, moving together like we'd rehearsed it a thousand times.

"Holy shit," I whisper, watching as the scene builds to its climax. Aimi and the visual effects team have outdone themselves, weaving magic and passion together seamlessly. But it's the raw emotion underneath that makes it so powerful to me.

Ashlyn's grinning like a cat that got the cream. "Told you she was the perfect replacement."

"You did good, Ash," Manu agrees, and I can hear the smile in his voice. "Really good. Even if you were also trying to push-"

Manu lets out a little grunt as Ashlyn jabs him in the ribs. "The fuck was that for?"

I can't take my eyes off the screen, watching our performance transform into something magical. Something real.

"Is Shelly downstairs getting something to eat?" I ask, still staring at the screen where our performance has me transfixed. The last few days, she's been splitting her time between helping me with physical therapy and making sure I actually eat the hospital food.

Ashlyn practically vibrates with excitement, nearly spilling her coffee as she bounces in place. Her eyes are bright with that particular gleam she gets when she's pulled off something spectacular. "Actually, she's at Eldritch Magic right now. We're getting her all set up with the moderator team – full time position." The way she's looking at me, you'd think she just solved world hunger instead of getting Shelly a job. Though honestly, given how protective I've become of Shelly, maybe in Ashlyn's mind they're equivalent achievements.

My heart does a little skip that has nothing to do with my healing wounds. "You got her to accept a real job offer this time?"

"Actually, it didn't take much convincing," she grins. "After that your joint performance and how quick she was with content moderation that day... plus, you know, saving the CEO's life probably didn't hurt her resume. HR didn't even say they needed to speak with you first for verbal approval."

"Regardless, she earned it fair and square. The girl's got skills." He takes another sip of coffee. "Though I'm pretty sure watching you almost die made her a lot more willing to accept help than before."

He's right. The stubborn independence, albeit a necessary learned behavior, that kept her sleeping on streets rather than accepting charity has softened since everything happened. Not gone completely – she's still Shelly after all – my Shelly, but she's learning to let people care for her.

"I did pull a few executive decision threads on your behalf and got her set up in the corner moderator booth by the break room," Ashlyn adds with that knowing smile she gets when she's particularly pleased with herself. "You know, the only one with a window to the outside and the good view of the Sound? The one all the other moderators have been eyeing." She leans forward, clearly waiting for my approval of her machinations. "I figured someone who spent a year without walls deserves a room with a view."

I smile, picturing Shelly in that space, making it her own. "Perfect spot for her."

"Thank you, Ash," I say, letting my gratitude show through. "Not just for getting her set up with the job, but for taking her in. After everything that happened..." I trail off, remembering how close we both came to not making it.

"Please," she waves it off with a smile, "having her around

has been amazing. Did you know she's actually interested in hearing about Liv and Des?" Ashlyn's eyes light up. "Most people tiptoe around mentioning them, but Shelly... she gets so excited when I tell her stories. Yesterday, I showed her the video of Des's first jiu jitsu competition, and she was practically bouncing."

I feel warm spread through my chest at that. Something that I've been getting used to feeling again. The idea of Shelly wanting to know about them, to understand that part of my life...

"She's like the little sister I never had," Ashlyn continues, her voice soft. "Though honestly?" She meets my eyes with that direct look I've known for years. "Even if we didn't get along at all, I'd still want her staying with me. The way you look at her, Connor... I'm glad you've stopped torturing your-self." She squeezes my hand lovingly.

"Besides," she adds with a playful smirk, "someone needs to make sure she actually eats regular meals instead of sur-viving on coffee and protein bars like a certain CEO I know."

Chapter 30: The Maiden's Recipe

Connor

THE KEY TO MY apartment clicks and I pause, bracing my-self. After weeks in the hospital, coming home feels...strange. Manu steadies my arm as I step inside, though I don't need it anymore. Shelly hovers nearby, ready to futility try and catch me if I stumble, while Ashlyn brings up the rear with my bag.

The familiar scent of citrus and pine cleaning products hits me first - Alicia's signature touch. The place is immaculate, not a speck of dust in sight. But what catches my eye is my dining room table, practically groaning under the weight of gifts, cards, and flower arrangements.

"Holy shit," I mutter, taking in the spread. There's a massive fruit basket from Adrian Chen, the voice of General Bracus Redthorn in Tales of Fallen Embers. A handmade get-well card from GrungeApeCodex, one of our most popular streamers. Even a vintage bottle of scotch from Sarah Mitchell, who voiced most of the female characters in CCC.

"Your fangirls really came through," Manu quips, picking up an elaborate arrangement of dark roses.

I spot Alicia's familiar handwriting on a note propped up against a vase: "Welcome home. Don't worry about the mess - I'll handle the cleanup when I'm back. Try not to die before then. - A"

"Classic Alicia," I chuckle, running my fingers over her neat script. The woman's been taking care of me for years, and her particular brand of tough love is exactly what I like about her.

My eyes catch on a small package wrapped in simple brown paper. The tag reads "From the Moderator Team." I glance at Shelly, who's trying and failing to hide a smile. I suppose I know which one I am opening first.

Home. After everything that's happened, I'm finally home. And somehow, impossibly, I'm not alone anymore.

I watch as the others move around my apartment putting away some of the things they brought to the hospital for me. They are moving as if they somehow practiced the choreography of it before. I find myself slowly walking around the massive place, taking in everything as if I have been gone for months and I need to reconnect with it all.

"You know," Manu says, carefully placing my laptop on my desk, "most people would take this opportunity to rest."

I ignore him, making my way to my custom-built gaming PC. The matte black case with its subtle purple LED accents (they're subtle to me anyway, I have however been informed on a few occasions that I am wrong) sits exactly where I left it. It is spotless of any dust, thanks to Alicia's careful cleaning. I wrap my arms around the tower in an exaggerated embrace.

"Oh Rebecca, my sweet mistress. Daddy missed you so much."

"Rebecca?" Shelly asks, poking her head out of the bathroom.

"Don't ask," Ashlyn groans. "He's been calling that machine Rebecca since he built it three years ago. Claims it's the most reliable woman in his life."

"Hey now," I protest, still hugging the PC, "Rebecca has never let me down. Have you, baby?" I pat the case affectionately.

Manu rolls his eyes. "And this, children, is why we don't let Connor name things anymore. Remember when he wanted to call Critical Chaos in Chains 'Bouncy Murder Fun Time'?"

"That was a perfectly good name," I mutter, finally releasing my grip on Rebecca. "Marketing just didn't appreciate my sense of humor. Not my fault they requested a meeting to discuss my 'vision' for the game and wasted half an hour of our time dancing around trying to tell me we shouldn't call it that."

Shelly laughs, and it sends pleasant ripples through my body. Laughter in this apartment after all these years. I would start to cry if I wasn't so damn happy right now. Happiness, that's another thing these walls haven't seen in a long time either. It's still new, this feeling, but I'm starting to get used to it. Liv and Des's visit, whether otherworldly or a trick of all the medication is making me believe that maybe I deserve all of this.

Manu and Shelly debate the merits of various gaming peripherals which brings a smile to my face. Shelly has dove head first into the gaming world and I love seeing her interest in it skyrocket. Ashlyn sidles up next to me while and her shoulder bumps mine gently. She follows my eyes to Shelly.

"So," she says quietly, "how does it feel to be home?"

I catch the weight in her question immediately. Ashlyn's known me for so long, been through too much with me, for this to be casual conversation. She was there for the aftermath of losing Liv and Des, watched me slowly wall myself off from everything except work. The way she's looking at me now tells me exactly what she's really asking.

How is it to let yourself feel again? To risk your heart after keeping it locked away for so long?

I swallow hard, my eyes suddenly moist. Across the room, Shelly's animated voice carries as she explains to Manu why mechanical keyboards are superior with their tactile stimulation. The sound fills spaces in my apartment that have been empty for years, brings life to corners that have only held echoes.

Meeting Ashlyn's knowing gaze, I give her a small nod and my face reddens and drops to my feet. "It's like..." I pause, searching for the right words. "Like I've been holding my breath underwater for years, and I'm finally coming up for air."

She squeezes my arm, and I see tears gathering in her eyes. "Liv would be so proud of you right now," she whispers.

For the first time, those words don't feel like daggers in my chest. Instead, they settle warm and true in my heart, because I know she's right. After the ICU vision I finally understand that moving forward doesn't mean moving on and leaving them behind.

"So, living arrangements," Ashlyn whispers, her eyes darting to make sure Manu and Shelly are still deep in their mechanical keyboard debate, "have you asked her yet?"

I run my hand over my face, feeling the rough scratch of my beard. It's grown out more than usual during my hospital stay. "Not yet."

"Connor..." There's that tone, the one she uses when she thinks I'm being particularly dense.

"I know, I know." I hold up my hands in surrender. "I just... I want to make sure she's ready. The last thing I want is to spook her by moving too fast."

Ashlyn snorts, not even trying to hide her eye roll. "You're ridiculous, you know that? That girl would absolutely freak out if you asked her to move in."

"That's what I'm worried about-"

"No, you idiot," she cuts me off, jabbing a finger into my chest. Thankfully in a spot that didn't get shot. "She'd freak out in the best way possible. She'd probably launch herself at you so hard we'd have to take you right back to the hospital. The two of you have been through at least a few years worth of shit together at this point."

I can't help but chuckle at the mental image, even as my chest tightens with hope. "You really think so?"

"I know so. I've seen how she looks at you when you're not watching." Ashlyn's voice softens. "And I've seen how you look at her. Stop overthinking everything."

She's right, of course. Ashlyn has an annoying habit of being right lately. I glance over at Shelly, who's now demonstrating different key switches to an increasingly bemused Manu, and feel well and truly loved.

"I'll ask her," I promise. "Soon. When the moment feels right."

Ashlyn claps her hands together, breaking through my thoughts. "Alright, time for us to head out. Let you get settled." She grabs Manu by the sleeve of his polo shirt, practically dragging him away from Shelly's impromptu keyboard seminar.

"But I was just learning about..." Manu protests weakly.

"You can geek out about clicky keys another time," Ashlyn cuts him off, already steering him toward the door. She turns back to me. "Call if you need anything, okay? And I mean anything."

Manu nods in agreement. "Seriously, man. Don't try to be a hero. You've filled your quota on that for a while."

"Oh!" Ashlyn stops suddenly, nearly causing Manu to crash into her. "Almost forgot - are you still good for the PVGAs next week? I know it's soon, but the organizers need to know if they should find a replacement presenter."

I straighten up slightly, ignoring the twinge in my chest. "Wouldn't miss it for the world." The thought of backing out of presenting Game of the Year hasn't even crossed my mind, and, after everything that's happened, standing on stage next to Dahlia Nightfall and getting to see Shelly's face when she meets her rock star idol feels like a perfect end to the month.

"Connor..." Ashlyn's voice carries that warning tone.

"I'm fine," I assure her. "Doctor cleared me for normal activities, remember? And standing at a podium reading from a teleprompter definitely counts as normal. Unless presenting now includes running out on stage and doing somersaults."

"If you're sure," she says, though I can tell she's not entirely convinced.

"I am." I meet her concerned gaze steadily. "Really. Now go home. The two of you have done enough for me today. Go do something fun, like knitting."

"Jackass." Ashlyn retorts.

Manu says matter factually, "I hear there is a drunken knitting class at that one pub with the dancing boar on the sign. Can't remember what the hell it is called."

Ashlyn raises an eyebrow. "You mean The Dancing Boar?"

"That's it!" Manu says as she pushes him out the door and shuts it behind them.

Suddenly the apartment feels different - not empty, but charged with a new kind of energy. Shelly stands near my gaming setup, fingers trailing absently over Rebecca's case, her eyes darting around like a bird that's not quite sure where to land.

I recognize that look. It's the same one I used to get when visiting Liv's parents for dinner in those early days - wanting to help but not knowing your place yet. Of course they didn't think I had a place, assholes.

"You hungry?" I ask, already moving toward the kitchen. "I could whip up something quick. Maybe a club sandwich like the one you enjoyed from the cafe in the hospital. Mine will be much better though." I'm trying to keep my voice casual, like this isn't the first time I've made food for someone in my home since... well, since everything.

Shelly's head snaps up, and suddenly she's moving, placing herself between me and the kitchen entrance. "Oh no you don't," she says, her voice firm but gentle. "You just got out of the hospital. Sit down, play a game or something."

I start to protest, but she reaches her hands up to my shoulders and physically turns me around (I have to assist her with it, I don't think her much smaller frame could turn me around on her own).

"Let me take care of you for once," she says softly. "You've done enough of that for me lately."

Her stern determination causes a flush of heat in me again. "You sure?" I ask, even as I'm allowing her to guide me toward my favorite chair. How does she know this is my favorite. I mean, hell, there are five scattered around the open living area, not including the couch. My favorite isn't even in front of the TV, where most people would think it was.

"Connor," she says, and I can hear the eye roll in her voice, "I may not be able to make you anything fancy, but I can handle feeding you without burning down your kitchen. Now sit."

I raise my hands in surrender, sitting down carefully into the chair. "Yes ma'am."

I sink deeper into it, letting the familiar comfort envelop me. My eyes drift to the photo of Liv and Des on the wall - one of my favorites, caught mid-laugh during a day hike. *Thank you*, I think silently, watching Shelly move through my kitchen with surprising confidence.

She's not just throwing together a sandwich like I expected. Instead, she's pulling out my stockpot (how did she even know where that was?), gathering chicken stock and vegetables from the pantry. The sight of her selecting chicken tenderloins from the fridge makes me smile - she's actually cooking. Really cooking.

The worn copy of The Maiden and the Lycanthrope sits on the side table where I left it before... everything. I pick it up, finding my bookmark still in place. Just one chapter left. Might as well finish while she works her magic in the kitchen.

The final chapter pulls me in immediately. The writing is beautiful and poetic in its alliteration, and manages to capture complex emotions in a way that tugs at my heart strings. I understand fully now why this book means so much to Shelly. The parallel between the Maiden learning to trust again and the Lycanthrope allowing himself to be vulnerable - it hits closer to home than I expected and I wonder if that was another reason she gave it to me.

I stow away a particular scene from the book in my mind vault for creative use later and close the book slowly, letting the ending settle over me. The sound of Shelly humming softly in the kitchen mingles with the gentle clink of utensils and the bubbling of whatever she's cooking. The familiar scents of home are mixing with new ones, creating something altogether different. Not better just fresh.

Looking back at Liv and Des's photo, I notice how the late afternoon light catches it just right, making their smiles seem to glow. For the first time in years, seeing their faces doesn't bring that crushing weight of grief. Instead, I feel... peace.

I reach for the stereo remote, a small smile playing on my

lips as I pull up my personal playlist of Japanese shamisen folk metal. The first song to play is a live song the Nightfallen played when they toured in Japan. It was only ever played live, and only in Japan. The opening riff of plucked strings resonates through the apartment, and I watch as Shelly stops cooking for a moment and just listens, then her whole body perks up instantly.

She freezes for a moment, wooden spoon suspended mid-stir, before her hips start swaying in time with the thundering taiko drum line. Her movements are natural, unreserved, like she's completely forgotten I'm here. The Nightfallen shirt she's wearing (one of their older tour designs) clings to her curves as she spins between the stove and counter, using the spoon as an air flute.

My mouth moistens as she shimmies and twirls, leggings hugging and accentuating every pop of her hips. She's singing along perfectly to Dahlia's haunting vocals, her voice carrying surprising power and control. I thought I might be introducing her to a song of theirs she didn't know but she proved me wrong almost instantly. The afternoon sun streaming through the kitchen windows catches her hair, creating a halo effect that makes my heart stutter.

I shift in my chair, allowing myself to feel the heat building in my core as she dances. There's something magnetic about her uninhibited joy, the way she owns the space that will hopefully soon be hers too - if she says yes when I ask her to move in. The thought of her here permanently, filling these rooms with her music and laughter, sends a surge of desire through me that has nothing to do with physical attraction (okay, maybe a little to do with it).

She catches me watching and instead of getting embarrassed, she just grins and dances harder, adding an extra sway to her hips that makes me grip the arms of my chair. The pure bliss radiating from her is intoxicating, and I find myself falling even harder for this beautiful, resilient woman who's brought so much light back into my life.

The song fades into something softer - something more traditional. It's calmer and my eyelids grow heavy as the gentle melody washes over me, and I find myself drifting off. The comfortable weight of contentment pulls me under, and for once, I don't fight it.

I must have fallen asleep because a light touch on my shoulder brings me back. Shelly stands before me, holding a tray that sends waves of mouthwatering aroma through the air. Steam rises from a bowl of creamy chicken soup, accompanied by perfectly arranged crackers and what looks like freshly warmed bread.

I carefully shift to sit up straighter, mindful of my healing wounds. "This looks amazing," I tell her, and her face lights up with a smile that reaches from ear to ear. The pride in her expression brings that warmth back again. The power this woman has.

Taking the spoon, I blow gently on the soup before tasting it. The flavors explode across my tongue - rich, thick, perfectly seasoned broth, tender strips of chicken, and vegetables cooked to just the right consistency. It's not just good; it's restaurant quality.

"Where the hell did you learn to cook like this?" I ask,

already reaching for another spoonful. The taste spreads out over every tastebud, and I feel my body tingle. I can't tell if it's from the soup or the way she's practically glowing at my reaction.

She fidgets with the hem of her shirt, that brilliant smile still in place. "Well..."

I watch as Shelly tucks the silver strand of her hair behind her ear, that adorable blush creeping across her cheeks. "After I turned thirteen I was usually the oldest kid in the house and cooking often fell to me. But there was one house, a temporary one unfortunately, where Mrs. Helms gave me a crash course on soups and stews. She said they were simple but tasted brilliant."

The way she says it, casual and matter-of-fact, makes my heart ache. But there's no sadness in her voice, just a quiet pride. She settles into the chair next to mine, tucking her legs underneath her.

"Plus," she adds with a little smirk, "Manu said you liked soups and I may have binged every cooking video I could find during my breaks at my moderator desk to see what kinds of tricks I could use to make this even better. Turns out you can learn a lot during those slow periods between banning toxic players."

I take another spoonful of soup, savoring the rich flavor. "Well, Shelly this is amazing. I always loved warm soup when winter hits."

"Really?" Her eyes light up, and I catch a glimpse of that younger version of her, quietly hoping for approval but not quite seeking it. "I mean, it's just soup..."

"Hey." I set down my spoon and reach for her hand. "It's not just soup. It's..." I pause, searching for the right words. "You. It's home. You made my apartment feel like a home again."

The words slip out before I can stop them, but I don't regret them. Not when I see the way her whole face softens, and her fingers tighten around mine.

"Connor I…I'm glad," she whispers, and there's so much meaning packed into those two simple words that my chest tightens.

We sit in comfortable silence for a few moments, my thumb tracing circles on the back of her hand while I finish my soup. The late afternoon sun paints everything in warm gold, and I can't remember the last time I felt this at peace.

Shelly gently takes the tray from my lap and sets it on the side table. Her hand finds mine again, our fingers interlacing naturally. Her freckles that I've grown so crazy about nearly sparkling in the apartment lighting. She keeps alternating between meeting my gaze and staring at our joined hands, like she's gathering courage.

"Connor..." Her voice is soft but steady. "We haven't really had a chance to talk. I mean, really talk, just us. Between all the hospital staff and having to pretend to be..." She trails off, a small smile playing at her lips. "…you know."

I squeeze her hand gently, encouraging her to continue. My heart rate picks up slightly, and I realize I'm holding my breath.

"I need to know..." She exhales fully, finally meeting my eyes fully. "I need to know exactly what this is between us.

What we are to each other. Because I meant what I said in the hospital, Connor. I love you. And not just because you saved me or helped me. It wasn't some overwhelming emotional response to trauma or adrenaline. I love you. I truly and deeply love you."

She traces 'I LUV U' on my palm as she speaks, sending little sparks of electricity through my arm. "I'm not Olivia and Desiree, and I would never try to replace them. The idea of that feels monstrous. But I still love you and want to be a part of your life. I just…I need to hear IT from you… I need to know if what I feel, if what I think is between us, is real."

The vulnerability in her voice, the way she's letting me see every emotion play across her face - it makes my chest tight in the best possible way. She's asking for clarity, for confirmation of something we've both been dancing around for what feels like months.

I slowly stand, pulling Shelly up with me. The soreness in my core protests slightly but I ignore it, guiding her toward the floor-to-ceiling windows overlooking the city and my balcony. The late afternoon sun bathes everything in a warm glow, making the glass and steel buildings shimmer like diamonds. The cold wind has given the glass a radiating coolness that I can see brings goosebumps to Shelly's arms.

Positioning her in front of me, I wrap one arm over her shoulder while the other slides under her arm to reach across her waist and hold her side. She fits perfectly against me, like she was meant to have been here all along.

"Look at the city," I murmur, my chin resting lightly on her head.

"Connor, please," she whispers, trying to turn around.

"Just... give me a moment." My voice is soft but firm. I need her to see what I see, to understand what this means.

We stand there, taking in the sprawling cityscape before us. The same view I've looked at thousands of times feels different now, charged with possibility rather than emptiness. I press a gentle kiss to the top of her head, breathing in the subtle scent of her hair.

Carefully turning her around to face the open expanse of my apartment, I keep her wrapped in my arms. She starts to speak again, but I quiet her with a gentle "Shhh." I feel the tension leave her body as she relaxes against me, trusting me completely.

Leaning down, I press my lips to the soft skin of her neck, still holding her close from behind. Her breath catches slightly, and I feel her pulse quicken under my lips.

I gently turn Shelly to face me, my hands sliding to rest on her hips. Her green eyes search mine, and for a moment I'm lost in them, in the way they reflect both strength and vulnerability. I almost forget what I'm going to say.

"I knew," I say softly, one hand moving up to cup her cheek. "I knew that first night at Books and Beans. There was something about you that called to me, but I kept trying to rationalize it away. Telling myself it was just because you reminded me of them, or that I was projecting, or a dozen other excuses. Trying to pack you away in a box like I told you about that night we filmed."

She leans into my touch, and I feel my heart skip. "But at the mall, watching you get so excited about everything, seeing how you lit up when I handed you that Nightfallen shirt, the smile on your face at the salon that I couldn't help but sneak a picture of, when we argued over Lord of the Rings, that's when I couldn't deny it anymore. I was in love with you. Not with what you could be for me or what I hoped you'd become. I was totally and helplessly in love with you."

My thumb traces the light dusting of freckles across her cheek. "I was scared of moving too fast, of frightening you away. And yes, I stupidly worried about, I don't know, dishonoring their memory? But they'll always be part of who I am, and you cared to ask me about them and learn who they were. That meant everything to me."

Drawing her closer, I rest my forehead against hers. "I love you, Michelle Lockhart. And I want... I want you to move in with me. Make this place ours, if you want to."

The words come easier than I expected, natural and right. Like they've been waiting to be said since I saw her crossing the street. Her hands grip the front of my shirt, and I can feel the slight tremor in them, matching the way my own heart is racing.

Her body melts against mine, and I feel the last traces of tension leave her frame as she wraps her arms around my waist. The sensation of her pressed against me numbs the lingering stiffness around all the recently closed holes in my body, and I have to remind myself to breathe.

"Yes," she whispers against my shirt. "Yes, I want to live with you. I want to make this our home."

My heart skips at the word 'our.' It's been so long since this place felt like anything more than walls and memories. Now, with her here, it's becoming something entirely new.

She pulls back just enough to look up at me, and I'm struck by the blush spreading across her cheeks, highlighting those sweet freckles. I want to kiss each individual one and name them like they are stars. Her teeth catch her bottom lip - that nervous habit I've noticed she has when she wants to say something but isn't quite sure how.

"Connor?" Her voice is barely above a whisper, vulnerable yet knowing. "Tell me. Tell me I'm your girlfriend?"

The request catches me off guard, not because it's unexpected of course, but because of how sweetly innocent it is. This fiercely independent woman who's faced down so much hardship is standing here asking me to make it official like we're teenagers at prom.

I cup her face in my hands, thumb brushing across her bottom lip. "You're my girlfriend, Shelly, and so much more."

Her face flushes an even deeper shade of red, but the smile that spreads across her face is radiant. She presses closer, and I can feel her heart pounding, matching the rhythm of my own.

I lean down, drawn by the magnetic pull of her lips. She rises to meet me, her mouth soft and eager against mine. My hand slides down her back, cupping the pleasing shape of ass with a gentle squeeze that pulls a moan from her throat. The sound vibrates against my lips, sending fire through my entire body.

Pulling her closer, I'm suddenly reminded of my limitations as sharp pain lances through my chest. I can't help the wince that escapes me, and Shelly immediately pulls back, concern flooding her features.

"Are you okay?" Her hands hover over my chest, afraid to touch where she knows the wounds are.

I nod, trying to catch my breath. "Yeah, just... maybe we should put a pin in where this was probably heading." The disappointment in my voice is obvious, but I force a smile. "I'd hate for our first time together to be... hell, right now I can barely manage three flights of stairs without feeling like I've run a marathon."

A small snicker escapes her, but her eyes are understanding and maybe a little relieved. "Actually," she says, fingers playing with the hem of my shirt, "after what happened in the alley... I think I might need a little more time to be fully ready myself."

Relief washes over me - not because I don't want her (God knows I do), but because we're both being honest about our needs. "Come on," I say, taking her hand and leading her to the bedroom.

We lie down under warm thick blankets facing each other, close enough that I can count her freckles in the dim light. Her hand finds mine between us, and we talk into the night, sharing soft kisses and gentle touches until sleep claims us both.

Chapter 31: Nice to Meet You, I'm Your Husband's Girlfriend

❦ ⸻ ◆ ⸻ ❦

Shelly

SOME MORNINGS OVER THE past week as I wake up I still expect to feel cold concrete against my back or the scratchy fabric of a shelter cot beneath me. Instead, there's the warmth of Egyptian cotton sheets and Connor's steady breathing beside me. Sometimes I have to touch the silk pajamas he bought me just to convince myself this is real.

The routine we've fallen into feels like something out of those cheesy romance novels I used to read at the library. Every morning, I slip into the master bathroom - *our* bathroom now - and take a shower with actual hot water that doesn't run out after two minutes. The shower gel smells like cinnamon and honey, and I use as much as I want because Connor insists on keeping it stocked.

Coffee in bed has become my favorite part of the day. Connor brings it in on this ridiculous silver tray he claims was a gag gift from Manu, but I've seen the way his eyes crinkle when he sets it down. We sit there together, sharing the morning quiet, sometimes talking about nothing in particular, sometimes just existing in the same space.

Work at Eldritch Magic feels surreal. I have my own desk, my own computer, my own security badge with my picture on it. The other moderators treat me like I've always been there. Connor has started coming in for half days now and sometimes I catch him watching me through the little glass window of my booth when he thinks I'm not looking. He gets this soft smile that makes me want to turn into a puddle in my chair.

Coming home - *home* - is the best part. Some nights we cook together, bumping hips in the kitchen while music plays. Other nights I'll find him waiting with takeout from places I'd never even dreamed of trying before. He always orders extra, knowing I like to try everything.

I still catch myself wondering if this is all some elaborate dream, if I'll wake up back on the streets. But then Connor will brush my hair back, squeeze my hand or caress the small of my back while kissing my neck and I know this is real. This is my life now. Our life.

But little did I know that our semi-established routine would change this morning. I let the hot water cascade over me, working out the knots in my shoulders from sleeping curled up against Connor's chest. The glass door fogs up, creating a dreamy haze around the bathroom. That's when I see him - a tall silhouette approaching the shower door through the steam.

My breath catches as Connor places his palm against the glass. I feel his request at my very core. He's asking permission. Permission to move a little past the late night make out sessions on the couch and in our bed. Our bed. Without hesitation, I press mine against his, our hands separated only by the glass between us. The hunger in his eyes makes my skin tingle, and I watch, transfixed, as he hooks his thumbs into the waistband of his boxers.

I bite my lower lip as they fall to the floor. God, he's beautiful - well muscled but thick with broad shoulders. My eyes trail down his body, drinking in every detail I'd only glimpsed through the mo-cap suit before. As my gaze drops to his waist, the sight of him hanging there makes my mouth smack as I part my lips and let loose a breath of desire. Suddenly I'm back in Heidi's bathtub, imagining him taking me at the empty Books and Beans while touching myself.

The memory makes me flush hot despite the shower's spray. I press my thighs together, remembering how many times I've fantasized about him like this. But fantasy pales in comparison to reality - to actually seeing him, wanting him, knowing he wants me too.

The shower door opens with a soft click, and steam billows around Connor as he steps inside. My heart hammers against my ribs as his eyes travel over my body - not with the predatory gaze I've known from others, but with something deeper, more reverent. The way he looks at me makes me feel like a masterpiece, like every perceived flaw is actually something precious to be worshipped.

His hands find my hips, and the contact sends electricity

through my skin. They're strong and sure, but gentle - so different from the rough handling I've feared in the past. When he pulls me closer, I can't help but rise up on my toes, desperate to taste his lips. The water runs between us as we kiss, making everything slick and warm. I am so blown away by how easily he has awoken this side of me. The side of me that craves physical contact, a side I don't know if I ever knew was there. Perhaps because I have never felt safe enough to explore it before.

Those magnificent hands slide down to cup my ass, and this firm grip makes me moan against his mouth. It's possessive but tender, claiming me while promising safety. I break away from his lips, trailing kisses down his neck to his chest. My teeth graze his skin, and I feel more than hear his sharp intake of breath.

The water continues to cascade over us, but I barely notice it anymore. All I can focus on is the feel of his skin against mine, the way his muscles flex when he shudders under my exploring mouth, and how perfectly our bodies fit together. This isn't just lust - though there's plenty of that - it's something far more profound. Every touch feels like coming home.

He turns me around and pulls me back against him. I can feel his pulsing girth against the middle of my back. Connor's hands on me send shivers down my spine, and I can't help but arch into his touch.

He brings my chin up and to the side and leans down to kiss me. His lips are soft yet gently demanding against mine, he's telling me I'm safe without ever saying an actual word.

That turns me on even more and I melt into him as he deepens the kiss. His other hand leaves my ass, and I whimper (Holy shit, I whimpered!) in protest until I feel it slip under my arm and to my breast, pulling me back against his stomach and chest.

His large hand engulfs me, cupping the soft mound in his bestial palm. He gently kneads me, sending an electric current straight to my core. My nipples harden under his ministrations, and I moan into his mouth.

That's when he does it - he rolls the sensitive bud between his thumb and forefinger. A low moan escapes my lips that nearly turns into a purr, and I throw my hand up and grab at the back of his neck, digging my nails into him, surprising even myself with my own aggressiveness. The sensation is almost too much to bear, but at the same time, it isn't enough. Greedy as it sounds, I want more of him - all of him.

His erection presses hard into my back. My other hand moves behind me and I wrap my fingers around him. I feel his breath catch in my mouth and when I start to stroke him, he lets out a low growl.

Connor's hand leaves my breast, and I feel a momentary pang of loss before his fingers trail down my stomach. My breath hitches as they reach the apex of my thighs, and I can't help but press myself into his touch. The water from the shower runs down my body, making my skin slick and sensitive.

His fingers slide between my legs, and I shudder at the contact. My knees tremble, and I grip his neck harder, nails digging into him more. Thankfully, he doesn't protest. Instead I feel his teeth begin to nibble at my neck. The sensation is overwhelming, and I can't help but let out a squeal of pleasure.

Connor's other hand tightens around my waist, holding me steady as his fingers explore my folds. I feel myself growing wetter under his touch, and I rock my hips against him. I reverse my grip on his cock, placing him between my palm and back. I rock my hips forward and backward, letting him slide against my skin. My other hand moves behind me, gripping his hip as I try to steady myself.

His fingers find my clit, and I gasp at the sudden sensation. He circles in a repeating slow motion that explodes into several fast and the back to slow, and I feel myself growing closer to the edge. My breath comes in short gasps, and I can feel my heart racing in my chest.

I tighten my grip on him, and I can feel him throbbing against me. It's a delicious reminder of his desire for me, and it only serves to heighten my own arousal. I rock my hips more forcefully, feeling him twitch in my hand and moan into my ear.

I'm shaking in his grip and just when I think I can't take it anymore, Connor's fingers slide inside me. I cry out at the sudden sensation, my body tensing around him. Everything stops and I gasp for air. He moves slowly at first, giving me time to adjust to the feeling. But soon, he's moving faster, his fingers curling inside me in a way that makes my legs tremble.

I can feel myself growing closer and closer to the edge, and I know I'm not going to last much longer. My hand tightens around him, and I can feel him growing harder in my grip. I know he's close too, that low growl building in my ear.

Suddenly, I feel myself tipping over the edge. My body convulses as wave after wave of pleasure washes over me. I cry out, my voice echoing in the small shower. Connor's fingers continue to move inside me, drawing out my orgasm until I'm left trembling and breathless.

As I come down from my high, I feel Connor's own release. He groans, his body tensing against mine as he cascades across my back. I can feel him pulsing in my hand, and the sensation sends aftershocks through my own body.

We stand there for a moment, panting and trembling in each other's arms. The water continues to run down our bodies, washing away any lingering tension. I feel myself growing tired, my legs still shaky from the intensity of my orgasm.

Connor's arms tighten around me, and he whispers something in my ear. I can't make out the words, but the sound of his voice is enough to make my heart flutter. I lean back against him, feeling safe and secure in his embrace.

For the first time in my life I have had an orgasm that didn't result in a feeling of awkwardness, shame or regret. Right now, with Connor, this is bliss. My whole body feels limp from released pleasure and being held in the arms of the man I love. A man that without question in my mind loves me.

I gaze into Connor's eyes, still catching my breath. The water continues to rain down on us, but I barely notice it anymore. His smile is so genuine, so full of warmth that it makes my chest ache in the best possible way.

"I love you," I whisper, meaning it more than I've ever meant anything in my life.

"I love you too, Little Lysa," he responds, his voice soft and tender. The nickname makes my heart flutter every damn time he says it - it's become something precious between us, a reminder of how far we've come.

We reluctantly separate and step out of the shower. Connor wraps a fluffy towel around me before grabbing one for himself. Even this simple gesture feels intimate, caring. I can't stop smiling as I dry off and start getting ready for work.

As I brush my hair out, I catch Connor watching me in the mirror. There's profound peace in his expression that it makes me pause. This is real. This is my life now. I'm loved, truly loved, by this incredible man. If ever there comes a day when I stop being thankful for this then I won't deserve him anymore.

I finish getting ready, and Connor helps me with my necklace, a little white gold laptop charm - another gift from him, though I've stopped protesting those. I've learned that giving makes him happy, and his happiness has become as important to me as my own.

"Don't overexert yourself while I'm gone." I say as I lean into his arms one more time.

He chuckles at me. "Where was that concern ten minutes ago?"

With one last kiss and an "I love you," I head out for work, feeling like I'm floating rather than walking. The memory of our shower and those tender moments after will keep me smiling all day.

Shelly

I reflect on how much I enjoy my job as Ashlyn and I take the elevator up to Connor's and I's apartment. The elevator ride feels different today - Ashlyn's been quiet the whole way, which isn't like her. Usually she's bubbling with stories about work drama or asking me how I'm settling into my role as moderator or even fishing for details about how Connor and I are 'getting on.' I'm pretty sure she knew something had changed this morning because she remarked about my face still being flushed when I got in her car. She seems lost in thought, like she knows something I don't.

When we walk in, Connor's dressed in a charcoal peacoat that makes him look like he stepped out of a magazine. He is his usual handsome self, but I notice something's different in his expression - a gentle melancholy that I've come to recognize on occasion.

"What's up?" I ask, dropping my bag by the door and moving to kiss him hello.

He pulls me close for a moment, his beard tickling my forehead. "Books and Beans starts their dark chocolate mint latte run today. They always start it a few weeks before

Christmas," he says softly. "I was hoping you'd want to come with me to the cemetery. It was Liv's favorite - she used to say it tasted like the holidays in a cup. I always bring her one and Desiree her hot chocolate."

My chest floods with emotion. These moments when he shares pieces of Liv with me are precious, sacred almost. "Of course I want to go," I tell him, squeezing his hand.

"Would it be okay if I came too?" Ashlyn asks from behind us, her voice unusually hesitant. "I miss her extra around the holidays."

Connor's eyes soften as he looks at his wife's best friend. "You know you don't have to ask, Ash. You don't need my permission."

The drive to Books and Beans is filled with laughter, which surprises me a little. I'm curled up in the passenger seat while Connor drives, listening as he and Ashlyn trade stories about Liv and Des like they're passing around precious gems.

"Remember when Des convinced Liv that the best way to teach you Brazilian jiu-jitsu was to attack you with surprise submissions while you were cooking?" Ashlyn's giggling from the backseat.

Connor's eyes crinkle at the corners. "Yes. I nearly burned the apartment down when they both jumped me while I was making a stir fry. Liv had Des on my back trying to get a rear naked choke while she went for my legs."

"Did they get you?" I ask, already grinning at the mental image.

"Are you kidding? They worked together like tiny ninjas. But I ended up tickling them into submission while trying not to knock over a wok full of hot oil."

The stories flow naturally between them - Liv's failed attempts at making macarons that somehow always came out looking like "cat buttholes" (Ashlyn's words), Des's determination to learn every single Pokemon name and type combination, the time they all went camping and Liv insisted on bringing her tarot cards to do 'spooky' readings by the campfire.

Something warm unfolds in my chest as I listen. These memories they're sharing, they're not just stories - they're giving me pieces of the people who helped shape the man I love. I've heard other people talk about feeling jealous of their partner's past life, like it somehow diminishes what they have now. But sitting here, watching Connor's face light up as he remembers Des trying to teach herself to skateboard, all I feel is grateful. Grateful that he had such love in his life, grateful that he's willing to share these precious memories with me.

I reach over and slip my hand into his free one. He squeezes back without breaking his story about Liv's obsession with 80's power ballads, and I feel like I've known them all along.

The walk from the car feels surreal. I've imagined visiting them so many times over the last week, but nothing quite prepares me for the actual moment. Connor's hand is steady in mine as he leads us through the quiet paths between the headstones, two coffee cups balanced carefully in a carrier in his other hand.

When we reach them, my breath catches. The stones are

beautiful - polished black granite with gold inlay. A small cherry blossom tree, still young but growing strong, stands barely peeking out from behind them. Connor sets down the drinks with practiced care - the dark chocolate mint latte at Liv's stone, the white hot chocolate at Des's. The gesture is so tender it makes my spirit ache.

We stand in silence for a moment, the Possession Sound stretching out before us like a sheet of silver glass. A container ship moves slowly across the horizon - the kind of sight Des used to love watching, according to Connor's stories. The wind carries the scent of the nearby trees and coffee, and somewhere nearby a gull calls out.

Ashlyn steps forward first, pressing her fingers to her lips before touching each stone in turn. "Miss you both," she says softly, then adds in a whisper that nearly breaks my heart, "You don't need to worry about Connor anymore. He's stopped being a vault of depression. She makes him happy."

She straightens up, touching Connor's arm briefly. "I'm going to give you guys some time," she says, and heads off down one of the winding paths, leaving us alone with the stones and the sound of waves.

Connor leads me to the bench across from their stones, his hand warm and steady in mine. I curl into his side as we sit, wrapping myself around his arm in that way that makes me feel safe and grounded. His lips press against my hair, and I close my eyes, savoring the gentle intimacy of the moment.

"You know what amazes me?" he says softly. "How easily you embrace them as part of who I am. You don't try to compete with their memory or push them aside. It makes moving forward feel... right."

I squeeze his arm gently. "They're part of your heart, Connor. Loving you means loving all of you, including the parts that will always belong to them."

He's quiet for a moment, his thumb tracing circles on my hand. "I need to tell you something that happened to me," he says finally. "When I was in the ICU, before you came to my room... I had this experience. Maybe it was the medication, maybe it was something else, but Liv and Des were there."

My breath catches, but I stay silent, letting him continue.

"Liv told me I was being thick-headed," he chuckles softly. "That I was killing my soul trying to hold onto grief instead of love. I thought I was dying, but Des... she said she didn't want me to join them until I was happy again." His voice breaks slightly. "Liv said she knew I loved you, and that it was okay. That she could share a piece of her soul if it saved the man she loves."

He tells me about the tarot cards falling, and the meaning of each of them. About the cherry blossom tree suddenly thriving after years of seeming dormant. About how I appeared in his life just when he was finally ready to see the signs. About the song that Liv had insisted must have the windows down no matter when it came on. But I think what hits the hardest is when he tells me that the night we first met at the Books and Beans, the whole reason that he saw me and helped me in the first place, was that I was sitting in the same seat Olivia always sat in when they would go there.

"They've been trying to tell me it was okay to love again," he says. "I was just too afraid to listen."

I lean up and press my lips to Connor's, tasting the remnants of his coffee and feeling the gentle scratch of his beard. "I'm so grateful you're finally listening," I whisper against his mouth.

Standing up, I take his hand and guide him to stand with me in front of the headstones. My heart pounds as I look at their names etched in the black granite.

"Olivia, Desiree..." My voice catches, but I steady myself. "I love him. I love him so much it terrifies me sometimes." Connor's hand tightens around mine as I continue. "I promise I'll do everything I can to keep him happy, to give him reasons to smile every day. He's... he's given me a world I never thought I'd have, the same kind of world I know he gave both of you. The kind of world I wish he could still give you."

Tears blur my vision but I blink them away, needing to get this out. "Thank you for sharing him with me. I know that sounds strange to say, but I mean it with everything I am. Having him in my life..." I have to pause, overcome for a moment. "It's literally saved me. I was so lost before him, and now..."

Connor's arm slides around my waist, pulling me close against his side, and I lean into his warmth as the sound of waves fills the comfortable silence that follows on the breeze.

"Thank you." Connor whispers into the air, and I know he is talking to all three of us.

I spot Ashlyn first, her figure moving carefully between headstones as she makes her way back to us. The late afternoon light catches her hair, making the highlights shimmer.

Connor notices her too, his body shifting slightly beside me.

"We should head back," he says softly, his hand warm against my lower back. "Tomorrow's going to be a long day at the awards ceremony. These things always turn into marathon events."

The mention of the awards show sends a little thrill through my stomach - a mix of excitement and nerves. I still can't quite believe I'm going to be there, let alone as Connor's plus one. I have an urge to give myself a sharp pinch, just to verify that I haven't conjured up this entire scenario while dozing in that backstreet near the mall. I wonder if I'll ever just accept that this is my life now?

"She's right," Connor adds, and I realize I must have missed Ashlyn saying something about getting rest. He gives my hand a gentle squeeze. "The red carpet alone can be an hour or more."

I take one last look at the headstones, at the cherry blossom tree swaying gently in the breeze, and whisper a quiet "goodbye" before letting Connor lead me back toward the car. The coffee cups stay behind - a tradition, he'd explained earlier, that started with when he finally found the courage to get out of bed and visit their graves all those years back, it was the closest he would ever get to their morning family coffee dates again.

As we walk back through the winding paths, I lean into Connor's side, grateful for his steady presence. Tomorrow might be a whirlwind of cameras and celebrities, but right now, in this peaceful moment between the stones and the sound, everything feels perfectly aligned.

Chapter 32: Gaming Royalty

Connor

THE MASTER CLOSET FEELS different these days - warmer, lived in. Ashlyn took Shelly clothes shopping several times while I was in the hospital so she wasn't limited to the three sets I bought her at the mall weeks ago. I think it was also an excuse for Ashlyn to feel like she had a sister. Shelly's clothes have started migrating over, creating splashes of color among my monochromatic collection. I'm adjusting my Knuckledraggers beanie when she sneaks up behind me, wrapping her arms around my waist.

"You sure you don't want to wear something fancier?" I ask, watching her reflection in the full-length mirror. She's gorgeous in dark jeans and another vintage Nightfallen shirt that she found at that little thrift shop downtown. I wonder if she is going to fangirl hard over Dahlia when she meets her.

"Nope." She pops the 'p' and grins, reaching up to straighten the cord on my matching Nightfallen hoodie. "I want to be comfortable. Plus, this way we match."

I turn to face her, unable to resist stealing a quick kiss. Her lips are soft, tasting faintly of coffee and the cherry lip balm she's become addicted to. When I pull back, she's already got a cat-eared beanie pulled on, making her look impossibly cute.

"The press is going to have a field day," I chuckle, helping her adjust the floppy ears. "CEO of Eldritch Magic shows up to the PVGAs looking like he raided Hot Topic and stole one of their employees."

"Good." She slides her hands up under my shirt to my chest, fingers playing my chest hair. She says it's what she imagines a werewolf might feel like. As most men would, I took it as a massive compliment. "Let them talk. I like how we look together."

I catch her hand and press a kiss to her forehead. The morning light streaming through the window catches her hair just right, turning it to fire. For a moment, I'm struck again by how natural this feels - getting ready together, steal-ing touches, sharing space.

"What are you thinking about?" she asks, tilting her head in that way that always makes me want to laugh. It reminds me of a puppy that doesn't understand something.

"Getting undressed and carrying you to the bed," I reply honestly, pulling her close for another kiss. My hand slides under her the back of her shirt and pushes under her jeans to her silk panties. She melts against me, and I lose myself in the warmth of her presence, the way her fingers tangle in my hair as she caresses my chest, the soft sound she makes when I deepen the kiss.

My watch beeps. "We're going to be late." I speak the words into her mouth.

"You're teasing me, Mr. Ebin." She bites my lower lip, sending lightning all the way to my toes.

I spin her around, hands settling on her hips as I guide her toward the front door. My lips brush against her ear, and I feel her shiver. "By the way, the doctor cleared me for *all* activities yesterday."

She stiffens in my grip, then turns to face me with narrowed eyes. "You went without me? You promised I could come to all your appointments."

"I know, Little Lysa." The nickname slips out naturally now, and I see her expression soften despite her attempt to maintain her stern look. "But I needed to ask some very specific questions, and I wanted to be sure of the answer before..." My hands slide down and pinch her through her jeans. "Before I made any promises about tonight."

She tries to maintain her pout, but I can see the heat building in her eyes. "That's still not fair. What if something had been wrong?"

"Then I would have called you immediately." I press a kiss to her neck, right below her ear. "But nothing was wrong. And now I have plans for when we get back from the awards show. If you're ready."

Her breath shudders, and she presses herself against me. Then with the most Victorian era voice she can manage, "My dear chivalrous Quinn, if I said I was pinning for your touch, what kind of plans would you tell me of?"

"The kind that involve finding out how every inch of you

responds to my touch." I feel her whole body tremble against mine.

Shelly steps back from me, her expression shifting from playful to something deeper. Her fingers trail down my chest, coming to rest over my heart. Her eyes alight like emerald fires.

"Connor, I'm ready." Her voice is soft but sure. "Not just for tonight, but for everything. I want to share all of myself with you - body, heart, soul. No more waiting."

My heart pounds against my ribs and I wonder how many more times she can make that happen before I have a heart attack. She continues, "I know we've been taking it slow, being careful fully moving forward physically. And we have had good reasons. But I don't want to be careful anymore. I want to dive in completely. The other morning in the shower…I've never felt more fulfilled. "

I press my forehead to hers, breathing in the scent of her lips, feeling the warmth of her skin. "Are you sure?"

She nods against me. "More sure than I've ever been about anything. I love you, Connor Ebin. All of you - your strength, your pain, your past, your future. I want it all." She grabs my ass and kisses over my heart. Shelly, my Shelly, is really stepping out of herself, or perhaps she is finally stepping into herself.

The raw honesty in her voice steals my breath. I've been so careful, so concerned about moving too fast, about making sure she feels safe and in control. But looking into her eyes now, I see nothing but certainty and love.

"Then tonight, we explore each other fully. I will map every inch of you and commit it to memory, tracing constellations in your freckles." Her eyes roll back and she groans, jumping into my arms and wrapping her legs around me. I smile one of the biggest smiles I have ever made and walk out the door with Shelly wrapped around me like a koala on a tree.

Connor

The blacked out SUV with the Eldritch Magic logo rolls to a stop, and I can feel Shelly's grip tighten on my hand. The door opens, and I step out first, turning back to help her. The flash of cameras starts immediately - not the overwhelming wall you'd see at the Oscars, the PVGAs are only important to the gaming community with small sub-interests from other entertainment outlets. Nevertheless it is enough to make an impact.

Shelly emerges like a gamer's dream girl, if I am being honest. I don't think she even knows how much male gamers like the casual gamer girl look. She blinks at the sudden attention, and I lean close to her ear.

"Don't worry, this is actually pretty tame. You should see the chaos at mainstream awards shows." I rest my hand on the small of her back, steadying her. "Gaming press is much more civilized."

Her eyes widen as she spots familiar logos. "Is that... IGN? And Kotaku?"

I nod, guiding her forward. "Plus GameSpot, Polygon, and probably some streamers doing red carpet coverage." The familiar faces in the press line nod at me - I've known most of them for years through various industry events.

"Mr. Ebin!" One of the reporters calls out. "Can we get a photo?"

I glance at Shelly, making sure she's comfortable. She gives me a small nod, and we pause for the cameras. The flashes increase, and I hear murmurs as they notice my cane. I hadn't been using it because I haven't been on my feet for very prolonged periods of time, but my physical therapist suggested it for the event because of how much we would be walking around. I'd insisted, at least, on walking without it for the red carpet, but Ashlyn had threatened bodily harm if I didn't bring it.

"I feel like I'm in a movie," Shelly whispers, and I can't help but smile at the wonder in her voice.

"Just wait until you see the after-party," I tell her. "That's where the real fun happens. All the gaming industry's biggest nerds in one room, trying to pretend they know how to be fancy."

A familiar voice calls out from the press line. "Connor! Over here, man!"

I turn to see Edward Hayes from Righteous Bytes waving at us. Edward has been covering Eldritch since our first game, and he's one of the few gaming journalists I actually trust to report things accurately. I guide Shelly over to his spot.

"Edward, good to see you." We clasp hands warmly. "How's the family?"

"All good, all good. More importantly, how are you? The whole industry was worried sick." His eyes flick to my cane, then back to my face. "You had us scared there for a while."

I feel Shelly's grip tighten slightly on my arm. "Takes more than a couple bullets to keep me down it would seem. Besides," I bring Shelly's hand to my lips with a kiss, "I had excellent motivation to recover quickly."

Marcus's professional smile widens into something more genuine as he looks at Shelly. "And who might this be?"

"This is Shelly," I say, feeling a warmth spread through my face. "My girlfriend."

"Pleasure to meet you," Shelly says softly.

"As it is to meet the woman that stole the heart of our Eldritch magician. So Connor," Marcus shifts back into interview mode, though his eyes are kind, "everyone's wondering - will this affect Rune Beast's release schedule?"

I shake my head. "Not at all. The team at Eldritch is incredible, and they kept everything moving while I was recovering. We're still on track for our spring release date."

"That's great news," Marcus says. "The beta feedback was phenomenal. People are really excited about the new mechanics."

I catch the subtle question there - he's fishing for details about the Seidr Witch scenes. I just smile. "We're excited too. Don't worry, I'll send you an advance access key for your brutally honest review and then you can see it all for yourself."

Marcus laughs. "Always appreciated, Connor. Well, don't let me keep you. Good to see you back on your feet."

We make our way inside, and I spot our table near the front - one of the perks of being a presenter. Ashlyn waves us over, and I can see Manu and Aimi already settled in. My eyes catch the striking figure of Dahlia Nightfall, her signature black Victorian-style dress making her pale skin seem almost luminescent under the venue lighting. She's chatting with James, their bassist, both of them looking perfectly at home despite being out of their usual concert environment.

"There's our warriors," Manu says, standing to help me with my chair. I wave him off - I'm not that fragile anymore.

"Connor!" Ashlyn hugs me carefully, then pulls Shelly into a warmer embrace. "You both look cute as hell. Matching hoodies is a bit on the nose but the world will forgive you I think."

I start to make introductions, but I notice Shelly has gone completely still beside me, her eyes wide as saucers as she stares at Dahlia. I can practically feel her vibrating with contained excitement.

"Dahlia, James, this is my girlfriend, Shelly," I say, squeezing her hand gently. "She's actually a huge fan of The Nightfallen, in case the sudden voicelessness wasn't a clue."

Dahlia's melodic laugh fills the air as she stands, her movement graceful despite her elaborate dress. "Oh, sweetheart, remember to breathe," she says, pulling Shelly into a warm hug. "Connor told me about what happened. I understand we have you to thank for keeping this wonderful man among the living."

Shelly makes a small squeaking sound that might be an attempt at words, and I can't help but laugh. It's endearing to see her this starstruck, especially given how composed she's been.

I watch with quiet joy as Shelly finally finds her voice, telling Dahlia and James how The Nightfallen's music helped her through some of her darkest nights. Her hands move animatedly as she describes specific songs that meant the most to her, and I see genuine warmth in Dahlia's eyes as she listens.

The ceremony itself passes in a pleasant haze. I've been to enough of these that the rhythm is familiar - the awards, the speeches, the carefully orchestrated moments of surprise and celebration. But tonight, I find myself watching Shelly more than the stage. Her face lights up at each reveal, and she grips my hand tightly when games she recognizes are announced. She even remembers to remind me to use my cane when I shift in my seat, which makes Ashlyn shoot her an approving look.

The voice of Bennie Jonson, the Game Master for one of the most popular ttrpg streams of all time and the MC's for tonight's awards cuts through my reverie: "And now, to present our final award of the evening, please welcome the CEO of Eldritch Magic Gaming, the voice and motion behind the Rune Beast and the illustriously beautiful and talented voice of the Seidr Witch in the upcoming Rune Beast game, Connor Ebin and Dahlia Nightfall."

I stand carefully, mindful that although I am mostly healed it would be terrible to move too fast and have everyone on live TV see me double over from missing a step. Shelly looks up at me with her hypnotizing green eyes that will forever take my breath away. I bend down, cupping her face gently, and kiss her. The cameras catch the moment, of course - they're meant to - but I barely notice them. When I pull back, her smile could light up the darkest night in any realm of the gaming worlds.

Dahlia appears at my side, resplendent in her gothic elegance, and takes my elbow. Together, we make our way toward the podium.

The steps feel awkward with this damn unnecessary cane, but Dahlia matches my pace perfectly. As we reach our position, I pull out the envelope containing the winner and prepare to read our scripted introduction. But something changes in the atmosphere - a shift in energy that makes me look up.

The entire venue is on their feet.

For a moment, I think there must be someone important behind me, but then I notice Dahlia has stepped slightly aside, joining in the applause. The realization hits me like a gentle wave - they're standing for me. For surviving. For being here.

My throat tightens as I see faces I've known for years in the gaming industry, all of them wearing expressions of genuine relief and joy. Even the typically stoic journalists are on their feet. In the front row, Shelly's eyes shine with tears as she claps, and beside her, Manu and Ashlyn are beaming.

"Thank you," I manage into the microphone, my hand pressed against my heart. The applause continues, and I feel my composure starting to crack. "Thank you, truly." My voice wavers slightly, and I have to take a breath. "Thank you all so much."

The moment stretches, filled with genuine warmth that cuts through all the usual industry politics and competition. In this moment, we're just a community of people who make and love games, grateful that one of our own is still here.

I catch sight of Shelly again, and she mouths 'I love you.' It helps to ground me, helps me find my center again as the applause finally begins to die down.

I lean into the microphone, my heart full. "If you'll indulge me for just a moment more - I need to acknowledge the true hero of this evening." My eyes find Shelly in the crowd. "Michelle Lockhart, would you please stand?"

She looks like she wants to sink into the floor, but slowly rises to her feet. The spotlight finds her, and even from here I can see the blush creeping across her cheeks. She's adorably awkward, fidgeting with the sleeve of her hoodie.

"Without this remarkable young woman's selfless act of heroism, I wouldn't be standing here tonight." My voice catches slightly, remembering those terrifying moments. "She saved my life in more ways than one."

The crowd erupts again, rising to their feet in another standing ovation. Shelly's face is now bright red, and she's looking everywhere but at the crowd. Her eyes finally lock with mine, a mix of embarrassment and love in her eyes.

I mouth "I love you" to her, and her whole face lights up. She brings both hands to her lips and blows me an exaggerated kiss that makes several people around her chuckle warmly.

The moment perfectly captures everything I love about her - her genuine heart, her endearing awkwardness, and that spark of playfulness that shows through even when she's uncomfortable. Standing here at this podium, watching her receive the recognition she deserves, I've never been more certain about anything in my life.

The applause finally settles, and I clear my throat, sharing a quick glance with Dahlia. She gives me a subtle nod, and we turn our attention back to the teleprompter.

"Gaming isn't just about entertainment," I begin, following the script. "It's about creating worlds that inspire, challenge, and connect us. This year's nominees for Game of the Year have all pushed boundaries in their own unique ways."

Dahlia's melodic voice takes over smoothly. "They've given us stories that moved us, gameplay that challenged us, and moments we'll never forget."

"The nominees for Game of the Year are..." I pause as the screen behind us lights up.

"Stellar State," Dahlia announces, "from Hybrid Quantum Studios."

"Chronicles of the Plagued Moon," I continue, "by Yonara Entertainment."

"Trail of the Ancient Gift," Dahlia reads, "from Mudd Hat Studios."

"And finally," I say, "Echoes of Desecration, from Morning Star Light Games."

I break the seal on the envelope, careful not to fumble it despite my slightly shaking hands. Dahlia leans in close as I open it, and we read the winner's name together.

"And the Game of the Year goes to..." we say in unison, pausing for dramatic effect, "Chronicles of the Plagued Moon by Yonara Studios!"

The room erupts in applause as the Yonara Studios team makes their way to the stage, their CEO leading the group with tears already streaming down her face. I can't help but smile - I remember that feeling from our first win years ago. Dahlia and I return to our seats for the closing ceremony.

The after-party is exactly as it always is - a bunch of us brilliant nerds trying to navigate an open bar while discussing polygon counts, frame rates and story details. I'm settled into a comfortable corner booth, watching Shelly chat with one of our streamers about gaming strategies for CCC. She's absolutely glowing, and I can't help but smile at how naturally she fits into this world.

"You look disgustingly happy," Manu says, sliding into the seat next to me with two cocktails. He passes one to me. "It's about time."

I accept the drink with a nod. "I am happy. Genuinely happy."

"Good." He clinks his glass against mine. "You deserve it."

Shelly makes her way back to us, her cheeks flushed from excitement or maybe the glass of wine in her hand, which I suppose is technically illegal, but no one here is going to say anything about it. She settles next to me, and I slip my arm around her waist.

"Having fun?" I ask, pulling her close.

"So much," she beams. "Though..." she leans in, her lips

brushing my ear, "I wouldn't be upset if we headed home soon. I'm curious about these plans you mentioned."

My body responds immediately to her whispered words, and I have to take a slow breath. I catch Ashlyn's knowing smirk from across the table and decide to take the out Shelly's offering.

"Actually," I announce, shifting slightly and reaching for my cane, "I hate to be the old man, but it's been a long day on my feet. I think we should probably head out."

"Of course," Ashlyn says, immediately understanding. "You shouldn't overdo it." She winks.

We make our rounds of goodbyes, accepting congratulations and well-wishes from various industry friends. Shelly's hand never leaves mine as we make our way to the waiting SUV, and I can feel the anticipation building between us.

As the door closes behind us and the driver pulls away from the curb, Shelly snuggles into my side. "Home?" she asks softly.

I kiss her temple. "Home."

Chapter 33: Whispers & Fairy Tales

Connor

I FUMBLE WITH MY keys at the door, my hands trembling slightly - though whether from anticipation or lingering weakness, I'm not sure. Shelly stands close, her warmth radiating against my side, making me suddenly and keenly aware it's my own anticipation. Maybe a little trepidation too, it's been five years since I have been with anyone.

"Before we go in..." I reach into my hoodie pocket and pull out a silk blindfold. Shelly's eyes widen slightly, and I catch the quick flutter of uncertainty across her face.

"Trust me?" I ask softly, holding it up.

She nods, though I can see her shoulders tense slightly. "But if this is a big reveal that you're a serial killer…"

I chuckle softly and lean in to kiss her gently, letting my lips linger against hers until I feel some of that tension melt away. Then I carefully slip the blindfold over her eyes, making sure it's secure but not too tight.

She shakes as though a cool draft just came through the

hallway. "I wasn't sure I'd like being blindfolded," she admits quietly, her hand finding mine and squeezing. "But someh ow... with you, it feels exciting."

My heart clenches at the simple trust in those words. I kiss her again, just because I can, just because she's here and real and choosing to let down her walls for me.

"Ready?" I ask, turning back to unlock the door.

"Ready," she whispers, and I can hear the smile in her voice.

I guide Shelly carefully through the apartment, my hands steady on her shoulders. The familiar scent of eucalyptus and vanilla hits me as we enter the bedroom - scents mentioned in Shelly's book, The Maiden and the Lycanthrope. Even in the dim lighting, I can see Alicia's outdone herself.

Dozens of flickering LED candles (this many real ones left briefly unattended would've given Alicia a heart attack) cast a warm glow across the room. Orchid petals are strewn about the floor and scattered across the dark blue silk sheets I splurged on yesterday. The air feels different somehow, charged with possibility.

I have to bite back a laugh, remembering Alicia's reaction when I nervously explained what I wanted. She'd just held out her hand for the credit card and muttered "Finally" under her breath, like she'd been waiting years for this moment. Maybe she had been. The knowing look she gave me when I handed over the money for supplies made me feel like a teenager again.

My hands tighten slightly on Shelly's shoulders as we pass through the bedroom toward the master bathroom. The soft gasp she lets out tells me she can smell the scented candles too. I'm grateful for Alicia allowing me to do it right in the bathroom where a turned over candle would likely go out without burning down the apartment if it feel over on the tile somehow- though I'd felt ridiculous discussing romance with my housekeeper, her expertise is obvious in every detail.

"Almost there," I murmur close to her ear, carefully steering her toward the tub. I can feel her trembling slightly under my hands, and I run my thumbs in small, soothing circles against her shoulders, the scent of essential oils in the bath dance into our nostrils. I can see Shelly biting her lip, she's so damn cute when she does that.

I slide the blindfold off slowly, my fingers brushing against her cheek bones. The soft gasp that escapes her makes my heart skip one more beat closer to a heart attack - I know she's recognized it before she even speaks.

"Connor..." Her hands fly to her mouth, and I can see her eyes growing wide in the mirror as they adjust to the flickering candlelight. The bathroom has been transformed into something out of a gothic romance - exactly as described in her book. Ivy vines trail along the walls, weaving between strategically placed LED candles. Delicate orchids rest in vintage-looking vases, their pale petals catching the light. Decorative silver skulls peek out from between the flowers, adding that perfect touch of darkness that made the scene in her book so memorable.

Wisps of sandalwood incense curl through the air from ornate censers, creating an otherworldly atmosphere. The large soaking tub is filled with steaming water tinted slightly purple from bath salts, and rose petals floating on the surface.

"You... you recreated the scene," she whispers, her voice thick with emotion. "From the book."

I wrap my arms around her chest from behind, resting my chin on her head. "I wanted tonight to be so memorable we'd never forget it," I murmur against her ear. "And what better way than bringing your favorite scene to life?"

She turns in my arms, and I can see tears glistening in her eyes. "You actually read it. And remembered all the details. How did all this get done?"

"Of course I did." I brush away a tear that's escaped down her cheek. "Magic got it done…or Alicia helped with the setup while we were-"

She cuts me off with a kiss that makes me forget what I was going to say.

I gently tug at the zipper of Shelly's hoodie, pushing it off her shoulders and letting it fall to the floor. Pulling her shirt over her head and watching her wavy hair cascade back down to her shoulders, I trace my fingers down her spine as I unlatch her bra. She kicks her shoes off and I push her pants down over her hips. She turns to face me and I kneel to grip her panties and slowly reveal her fully to my eyes. Before I stand I nuzzle my face against her folds and breathe in her scent. I am instantly intoxicated. My lips press just above her clit and I kiss up her body to her mouth. Her skin glows in the candlelight, making me cease all external thought. She is all that exists now. Her emerald eyes are dark with desire as I strip off my own clothes.

Her fingers trail across my chest, she traces the scars. The touch is feather-light but sends electricity through my nerves. "My protector." She says and I catch her hand when it lingers too long on the bullet wound, bringing her fingers to my lips.

"Mine." I whisper into her ear, as the lycanthrope did to the maiden.

Taking a deep breath, I steady myself. The secret gym sessions should pay off - I've been careful to rebuild my strength without pushing too hard. I'm not back to where I was but Shelly's small frame is far from my peak strength, even in this condition. The last thing I need is Shelly worrying about me overdoing it.

Before she can protest, I scoop her up in my arms. She's lighter than I expected, though maybe that's the adrenaline coursing through me.

"Connor, don't! Your wounds-" she starts, but I silence her with a look that makes her breath hitch. The mixture of concern and desire in her eyes only fuels my determination.

I step carefully into the Jacuzzi tub, the warm water embracing my legs as I lower us both in. Settling onto the built-in seat, I guide Shelly down onto my lap, the water swirling around us as she adjusts her position.

The scented water laps at our skin as I pull her closer, my hands spanning her waist. She fits against me like a puzzle, she was made to be here.

I capture her lips with mine, feeling her soft moan vibrate against my mouth. My hands glide over her skin beneath the water, memorizing every curve and contour. The warmth of the bath pales in comparison to the heat radiating between us.

She shifts in my lap, her fingers tracing patterns across my chest and shoulders. I deepen our kiss, tasting hints of the wine from earlier. Her hands tangle in my hair, sending shivers down my spine.

Breaking away to catch my breath, I reach for the loofah and citrus body wash. "Let me take care of you," I whisper against her ear. She shivers and nods, eyes half-lidded with contentment.

I guide her to turn, her back pressing against my chest. Starting at her shoulders, I massage gentle circles with the soapy loofah, dropping soft kisses along her neck. She sighs, melting back against me as I work my way down her arms.

"This has to be a dream," she murmurs, tilting her head to give me better access to the sensitive spot below her ear. I smile against her skin, overwhelmed by how right this feels - having her here in my arms, caring for her, loving her.

The rose petals swirl around us as I continue washing her back with reverent attention, punctuating each stroke with tender kisses along her spine. Her breathing grows deeper, more relaxed with each passing moment.

My hands glide down Shelly's legs beneath the warm wa-ter, my fingers tracing patterns along her inner thighs. She shivers against me, her breath catching as I brush against her sweetest spot. I can still smell it and I unconsciously lick my lips.

"Wait," she says suddenly, turning to face me with that

playful sparkle in her eyes I've come to adore. "If we're recreating the book, we can't forget the next part."

She stands, water cascading down her body in the candlelight. "The maiden had to tend to the lycanthrope's wounds," she says softly. "Stand up."

I rise carefully with a smile, this woman is a treasure. Shelly's eyes travel over my scars - both old and new - with such tenderness it makes my chest ache.

"Your turn," she whispers, reaching for the loofah. Her hands are gentle as she begins washing my chest, paying special attention to the fresh scars. Each touch is reverent, healing. She presses soft kisses to the marks left by the bullets, just as the maiden did to the sword wounds on the lycanthrope.

The parallel isn't lost on me - how we both fought to protect each other, bearing the scars to prove it. Her lips brush against the longest scar, and I have to steady myself against the edge of the tub, overwhelmed by the intimacy of the moment.

"My brave protector," she murmurs against my skin, echoing the words from her beloved book. But there's nothing scripted about the emotion in her voice or the way her hands tremble slightly as they trace the evidence of how close we came to losing each other.

I feel Shelly move behind me, her delicate hands gliding across my shoulders with the loofah. The warm water trickles down my back as she works, each touch filled with care and tenderness. Her fingers trace the muscles along my spine, and I close my eyes, letting myself sink into the sensation.

A sudden sharp but pleasant feeling makes me inhale as she drags her nails lightly down my back. Her hands drift lower, giving my ass a playful squeeze that makes me chuckle.

"I don't remember that part being in the book," I say, glancing over my shoulder to catch her impish grin.

"Hush," she scolds, though I can hear the smile in her voice. "I'm working here."

Her arms slip around my waist from behind, and I feel her press against my back, her soft breasts and hips warm and comforting against me. The water laps gently around us as she holds me, her hands beginning to explore.

She moves them with agonizing slowness to my aching arousal and grips it lightly. Her hands lock over me, stacked one above the other and she begins to stoke me slowly. I shudder against her and I hear her light giggle, like someone that just discover they have power over someone. She definitely does.

Shelly's hands continue their slow, teasing strokes, she takes one of her hands away and begins tracing patterns across my chest and stomach. I can feel her breath against my back, warm and steady. I'm not sure how much longer I can last before I lose control and take her.

She moves in front of me, her eyes meeting mine with a mixture of vulnerability and desire. "I haven't done this much," she admits softly, biting her lower lip. "...or what we'll be getting to shortly."

I take a deep breath, trying to steady myself. "It's been five years for me, Shelly" I confess. "And before that... it was only Liv for eleven years."

Shelly nods, understanding in her eyes. She leans forward, pressing a gentle kiss to my chest, right above my heart. Then she slowly sinks to her knees in front of me, the water swirling around her.

She looks up at me, her gaze full of trust and longing. I can't help but feel a surge of protectiveness and love for this woman who has managed to break through the walls I've built around myself like an expert demolitionist.

With a soft sigh, Shelly leans forward and kisses the length of my cock, her lips warm and tender against my skin. I can't help but let out a low growl as she licks the head, her tongue swirling around my sensitive tip.

Then, with a look of determination in her eyes, she takes me into her mouth. I can feel her hesitation, her fear of being inexperienced, but it only makes this moment more precious. She's trying, for me, and that's all that matters.

I thread my fingers through her hair, guiding her gently as she finds her rhythm. I can feel the tension building in my body, the pleasure mounting with each stroke of her tongue. But I don't want this to end too quickly. I want to savor every moment with her.

"Shelly," I whisper, my voice strained. "You-"

But she shakes her head, her eyes meeting mine as she continues to move her mouth along my length. I can see the determination in her gaze, the desire to please me. And I can't help but feel an even greater surge of love and gratitude for this woman who has come into my life and turned it upside down in the best way.

I lean my head back, letting myself sink into the sensation of her mouth on me. The water laps gently around us, the candles flickering in the dim light. It's a moment of pure, unadulterated pleasure, and I never want it to end.

But eventually, I can feel myself getting closer to the edge. I lightly grip Shelly's hair, my breath coming in ragged gasps as I force myself to stop her. I pull her mouth from me and stand her up. She has a mischievously satisfied smile on her face that makes my knees feel even weaker.

I scoop Shelly up again, cradling her against my chest as I reach for one of the plush towels. The Egyptian cotton is impossibly soft as I pat her skin dry with careful attention, watching goosebumps rise wherever the air touches her damp skin. After drying myself quickly, I lift her into my arms once more, loving how naturally she fits there.

Using my foot, I nudge open the door to the bedroom. Shelly's sharp intake of breath makes me smile - I'd hoped the setup would have this effect. The room has been transformed into our own private forest grove, just like from our book. Small potted trees line the walls, their leaves creating dancing shadows in the candlelight. The same trailing ivy from the bathroom continues here, weaving between more LED candles and vintage-looking lanterns and the scattering of orchid petals.

"Connor..." she breathes, her eyes wide as she takes in every detail. The flickering lights catch the tears welling in her eyes. "It's exactly like in the book. The forest where they..." Her voice trails off as she notices the scattered petals leading to the bed.

"Where they finally admitted their love wasn't just about protection or lust," I finish softly, carrying her toward the bed. "Where they chose each other, scars and all."

The look she gives me - wonder mixed with such deep affection - makes my heart swell, well, everything swell. I've spent the whole week planning this, ever since I read that final chapter of The Maiden and the Lycanthrope while she made dinner for me in the kitchen the day I came home. I wanted everything to be perfect, wanted to show her that I understand what this story means to her. That I understand her.

I lay her gently on the bed, watching how the candlelight plays across her skin. The soft glow transforms the room into something magical, making it feel like we've truly stepped into the pages of her cherished novel.

I kneel by the bed, my hand resting gently over Shelly's heart. I can feel its rapid beat beneath my palm, a testament to her excitement. I lean down and press a tender kiss to her stomach, feeling her muscles quiver in response. My lips trace a path downwards, and I can't help but growl lightly when her body shivers beneath my touch.

As I reach her pussy, I pause for a moment, taking a deep breath to savor her scent. It's thrilling, and I can't help but growl in response. She squeaks in surprise as I lick from her opening to her clit, her body tensing beneath me. I can feel her trying to hold still, but the sensation is too much for her.

I start off gently, teasing her with soft licks and nibbles. But as her moans grow louder, I find myself losing control as I suck at her clit. I'm forced to hold her legs still as I feast upon her womanhood, my tongue darting in and out of her folds. She's writhing beneath me, fighting the pleasure of pent up energy that needs to escape her hips, her fingers gripping my hair as she tries to pull me closer.

"Connor," she gasps, her voice barely above a whisper. "I can't...I've never felt this good before."

I reluctantly pull away, scooting her further up on the bed as I climb over her. She looks so beautiful beneath me, her eyes wide with desire and trust. I press my lips against hers, feeling her body tremble as I push myself slowly inside her.

She lets out a whimpered moan, her mouth falling open around my lips. After I'm inside her as far as her space will allow I pause and feel myself pulsing within her. She grabs my face in her hands and kisses me deeply between breaths. I start off slow, savoring the feeling of being inside her. But as her hips begin to rock against mine, I find myself fighting to keep control once again.

Shelly's nails dig into my back, her moans growing louder with each thrust. I can feel her body tensing beneath me, and I know she's close. I reach down between us, my fingers finding her clit and rubbing it in tight circles.

With a final cry, she comes apart beneath me, her body shaking as wave after wave of pleasure washes over her.

I can't get enough of her. I'm consumed by the taste of her skin, the sound of her moans, and the way her body responds to mine. As she quivers beneath me, still recovering from her orgasm, I kiss and bite at her neck, leaving a trail of marks that I know will make her blush when she sees them in the mirror later.

She's breathless, whispering "too much" with a ridiculously wide smile on her face. But I know she doesn't mean it. I can feel the way her body arches into mine, the way her hips grind against me, begging for more.

I move to take her small perky nipples into my mouth, my hand clutching lightly at the back of her neck. I look up at her, my eyes meeting hers, and I tell her what I need. "I need more of you," I say, my voice low and rough with a deep craving. I'm seeking permission, but I can see in her eyes that she wants this just as much as I do.

She nods eagerly, biting her lip with a smile. I roll her over, positioning myself just below her cute ass, and push myself inside her from behind as she tilts her hips back to present herself to me. Once I'm fully seated, I gently put my weight on her back, my hands holding her shoulders as I smell her hair and begin to slowly thrust again.

I can feel the tension building in my body, the pressure that's been accumulating since the moment I first saw her. But I don't want this to end. I want to stay here, inside her, forever.

Bringing my mouth close to her ear, not sure what has come over me, I murmur words that cause her to writhe and gasp under my weight. I describe how incredible she is, how perfectly she feels around me, and how much I adore every sound she gives me. I express my burning desire for her, my desperate craving, and my wish to keep her forever in my arms.

As I continue to move inside her, I can feel her body starting to tense again. She's close, and I know it. I reach underneath her and take her soft breast into my hand, squeezing it while I nibble at her neck.

"Connor," she whispers, her voice shaking with pleasure. "Again…"

I smile against her skin, feeling a surge of pride and satisfaction. This is what I want. I want to make her mine and show her that I am hers. I want to bring her pleasure, until she's too exhausted to move. I want to show her how much she means to me, how much I love her, and how I'll never let her go. This possessive feeling washes over me and I remember the description of what the lycanthrope felt for the maiden in Shelly's book.

But for now, I just focus on the feeling of her body beneath mine, the sound of her moans in our bed, and the knowledge that we belong to each other in this moment. I thrust harder, faster, my movements becoming more urgent as I feel my own orgasm building. There's a small twinge of pain in my chest but my pleasure brooks no argument over who is going to win that battle.

And then, with a final cry, she comes apart beneath me, her body shaking and trembling as wave after wave of pleasure washes over her again. I follow her over the edge, my own release crashing through me like a tidal wave.

I hold myself over her back and kiss her neck, gently nuzzling her ear as I whisper to her that I love her. I trail kisses down her back and give her ass a sharp little bite that causes her to squeal and turnover, laughing.

I realize in this moment, the afterglow of our love acted out in the sweetest and most passionate way, that I am finally at home in my own skin again.

Shelly

I rub at my recently bit ass, a playful smirk tugging at my lips as I smack Connor's side. We stare at each other for several moments, lost in the depths of each other's eyes, just appreciating where we are. The room is filled with the scent of orchids and the soft glow of little lights that dance like the willow-wisps in my book, creating an atmosphere that feels like a dream.

Then, with a mischievous glint in my eyes, I push Connor over onto his back and climb on top of him. I lean down, my hair cascading around us like a curtain, and kiss him deeply. When I pull back, I can't help but smile. "That was... incredible," I whisper, my voice barely above a breath. "The decorations, making sure I felt safe, taking care of me... you're just... you can't be real."

Connor's hands rest on my hips, his thumbs gently tracing circles around the dimples in my lower back. His eyes, filled with a mix of love and desire, never leave mine. I can feel his heart beneath my palm, steady and strong, just like him.

"I may never believe this is real," I confess, my voice soft. "You, us, this... it's all too perfect. It's a dream I never want to wake up from." I lean down again, pressing my forehead against his, our breaths mingling. "I love you, Connor Ebin. More than I'll ever be able to tell you."

In this moment, everything feels right. The world outside could be crumbling, but here, with Connor, I'm safe. I'm home. And that's all that matters.

I drift in and out of consciousness, wrapped in a cocoon of warmth and safety. Connor's lips press against the top of my head, and he pulls the covers over us both. Just before sleep claims me completely, I hear his whispered words: "You made me whole again."

My heart swells, and I try to burrow even deeper into his embrace, as if I could somehow merge our souls together. The steady rhythm of his heartbeat becomes my lullaby, and I surrender to sleep.

Morning light filters through the blinds when I finally stir. I'm still sprawled across Connor's chest, exactly where I fell asleep. We haven't moved an inch all night, as if our bodies knew this was exactly where we belonged. I tilt my head up, drinking in the sight of his peaceful face bathed in the soft golden glow of dawn. The worry lines that sometimes crease his forehead are smooth, and there's a hint of a smile playing at the corners of his mouth even in sleep.

He stirs beneath me, those beautiful eyes that are mine now fluttering open. When he sees me, his smile grows wider, and his arms tighten around me. "What do you want to do today?" he asks, voice still rough with sleep.

I feel my face heat up as I lay my head back down on his chest, listening to the life within him. "This," I whisper. "Everyday. Just this."

www.ingramcontent.com/pod-product-compliance
Lightning Source LLC
Chambersburg PA
CBHW070205310726
48976CB00001B/219